The

SOUND

of

HER

NAME

Also by Mary Morgan

Deeper Waters

The House at the Edge of the Jungle

Willful Neglect

The
SOUND
of
HER
NAME

Mary Morgan

THOMAS DUNNE BOOKS
St. Martin's Press
New York

THOMAS DUNNE BOOKS.
An imprint of St. Martin's Press.

www.stmartins.com

Book design by Kathryn Parise

ISBN 0-312-34135-0
EAN 978-0-312-34135-0

First Edition: June 2005

10   9   8   7   6   5   4   3   2   1

For my brother,
William Michael Gordon Braund

Acknowledgments

.

I would like to thank Ruth Cavin, senior editor at St. Martin's Press, who has been gentle in her editing, and also my agents, Anna Cottle and Mary Alice Kier of Cine/Lit, for their encouragement and for staying the course.

My thanks also go to Susan Cooke at the University of Washington, who was kind enough to help with the Welsh language.

Oh! No! We never mention her,
Her name is never heard;
My lips are now forbid to speak
That once familiar word.

—THOMAS HAYNES BAYLY

The

SOUND

of

HER

NAME

$\mathcal{P}$rologue

1968

·

The sound of a name, jostled out of memory by a stranger and overheard by mere accident, altered the direction of Tim Bruce's journey. An impulsive decision on his part, he wasn't to know that changing the direction of a journey would also change his life and the lives of other people. People as yet unknown to him.

The name, and the few words accompanying it, almost drifted away on a gentle evening breeze warmed by flaring tiki torches amongst the rhododendrons and azaleas in his parents' backyard. The torches transformed the backyard into something resembling a Hollywood film set, probably what his mother intended, of course. She was fortunate that the weather was mellow enough for the party to take place outdoors. May is an uncertain month in the Pacific Northwest.

The party was for Tim's father, Carlton Bruce. For his students and colleagues. The guests spilled across the freshly mown grass, barbecue coals glowed in the brick fireplace pit, laughter and conversation rose and fell in the gathering dusk, to all appearances a happy and relaxed celebration of the end of the academic year. Conversation sounds less serious outside, but to Tim, all conversation was serious these days—the war, the draft, the protests, the riots, and he tried not to listen to any of it. He was almost surprised to hear people laughing. He found little to laugh about these days.

Tomorrow he was off to Europe. Tomorrow. He couldn't wait.

Meandering silently among his father's guests, perhaps too tall and too fair-haired to be invisible but doing his best to fade into the background, he poured wine and beer, smiled and nodded without engaging in any of the small talk. He didn't know these people, anyway; this was his father's event, the wrap-up of the year at the law school. As Tim wandered around with the tray of drinks, he came upon his father in close conversation with someone near the flaming torches. The light flickered on Carlton's face, and the expression in his eyes, the way he bent his head so intently to listen to the person standing beside him, made Tim pause in the shadows for a moment.

The person next to his father wore a dark suit and tie, too formal for a backyard barbecue, and he spoke with a precise, definitive British accent that carried clearly between the rhododendrons.

"Why, yes," he was saying, "that's exactly where I'm from. Fancy you knowing it. Quite a coincidence."

"I thought Clarrach was the loveliest place I'd ever seen," Tim heard his father say, an odd nostalgic wistfulness in his voice. Carlton Bruce was not a wistful man. Whenever he spoke to his family, particularly to his elder son, it was with conviction and decisiveness, but in that moment he sounded uncertain, almost hesitant. "I met a girl in Clarrach. A beautiful Welsh girl. Her name was Gwyneth. Gwyneth Griffiths." Carlton lingered over the name, rolling it in his mouth, as though he wanted to listen to the sound of it again. "Yes, Gwyneth," Carlton repeated. "Gwyneth Griffiths."

"Gwyneth Griffiths? Fancy that! She's still beautiful. She still lives in Clarrach. She married the local doctor, Rhys Edwards."

The strong lines of Carlton's face crumbled into a semblance of youthful uncertainty, softening and smoothing it. He kicked at the grass with the toe of his shoe. "Of course she'd be married by now. Of course. To tell you the truth, I'd have married her myself if it hadn't been for the war."

Standing in the shadows, Tim clutched the tray of drinks to his chest. A woman called Gwyneth that his father might have married? In a place called Clarrach? Where the hell was Clarrach? Who the hell was this Gwyneth? How was it that he'd never heard either of those names before?

At that moment, Carlton glanced up and caught sight of his son, and waved one hand impatiently. "Well, don't just stand there," he said. "Offer our guest a glass of wine."

Tim stepped forward with the tray, the glasses rattling.

Carlton said to the stranger, "This is my son, Tim. He's just graduated. From Berkeley. You know, where the students have nothing better to do than march and protest. As a matter of fact, he's off to your part of the world tomorrow. Off to play again until it's time to join the army."

The man raised his eyebrows. "Your father was telling me he was stationed in Wales before D-Day. Are you planning to visit Wales?"

"Wales?" Tim echoed. Was that where this place called Clarrach was? "Wales isn't on my list." Then he added, "The army isn't on my list, either."

His father frowned at him. "In my day," Carlton said, "young men did their duty without question."

The smoke from the torch blew into Tim's face and made his eyes sting.

"Yes, but then was then and now is now," he said, stopped, and turned away. This wasn't the time or place for more arguments. Tomorrow he'd be off. Tomorrow.

Right there and then Tim Bruce made the rash decision to go and look for this place called Clarrach, for this woman called Gwyneth. Maybe he'd discover something about his father he didn't know already. Then maybe he and his father would have something different to argue about.

One

But when Tim arrived at the town of Clarrach, in the far west of Wales, it was not in the least how he'd pictured it, not the quintessential English village with half-timbered, deep-thatched cottages and riotous flower gardens, with a green pasture and a pond at its heart. Clarrach was an undistinguished gray town hanging on a cliff above a pallid and empty expanse of ocean. It just went to show how flawed memories could be. Even those of his father.

The town appeared to be totally carved out of stone, with narrow stony streets that wandered chaotically up and down steep hills, stone houses that abutted directly onto the sidewalks with no front yards or lawns to soften them and no trees for shade. Not that shade was necessary that day. A damp gray mist hung low over the dark slate roofs, muffling sounds, obscuring the light of morning.

Not in the least how he'd pictured it.

Nothing was turning out the way Tim had pictured it. Instead of an ancient grandeur, the British Isles seemed undersized and miniature to him, everything too small and contained. Pinched. Claustrophobic. Even in London, where he'd hoped for great things, buildings crowded into less than noble streets that meandered around in a circuitous fashion, following no grid or discernible pattern, so he rarely knew if he was heading north or south, east or west. The randomness of direction confused and disconcerted Tim and made him more aware that he hadn't much idea where he was going or what he was heading for. Or why. He'd come to Clarrach on a whim, because he'd heard his father speak a woman's name. At least he could catch the ferry to Ireland from here. Except he didn't have much idea what he was going to do in Ireland, either.

He'd hitched a ride on a truck from Cardiff, early in the morning. Lorry, he told himself, remember to call it a lorry. The journey was slow, the truck laboring up the hills, unable to pass the other traffic, but beggars couldn't be choosers and the truck driver was cheerful enough and told jokes until Tim had fallen asleep. Now he'd been dropped in the middle of the town of Clarrach, and it might have been better if he wasn't standing right by another of those unsettling war memorials that haunted every town center of every town and village in Britain. This one was a group of stone soldiers, stony heads bent in sorrow, stone rifles turned downwards. After only one week, Tim had already seen too many memorials. Most of them dated from World War I, an unimaginably distant war to Tim, but his stomach still twisted in a knot whenever he came upon one of them, each an echo of tragedy and human stupidity, a grim reminder of unbearable loss in every small community. Somehow he'd imagined he'd come to Europe to escape such reminders.

As he lingered uneasily beside the stone soldiers, the damp sea mist clung to Tim's face and hair, seeped around his neck, and dampened his spirits. What he needed was a cup of coffee, hot and strong and black. He was pretty sure he wouldn't find any decent coffee, but at least he might find somewhere to get inside off the street. Tim was discovering he didn't enjoy hanging around streets by himself. Travel, they said—his father had said—broadens the mind, but he wasn't too convinced about that anymore. So far, travel had made his mind shrink down and concentrate on minutiae, whether the coffee would be strong, whether the bed in the hostel would be lumpy, whether he'd find anything resembling real orange juice for breakfast. He might not be cut out for traveling.

Around the square, several small stores were opening their doors, a newspaper and candy store, a dress shop with old-fashioned, blank-faced mannequins, a shoe store, a greengrocer's, a butcher's. Tim sniffed at the morning air for a hint of coffee and caught instead a pervasive odor of fried fish and chips and stale beer, and from the dark stone church opposite, a cloying, funereal scent of lilies. This highly developed sense of smell was proving yet another handicap on his foreign travels, his sensitive nose detecting, all too readily, unwashed bodies, unsanitary restrooms, centuries of dust and soot in the old buildings, the unsettling redolence of bloody unwrapped meat in the butchers' shops. Never before had Tim realized how deodorized daily life was in the United States, so wrapped in plastic, so safe. And if it was like this in Britain, a country supposed to be the most akin to America, how would it be when he got to France? He'd heard about France, garlic and Gauloise cigarettes on everyone's breath, toilets mere reeking holes in the ground, just thank heaven not to be female in those conditions.

He couldn't smell any coffee, good or bad, but set off in search of it anyway, because he had to head somewhere. He was fairly confident he'd come across one of those places that catered to people much smaller than he, lintels too low at the door, tables too tiny to accommodate his knees. The whole country made him feel like an awkward giant. He wandered down a side street and came upon a door bearing the sign, "MORNING COFFEE," and pushed at the door. A bell tinkled above his head, reminding him, just in time, to duck, and a mouthwatering aroma of newly baked bread wafted over him, mixed with the unmistakable, unbelievable smell of fresh percolating coffee. He could hardly believe his luck.

Easing the backpack off his shoulders, Tim dropped it with a thud on the ground. The café was tiny and crammed with dark wooden tables and chairs, all empty of customers, but a girl with dark curly hair and rosy cheeks, pretty in an unformed teenage way, was mopping the counter, almost hidden behind glass cake stands and heaping white china cups and saucers. Her mouth dropped open at the sight of his backpack, as though she'd never seen anything like it before. "Goodness!" she exclaimed. "What on earth do you have in that enormous thing?"

She spoke with a funny lilting accent, up and down a scale in a singsong fashion that made Tim smile. She smiled back at him, shyly, her teeth crooked. It felt as though weeks had passed since anyone near his own age had spoken to him.

"Sleeping bag, bedroll," he explained. "A change of socks."

"Goodness!" she said again. "And how far are you going to carry it?"

"To Ireland. I'm taking the boat to Ireland. Then after that I'm going to France and Italy, perhaps Greece. Ever been to Greece?"

"Greece? You must be joking. I've never even been to London."

"Not been to London?" Tim was amazed. "I just came from there. Via Oxford and Bath and Cardiff."

The girl leaned on the counter and wriggled her shoulders. "Oh, Cardiff. I've been to Cardiff. But London's hundreds of miles away. Are you American, then?"

"American," Tim agreed. "And what I'd like is a cup of coffee, hot, strong and black, no sugar, no cream, just the way they make it in America. Can you do that for me?"

"I don't know. I've never been to America, have I, so I don't know how they make their coffee there, do I?"

"Okay, I'll take whatever you've got."

She swiped at the crowded countertop with the damp rag. "It's not ready yet. Not for another few minutes. People don't usually come in till well after ten, you know." There was a faint accusatory note in her voice, as though he'd violated some unwritten rule of coffee shop hours, but she lifted the glass lid of a cake stand with dainty fingers. "Want a sticky bun?"

Tim gazed at the array of luridly colored cakes. "Sure. Why not?" As he settled on one with the least amount of frosting, the girl wrinkled her forehead.

"Is it today you're catching the boat to Ireland? It doesn't go till three, you know. That'll be one and sixpence, please."

By now he'd learned how to cope with the complicated currency, pulled a heap of coins out of his pocket, let them lay on his open palm, and watched as she picked out a few, delicately, so her fingers didn't touch his. He smiled again. Most girls he knew weren't that way at all. Not at all.

"I know the boat doesn't go until three. Only five hours to kill. But as a matter of fact, I was hoping to look up someone my father knew during the war."

"The war?" Her voice flew upwards, high and amazed. "The war's been over for more than twenty years. It's far too long for anyone to remember that far back." She thought about it for a moment. "Was your dad a soldier, then? I've heard there were American soldiers stationed here before D-Day."

"I guess that's when it was."

"So who is he, this friend of your dad's? Maybe I know him?"

"It's a she. Her name was Gwyneth Griffiths. I believe she's married to a Dr. Edwards." But Tim knew without doubt it was Dr. Edwards because he'd listened carefully to what the stranger had told his father.

"I know who Dr. Edwards is, of course. Everyone knows Dr. Edwards. I don't know what his wife's name was but I bet my da will know. He knows everybody for miles around." Opening a door behind the counter, she called out, "Dada, are you there?" and then she strung together a bunch of totally incomprehensible words in a completely foreign language. From somewhere in the depths of the building came a muffled reply and the girl closed the door. "He'll be right down."

"What was that?" Tim asked. "That language?"

She stared at him as if he were some kind of idiot, her eyes round and astonished. "Welsh, of course. Haven't you ever heard Welsh before?"

"Welsh? It's a language? A whole different language?"

"You didn't know that? Fancy not knowing that! Fancy! Don't you know you're in Wales?"

"Forgive me." Tim was humble. "I thought Wales was just a part of England."

She laughed then, spots of color running high in her cheeks, like a pretty painted china doll. "You'd better not say that to my da."

Placing his elbows on the counter, Tim leaned closer to her. "So what's your name?" She blushed and turned away, lifted the glass pot, poured the coffee in an unsteady stream into a thick white cup, pushed it towards him, and in an embarrassed whisper, as though she'd never had to confess her name to anyone before, muttered, almost under her breath, "Eirwen. Eirwen Price."

"Eirwen?" Tim repeated. "How do you spell it?"

"E-I-R-W-E-N."

"That's charming. Eirwen. I've never heard it before. Is it a Welsh name?"

"Of course it is." The color in her cheeks deepened. "I think it's a stupid name."

"But we all think our own name is stupid. Or too ordinary. Mine's ordinary. Tim. Tim Bruce." He reached out across the counter to shake her hand.

She seemed uncertain what to make of such confidences and

moved away from the counter cautiously, putting distance between the two of them, and at that moment the door behind the counter creaked open and a short, thickset man came through it. His face was the same round shape as the girl's and he glowered at Tim. The street door tinkled and two women came into the café, immediately launching into an animated conversation in the same strange tongue. Retreating to one of the tiny tables with his coffee and frosted cake, Tim listened with uncomprehending interest. Fancy, indeed, not knowing there was such a language. Wales might be more amusing than he'd thought so far.

The women wore identical short tweed coats and little felt hats. They were small and dumpy, just the right size for the tables and chairs, and as they collected their coffee from the counter, they glanced surreptitiously at Tim and looked away just as quickly. He smiled at them, but they didn't smile back, as if unwilling to acknowledge his presence, as if he were an intruder on private territory, and they carried their cups and saucers to a table in the window and whispered to each other with furtive bent heads.

Eirwen said, "Dada, this chap is looking for someone his father knew in the war." She said "war" as though there were only ever one war, as if right now there wasn't another war going on that threatened to engulf and doom someone like Tim, as wars had always engulfed and doomed young men. The women at the table in the window paused in their conversation.

"World War Two," Tim explained.

Eirwen's father frowned. "Are you American?" There was a challenging note in his voice and Tim wanted to say, "Something wrong with that?" but instead he said, "Yes, sir. My dad was stationed here in the war."

One of the women at the window spoke up. "There were Americans up by Cwm Glas, right before the invasion. You remember, Billy. In that big camp up by Cwm Glas."

"Of course I remember," he said, and there was a pause as they all seemed to think about it.

"So who was it your father knew?" Eirwen's father asked at last. He sounded suspicious, as though Tim was trying to pull some kind of scam. "I know everyone around these parts."

"Her name was Gwyneth Griffiths. I'm told she married a Dr. Edwards."

Over by the window, the women sat up straighter and exchanged sideways glances, their eyes small and somehow disapproving.

Tim looked at them. "You know who I mean? Someone called Gwyneth who's married to Dr. Edwards?" Their eyes slid away from his.

"Everybody knows Dr. Edwards," Eirwen's father said. "That would be his wife. Her name is Gwyneth."

The women looked at each other again, mouths tight and pursed, and one of them nodded knowingly. "Yes, Gwyneth Griffiths. That's who she was."

Tim couldn't believe his search had proved to be so easy, and after all, wasn't sure he really wanted it to be. So what if he found this Gwyneth, what was he going to say to her? Maybe it had all been a stupid idea. But the women's reaction made him curious. "You know where I can find her?"

"Well, she'd be at home, wouldn't she?" one woman said.

"And where's home?"

"Well, they live out at Llanberis. Isn't that right, Billy?"

"That's right. Llanberis."

"Is it far?" Tim was uneasy now. "Will there be time to get there and back before the ferry leaves?"

Everyone looked at the clock on the wall behind the counter, a big and old-fashioned clock with large black hands, like a school clock. It was ten-fifteen.

"Llanberis is four or five miles away. Easy with a car. I'll give you directions."

"I don't have a car. I've been hitchhiking."

There was another small silence, as though no one was willing to believe him. Their faces seemed to say, "You're American and you don't have a car?"

Eirwen smiled at her father, a toothy, winning smile. "You could give him a lift, couldn't you, Da? You're going that way. It wouldn't be any trouble, would it now, Da?"

Tugging at the peak of his tweed cap, he cleared his throat reluctantly. "I suppose not. I was just leaving, as a matter of fact."

"I wouldn't want to take you out of your way, sir. Perhaps we should call first?"

"No, no. I don't think that'll be necessary. If she isn't there, you can just come on back with me, can't you? I've only got a few deliveries to make."

"Well, thanks a million." Tim wasn't sure quite how thankful he was really, and hesitated for another moment, but since he seemed stuck with the decision, he heaved the backpack off the floor and drew little gasps from the women in the window.

Staring at the backpack, Eirwen's father laughed suddenly. "Dew, boy, I don't know there's room in my little van for that monster. Come on, though, we'll give it a go." He lifted the flap of the counter to let Tim through.

"See you later," Tim said to Eirwen as he passed close by her and she blushed again, winningly. He followed her father along a narrow dark hallway, the backpack lurching against the walls, and emerged into an alleyway where a parked white van almost filled the space between buildings. He squeezed the backpack behind the passenger seat, among baskets of sweet-smelling bread, and crushed himself into the front seat, knees bent toward his chin at an absurd angle.

"Hold on tight, boyo," Billy Price said, throwing in the clutch, and rocketing the little van down the alley as though there was no time to waste, skidded around the corner, past the front of the café, around the square and the war memorial, down a steep hill out of the square, and over a narrow, humped one-lane bridge. The oncoming traffic seemed to pass only inches away from Tim as he huddled nervously in the passenger seat.

On the other side of the bridge, after another steep hill rising between high fuschia hedges, they were all of sudden out of the town, on a smooth and empty road in brilliant sunshine, the mist left behind. For a moment, the sun blinded Tim and he had to blink away from it. Ahead of them, a radiant expanse of water met the horizon in a shining blue arc; on the right-hand side of the road, smooth green hills rose to craggy tops and were dotted with whitewashed cottages, and on the left-hand side of the road, the hills swept down to sharply defined cliffs, each indentation and curve clearly etched in the bright morning light. Far below, the ocean's edge tumbled and curled against black rocks and slivers of pale yellow sand.

"Jeez!" Tim leaned forward in the seat. "It *is* beautiful. After all, it is beautiful."

Billy Price grinned. "Yes, it's pretty enough round here. Lived here all my life. Wouldn't dream of living anywhere else."

"Were you here in the war?"

"I was off fighting Rommel in the desert, boyo. With Monty. You heard of Monty?"

"Montgomery? Sure I've heard of him."

"Bloody marvelous general, he was. If you want to know how to fight a war, go ask someone like Monty."

Tim had absolutely no desire to fight in any war, and that wasn't what he'd heard about Montgomery. He'd heard Montgomery was nothing but an arsehole, a pain in the butt, a thorn in the side of the people who'd done the real fighting, the Americans, but he guessed it was probably wiser not to voice that particular opinion at this particular moment. Before he could think of something diplomatic to say, Billy Price swung the van across the road into a narrow opening between high hedges, and the abrupt maneuver threw Tim hard against the door. Downshifting the gears in quick succession, Billy Price revved the small engine hard, and hummed to himself as though he'd forgotten he had a passenger.

Soon they were climbing even more steeply, higher and higher, the engine laboring. The hedgerows and houses vanished, the fields turned to open heath, and black-faced sheep lifted their heads to watch them pass. Tim could hardly credit it was still the same country, the scenery had changed so abruptly and dramatically. The van climbed the narrow curving road towards the crags.

Pointing to the rocks, Tim remarked, "They look exactly like castles."

Billy laughed. "No, no. They're just rocks, that's all. But we do have a few castles round about. The English built them, you know, to keep the Welsh down. Didn't succeed, of course. The Welsh were always a problem for the English."

They seemed to be going nowhere, the landscape growing emptier, and the houses vanished, when Billy Price suddenly announced, "Here we are then, boyo." He brought the small vehicle to a screeching halt before a wide iron gate. "This is where she lives. Gwyneth Griffiths as was. Hop out and open the gate for me, there's a good lad."

Uncoiling from the passenger seat thankfully, Tim climbed out of the van, wondering what the hell he was doing here, why on earth he'd come so far on a foolish whim. He stood at the gate for a moment and the air smelled sweet and fresh, of hawthorn and bracken and the faint tang of salt water. Pine trees rustled overhead and there was the sound of birds high on the hillside, but otherwise everything was extraordinarily quiet. Far from anywhere.

He swung the gate open.

Beyond the gate, a graveled driveway wound up to a long, low, whitewashed house, a house with small deep-set windows and a steep roof of dark slate. The front door was painted a shiny bright blue and it stood open. Like an invitation. As though he were expected.

Two

·

Gwyneth heard the van grinding up the hill before she ever saw it. When the wind was from the right direction, it was almost impossible for any vehicle, let alone one whose engine strained and labored like this, to approach the house without being heard. The advance warning gave her a feeling of security. No one could arrive unexpectedly, so it gave her a chance to escape, to pretend she wasn't home. Gwyneth preferred not to be surprised.

She watched from the window as a small white van stopped before the gate into the driveway. Billy Price's van. What was Billy Price doing here? She hadn't ordered anything from him. The passenger door of the van opened and a tall young man, broad-shouldered and narrow-hipped, in a faded plaid shirt and a pair of equally faded jeans, sprang out to unlock the gate. Someone she'd never seen before. At least, she was almost certain she'd never seen him before, although there was an elusive familiarity to him. As he stood holding the gate, he stared up at the house and then down the mountain towards the sea; the breeze lifted his floppy bright hair and the sun glinted on it, across the sharp angles of his face. Uneasily, Gwyneth thought, he reminds me of somebody, somebody . . .

The van drove in, the young man swung the gate shut and strode up the curved gravel drive behind the van, his gait easy and loping, his head high and somehow arrogant on his neck, and in that instant, in the way he walked, in the carriage of his head, in the slant of sunshine on his face, an abrupt jolt of recognition crashed through Gwyneth. Alternative waves of heat and cold battered her, freezing and burning, cramping her stomach, banging her heart against her rib cage; her legs and arms turned to blocks of wood, to carved stone so she was unable to move, do anything to prevent this . . . this apparition approaching her house, her home, her castle. She wanted to throw herself on the floor, to melt away so she was hidden from his eyes and the eyes of Billy Price, but she couldn't take a step, couldn't breathe, could only just manage to keep upright. And it was already too late, because she'd forgotten the front door was wide open and Billy Price was rapping on it with his knuckles, stepping through into the hallway, so that he could see her pinned against the window of the dining room, impaled like an insect. Trapped.

"Oh, there you are, Mrs. Edwards," Billy Price said. "Forgive me for walking in like that but the door was open."

He paused awkwardly in the hallway and removed his cap, an oddly unfamiliar gesture. Gwyneth thought, irrelevantly, that she'd never seen Billy Price without his cap before. He was waiting for her to say something but her voice had been snatched away, as if she was in one of those dreams where you have to speak some special word in order to be saved from some peril, but the word won't come out of your mouth and you wake up, sweating and fighting with the bedclothes. In a moment, she would wake up, she knew she would . . .

"I brought this young fellow with me, Mrs. Edwards. He

wanted to meet you. Says something about you knowing his father in the war. So I gave him a lift up here." Billy raised his voice upwards, uncertainly. "I hope that was all right? I mean, perhaps we should have phoned first?"

Of course, he should have phoned first. Of course. And then she could have said don't come, I don't want him coming here, bringing those memories, invading my home. I could have said something, anything. But phoning first wasn't the way of the locals, she knew that. They liked to surprise you, catch you unawares. Now she was a prisoner in her own house, a fish caught on the end of a line, gasping for air.

Behind Billy Price, a long shadow stretched across the black and white tiles of the hallway. At first, Gwyneth dared not raise her eyes to look at its source, but when at last she did, it was as if a ghost had been conjured from the past. This living image of the past was smiling at her, a wide cheerful grin, full of innocence and the expectation of welcome, was reaching out a hand to grasp hers, and somehow her own hand was taking hold of his, as if she couldn't keep from touching him. His hand was warm and firm and strong, and with her hand in his, the years seemed to spin away so she was a girl again, treading on air, drifting in a daze of desire, her hair soft on her shoulders, her flesh on fire. Mad, out of control, wild and crazy for love with a stranger from across the sea.

"Hi!" The apparition smiled more broadly. His teeth were very white and even. "I'm Tim Bruce. I believe you knew my dad, Carlton Bruce. A long time ago. In the war."

His voice had exactly the same deep timbre, the same American accent, as though Carlton Bruce, gone and forgotten for so long, had suddenly materialized, unchanged, unmarked by time, had come sauntering back into her life with a grin and a cheery word, everything ready to be forgiven and forgotten. The shape of his mouth, the tilt of his chin, the angles of his cheekbones, those gray-green eyes . . . so incredibly familiar. She couldn't believe she hadn't recognized him instantly, the very first moment she'd set eyes on him down by the gate. How was it possible to have forgotten someone so completely and then recall him so clearly, as though the years had never passed?

She had to say something. She should attempt to be civilized, at the very least. But what? What could she possibly say to this echo of the past? Oh, how nice to meet you? Do come in. How's your father? I've been waiting to hear for more than twenty years? The silence stretched into seconds and she was acutely conscious that Billy Price was staring at her, listening to the peculiar silence, waiting, no doubt, to report on her down in Clarrach. She was always an object of interest in Clarrach.

Gwyneth took a long deep breath. "Why, yes," she said. "Yes, I believe I do remember," and was amazed how normal, how ordinary her voice sounded.

"I'm glad," the boy said, "because he's often spoken of you."

It wasn't true. He'd only heard Carlton speak of her that one time. Until that moment, Tim had never heard her name, had never known of her existence. But he could see immediately she hadn't forgotten Carlton, the way the color left her face, the way the pupils enlarged in her light brown eyes, how her hand trembled in his. He also understood in a heartbeat why his father hadn't forgotten her. In that overheard conversation, he'd said she was beautiful, but Tim hadn't for a moment expected to find her so, not merely because she must be middle-aged by now, but because his father's idea of beauty was surely different from his own. But this woman *was* beautiful. Incredibly, unbelievably so, with a smooth pale face and high, curving cheekbones, heavy-lidded, shadowy eyes of a strange amber color, a long, slender neck and a cloud of soft brown hair tied back with a ribbon. Like Sleeping Beauty, Tim thought ridiculously. Untouched by the years. Waiting to be wakened. She couldn't be his father's age, couldn't be. There must be some mistake. In that instant, treacherously, Tim couldn't help comparing his mother's teased and bouffant hair style and her stiff tailored clothes, shiny and deliberately put together, with this woman who was dressed with a casual grace, long skirts flowing and eddying, silky shirt clinging to breasts he knew would be blue-veined and white.

Absurdly dumbstruck, Tim was smitten into silence, his hand holding hers. He felt the two of them were frozen into a tableau, fixed in a frame, as though they were being photographed and preserved forever, just like this, sunshine filling the hallway of the house, gleaming on the black and white tiled floor, glinting off the gold chain around her white neck.

Billy Price cleared his throat, his boots scraping loud on the floor. "Well then, I'll be getting on my way. You two will have a lot to talk about, no doubt." Cramming his cap back on his head, he moved sideways around them. "Give my regards to the doctor," he said to Gwyneth.

She seemed startled when he spoke and she dropped Tim's hand, turned the wide eyes to Billy Price. "You're leaving?"

"Got my deliveries to make. I just gave this young fellow a ride, like."

There was another moment of silence.

Tim said, "I'm catching the ferry to Ireland this afternoon. It was kind of Mr. Price to bring me up here. Just on the off chance you were home."

"The ferry to Ireland?" she echoed, as if Ireland was a place she'd only vaguely heard of.

"He doesn't have a car," Billy Price explained. "Perhaps you or the doctor could give him a lift to the boat later on?"

"I could hitch a ride," Tim said. "It isn't far. I could even walk it."

"Well then." Billy Price rubbed his hands together briskly as if ridding himself of a problem. "I'll be off, then. Good-bye,

Mrs. Edwards. Good luck to you, *bach*." He slapped Tim on the shoulder, stepped out of the hallway.

There was the sound of the van's engine revving up, a screech of tires on the gravel as it turned and headed back down the driveway. "Oh, my God!" Tim exclaimed. "My backpack!" He suddenly jerked into action, hurling himself out of the door and down the driveway after Billy Price.

Moving slowly, almost painfully, to the door, Gwyneth leaned against it, lifted her hand to shield the sun from her eyes, watched him running with an easy loping stride to catch the van at the gate. He reached into the back and hauled out a huge rucksack, heaved it onto one shoulder, and started up towards the house again. The unexpected flurry of movement and the absurd size of his burden broke the spell; she stepped out of the door, and the breeze blew up the hillside, lifted her hair, and blew away the fantasies. Her arms and legs became flesh again, connected again, the blood circulating in her head so she was no longer in a trance. But she was too late to stop Billy Price driving away without his passenger.

Before he reached the front door again, the boy turned to look down the hill at the indented coastline far below.

"It's stunning up here. I didn't appreciate it down there in the town. Up here it's quite different. Look at that! You can see for miles."

Gwyneth said, "On a clear day, you can see all the way to Ireland," and thought it was the first normal thing she'd said since he walked up to the house. She made an effort to say something more, pointed to the west. "Over there. See that smudge on the horizon? That's Ireland. And that way . . ." She gestured to the north. "Over there is Snowdon."

"Snowdon?"

"Our highest mountain."

"How high is it?"

And with an alarming sense of déjà vu, Gwyneth knew where

the conversation was going because she'd had this same inconsequential conversation before. A long long time ago. "About three thousand feet," she said, and waited for him to throw back his light-colored head and laugh. Which he did.

"Where I live," he said, "the highest mountain is over fourteen thousand feet."

It made Gwyneth's head spin to hear him say it, because Carlton Bruce had said the very same thing all those years before. The thought of so many years made her dizzy, time and reality sliding away from her once more, her life telescoping suddenly, compressing, as if she was still a foolish and starstruck girl. Sitting down quickly on the bench outside the front door, specially positioned to admire the view, Gwyneth couldn't look at the view, could only stare at her feet, her mind running in tiny scrabbling circles, ineffectually and nonsensically.

She didn't raise her head, didn't look at him. "Can I ask . . . ? How old you are?"

"Almost twenty-three," he said.

Almost twenty-three. Like a child, telling his age that way. It was now 1968 and Carlton Bruce was here in 1944. Twenty-four years ago. Twenty-four years! A lifetime—more than this boy's lifetime.

His feet scrunched on the gravel. He wore enormous hiking boots, laced up around his ankles, and she thought, he'll be off to Ireland in a couple of hours, I can manage to be polite until then. He's only a boy, he knows nothing, why should he? Nobody knows. Not even Rhys. And then she thought, Rhys will be home soon, for lunch. Do I want them to meet, this stranger who isn't a stranger, my husband who doesn't care for strangers? I can ask this boy to go now. I can look him in the face and say, sorry, but you called at an inconvenient moment, and I'll phone for Jenkins the taxi to take him down to Clarrach and then he'll be gone, out of my life, as though he never came into it, and everything will go on in the same old way. Undisturbed, peaceful, humdrum. And safe.

Out of the corner of her eye, Gwyneth saw his boots scuffing at the gravel, little bursts of dust flying in the air. "Would you mind?" he said tentatively, "if I had a look round? You've got such an incredible view and I've never been to Wales before. I've never even been inside a Welsh house."

She looked past him and then up at him. Now was her chance to say "go." Now.

He smiled at her, the corners of his mouth drawn down humbly. "I didn't mean to be disparaging about your mountain."

His smile was infectious. It was such a relief to feel herself smiling that she rose to her feet involuntarily. Soon he would be gone, soon. He was a stranger in the country, a visitor, and she didn't want to be uncivil, but even as she ushered him through the front door, she thought, no, this is a mistake, and by then he was already inside the house. She hesitated for another moment, still uncertain, took a deep steadying breath and showed him through the hallway and into the long sitting room. She started to tell him about the house and suddenly it was easier because she had something definite and limited to say. She heard herself saying too much, breathlessly, too fast.

"This was a farmhouse, once upon a time, practically in ruins when Rhys and I bought it. I suppose we've wasted an awful lot of time and effort doing it up, saving it, but it's so peaceful up here on the mountain. Of course, it seems wonderful in the summer when the sun is shining like this, but in the winter the winds howl in off the sea and storms blow up the mountainside and it can be quite bleak. Lonely, some people think. The people who lived here probably couldn't wait to get away, back down to civilization and neighbors. But I like it. Far from the madding crowd and all that. And now that we have conveniences like central heating and electric light and running hot water, life's easy, isn't it? The people who lived here before didn't have any of those things, of course."

Tim couldn't imagine life without electric light or running hot water. He watched her talking, listened to her voice running up and down a scale like the girl's in the café, but the lilt of it softer and gentler, the accent fainter. Her hands flew in and out as she talked, nice hands, long thin fingers, the amber eyes glowing, and as she talked she seemed to become even younger, almost his own age. He followed her round the house, exclaiming over the thick stone walls, the tiny deep-set windows, and wanted to know all about the house, how old it was.

"Oh, not more than a couple of hundred years," she replied casually, and Tim laughed and told her there weren't any houses near as old as that where he came from. He told her how he liked to build things himself, how the houses where he came from were built of cedar and fir, not great heavy stones like this, and he inspected with minute interest the iron latches on the doors, the hand-hewn beams in the ceilings, the cool flagstones on the kitchen floor, the huge hooks in the ceiling beams of the kitchen. She explained that bacon once used to hang there, for curing. A steep and narrow staircase with dark blue carpeting and brass rods curled up from the hallway, but she didn't offer to take him up there.

It wasn't a large house, but it was fragrant with wax polish and the scent of flowers, of herbs and something delicious cooking in the oven. The sun streamed in through the windows. It was the first time the sun had shone on Tim since he'd been away from home. The ceilings and doorways felt too low for him; he had to remember to duck his head every time he went through a doorway, but there was a warm settled feel to the whole house, as though it had always been this way, not as if someone had gone out to search for special objects to furnish and decorate it. There were old maps and prints on the walls and faded chintz covers on the chairs, lots of books and a piano in the living room. He noticed how the top of the piano was bare, no clutter of photographs on it, which surely meant there weren't any children in this house. The piano in his parents' living room bore an extensive pictorial history of the Bruce family, weddings, graduations, stylized and posed photos, his father, his mother, his sister Annette, his brother Mark. And himself, of course. Tim had a sudden unexpected twinge of homesickness.

Finally Gwyneth led him out through the kitchen door at the back of the house, away from the ocean view, and as they stepped outside, house martens dipped and swooped around their heads. On this side of the house, there was shelter from the sea breezes. A high stone wall surrounded a hidden secret oasis, an emerald green lawn, curved beds with flowers, straight lines of berry bushes and vegetables and tall growing shrubs; peaches and apple trees were espaliered against the wall and old-fashioned roses climbed on trellises. From beyond the walls came the plaintive sound of sheep and birds were singing somewhere high above, and the whole garden was filled with the gentle soporific drone of bees and a heady scent of lavender and sage. Tim was sure this garden must have been here for centuries, that people must have tended plants inside these walls since before history was written. He sensed, for the first time, an overwhelming longevity that he'd been seeking and hadn't discovered so far, not in London, not even in Oxford with its ancient mellowed buildings. Perhaps because in this sheltered enclave, there was no sound of hurtling traffic, no crowds and no streets, no intrusions of the twentieth century; here were only the muted sounds of the garden and the hillside beyond. Here he felt he could listen for what he'd been hoping to find, all those yesterdays of mankind, that long stretch of history to put the realities of today into perspective. Even if by now he'd seen too many of those gut-twisting memorials not to be aware that the yesterdays of mankind were drenched in blood.

"Just beautiful," Tim murmured, inadequately and awkwardly, standing in the sunshine in the garden. "Jesus, so beautiful."

The even more beautiful Gwyneth seemed gratified by his reaction. She was almost smiling at him now, the shadows chased
away from her eyes. As he followed her along the grassy paths between the flower beds, he watched the sway of her skirts against
her legs, the shape of her narrow bare feet in the open sandals.
There was something medieval about her, he thought, with her
cloud of hair and pale serious face; she made him think of Arthur
and Guinevere, Merlin and Excalibur.

At the end of the path where it met the wall, Tim stretched to
look over the wall, up to the craggy tops of the hillside. They still
reminded him of ancient castles.

"Merlin?" he asked. "Wasn't he a Welshman?"

"Why, yes." The sudden brilliance of her smile was dazzling.
"So you *do* know something about Wales, after all."

"No, I know nothing. Nothing. I didn't even know there was a
Welsh language until the girl in the café started speaking it. Billy
Price's daughter. She had a pretty name. Eirwen. Do you speak
Welsh?" He wanted to call her Gwyneth, wanted to roll the sound
of it in his mouth, didn't quite dare to.

She smiled again. "I know a few words but I can't really speak
it. I didn't learn it while I was a child. It's quite a difficult language, you know. But Rhys, my husband, was brought up in a
Welsh-speaking household. He didn't use English until he went to
school."

Tim shook his head in disbelief. "To think I never knew."

"There was Welsh in Wales before there was English in England. It's a very old tongue."

"Teach me a word," Tim said. "Just one."

"What word would you like to know?"

He thought about it for a moment. "Thank you. Thank you
would be useful."

"Yes," she agreed. "It would be. *Diolch.* That means thank you."

"*Diolch?*" Tim struggled with it. "So I can say *diolch* to you? For showing me your beautiful house. What is house? What is beautiful?"

"You said just one word. Anyway, this house is hardly beautiful, even though it's kind of you to say so. It's just an ordinary Welsh farmhouse."

Ordinary, Tim thought. Like you are ordinary? Turning to look at the house again, the small windows set deep in the stones, the long sloping roof, the martens swooping around the eaves, he noticed another building, also slate-roofed but windowless, attached to the wall at the far end of the garden. "What's that building?"

"Once upon a time, it was a barn and an old pigsty." She made a small movement with her shoulders under the silky shirt, and Tim tried not to watch the rise and fall of her breasts. "Now it's been converted. Into a kind of studio."

"A studio? Someone paints? You?"

Gwyneth spread her hands in a dismissive gesture. "I try."

He might have guessed it from the way she dressed, the flowing clothes, the fluid movements. Like an artist. Or an artist's model, that grace, those moments of stillness. He stared from her to the building. "But there aren't any windows."

"They're on the other side, the north side. And there are skylights in the roof."

"I'd like to see your paintings," Tim said. Boldly. Though he didn't feel bold. He felt awkward and gauche and out of his depth. "Would you show them to me?"

She looked startled, almost alarmed, and shook her head. "I don't show them to anyone. It's something I do just for myself."

"No one?"

"No one."

He was disappointed, but in a way relieved. He wanted to believe that everything she painted would be a masterpiece and wouldn't know how to react if it wasn't.

Turning away from the wall, Gwyneth headed back towards the house, down a path between orderly rows of raspberry canes. Berries hung heavy on the branches, and she paused along the way to finger the fruit, as if testing its ripeness. For a few seconds she remained very still, then she looked at Tim. A small frown creased her forehead and she said slowly, as if it was important, "Do you like raspberries? Some of these seem to be ripe."

"Raspberries? Love 'em."

"I could pick some for lunch." She hesitated again, peering at him, then at the berries. "Perhaps you'd like to stay for lunch?"

Taken by surprise, delighted, Tim said, "Why, that'd be great. Great. Are you sure?"

She turned with flurry of skirts. "Wait. I'll get something to put them in," she said and hurried away. Tim waited among the raspberry canes and the thrumming bees, but without her the garden felt empty and deserted. Never in his wildest dreams could he have imagined the woman his father had spoken of would turn out to be like this, like some sort of . . . witch. That's what she was, a beautiful Welsh witch. A female Merlin. He'd never before understood the real meaning of the word bewitched, but now he knew. Because this Gwyneth had bewitched him. Totally.

He was still standing there, befuddled and dazed, when she reappeared with a bowl in her hands. Handing it to him to hold, she began plucking the bright red berries from the canes. Tim watched the quick movement of her fingers, the delicate way she handled the berries, but before the bowl was half full, she straightened up and lifted her head, as though she was hearing something he couldn't hear. After a moment, Tim made out the sound of a car engine coming close, stopping, starting again.

Gwyneth said, "That'll be Rhys, my husband, home for lunch."

It seemed to Tim that a cloud had suddenly skidded across the sun and cast a shadow over the garden, silencing the bees and the birds, as though a spell was broken, as if the magic web wrapped around him was breaking apart. He wouldn't be alone with her any longer. He had so little time.

Soon he'd be on his way and he'd never see her again.

Three

Rhys Edwards was late getting home for lunch. But then he was late for lunch most days; late for lunch, for dinner, for appointments, running perpetually behind the clock. A way of life. Secretly, to himself, Rhys acknowledged it could be a defense mechanism, a manipulative device. Not that he considered himself a manipulator, of course, not at all, but when he was trapped by the endless demands, the recurring emergencies, it was the ability to make others wait for him, even Gwyneth, perhaps especially Gwyneth, that made him feel he might be in control of his own life.

Rhys liked going home to the house up the mountain, enjoyed racing the car too fast up the narrow lanes with the heavy scent of hawthorn blossom in the air, air washed clean by storms sweeping in from the southwest, sudden rushes of wind and rain gone as quickly as they came. He liked his house, his own little piece of history, two hundred years old, built of ancient stone from the quarries on the other side of the mountain. The walls were repaired now, the rotting window frames made new, the antique kitchen updated, the long low roof retiled with fresh blue Welsh slate. A simple house, reborn and proud, high on the hillside between slanting Scotch pines. Gwyneth had done it all, of course. Rhys had neither the time nor the inclination to have devoted his energy to the project, but now it was done, he was content with it, delighted with his own little bit of Wales saved for the future.

Whistling, he skimmed close by the hedges, slammed on the brakes to avoid the red mail van driving equally quickly down the hill, waved to Harries the postman, flung the car round the last corner, and stopped short at the tight space between the gateposts. He leapt out to open the gate and smiled at his good fortune. If it had been up to him, right at the beginning, he'd as soon have continued living down in the town, but it was Gwyneth who persuaded him to come all the way up here, and now he loved the freshness of the mountain, away from the traffic and the people he saw quite enough during the day, thank you very much. Up here he could kick back and relax, not have to be on duty all the time. Up here, he was king of the castle.

The blue front door with the shiny brass knocker stood ajar. Rhys shut it carefully behind him. A nice day, but not that nice, a waste to let the expensive warm air inside the house wander outside. He called out, "Hello, Gwyneth, sorry I'm late," same as always, draped his jacket on the newel post, crossed the hallway into the kitchen, lifted the lid of a saucepan. "Gwyneth, I'm home."

The sun was bright through the windows, almost balmy, almost like summer, and Rhys guessed she was out in the garden, playing around with her plants as usual. He wasn't a gardener himself and couldn't appreciate the joy of dirt under one's fingernails, but it pleased him that Gwyneth seemed to like growing vegetables for the kitchen and flowers for the house. But then everything about Gwyneth pleased him. Her creative touch with flowers pleased him, her habit of stuffing large, untidy arrangements into every sort of odd container, copper bowls or brass jugs or ceramic vases, anything that took her fancy, so the house was always full of heady fragrances Rhys couldn't quite identify. The looseness, the abandon of the arrangements revealed a side of Gwyneth that normally wasn't apparent; she was otherwise so neat, so contained, so careful not to spill over any edges. He might understand more of that creative side if he could ever see any of those paintings she never wanted him to look at, though sometimes he wondered whether she ever really painted anything at all, didn't just disappear into her inner sanctum and stare at the walls. Sometimes he was tempted to go in the old pigsty to check on what she really was doing, but he supposed she was entitled to stare at walls undisturbed if that's what she fancied.

Pausing at the back door, Rhys shaded his eyes against the sun, and saw Gwyneth standing among the raspberry canes at the far end of the garden. He opened his mouth to call and then realized she wasn't alone. Gwyneth was almost always alone—she claimed she preferred it that way—but now there was a tall, fair-haired fellow with her, someone Rhys didn't recognize, a tall and lean young man in blue jeans and a plaid shirt, blond hair gleaming bright in the sunshine. Someone Rhys was certain he'd never seen before. Gwyneth was plucking raspberries off the canes, dropping them into a bowl that this stranger was holding for her, and she was laughing, the color running high in her face, the wild brown hair curling out of a ribbon at the back of her neck. As she laughed, she threw her head back and her white throat lengthened and the sun and the wind caught her hair into a hazy transparent cloud, and Rhys was suddenly struck anew by her beauty, as if he was looking at someone he'd not seen for a long time.

Who the hell was he, this fellow who was making his beautiful, melancholy wife laugh like that?

Rhys stood in the doorway and watched her. It was the first thing he'd ever known about her, of course, her beauty. And her melancholy. That very first time he'd gone to visit Gwyneth's mother in her little house in Clarrach, he'd noticed the photographs. It would have been impossible not to notice them, so many around the bedroom, on the walls, in silver frames on the dresser, on the nightstand beside the bed, striking photographs of a cool, poised young woman in odd unnatural poses, eyes and cheekbones emphasized by artful lighting, by the extraordinary clothes she was wearing. His eyes kept wandering to the photographs even as he placed his stethoscope on Mrs. Griffiths' chest and listened to her heart, tapped her chest, felt her belly.

"My daughter," Mrs. Griffiths said. Proudly. Proprietorially. "My Gwyneth. She's a model, you know."

On that first visit, he'd picked up one of the photos and stared at the sad shadowy eyes and the hollowed curving cheeks. "She's very beautiful," he'd said inadequately, and put the photo down quickly because he should be paying all his attention to his patient. But Mrs. Griffiths was pleased, though he detected a hint of acerbity in her voice. "Most of them don't really look much like her," she said. "All that makeup. Those funny clothes. Extraordinary what those designers think up, isn't it?"

"Where does she live?" Rhys wanted to know. Because one day soon, sooner rather than later, he'd have to summon her home if she wanted to see her mother before it was too late, and somehow he wasn't surprised when she told him, "Sometimes in London. Sometimes in Paris. I never know where she is half the time."

"Does she ever come back to visit?"

"Oh, no. Gwyneth hardly ever comes to Clarrach. Not since the war. But I've been up to see her in London. And she bought this house for me when I had to give up the shop. I used to keep the newsagent's on the square. Do you remember?"

Rhys didn't remember. He hadn't lived in Clarrach as a boy,

even though his father and grandfather were doctors in the town, and he'd been away for so many years, at boarding school and medical school and in the army, that he barely remembered the town in the old days. Afterwards, during the weeks before the disease finally caught up to Mrs. Griffiths, before he had to insist she send for her daughter, the model, she'd bring old magazines out of cupboards and drawers, glossy womens' magazines that Rhys would never have looked at himself, and she'd show him more photos and Rhys would fantasize about the day he'd get to meet this rare and glorious creature.

She was still rare and glorious.

He stepped out into the garden and Gwyneth turned to look at him as though she hadn't been expecting him. She spoke hurriedly, almost breathlessly.

"Rhys, darling, this is Tim Bruce. He's American. The son of someone I knew a long time ago."

The young man held out his hand and Rhys realized that after all, he was only a boy, young and eager, expecting to be welcomed, his smile wide and trusting.

❦

Tim saw a tall, thin man with a blank unwelcoming expression, as if he didn't care for the sight of a stranger. His eyes were dark and deep-set, his hair thick and black and tipped with gray as though he'd been out in a snowstorm. He shook Tim's hand, perfunctorily.

"An American? So what brings you to our part of the world?"

"He's just passing through," Gwyneth explained. "On his way to Ireland."

"Ireland? Ah, yes, that's where all Americans want to go, isn't it?"

The doctor had a deep rich voice, like an actor's, each consonant and syllable clearly defined and accented. Tim thought he could have been an actor with that lean, sardonic face, those hooded, brooding eyes.

"Are you on your way to Ireland at this precise moment?" Rhys Edwards wanted to know, and Tim was at a loss. Was he expected to leave at this precise moment?

Gwyneth said, "He's catching the ferry this afternoon."

"So soon?" Rhys Edwards ran his fingers through his hair, brushing it back from his forehead. "Well, then, let's not stand around in the garden wasting precious minutes," he said and spread his hands wide, sweeping Gwyneth and Tim before him, as if shepherding geese, through the flagstoned kitchen and into the room with the faded chintz furniture. Gesturing Tim to one of the chairs, he sat on the opposite side of the fireplace, crossed his legs and folded his arms and peered down his nose at Tim as at some sort of lab specimen. His dark flannel trousers were sharply creased and he wore a soft checked shirt and striped tie, so that Tim, in his jeans and hiking boots, not only felt scruffy by comparison, but knew he *was* scruffy. Especially in this man's eyes.

Tim said, "I must apologize for dropping by in this way. It was just on impulse and I had so little time."

"Indeed, if you're catching the boat, you do have very little time." Dr. Edwards looked pointedly at the watch on his left wrist. "The ferry leaves at three o'clock sharp." He cleared his throat and glanced up at Gwyneth. "And Gwyneth, my dear, I'd remind you that I don't have much time either. I must be back at the surgery by one."

"Lunch is almost ready. Actually, I've invited our visitor to stay for lunch."

She tossed the announcement over her shoulder as she left the room, not giving Tim a chance to say, "After all, perhaps I should go," because somehow he didn't believe Gwyneth's husband wanted him to stay for lunch. He waited a moment for Rhys

Edwards to say something and then ventured, "The surgery? Does that mean you're a surgeon?"

"No, just a common-o-garden GP, I fear. None of that high-flying stuff for me. The surgery is how we refer to the rooms where we see the patients. A hangover from the old days, when all physicians were surgeons of some kind or other." There was another moment of protracted silence. "So what is it that *you* do?"

Tim stared down at his knees, his jeans worn, his feet big and clumsy in the hiking boots, drew his legs and feet closer to his chair, and rested his elbows on his knees. "I've just finished undergrad school. At Berkeley. You know, in California. As a matter of fact, I'm thinking of going to medical school in the fall. I've been accepted at Harvard."

Dr. Edwards didn't seem particularly impressed, apparently not understanding that being accepted at Harvard was a big deal. He leaned back in the chair and half closed his eyes. "Harvard? Even I know about Harvard. And medical school? So you plan to be a doctor? What sort of doctor? A surgeon? A GP?"

Tim hesitated. The truth was he didn't have any idea what sort of doctor he might be. Or even if he was going to be a doctor at all. That wasn't why he'd applied to medical school. He'd applied to medical school to get out of the draft. He had to say something other than the truth. "I thought perhaps I might do research."

"Really? Research? What type of research?"

Tim desperately searched his mind for something he was at all familiar with. He knew very little about any form of medicine, research or otherwise. "Trypsin inhibitors," he said blindly. He'd heard of trypsin inhibitors when he was working in those awful dog labs at the hospital and he hoped a country doctor in Wales wouldn't know anything about such an esoteric subject. He knew absolutely nothing about it himself.

"Trypsin inhibitors? Well, that's certainly something no one else understands, so the field is wide open for you. But if that's the sort of medicine you want, wouldn't you be better off with basic sciences? It seems a bit of a waste to go to medical school unless you're interested in treating patients, don't you think?"

Tim was at a loss for words. Rhys Edwards had gone right to the heart of the matter. He'd very little interest in treating patients. The truth was that he had little interest in medicine, or in medical research, and somehow he was sure this man could see straight through the pretense.

"My father wanted me to go into law but it doesn't do to emulate one's father, does it?"

Dr. Edwards raised his eyebrows. His eyebrows were very dark, straight and black across his forehead, and they swept up at the ends and lent a faintly satanic expression to his thin face. "Oh, I don't know. I come from a long line of general practitioners myself, following in the family business, so to speak. So your father's a lawyer?"

"Yes."

"I've always understood doctors and lawyers don't get on too well in the United States. Is that correct? So what does he think of your taking up medicine?"

"He thinks it's great." But that wasn't true either. Carlton Bruce thought Tim should go to Vietnam and do his duty by his country, just as Carlton had done his duty in World War II. Carlton Bruce considered the whole antiwar movement as treachery.

Abruptly, startling Tim, Dr. Edwards leapt to his feet, as though he couldn't bear to sit still for another moment. He rubbed his hands together. "But I forget my duties as a host. Would you care for a glass of sherry?"

"Sherry? I don't believe I've ever had any."

"Never had sherry? My dear boy! Then you must certainly try some of this." Striding across the room to a large black oak cupboard in the corner, he rattled glasses and bottles. "I don't usually indulge in the middle of the day, but then it isn't everyday we have a guest from America, is it?"

He seemed to finish every sentence with a question, like the girl in the café, like Billy Price, her father. When they'd done it, it was somehow disarming, but there was nothing disarming about Dr. Edwards. Tim was accustomed to people liking him and he had the distinct and uncomfortable feeling that Gwyneth's husband had taken against him for some reason. He tried to imagine this cool sarcastic man as a country doctor and wondered how his patients related to him. He wondered how his wife related to him.

Handing Tim a small crystal glass filled to the brim with pale golden liquid, Rhys Edwards raised his own. "Well, *iechyd da,*" he said and knocked it back in one gulp. Tim took a cautious sip and didn't like what he tasted, too tart, too aromatic. He'd prefer a beer any day.

"Pity you don't have more time," Dr. Edwards said. "I'd take you on rounds with me. Show you how we do medicine in this country."

Immediately intrigued by the idea, Tim decided the suggestion was made only because Dr. Edwards knew he was leaving in a couple of hours and wouldn't be able to accept.

"Rounds? You have to see your patients in the hospital?"

"No, of course not. That's not my purview. I see my patients in their homes. Those that can't make it to the surgery, that is."

"You mean . . . house calls? I didn't know anyone did those anymore, not in this day and age."

"This is an old-fashioned country, Mr. Bruce. Except for the National Health Service, of course. That's a fairly up-to-date idea."

Tim took another polite sip of the unpleasant drink. "The National Health Service? Don't you hate it?"

"Hate it? Why should I hate it?"

"Well, that's what everyone says in the States. That it's a terrible system, that no one gets proper treatment. That all the doctors despise it. There are a lot of British physicians coming to the States these days."

Rhys Edwards poured himself a second glass of sherry. "My dear boy, I can assure you that I and most of my colleagues wholeheartedly admire the National Health Service. I happen to believe firmly in the principle of free medical care. The standard of medicine in this country has improved immeasurably since the bad old days of private practice. And if you're speaking of medicine in the same breath as the profit motive, God forbid, many of us are a great deal better off than we used to be. At least we get some form of compensation nowadays. Farmers and shopkeepers could rarely afford to pay their doctors in the bad old days. And if nothing else, the NHS has raised the standard of surgical treatment. No fly-by-night surgeons butchering the patients anymore, thank God. Now, at least, they have to be properly trained. Nowadays one can refer a patient with some degree of confidence."

His forbidding cool demeanor slipped a little, the dark eyes gleaming with some sort of messianic fervor, and he almost smiled at Tim, as though he'd won him over to his side of the argument. Tim was relieved, as though the ice had literally broken. The room began to feel a touch more comfortable and hospitable and he eased himself off the edge of the chair, settled back into the cushions. But he remained wary of Rhys Edwards, intimidated almost.

"It's interesting," he said politely, "to hear a different viewpoint."

Dr. Edwards smiled, a mere stretching of his mouth, the light not reaching his eyes. "There's nearly always a different viewpoint, isn't there? About almost anything." Another small silence hovered in the room. "So your father knew my wife? When was that?"

"During the war, I believe. Before D-Day. He was stationed in these parts."

"Really? I'd no idea Gwyneth had kept in touch with anyone."

That's why he doesn't like me, Tim suddenly thought. Because my father knew the beautiful Gwyneth. He probably wants to think of her as belonging to himself alone. And who could blame him? Tim realized he might be treading on dangerous ground, slippery territory. He'd deliberately misrepresented his father's connection to this man's wife. Maybe it was unwise to leave the wrong impression with her forbidding husband.

"Oh, I don't believe they ever kept in touch. But my dad said I should take a look at Clarrach if I was ever this way. He said it was the loveliest place he'd ever seen."

Rhys Edwards stared at Tim for another long moment. "Is that so? Well, I happen to think that myself, but then, of course, I'm prejudiced. There *were* Americans here before D-Day. There were Americans all over this country then. Still are, for that matter. You could say we're occupied, just like Germany."

"Occupied?" The suggestion shocked Tim. "I thought there was some sort of pact. NATO or something."

"Perhaps you won't agree with me but I happen to believe America has an agenda for taking over the world. They haven't left Europe and now they're involved in that mess in Vietnam. What do you have to say about that?"

Opening his mouth, closing it again, Tim didn't know what he had to say. If he were back at Berkeley, he might have said exactly what this man was saying now, but it was an entirely different matter when some foreigner voiced the same opinion. "I thought we came to fight in Europe because Europe needed us."

"We did. Oh yes, indeed we did, and we're grateful you came to the rescue. But don't you think it's time to go home now?"

Tim spread his hands helplessly. "To tell the truth, I really haven't thought about it. I'd assumed we were allies. Friends, you know."

"Like the Vietnamese? You think the Vietnamese want you there? They got rid of the French, you know."

Tim knocked back the rest of the tart sherry in one gulp. Vietnam was the last thing in the world he wanted to talk about. "I don't know what to say about that. It's not a subject I feel qualified to discuss."

"Then we should talk about something else," Rhys Edwards said. "What would you prefer to talk about?"

Tim couldn't think of a single thing he wanted to talk about to this man. He was sure it was deliberate, this only slightly veiled hostility, this needling of his guest, and it offended Tim's sense of propriety. A guest was a guest and Tim had been brought up to treat guests with courtesy. He was relieved and grateful when Gwyneth drifted into the room and said, "Rhys, are you bullying this young man? But if he's berating you about being American, rest assured it's no worse than you'd get if you were English. He's a Welsh nationalist, you know. He thinks all foreigners are a curse on this land. Don't you, Rhys darling?"

Rhys darling laughed and said something in the strange Welsh language, and Tim was humiliated and confused by his ignorance of it. He knew some Spanish and a few words of French but he hadn't expected to be floundering around with a foreign tongue while he was in Britain.

"Can I ask what that means?"

"*Cymru a Cymraeg?* It means, Wales for the Welsh. Down with the English. You'll find the same thing in Ireland. In Gaelic, no doubt. Down with the English. And the Yankees, come to that."

"Oh, Rhys, do stop that," Gwyneth said without rancor. She was probably used to his sardonic humor and better able to ignore it. Tim wanted to jump in and explain that Yankees come from the East Coast and that he was from the West Coast, but Gwyneth said, "Come on, time for lunch," and ushered them into the dining room.

It was cool and hushed in the dining room, as though it was rarely used, a handsome room with plain white walls and deep-set windows and polished black and red tiles in a diamond pattern on the floor. The long narrow table was set with silverware and glasses and cloth napkins in silver holders, and an elaborate arrangement of flowers in the center. Gwyneth sat Tim in a high ladder-backed chair opposite one of the small windows so that he could look out at the ocean in the far distance, but he wasn't comfortable, unaccustomed to sitting down so formally at lunchtime, and he was beginning to dread more of Rhys Edwards's barbed conversation. Gwyneth trailed in and out of the room with covered dishes, setting them on the table, and he offered hopefully, "Can I do something to help?"

She seemed surprised at the suggestion. "Oh, no, thanks. I can manage. Do start. The food will get cold."

She handed him a heaped platter of crispy broiled lamb chops and a bowl of small buttery potatoes and quite suddenly Tim was ravenously hungry. But he was careful to take only politely small portions and he watched Gwyneth's every movement as she passed the food, first to him and then to her husband, noticed how she performed even that small task with elegance, her hands quick and quiet, her back very straight. She saw him watching her and looked away.

"The peas are from the garden," she said. "And the lamb chops are Welsh lamb." Tim gazed down at his plate with interest. As far as he knew, he'd never before seen peas that hadn't come from a package and hoped the lamb chops didn't come from the offspring of those sheep he'd seen on the hillside.

"So," Rhys Edwards said, unfolding his napkin, picking up his knife and fork, "tell us exactly why you're going to Ireland?"

This was something else Tim wasn't entirely sure about. He had a vague and indistinct picture of Ireland in his mind, of stone cottages and skirted Catholic priests, donkeys, peat fires and whiskey, and was uncertain how it would translate into reality when he finally got there.

"Well, you see, my mother's family originally came from Ireland. County Cork. I thought I'd like to see where they came from. Though I don't expect any of them are left, of course. It was a long time ago."

"In the famine, of course?"

"Yes. How did you know that?"

"Wasn't that when all the Irish left? The Fitzgeralds and the Kennedys and all the rest of them?" Rhys Edwards broke off suddenly, put down his knife and fork. "You heard the news, I suppose? About Robert Kennedy?"

Something in the hooded eyes made Tim uneasy. "News? What news?"

Wiping his mouth deliberately with the linen napkin, Rhys Edwards scrunched it into a heap on the table. "Oh dear. Somehow I imagined you'd have heard. You didn't know, Gwyneth? Robert Kennedy was shot last night. It was on the radio when I was driving home."

Tim heard the words and somehow couldn't make sense of them, as if once again Rhys Edwards was speaking in a language he couldn't comprehend. He stared helplessly around the room, searching for some other meaning to the words. "Shot?"

"In a hotel kitchen in Los Angeles, I believe. An ignominious place to be gunned down, don't you feel? Apparently he'd just made some sort of victory speech and when he left the podium, someone shot him. He's in the hospital."

"In the hospital? So he's alive?" Tim laid down his own knife and fork carefully, and felt a wave of relief wash over him, even as the news left him gasping for air. Not dead? Not like the other times? The nightmare wasn't recurring; after all, it wasn't going to happen again, not another Kennedy dead. This had to be a false alarm, one more awful event that couldn't possibly turn out as disastrously as the others . . . John Kennedy, Martin Luther King. Couldn't possibly.

Now Rhys Edwards spoke more gently, as though attempting, in spite of himself, to soften the news. "But it doesn't look good, I'm afraid. It seems he was shot in the head."

"In the head?" Tim stared at his plate. Another Kennedy head blown to bits by a bullet? Another death among so many deaths? Another voice in the wilderness silenced?

"I'm sorry," Rhys said. "Of course, I shouldn't have broken it to you like that. I didn't think . . . Did Robert Kennedy mean something special to you?"

Tim started to say, "I worked on his campaign. In California," but he couldn't continue. The smell of the food, the flowers in the vase, the polish on the table, everything revolted him. He felt his gorge rising and was afraid he was going to throw up, right here, right in front of these strangers. He stood up shakily, his legs barely supporting him, and he had to lean on the table, the sweat prickling on his forehead, in his armpits.

Jumping to her feet, Gwyneth seized his arm, murmuring something in her soft Welsh voice, and she pulled him quickly out of the room and across the hallway to a small cold restroom where he could shut the door and kneel down on the cool tiled floor and throw up into the toilet.

Four

All the food he'd just eaten, the lamb chops and the fresh peas and the sweet new potatoes, came up. He hadn't been sick like that since he was a kid, and he was humiliated and embarrassed. When he flushed the toilet, the cistern made a loud gurgling noise that seemed to draw more attention to a shameful weakness. The chill of the tiled floor seeped into his legs and they started cramping, and he had to stretch them out, dig his fingers deep into the calf muscles, trying to massage the charley horses out.

The small space smelled musty and mildewy, and was so narrow his arms reached from one side of it to the other. High up in the wall, a barred opaque window made it seem more like a jail cell than a bathroom, and it was as though he'd been incarcerated, locked away from the world. His guts were aching, the same way they'd ached after the confrontation with the cops in Berkeley, when the cell was really a cell, when he'd been punched in the gut, but then he'd been angry and excited with the aphrodisiac of rebellion. And he hadn't been all by himself. Now he wasn't angry or excited, only lonely and sickened by anguish, all the joy gone out of his world, leaving him in darkness. Tim's stomach revolted at the image of another bloody Kennedy head and there was a bitter, nauseating taste in his mouth. He wanted to bang his head against the wall and yell aloud at the dreadful mess, the dangerous feral place his country had become, running out of control, all the compasses gone haywire.

Tim stayed on the cold floor for a long time. Somewhere above his head he could hear the clattering of dishes, a low murmur of voices, and he resented that those people up there were still sitting at their table, still eating their food, not understanding how it was to have death and disorder abroad in one's land. He waited until he heard the sound of a car driving away and when everything grew silent, he unlocked the door.

Gwyneth was sitting alone at the end of the long black table, her hands folded in front of her; she didn't move when Tim came into the room, just turned her head towards him, her eyes darker and more shadowy. "Rhys had to go on his rounds," she said, and looked down at her hands. "He wanted to apologize for breaking the news to you like that. And I'm sorry, too. About Kennedy, I mean. Yet another dreadful shooting. It must be terrible for you."

Sliding into the chair where he'd sat before, Tim put his elbows on the polished surface of the table and held his head in his hands. Somewhere nearby, he could hear the deep throaty ticking of a clock, regular like a heartbeat, falling slow and steady into the quiet air, everywhere and everything else so silent he could hear the sound of his own breathing. He dropped his hands. "Have you heard any more news?"

She shook her head. "The one o'clock news will be on the radio in just a few minutes. We can listen to it in the kitchen. Perhaps you'd like a cup of tea? Or would you prefer coffee?"

"Oh God, I could really use some coffee."

"I'll put the kettle on," she said, and jumped out of her chair to go into the kitchen. Tim got up, too, not wanting to remain alone in the room, too cool and too quiet, the smell of food still lingering, and as he followed her the sun came dazzling through the opening of the doorway and he forgot about the height of it. His head cracked on the thick wooden beam above the door, a sharp resounding blow that brought tears into his eyes and a ringing in his ears. He saw stars, literally, jagged bursts of white light behind his eyes, and he staggered and must have cried out, because Gwyneth was immediately at his side, catching hold of his arm again. "Are you all right? Oh no, look, your forehead's bleeding."

Once more, his knees didn't seem to be holding him up too well. He tried to blink the starbursts away, opened his eyes and quickly closed them again in painful reflex, and was conscious that Gwyneth was pushing him onto a chair, her hand a steadying weight on his shoulder. "Hold still," she ordered quite calmly, and he heard the sound of running water, felt a cold wet cloth pressing against his forehead. "Keep it there for a while," she said. "That should stop the bleeding. Don't worry. It isn't bleeding too much."

Tim was grateful she wasn't making a big deal out of it. He clutched the towel to his head, the cool and the damp comforting, and when she leaned over him, he smelled her faint, flowery perfume. "It's okay," he muttered. "I'll be fine in a moment."

But he didn't feel fine. The room was still swirling around him and when he touched his fingers to his forehead, he could feel a huge tender swelling. After a while, the room settled down, the white flashing lights went away, and he opened his eyes cautiously. He was sitting on a chair in the middle of the kitchen beside a scrubbed pine table, the sunshine too bright through the windows. Gwyneth leaned foward very close to him, peering into his face.

"How do you feel?"

Tim squinted around the towel. "Extremely foolish."

"We're so used to the height of the doorways. I should have reminded you."

"God! What an idiot. One minute throwing up, the next knocking myself out."

"Perhaps you'd like to lie down?"

He started to shake his head but immediately the swirling sensation came back. "Maybe an aspirin or something?"

"Oh dear! I'm not certain we have any."

He tried grinning. "No aspirin? I guess that's one sure way of knowing this is a doctor's house."

"Still want that cup of coffee?"

He was careful not to nod too vigorously, and watched as Gwyneth filled a kettle with water and plugged it into a socket. "I'll see if I can lay my hands on some aspirin," she said, and her light rapid footsteps ran up the stairs and he heard the sound of movement above his head. He took the towel from his forehead and stared at the spreading splotch of blood on the white terry cloth, looked around for a mirror but even that slight movement made him dizzy again. God, how stupid! He felt like a total fool. A great lumpkin, his mother used to call him when he was a teenager, and that's exactly what this country was reducing him to, a great stupid lumpkin. Groaning, Tim pressed the towel back on his throbbing forehead. Through it, he could hear birds singing somewhere outside, out there in that other life where he'd stood in the sunshine with the enchanting Gwyneth. Before he'd heard about Bobby Kennedy. It was as though his world had made a sudden unsettling shift on its axis. He'd believed Bobby Kennedy could do something to stop the war in Vietnam, had come to believe his own future depended on it. Now God knew what was going to happen. To Kennedy and to himself.

He groaned again and didn't realize Gwyneth was back in the kitchen. Her feet made hardly a sound. She put a hand on his shoulder, two large white pills on the table beside him. "Codeine. Better than aspirin. Let me look." She took hold of his wrist firmly, lifted the towel away from his face. "It seems to have stopped bleeding. I've got a plaster. Shall I put it on for you?"

Closing his eyes, Tim tipped back his head and felt her wipe his forehead, deftly and gently, smoothing his hair back. Her hands ran swiftly and gently across his forehead, then she applied the plaster with soft pressure, and when he opened his eyes, her face was very near to his, the pupils of the amber eyes enlarged and darkened, a tender expression on her face. He could smell her skin and hair. He'd never been so close to such a beautiful woman.

His face was white and troubled where it had been tanned and healthy before, so wonderfully confident and youthful. A large discolored bruise swelled on the thin skin of his forehead and blood was congealing among the thick blond hair. She wiped the blood away and wanted to soothe his brow. Poor thing! So far from home, so upset by more of this dreadful news that seemed to come out of America almost daily. What a terrible place it must be to live, guns and madmen lurking around every corner.

Dear God in heaven, how like Carlton he was! Serious and polite, just as Carlton had been. Courteous and gentle. A gentle giant. It was almost overwhelming, this curiosity to hear something about Carlton Bruce, what he'd been doing all these years, whether he really talked of her. If he really remembered. Somehow it might make it easier if she knew he'd truly been thinking about her. Not better, but easier. Nothing could undo the harm already done.

The boy's eyes opened, gray-green, blond lashes, and she snatched her hand away.

"It doesn't look too bad," she said quickly. "I think you'll mend."

"Thank you." He smiled at her, and she moved across the kitchen to unplug the kettle, heap spoonsful of instant coffee into a pot, pour in the water, stir.

"I'm sorry it's only instant. We don't drink much coffee." She reached out to the small black radio on the windowsill, among the pots of herbs and rooting geranium cuttings, paused. "You're sure you really want to listen to the news?"

The green eyes turned bleak with anxiety. "I don't know. Is it better to know or not to know? Whether he's . . . not alive, I mean."

Gwyneth found herself saying briskly, as though she knew what she was talking about, "Isn't it always better to know? Isn't knowing always better than just imagining?" and wasn't at all sure why she should make a pronouncement like that. Hadn't she avoided the truth all her life? But she turned the knob on the radio anyway and a measured BBC voice came floating into the kitchen, intoning solemnly, "Ross and Cromerty, Firth and Dogger, the Outer Banks, winds light and variable." She saw the puzzled expression on the boy's face. "The shipping forecast. It comes on every day just before the one o'clock news. The news will be next."

As she poured a mug of coffee and placed it on the table by his elbow and he reached out a hand for it, the time signal at the beginning of the news beeped sharply through the room. "This is the BBC Home Service," a voice said. "Here is the one o'clock news for today, June 6th, 1968." They both turned to look at the radio, their movements frozen, her hand still setting down the coffee, his hand still stretching for it, and in the correctly funereal tones of a BBC announcer, the words fell heavily into the room. "Robert Kennedy, brother of the late president, remains unconscious in a hospital in Los Angeles, gravely wounded."

They stared at the radio, listened to descriptions of the assassination attempt, "an unknown assailant," someone reported, and then came the familiar Kennedy voice proclaiming victory in California, the sounds of shouts and screams and sobs, accounts by eyewitnesses, an update from the hospital. Robert Kennedy had not yet regained consciousness. "The prognosis," said someone who seemed to know what he was talking about, "is poor." That person didn't say, "He's going to die." Merely "prognosis poor." But Gwyneth sucked in her breath because she knew what that must surely mean and assumed that Tim Bruce would know, too. She wanted to take hold of his hand, but didn't.

He sagged in the chair, his shoulders slumping, the fair hair flopping on the bruised and battered forehead. "I don't know what to do now. How can I possibly think of tramping around Ireland, pretending to enjoy myself? Or going to France? Or Italy? Or anywhere? I feel I should go home. But that's stupid, isn't it? As though going home would make any difference." His eyes clouded and he stared down into the coffee mug. "I don't know what the hell to do."

The words spilled out of Gwyneth before she considered them, reckless words, ill-conceived. She never spoke like that, unthinkingly. "Listen," she heard herself say, "you can't possibly go on the boat this afternoon. You're not in a fit state to travel at the moment. You can stay here. We've got a spare room. You'll feel better soon. Tomorrow you can decide what to do."

Even before she finished speaking, she knew how dangerous it was. This boy carried all that baggage with him, even if he wasn't aware of it, that past she'd buried under her careful, protected life with Rhys, a past that lurked in those familiar smiling eyes, in that graceful, lanky American body. It wouldn't take long for the memories to rise up and swamp her painfully reconstructed existence. She should have kept her home safe from those memories. She shouldn't even have invited him to stay for lunch. Only the sudden foolish urge to hear something about Carlton Bruce had made her invite him in the first place.

After all, she didn't want to know anything about Carlton Bruce. He'd almost ruined her life. Now she'd have the memories here in this house where they had never been before, rising unbidden from the corners of the rooms, lurking behind the furniture. No amount of scrubbing and polishing would remove them.

She wasn't sure who was in more danger, herself or the boy.

But it was already too late. He was smiling gratefully, relief in the green eyes.

"That's very kind of you, Gwyneth. You don't mind if I call you Gwyneth, do you?"

Five

Gwyneth insisted he lie down on the sofa in the sitting room. Lying there on the sofa made him feel even more foolish, not only like some sort of pathetic invalid, but far too long for the sofa, his feet sticking out over the end absurdly. He sat up and unlaced his boots, lay down again.

"As a matter of interest," she wanted to know, "how tall are you exactly?"

"Six four. It doesn't seem quite so extreme back home."

She arranged the pillows behind him. "At least you can keep your head lower than your feet. I believe that's the right treatment for a bang on the head. Just watch out for our doorways in the future."

She also brought in the radio from the kitchen so he could listen for more news, and for a while Tim listened obsessively, but once the newscast was over, the BBC resumed its normal programming as though the world wasn't falling apart. But the English voices were calm and somehow reassuring and the room was warm and sunny, and soon he drifted into a dreamless sleep. When he awoke, he sat up with a start, with no idea how long he'd been sleeping, and immediately his head throbbed violently. A wave of guilt washed over him, as if he'd been asleep on duty instead of alert and ready. But ready for what?

On the radio, another soothing English voice was reading a book aloud, like a mother reading a bedtime story to her child, and somewhere the clock was ticking, but otherwise the house was langorously silent. Filmy curtains stirred in a breeze at long open glass doors, the sun shining through the thin material, sending a summery glow into the whole room. Tim lay on the sofa and stared around at the prints on the walls, the patterned Oriental carpet, the dark wooden beams in the ceiling. There was the chair where Rhys Edwards had sat earlier, the tall dark cupboard where he'd poured the drinks, the piano with no photographs on it. Tim wondered who played the piano and could picture Gwyneth sitting there, head bent, eyes abstracted. Playing Chopin, perhaps. She looked like someone who'd play Chopin. There was nothing jarring or out of place in the room, the sort of room he'd have been perfectly at home in if his head and his heart didn't hurt, if there wasn't this uneasy sense of guilt.

A round concave mirror hung above the fireplace and eventually Tim got up off the sofa to peer into it. The room tipped and swayed queasily and he had to hold on to the mantelpiece for a moment to steady himself, but the swaying soon ceased and he reckoned he couldn't have damaged his thick head too seriously. The mirror distorted his image, his nose and mouth looming at him, the plaster on his forehead magnified into a grotesque lump. He touched the tender spot, gingerly, then he wandered around the room, examining the framed prints on the walls. Most of the prints were old maps, very old, crudely and brightly colored with fancy cartouches and illustrations of fantastic animals. He'd never seen anything like them before and perused them with interest, then he stooped down to peer into a glass-fronted bookcase. It was filled with leather-bound volumes, among the books a full set of Dickens with gold leaf on the bindings, and a book entitled, *A Modern History of Wales. The Last Four Hundred Years.* Very modern!

After a while, bored with his own company, he went in search of Gwyneth. He found her stretched out in a long chair in the backyard, her eyes closed, her face tilted up to the weak sun, a newspaper drooping from her hand. He stood watching her for a few unobserved seconds, the shape of her mouth, the flaring wings of her eyebrows, and then as if she sensed someone was watching her, her eyes flew open and she sat up abruptly, the newspaper falling to the ground in disorganized sheets. Tim bent down to pick them up. He said, "I didn't mean to startle you."

Smoothing her skirt down over her legs, she brushed back the hair from her face, shaded her eyes with one hand to look up at him.

"So? How does the head feel now?"

He fingered the plaster. "Okay, I guess. Was I asleep for long?"

"Half an hour perhaps. You were probably tired. An afternoon nap is good for one."

"Were you having a nap?"

Color ran into her face, as though she, too, felt guilty for sleeping during the day, and she swung her legs over the side of the chair. "Usually I take a walk in the afternoon. Want to come? A bit of fresh air and exercise might do both of us some good."

"A walk? That'd be great." His whole body felt stiff and cramped, static for far too long, first in the truck on the tedious journey from Cardiff, then inert on that sofa for what seemed like hours. He wondered if she really wanted to go walking with him. It seemed to Tim that somehow he'd willed her into inviting him to stay, as though he'd never intended to move on in the first place, had found a way to delay his departure by cracking his head and making her sorry for him. Had it been a deliberate accident, like shooting yourself in the foot before a battle? Because he hadn't really wanted to leave? He certainly didn't want to leave. Not yet. There was a whole country here he was curious to explore. There was much more he'd like to learn about Gwyneth Edwards.

Whether she wanted to go with him or not, she jumped out of the chair eagerly enough, pulled on a light jacket, and led him through a wooden gate set into the wall at the back of the house. Outside the gate, there was a path on the hillside, a path that led past the building she'd told him was her studio. From this side, Tim could see high windows set into the thick stone walls, skylights in the slate roof. He was curious about her paintings and would have liked to press his face up to the windows to see what was inside, but Gwyneth walked past the building without stopping.

Beyond the studio and the walls of the garden, the long slope of the hill arced gently upwards, and after a hundred yards or so, the path began rising steeply toward the strange crags at the summit. Sheep with tattered woolly coats were grazing all around, and they froze for a moment, staring with nervous yellow eyes, then fled from the nearness of humans, skittering foolishly on skinny black legs. The hillside stretched ahead, quite bare of trees and hedges, the short springy turf soft and easy underfoot, the stone crags at the summit appearing and disappearing as the path wound round the slope of the hill. Tim tried not to think about what might be happening in the hospital in Los Angeles. Los Angeles! There seemed no relation between the world of Los Angeles and this place, as though they didn't occupy the same universe. He sucked in grateful breaths of the sweet clean air, and for the moment all he wanted was to go to the top of the mountain.

The light on the hillside was wonderfully bright, almost too bright, and Tim fished in his pocket for his dark glasses, new and expensive with gilt frames, bought specially for the trip. He'd begun to believe he'd never have need of them. When the crags loomed on the horizon once again, he pointed to them. "Are we heading up there?"

The breeze was blowing strands of the light brown hair into Gwyneth's face, and she held the hair away from her forehead with one hand, her arm held high, her wrist narrow and bony and blue-veined. "It's not very far."

"I thought those rocks were castles when I first saw them," Tim said. "I thought for sure people must have lived there once."

"They look exactly like the rock fortresses in France, don't they? People have been living in those forever. But I don't believe any trace of early man has ever been found in our rocks. Though there are prehistoric burial chambers around here. There's a wonderful one just a few miles away. A bit too far to walk from here, but we could take the car. Would you like to see it?"

"Now? Just now, I'd rather walk if you don't mind."

Gwyneth smiled. His heart seemed to miss a beat when she smiled. "Fine," she said. "Me, too. It's good to stretch one's legs and it's only a mile or so to the top. We can do it easily. And there's a marvelous view from up there."

There was a marvelous view from where they were now. Down below, the coastline stretched away for miles, dark carved headlands thrusting into a silvery sea, golden strips of sand under the shadows of the headlands. When he looked back, Tim could see all the way to the little town of Clarrach, huddled into the shelter of the harbor. How gray and dismal it had seemed not so many hours ago; now it nestled among the green hills, peaceful and picturesque, small and contained. As he stared towards the town, a ship came sliding out from under the lee of the cliffs, so far away it was nothing but a toy ship, a trail of white smoke from the funnel, an arrow-shaped wake braiding the water behind. He looked at his watch. Five minutes past three.

"The boat to Ireland?"

Gwyneth turned to look. "Yes, that's it. Think, you should have been on it. On the way to find your ancestors."

But Tim had already decided that Wales might prove much

more interesting than Ireland. "Who knows, maybe there are some ancestors in Wales I can look for. We Americans are always looking for ancestors."

She laughed. "Looking for ancestors is something we never have to bother about. We know exactly where ours are. Mine and Rhys's. They've been around here forever. Makes life a bit dull, I suppose."

Nothing about you could possibly be dull, Tim thought. Nothing.

He followed her up the hill.

The rough grass was eaten down to a lawnlike texture by the sheep, the surface gentle and undemanding so that Tim hardly had to look where to put his feet. He was used to long rugged hikes at six or seven thousand feet, and he was wearing hiking boots, sturdy and supportive, laced high around his ankles, so this was an easy stroll for him, but Gwyneth didn't seem to find any difficulty either, skimming over the turf in her strappy, unsuitable sandals. He noticed rabbit holes hidden among the grass and areas of erosion where the ground was cut into shallow crevices, and he said, "Shouldn't you wear something better on your feet? Aren't you afraid you'll turn an ankle or something?" Then he said, "Oh, I guess you've been walking around these parts for a long time. I guess I should mind my own business."

Gwyneth peered down at her sandals as though surprised by the sight of them.

"But you're quite right. In the winter, I wear proper shoes and warm clothes and always carry a torch. But in the summer . . ." She shrugged and her eyes flashed at him. "In the summertime, one forgets about the bad days, and that's silly because the weather can change very suddenly around here."

God, she was lovely! The longer he was with her, the more beautiful she became. He'd been dazzled that first moment he set eyes on her, by the shape of her mouth and the curve of her

eyebrows, the smoothness of her skin, but now that he'd spent—
what, three, four hours?—in her company, he could look at her
mouth when she smiled and notice one slightly crooked tooth that
made him smile in return, could take note of the way the light
hair sprang away from her temples, the way she held her head
on the long white neck. Now he could see there were tiny lines
around her eyes and mouth, lines that merely defined her mouth
and eyes, removing any hint of blandness. He wondered how such
loveliness could remain hidden from sight in this distant corner of
the world.

"Have you always lived here?" Tim wanted to know. "Even before you met my father?"

Gwyneth suddenly picked up her pace. She said sharply, an
edge to her voice, "Life didn't begin and end with the American
army, you know."

He'd annoyed her in some way. Perhaps he shouldn't have
brought up the subject of his father. God knows what the real
story might be, though surely it must have been her choice that
nothing ever came of it. Tim remembered that wistful note in his
father's voice and tried to imagine how she must have looked in
those distant days. She'd have been very young. That was the astonishing thing about her. That she didn't look old enough to have
known his father so many years ago.

He would have liked to pause and admire the sweep of the
cliffs, the tiny dots of cottages and fields far below, but Gwyneth
kept walking fast, her hands thrust deep in her jacket pockets,
then suddenly she stopped and came back to stand beside him.
"You see that farm with the big barn, there below the headland?"
She stretched a hand out, pointing a finger, and Tim lowered his
head to squint along her arm. "See? The long white house with the
trees around it and the barn with the high curved roof?"

He had to make an effort to concentrate on a faraway house
that he wasn't sure was the right one, tried not to stare instead at

the bend of her wrist where the jacket fell away, at the shape of her hand and the hollows between the bones.

"That's where I was born. My father's family farmed there for over two hundred years."

"Two hundred years?" It was difficult for Tim to imagine any family living in the same house for over two hundred years. A very un-American idea. "And do they still live there?"

"No. Not since I was a child. My father died rather young and my mother couldn't manage a farm on her own. There weren't any sons to carry it on, you see. Just me."

"And you wouldn't have liked to be a farmer?" But that was a stupid question. Imagine a woman who looked like Gwyneth being a farmer!

She thrust her hands back into her pockets and gazed at the distant house. "I was only a child when my father died. And no, I wouldn't have wanted to be a farmer. Though I did love the place when I was growing up and I did miss it when we left. But it was an impossible situation for my mother. She couldn't handle the work on her own and she couldn't afford to hire help and she didn't want to marry again, so she sold the farm and we went to live in Clarrach. She kept a shop there. On the square. Newspapers and sweets and things. She liked keeping a shop. It can be a lonely life on a farm, you know. In a shop you see people all day long."

"Your father? Did he die in the war or something?"

"Farmers don't go to war, Tim. Someone has to stay home and grow the food so men get enough to eat so they can go out and kill each other." She made a small grimace with her mouth, pulling it down at the corners. "No, my father died of a much more commonplace complaint. Tuberculosis. TB was rife among the population round here in those days, damp houses, poor nutrition. There was a lot of disease in Wales back then. Everyone was poor and they lived on potatoes and salt bacon and didn't get enough fresh fruit and vegetables, and so, apart from everything else, they suffered from deficiency diseases. Things you never see anymore. Rickets, for instance." She glanced at Tim. "You should ask Rhys about it. You might find that sort of thing interesting as you're going to go to medical school."

The idea that diseases could be caused by a lack of nutrition and decent housing wasn't exactly a revelation to Tim, but to him, the world of medicine had always seemed to consist of shiny operating rooms, of laboratories, institutions, and concrete buildings. Disease was something to be cured with pills and knives. Not merely to be prevented by good food and housing.

"To tell the truth," he confessed, "I was never terribly interested in medicine. That's about the first thing anyone has ever said to me that's brought it to some sort of life for me."

Gwyneth stared at him in astonishment. "Then, for heaven's sake, why are you thinking of becoming a doctor?"

He shrugged awkwardly, and avoided the question. "You know, your husband mentioned he might take me on his rounds with him. That he'd show me what it was like practicing medicine here. Do you think he meant it?"

"If Rhys said it, then he meant it."

"Does he mean everything he says?"

A glint of amusement came and went in the amber eyes. "Don't worry, not always. Rhys enjoys needling people but he doesn't mean any harm. At least, not usually." Then the smile disappeared and she frowned instead. "But I don't understand why you'd undertake a career like medicine if you're not enthralled by it. That's about the worst thing in the world, to be stuck in a job you don't like. Especially medicine. Apart from anything else, it's such a demanding life. If there's one thing I've learned, it's that a doctor's life isn't his own. So why do it if you don't love it?"

She seemed to be waiting for an answer, as though she really wanted to know, and Tim wasn't sure how he should answer the question. "I'm thinking of going to medical school because . . ."

He hesitated again, and decided to tell the truth. He wanted to tell someone. He wanted to tell her. "I'm thinking of going to medical school because then I won't get called up for Vietnam." There, he'd said it. Out loud. What he couldn't possibly say to his father. Or even to his mother.

Gwyneth stared at him for a moment longer. "Oh, I see. Well, it's certainly not the best reason in the world, but I suppose I can accept it as having some degree of sense."

"You can? My mother and father wouldn't agree with you."

"Yes, but then I'm not your mother, am I?" Suddenly bright splotches of pink appeared on the hollowed cheeks, almost like anger. Her eyes darkened and she turned her head away from him. "But if I were," she said quickly, "I certainly wouldn't want you going off to fight in a stupid war like that one."

Tim felt a wave of relief, of validation. "Stupid. Immoral. And wrong. That's what Bobby Kennedy says." He stopped suddenly, remembering. "Oh God! That's another reason it made me sick to my stomach to hear about him."

Gwyneth pressed her lips in a tight line and shook her head. "So terrible, these things that keep happening in your country. It's very hard for the rest of the world to understand."

He couldn't bear her to look at him like that, as though he were personally responsible for all the terrible things that kept happening, Bobby Kennedy and Martin Luther King and John Kennedy, the marches in the South and the dogs and the water cannons and the riots. The war in Vietnam. He blurted out, "Sometimes I'm ashamed of my country."

He heard the words come out of his mouth and immediately regretted them, because one shouldn't say that sort of thing, not about one's own country, especially not in someone else's country. He rubbed the side of his face and his head hurt again. "I shouldn't have said that. That's an awful thing to say. I *am* American, after all."

She shook her head again and regarded him carefully. "Nobody would ever mistake you for being anything else. But can't you criticize your own country? After all, every nation has done things it ought to be ashamed of."

The breeze blew around them and the birdsong carried on the air and Gwyneth touched his arm. "Come on. Cheer up. Let's keep going to the top. Walking clears the mind, empties it of things you'd rather not think about."

They walked in silence for a while. As the ground grew steeper, Tim thought, It's true, walking does make problems go away. Only the goal remains, the end of the journey. The top of the hill. At the top of this hill were the strange stone crags that he wanted to see. Soon the rocks were just a few yards distant, huge outcrops rising against the pale sky like battlements, jutting into the clear air, heaping massively one on another. In another hundred yards or so, Tim and Gwyneth were among them, the enormous rocks piled all around, their size somehow exhilarating and exciting, like an ancient ruined fortress. Between the outcroppings of rock were sheltered grassy spaces that seemed created especially for people to hide in, and it was easy to imagine ancient man up here, surveying the world, believing himself king of the world.

Once they reached the very top, the other side of the mountain came into view, more dark hilltops mounding into a purple distance. Tim paused in silence, gazing at the waves of ancient land and up at the surrounding rocks. Gwyneth, too, was quiet, almost as if she'd never been here before, as if she too were overwhelmed by the size of the rocks and the sight of the other hills.

After a while, she said, "Did you know that the stones for Stonehenge came from over there? Most of the stone at Stonehenge is bluestone, found only in this part of the country. It's a great mystery, why and how primitive man could have hauled those enormous stones all the way from here to southern England. Have you been to Stonehenge?"

"No, it wasn't on my itinerary. But I've seen the Tower of London and Oxford and Bath. I've been doing the tourist route."

"Europe in three weeks?"

He grinned. "Eight. It's a long way from where I live. I may never be this way again. If I come another time, I'll do Stonehenge. But I like the feel of this place. Maybe because we're on top of a mountain."

"Even a little mountain like this?"

"Oh. Yes. Well, I'm sorry I was rude about your mountains."

She laughed and seemed to be losing that air of gravity, of slight melancholy. "I suppose I can forgive you," she said.

Among the rocks, in the soft grassy hollows, they were sheltered from the wind, hidden from the rest of the world, in a warm secret spot. Tim was certain people must have lived here once. Or if they hadn't lived here, surely they'd fought battles here, here in this high place, this natural fortress, where no enemy could creep up without being seen. His knowledge of early Welsh history was as vague as his knowledge of present day Welsh history but he thought there had been Celts in Wales, way back when. Had they always fought the English, as Billy Price had said? Were there other enemies as well? He turned to ask Gwyneth. She was sitting on the grass, her arms around her knees, her skirts gathered together. She said, "Tell me about where you live."

He went over to sit down beside her. Her eyes were the color of the sherry he'd had before lunch, golden rather than brown, the irises translucent and flecked, changing all the time, so at one moment they were shadowy and mournful and at the next moment alight, glowing, amused. Now her eyes seemed deliberately cool, as though she was trying to keep emotion out of them. He knew he was staring too hard.

He cleared his throat. "Have you ever been to America?"

"Yes, as a matter of fact. Once upon a time. To New York."

Once upon a time. That fairy-tale phrase again. Tim wondered what she'd been doing in New York.

"Well, where we live isn't much like New York. We live in the Pacific Northwest."

The Pacific Northwest seemed very far away now. The mountains there were quite different from these hills, huge mountains, snow-covered above the tree line, blanketed with thick conifers below, no burial chambers or prehistoric ruins, only miles and miles of wilderness. Tim didn't know how high these Welsh hills were, even where they were sitting now couldn't be more than a thousand feet or so, but he had to admit there was the same exhilaration he always felt at the top of a very high mountain, just to be at the top, looking down on all the land below.

Hugging her skirts tighter round her knees, Gwyneth said without looking at him, "And what about your father?"

Tim didn't know what to tell her about Carlton. He'd never be able to explain he'd only heard him speak of her that one time. Now that Tim had met her, he knew something about his father he'd never known before, but he still didn't know anything about her, even though he was sitting here with her on a mountain in Wales, a place he'd never thought to go, amongst a pile of prehistoric rocks. He wished his father could know where he was and with whom, then hoped he'd never know because Tim guessed he wouldn't like it. Not at all.

"Well," Tim said at last, picking his words, "he's dean of law at the university. That makes him a bit of a big shot, I suppose. He teaches constitutional law, and consults on it, too. He goes off to the other Washington and advises the government. I'm not altogether sure what it is he advises them about, but if you ask me, they need plenty of advice."

Gwyneth gazed into the distance. "But you didn't want to become a lawyer, too?"

"Heavens, no! Lawyers lead totally boring lives. They don't seem to *do* anything, you know. Apart from reading heaps of documents and getting involved in cases that drag on for years. I'd rather do something that has a quicker turnover, with a bit more excitement in it."

"Like medicine?"

He grimaced. "At least it shouldn't be boring."

She was silent for another few moments. "And is your father boring?"

"Rigid, you might say. Very upright and honorable."

"Upright and honorable? Isn't that a good thing to be?"

Tim laughed. "It can be hard to live with."

Gwyneth fell silent once more. The silence stretched into minutes. Tim waited for her to tell him something about his father, but she seemed to have nothing to say. He stared up at the jumbled rocks heaped around, their tops another twenty feet or so above his head, and suddenly he felt strong and daring and foolishly excited and wanted to climb them, as though he had to prove something to her, had to perform some daring deed to win her admiration. Now that he was so close to the rocks, he could see they were pitted and full of footholds and handholds. He was used to rock climbing.

"I'm going to have to climb those rocks," he announced and leapt to his feet, strode over to the largest pile of stones, began to scramble upwards.

And he'd definitely caught her attention because Gwyneth jumped to her feet, too. "Oh, do be careful," she cried. "It's too easy to slip and fall."

Glancing over his shoulder, Tim grinned and waved to her, put his left foot in a crevice, stretched up his left arm to find a fingerhold, placed his right foot a few inches higher, flattened himself against the face of the boulder. The climbing wasn't difficult. The stones weren't upright but leaning this way and that, so all he had to do was to dig in his toes in his sturdy, supportive boots, and haul himself up their sloping sides. His fingers sought out the cracks and there was a thrill in mastering even such a minor challenge. Soon he could feel the rounded top of a boulder above his head, and he levered his shoulders over the edge, dragged his legs behind him, stood tall and triumphant on the rim, the sky blue above him, the ocean in one direction, the purple hills in another. He looked down to see Gwyneth staring upwards at him, shaking her head. He waved his arms.

"Look at me," he wanted to yell aloud, like a child proving himself, and then his head started to pound again, as though someone had hit him, and he felt dizzy and insecure. The piled boulders began spinning away from him. He knew he was going to fall, and before he had time to catch hold to stop himself, he was tumbling back down the rocks, slipping and sliding out of control, the hard surfaces banging the breath out of him.

He crashed to the ground at her feet.

Six

The long slow tumble down the rock face seemed to last forever, as if she were watching a film in slow motion. She cried aloud, "Oh my God, no!" as though that would somehow stop it happening, and ran to spread her arms in a fruitless effort to break his fall. He thumped on the ground at her feet and lay so still and silent on the soft grass, his long body in a crumpled heap, his arms thrown wide, that she was certain he'd done some dreadful damage to himself. Sinking to her knees beside him, Gwyneth peered into his face, at the closed eyes, the thick blond lashes, and tried not to panic, caught hold of his wrist to feel for his pulse. His fingers curled around hers, as though in a reflex, and after a moment, he opened his eyes and gazed up at her, smiling. She felt the blood wash away from her face in a tide of relief.

"I think I'll live." His voice was quite normal. But he made no attempt to move, just kept an insistent hold on her hand, staring at her, and she felt terribly responsible for him, as though he'd been put in her care, as though in some way she was in charge of his life. She found herself scolding him, like a schoolmarm. "I told you not to climb up there."

Beneath the torn shirt, the boy's chest heaved, and he closed his eyes again. Gwyneth had the alarming sensation that fate had delivered Carlton Bruce's son into her hands, as though this was her chance to take revenge on him. In spite of herself, she knew she'd wanted revenge. Once she'd been eaten up with it, all that anger and bitterness, and it must surely still lurk somewhere deep inside her, otherwise, may God forgive her, she wouldn't be thinking of it at this very moment.

She stared at Tim Bruce. She didn't wish him any harm. How could anyone wish harm to anyone so young and strong and innocent of the past? In the past, the wish for vengeance had almost destroyed her, and she wanted to put it out of her mind now. What if he'd broken his back? His neck? My God! His neck? She bent closer to him and whispered, "Can you move your legs?"

Groaning, Tim slowly sat upright and then clutched at his left ankle in the high, laced boot. His head sagged over his knees, and though he was obviously in pain somewhere, at least it wasn't his neck, thank God. He muttered through clenched teeth, "I think I've wrecked my damned ankle."

Gwyneth sat back on her heels. "Your ankle? That's all?" For some reason, she wanted to laugh. "Oh, Timothy Bruce, you do seem rather accident prone."

He groaned again. "It's not Timothy. It's Timpson. After my mother's father. Isn't it the most ridiculous name? Please don't laugh."

But when Gwyneth looked him in the eye, she couldn't help laughing. Not about his name. She thought it rather fine, actually, a very American ring to it. Timpson Bruce. The sort of name an ambassador might have. No, she was laughing because, after all, he wasn't badly hurt. For one dreadful moment, she'd thought he might be dead. For one dreadful moment, she'd thought of revenge. She couldn't believe such a terrible thought had crossed her mind. She didn't want harm to come to this boy. Of course she didn't. She had no desire for such vengeance. Nothing could heal old wounds. Better to wrap them up again in her safe life with Rhys and just thank God she'd been given a second chance. She had to forgive. Forgiveness, they said, brought one closer to God. Even if she didn't believe in God.

Gwyneth pressed her hand over her mouth to control the laughter, and then Tim Bruce started to laugh as well, and soon they were both laughing like silly teenagers, the kind of insane laughter that feeds upon itself, the very sound and feel of it infectious, hysterical almost. Gwyneth hadn't laughed in that uncontrollable way since she was a girl in school, and after a while she grew weak with it, drained by it, until she wanted to throw herself on the ground and weep instead. At exactly the same moment, as if at a signal, both of them stopped laughing quite suddenly, and it was silent for a few seconds up there on top of the mountain, only the faint sound of the breeze sighing among the stones and the distant mournful bleating of sheep.

Gwyneth said, "I'm so sorry. I don't know why . . . It wasn't your name, honestly." She held out her hand to Tim. "Can you stand at all? I can hardly carry you down from here."

He rose easily enough, pressed his weight on his foot, and winced. "Shit. It's got to be sprained or something," and he sat down again, started to unlace the boot, stopped. "Perhaps it's better if I keep this on. For support."

"Can you make it down the hill?"

Tim gazed around at the rocks, at the empty grassy spaces. "What else is there to do?"

"Well, I could leave you here and go for help."

"No. No, please don't do that." Standing up again, he leaned against her, and slung an arm around her shoulders. "Think you can bear my weight?"

Gwyneth didn't believe she could. It wasn't the physical weight, it was the emotional weight. To have to walk with his arm around her shoulders like this, have his body so close against hers, this ghost who wasn't a ghost but familiar flesh and blood, hair, teeth, eyes, voice. Too much to bear.

"Of course," she said. "No problem."

Tim lurched forward uncertainly. A searing pain shot through his ankle and up his leg. He could feel the flesh inside his boot swelling, the ligaments tearing, but he thought that if he concentrated on setting his foot down just so, tried not to lean on her so heavily that she'd crumple under his weight, he could manage. He could smell her skin and hair, and for a moment the pain in his ankle shrank to a bearable ache, a welcome test of stamina. Beneath his encircling arm, he could feel the delicate bones of her shoulder. Her arm was around his waist; if he'd wished it he couldn't have chosen a better way to get so close to her like this, matching his step with hers, her hair against his face. Was this just another accident? Or had he wished this? Perhaps he could have chosen an easier method than crashing from those rocks in such an undignified manner. He could have broken his stupid neck.

They started down the path towards the house, their forward progress slow. With the downward slope all Tim's weight was on Gwyneth, and on the steepest downward curve of the hill, she had to keep stopping to catch her breath.

"Are you all right?" he asked.

"Yes, all right. How are you doing?"

He tried to disguise his delight. "Jesus," he said cheerfully. "It really hurts."

But after a while his boot became too tight and full of aching flesh, burning, pulsing, throbbing. After a while, the pleasure in being this close to her was consumed instead with the effort of taking one more step. Sweat broke out on his forehead and under his armpits and ran down inside his shirt, and though by now he could see the house below on the side of the hill, it seemed beyond his reach, beyond the limits of endurance. He had to beg her to stop again, had to sit on the ground and take deep breaths, grit his teeth, stand up again, lean on her once more, this time merely for support, not for pleasure.

At last they reached the gate in the wall. At last. Limped together through it like a couple in an odd three-legged race, into the bee-droning haven of the garden, through the kitchen door, into the low-beamed kitchen. With a sigh of relief, Tim made it to the chair by the table where he'd sat before. He propped his foot up on an adjacent chair and stared at it with dismay. He was nothing but a pathetic bumbling idiot who ran into doorways and fell off rocks that probably no one had fallen off in a thousand years.

Gwyneth massaged her shoulders. "I suppose the sensible thing would be to drive you down to the surgery and let Rhys look at your ankle."

Tim groaned again. He'd be nothing but a figure of ridicule to the intimidating Rhys. Which he was already to Gwyneth, he supposed, when what he'd wanted was to impress her with some sort of all-American bravado, a brave young daredevil ready to risk himself to rescue her from . . . from what? A villainous husband? A life of drudgery? From the wilds of a country where the natives didn't even speak English?

"He'll think I'm nothing but a fool."

"I shouldn't worry about that. Rhys thinks everyone is a fool."

Tim examined the leg stretched out in front of him. There was nothing much to see, only the fleshy swelling above his boot. "I'm sure it's only a sprain. It'll be okay if we put some ice on it and wrap it in an Ace bandage. There's nothing else to do for a sprain anyway."

"How do you know it's only a sprain?"

"I know. After all, I am going to medical school."

Gwyneth laughed and touched his head with the barest fleeting gesture, almost a caress, which made him feel slightly better. "You'll do, Tim Bruce. You'll do."

She brought an Ace bandage and a plastic bag with ice cubes, unlaced his boot, and eased it away from his foot with difficulty. Tim was both alarmed and impressed to see how swollen his ankle was, how puffy and discolored the soft tissues were around the bones. He prodded at the swelling with a finger, carefully. "I've eight weeks of tramping around Europe ahead of me. Doesn't look too good, does it?"

"It doesn't." Gwyneth bent to peer at his ankle more closely, put one cool hand on the swollen flesh. "What are we going to do about it?"

"Good question."

"Rhys will know. When he gets home. It won't be too long now. He usually comes home for tea before he goes off to evening surgery."

Tim didn't look forward to Rhys getting home. Rhys Edwards would expect him to be on the boat to Ireland by now, sailing across that shining sea on the way to search for his ancestors. He was pretty sure Rhys Edwards wouldn't be at all pleased to find him still here. Not only still here, but incapable of movement.

"It's back to the couch for you," Gwyneth said. "I'll make you a nice cup of tea. That's the Welsh way of coping with trouble. A nice cup of tea."

Trouble. Tim remembered the radio and the news, and knew he wasn't ready for any more news, not unless it was good news. Gwyneth gave him her hand again, and he limped into the living room without protestation, lay docilely on the too short sofa while she wrapped the Ace bandage around his ankle, deftly and competently, raised his foot on a cushion, and draped the bag of ice on top of it. He wondered if she'd been a nurse. Doctors always married nurses, didn't they? So much to learn about her.

"I'll make some tea," she said, and left him staring dumbly at the rays of late afternoon sunshine filtering through the windows, spreading golden streaks across the ceiling. It had been a very long day.

He was still lying on the sofa, washing down more codeine pills with tea from a thin china cup and saucer balanced precariously on his chest, when Rhys Edwards arrived home. He marched in through the front door, straight into the living room, didn't even seem to notice Tim, announced, "Hello, Gwyneth, I'm home," dropped his coat over the back of a chair, and then stopped in his tracks. "Good God! What the hell's happened? I thought you'd be long gone by now."

"Now, Rhys darling." Gwyneth's voice was soft and chiding. "That isn't very nice of you. The poor boy fell off a rock. He thinks he's sprained his ankle."

Tim raised his head from the cushions and blinked at her. Poor boy? Was that how she thought of him? A boy? He was almost twenty-three. He'd marched in antiwar demonstrations, been arrested by the police, spent a night in jail. He'd smoked pot, had sex. He might soon have to go off to war. He was not a boy.

"Oh. I'm sorry," Rhys said, but he didn't sound that sorry. He sounded put out, disconcerted, distracted, much like Carlton did when he arrived home from his day's work. Not ready to greet a stranger or partake in small talk.

"No, *I'm* sorry," Tim said. "I'm afraid I'm being an awful nuisance. Gwyneth has been very kind." He saw Rhys frown when he said her name. He should have remembered that people didn't use first names so casually in this country. Someone had warned him about that. But he couldn't possibly call her Mrs. Edwards. So ridiculously formal. So ancient. As though she was a different generation.

Gwyneth poured another cup of tea from the silver teapot and handed it to Rhys. He took a mouthful, put down the cup and saucer, and leaned forward to peer at Tim's foot.

"Certainly looks swollen. Let me look at it." He started unwrapping the Ace bandage, quickly but gently. Tim was surprised at how gentle his hands were. He sat up to watch the bandage coming off and saw his ankle was already more discolored and swollen, purple blotches spreading up his leg, deep marks where the bandage had bitten into the swelling.

Rhys stared at the ankle, then looked into Tim's face. "I see you hit your head as well," he said, and touched a finger to the plaster on his forehead. Tim had forgotten all about his head. He prayed Gwyneth wouldn't want to explain how that particular injury had come about. Falling off a rock was quite stupid enough. Forgetting how tall you were was cretinous.

Cradling Tim's foot between his two hands, Rhys moved the ankle minimally backwards and forwards and Tim yelped with pain.

"Obviously sprained," Rhys pronounced. "But perhaps not broken. Looks like you've torn some ligaments, though. We can get it x-rayed and put it in a cast, but even so, you'll have to stay off it for a few weeks."

Tim gasped. "A few weeks? That's impossible. I've got plans to hitchhike around Europe. I'm meeting friends in Paris. It's all arranged."

"Well, then you'll have to hitchhike with crutches. That should get you a few rides."

Tim fell back against the cushions. Now what the hell was he supposed to do? This had been his chance to see Europe, to be free for a few weeks until he had to spend the rest of his life with his nose to the grindstone. He'd blown it. Now he'd have to skulk back home and spend the last free summer of his life with the folks. Fetch and carry for his mother. Or go back to work, cleaning those awful dog cages where the poor dumb animals led their miserable, smelly existence with tubes sticking out of their sides. God, how he hated those animal labs.

"Well now," Rhys said. "Don't fret. We'll not throw you out in the street. Not immediately, anyway. He could stay here for a couple of days, couldn't he, Gwyneth? Until he's mobile. We do have the spare room."

Tim saw Gwyneth's eyes widen and darken, a patch of color running onto the high cheekbones. She hesitated for what seemed a very long moment, then she said quickly, "Oh yes, of course. Yes, why not? If it's all right with you, Tim."

All right with him? Spend a few more days with the beautiful Gwyneth? Find out more about her. Maybe learn a little Welsh. Surely that was worth tearing a couple of ligaments for?

He said feebly, "Isn't that a bit much? Dumping myself on you?"

"Oh, I don't know." Rhys picked up the cup and saucer again, took a slurp of tea. "I could teach you a bit of history. Convert you to the National Health Service. Send you back to America as a prophet. Yes, I think we could have quite a good time, you and me. After all, you are going to be a doctor, aren't you? I'll take you on my rounds with me. They'd like that, the patients. I'll tell them you're a visiting guru from the States." He stopped suddenly. "By the way, have you heard about Kennedy?"

There was a small silence in the room. Gwyneth paused with a teacup halfway to her lips and Tim thought he knew exactly what the news was going to be by the expression on Rhys Edwards's face. He looked down at the cup and saucer rattling in his own hands, at the delicate translucent china, the pale green leaves twining up the cup and the gold leaf on the handle, stretched to place the cup and saucer on the table beside the sofa before he dropped them, and Gwyneth got up from her chair and took them from his hand.

"He still hasn't recovered consciousness. I'm afraid it doesn't look good."

Tim only felt relief when he heard what Rhys was saying. Kennedy wasn't dead. At least he wasn't dead.

Rhys said, "I wouldn't hold out hope."

But Tim did hold out hope. He'd hold on to it as long as possible. Where there was life there was always hope, wasn't there? But he could tell Rhys Edwards thought it was hopeless and knew he'd never forget where he was when he heard all this, just as no one forgot where they were when President Kennedy was shot. Tim had been in the middle of lab class, remembered the rotten smell of sulphur that was making them all gag and laugh, him and Joe Pignatti and Josh Bergman, remembered how the door had flown open and that girl with braces on her teeth stood poised in the doorway, tears streaming down her face, as though she was trying out for a part in the school play, how everyone stared at her and how for a moment there was a little silence, just like this silence, and then she'd cried out, the words muffled and choked. "Somebody's shot the president."

He'd never smelled sulphur again without bringing back that moment. Now he'd never drink tea out of a china cup and saucer without remembering this particular moment.

But he couldn't believe death would strike again. He had to hold on to that hope.

Otherwise he might never be able go home to America again. Never.

Seven

Rhys wasn't altogether sure why he'd been so quick to offer the American boy a bed. He didn't usually speak before thinking, and now, when he did think about it, the idea of having a stranger in the house was a little unsettling. He and Gwyneth weren't used to having other people around. After all, who was there? No parents anymore, no brothers or sisters or cousins, which he'd always considered a blessing, really; relatives could be such damn nuisances. On the other hand, on further thought, there was something appealing about having a young person in the house. Perhaps, after all, the house was too perfect, too neat and tidy. Too quiet. Perhaps it needed a little roughing up. And he felt sorry for the boy, that was the truth. A gangly, unwordly youth, but pleasing to look upon, with those good straight limbs and fine white teeth. Americans might be useless at many things but they were good at teeth. Rotten teeth were among the curses of the Welsh, who were a poor lot physically, on the whole. Bright enough in the mental department but stunted in the physical, not enough sunshine, not enough decent food in the years of deprivation. He, Rhys, should know, his entire professional life spent fending off the legacy of centuries of undernourishment, of damp houses and poverty and working lives spent underground in the damn coal mines, making money for the English. Coal mines and the English had been nothing but a curse on the country.

Yes, he must stay, this boy. Between them, he and Gwyneth would mend him, his leg and his awkwardness, and in return he'd reward them with a taste of another world, those things they didn't know too much about, about being young and American and having a future to plan for. He couldn't stay forever, of course. Only a few days and then he'd be gone, and then their lives, his and Gwyneth's, would return to normal, to the humdrum beat they'd grown accustomed to. But for a while it would be good to have a fresh face and a fresh voice around.

"So," Rhys announced briskly, "we'll take you down to the surgery and get that leg x-rayed and put in a cast, and then we'll decide where to go from there."

He caught the doubt and apprehension on the boy's face, intercepted his quick darting glance at Gwyneth, saw the way her eyes darkened and deepened, as though she were gazing into an abyss. Rhys knew she hated surprises, knew how she liked to tread some narrow path he didn't altogether recognize, and decided it would do her good to be shaken out of that secret world she'd been retreating into of late. He could tell she thought none of this a good idea but he also knew her innate good manners would keep her from saying so. He'd counted on it. Anyway, what else were they to do with the boy? Send him off to the hospital? They could do that, of course, ship him to the casualty department at the hospital and let strangers take care of him. Then what was to happen to him? They'd put his leg in a cast and where would he go from there? On a plane back to America and never get a chance to learn anything more about Wales or the National Health Service or the way people here felt about that idiotic involvement in Vietnam. Education was what this boy needed. A broadening of his horizons.

Rhys rubbed his hands together. "Evening surgery starts at five. Drive him down, Gwyneth, we'll fix him up and then you can bring him back here afterwards." He looked at Tim. "You need help to get to the car?" He'd use his name except he'd forgotten what it was. Bruce something. Something Bruce.

The boy shifted uncomfortably on the sofa. "Isn't this a lot of trouble for you? Wouldn't it be easier if I just went to the nearest hospital?"

Rhys waved a dismissive gesture. "The nearest hospital is more than thirty miles away. I can assure you it'd be a lot more trouble to drive you all the way there than down to the surgery. Anyway, this sort of thing happens to be my job, you know."

Looking vaguely around the room, the boy said, "I have an insurance card in my backpack. Blue Cross. It covers any medical expenses while I'm overseas. At least, that's what Dad said."

"Expenses? What expenses? Everything's covered, lock, stock, and barrel. That's what we have a National Health Service for, my boy, to take care of poor unfortunate accident victims like you. I'll sign you on as a temporary resident and the Health Service will enrich me by a few paltry pence. Enough to buy a pint at the pub, no doubt. I might even treat you to one when we've fixed up that leg. Ever been in a Welsh pub?" Rhys drained the teacup, filled it again. "Do you have a pair of shorts in that backpack of yours? I suggest you change into them, otherwise we'll have to cut the leg off those pants you're wearing."

He popped another of the small cakes from the tray into his mouth and waited. Neither Gwyneth nor the boy made any attempt to move. "Well, are you coming or are you not coming? You can't just lie there and wait for nature to take its course, you know. Nature has a nasty little habit of taking the law into its own hands. Suppose it's broken, that ankle of yours?"

Gwyneth's eyes were mournful. "I'll fetch the car. We managed to get down the mountain so I'm sure we can manage to get to the car. We'll be there in half an hour, Rhys."

Tim said, "Thank you, Dr. Edwards. It's very kind of you."

"Just my job," Rhys said again, plucked his jacket off the back of the chair, thrust his arms into the sleeves and headed for the door. Pausing when he reached it, his hand on the knob, he glanced over his shoulder. "By the way, I'm damned sorry about Robert Kennedy. You're certainly getting yourselves into a bloody awful mess in that country of yours."

After he was gone, the room was very quiet. All Tim wanted was to stay there on the couch and not move. Not think. Not think about his own stupid situation and what his father would have to say about it, not think about another mortally wounded Kennedy or about the bloody awful mess his country was getting into. He wanted time to reverse itself, wanted it to be twenty-four hours ago, before Bobby Kennedy walked off that podium in the hotel and through the kitchen, where a bullet was waiting for him. If today were yesterday, Kennedy might have made a different choice, taken a different way, gone to the left instead of to the right, chosen to leave by the front door instead of the back door. It would have been so easy for him to have done something different, anything, to have made some small change that could have altered the course of history.

The awareness of the dizzying array of the choices available in life and the consequences of the smallest of them sent little nervous shocks through Tim. If yesterday were today, he himself might also have made a different choice, might have chosen not to come on this quixotic search for some woman his father once knew, once upon a time. He might have stayed in the truck and got on the ferry boat to look for his ancestors in Ireland. He wouldn't have ended up lying on a sofa in a strange house in the middle of nowhere with a wrecked ankle, not knowing what the hell to do.

If only today were yesterday.

For a few seconds, Tim was paralyzed by the enormity of tiny decisions. He fell back into the cushions, unable to move in any other direction. I'm having a panic attack, he thought. What would my father call it? Cowardice? Inability to make up one's mind? Lawyers don't suffer from an inability to make up their minds, their fingers don't freeze on the page, their voices fail in the middle of a trial. Or do they? What if he, Tim, were to become a doctor, after all, and get in a panic like this, and wonder what the hell he was doing with blood and disorder and another person's life in his hands? What sort of a doctor could that possibly be?

Tim took a deep breath, held it, and his heart rate slowed and steadied. It was an absurd way to react. He'd only sprained his ankle, for God's sake. He'd done far worse damage to himself before. That time he tore a ligament in the same knee skiing at Snowbird, that time he dislocated his shoulder playing touch football. This was nothing. Nothing. Was he worried about putting himself into Rhys Edwards's hands? He tried to think more rationally, thought how a surgeon friend of his father's had once invited him into the operating room to watch a surgery. He'd learned how calm everything could be in a place like that, under control, no panic or disorder, the room peaceful, almost soporific, just the steady sighing of the breathing machines and the muted clatter of the stainless steel instruments. Soft music had been playing low in the background, cool jazz, good music to operate by, the surgeon had explained. It calmed Tim to remember the operating room and the competence of the surgeon.

He looked over at Gwyneth, and when she smiled at him, he

wasn't sorry, after all, that he hadn't changed his own day. But God almighty, he wished he could have changed Robert Kennedy's day.

"I'll bring the car round," Gwyneth said, "while you get changed." She dragged his backpack in from the front hall where he'd dropped it a hundred years ago.

He rummaged around in the backpack, through the meager supply of clothes, the spare pair of jeans, the T-shirts, the one decent pair of pants and tidy shirt. "In case you go somewhere nice," his mother had advised. He'd packed for sleeping rough, a sleeping bag and ground tarp, the usual gear he'd have taken to the mountains for a camping trip, together with his passport, a wad of travelers' checks, an American Express card, and his health insurance card. Somewhere. He had to pull most of the stuff from the bag before he found the insurance card and a pair of shorts, then he pushed everything back in, in a haphazard fashion, changed into the shorts, and hopped to the front door. But when he saw Gwyneth's car, his heart sank again. It was one of those absurd toylike Minis with tiny little wheels that he'd seen all around the country, and already had wondered how anyone dared to risk their lives in such tin cans.

"I'll never fit into that," he protested.

"Oh yes, you will." Gwyneth pushed the passenger seat back as far as it would go and Tim scrunched into it. His head butted up against the roof, his knees were at an acute angle, but he did indeed fit. He couldn't say he was comfortable but at least he was very close to Gwyneth again.

She drove swiftly down the long driveway and through the open gate, accelerating down the hill, changing the floor-mounted gear shift quickly and smoothly like a racing car driver, barreling along the same road Billy Price had labored up in the bread-redolent van only a few hours ago. In his head, Tim knew it was only a few hours ago, but time had taken on an odd elasticity, stretching the day into an eternity, into a lifetime. Most days shrank into an insignificant and boring nothingness, time passing and yet seeming to stand still, nothing changing, nothing happening, but now it felt as though it was some other person who'd been a passenger in Billy Price's van this morning, in another day, in another life. That other person wasn't someone Tim particularly recognized anymore, as though he'd traveled an immense distance since then. Even his skin felt different, prickly and too aware of the woman next to him, the smell of her hair, the hollow curve of her averted cheek.

The lane wound down towards the wide and empty ocean, glittering now and then at the end of the tunnel of hedges. The hedges were banked so high on either side of the narrow lane that most of the corners were blind, and Tim, still nervous about being on the wrong side of the road, tried not to stiffen each time they zipped around another unheralded turn. Gwyneth glanced at him sideways. "Don't worry. I know this road quite well."

"Yes, but what happens if you meet someone coming the other way?"

"Well, then," she said and smiled. "I suppose all will depend on their brakes and mine, won't it?"

He wanted to explain he wasn't really worried, merely unaccustomed to this side of the road, being this close to its surface. It felt as if they were traveling about a hundred miles an hour, the hard pavement lurching and hissing towards the car, the hedgerows and tall grasses hurtling above their heads with hypnotic, sighing flashes. He tried to relax, to enjoy the sensation of speed and the thump of wind through the open window, the scent of blossom on the air, and then all of a sudden they were safely at the bottom of the hill and turning left onto the main highway, back towards Clarrach, down the steep hill to the one-lane bridge and up the other side, into the main square and the carved soldiers where Tim had started this day so long ago. Gwyneth swung the car into a parking space that was marked "No Parking."

"Here we are," she announced, "safe and sound," and dazzled him once more with her smile.

The door to the doctor's surgery, it turned out, was right there on the square, right where he'd been standing this very morning. This morning he hadn't noticed the large shiny brass plaque fastened to the dark stone wall with the name Rhys Edwards engraved in the brass, followed by a long string of letters: "MRCS, LRCP (Lond.), D. Obst., RCOG." Tim gazed at the impressive letters. He'd assumed the name would be spelled Reese, like the baseball player, and he rolled the Welsh sound of this Rhys on his tongue.

"What do all the letters mean?"

Gwyneth pushed the door open. "It means he's qualified to take care of your ankle."

The "surgery" turned out to be an unprepossessing waiting room with mismatched wooden chairs lining three sides of it, half a dozen or so elderly people sitting silently on the chairs, a careful distance between each person. All of them looked old and worn, and very patient, and they glanced up briefly as Gwyneth and Tim entered and then away quickly as if it wasn't polite to stare at fellow sufferers. In the middle of the floor was a large Oriental carpet, ragged round the edges, and two low tables strewn with tattered magazines; the walls of the room were cream painted and covered with thumbtacked notices that might have been there for years, and the fourth side of the room held a sort of reception desk with a window. There was no one at the window, and no one greeted Gwyneth, as though no one knew her. She took a seat beside Tim and seemed to expect to wait like everyone else.

None of this filled Tim with any degree of confidence. He was accustomed to far more impressive doctors' offices, to upholstered chairs and sofas and pictures on the walls, soft lamps, sculptured carpets, glossy magazines. He was used to receptionists and office personnel leaping to attention whenever anyone came in, if only to get them to fill in the insurance forms. He had to wonder if he was doing the right thing by allowing anyone with a waiting room like this to mess around with his leg, no matter how many letters there were after his name.

After a while, a small flurry of activity erupted behind the reception desk. A middle-aged woman in a dark blue dress, starched white apron, and white cap perched on her graying hair like a nurse out of some old movie, called out briskly, "Next please. Mr. Bert Williams." An elderly man inched himself slowly out of one of the wooden chairs and wheezed his way past the desk, and as he did so, the woman caught sight of Gwyneth and Tim, came bustling out from behind the window to stand before them, her hands clasped over the crackling apron. She spoke to Gwyneth in a hushed reverential tone.

"It's sorry I am to keep you waiting, Mrs. Edwards."

"That's all right, Mavis," Gwyneth said. "I'm sure you're busy."

"I was just in with the doctor and so I didn't see you come in. Is this the young man from America, then? Is this his bad ankle?"

Tim said, "I'm from America and this is my bad ankle." He stuck his bandaged leg straight out in front of her. "What are you planning to do with it?"

"Well, we're going to x-ray it. And then Dr. Edwards will put a cast on it for you. And we have some crutches you can use. Then you'll be as right as rain, won't you?"

"Will I?" Her voice had a mesmerizing quality, running up and down the scale in the same funny accent as Eirwen Price and her father. Tim found something oddly reassuring in her voice, something motherly and comforting. She crackled out of the waiting room and was back in a quick moment with a pair of battered wooden crutches that must have been passed down from one ancient cripple in the town to another, the rubber arm pads crushed and dark with sweat, the wood scuffed and chipped. Handing them to Tim, she said sympathetically, "Poor boy."

It was the second time in the same day someone had called him a poor boy.

"We'll just take you to the back for the X ray, then?"

The other people in the waiting room watched with curious sidelong glances as Tim rose to his feet and grabbed hold of the crutches. They were several inches too short for him and the nurse blinked up at him. "My, aren't you the tall one? Are you sure you can manage?"

"I can manage."

Tim and Gwyneth followed her along a dark corridor, through another door, and into a tiny room without windows, a single light hanging from the ceiling, an old-fashioned doctor's couch on one side of the room. On the other side, an odd-shaped machine that looked something like an old television set stood on a table beside a white sink, and there was a glass cabinet with an array of bottles filled with colored liquid. It all seemed incredibly primitive to Tim and his heart sank further, but when the nurse patted the leather couch, he slid his backside onto it obediently and she began to unwrap the Ace bandage.

"We've only got the portable X ray machine. The doctor takes it with him if he needs to x-ray someone in their home and we use it here for small things like wrists and ankles. Nothing major, of course. The doctor is very good with the X rays. But of course you knew that, didn't you, Mrs. Edwards?"

Gwyneth didn't look as though she knew much about anything just at the moment. She leaned against the wall and pushed the hair back from her forehead, her eyes cloudy and troubled. She seemed somehow diminished, less radiant and elegant, almost a little awkward, standing in the bare airless room and obviously wanting to escape from it, as though she was trapped in a place she didn't want to be. She should stay on her mountain, Tim thought, among the breezes and the flowers in the garden, where she was magical and enchanting. She didn't belong down here in the ordinary world.

"I'll just fetch the doctor," the nurse said, and when she rustled out of the room, Gwyneth said, "I think I'll wait outside in the car. Mavis will let me know when you're ready."

She drifted out of the room, her feet silent on the creaking wood floor, and Tim was left alone. He listened for some sounds from the corridor and heard nothing. There was nothing in the small room to distract him, the walls bare of any kind of ornamentation, not even any of the tattered notices that were pinned up in the waiting room, not even a single magazine. They certainly didn't believe in smartening up doctors' offices around here, he thought. He peered down at his swollen ankle, the bruising impressively livid now, great patches of purple and blue seeping down to his toes and up into his calf, and he hoped to God he hadn't torn anything important or broken something that would take years to heal. He hoped to God that Dr. Edwards was capable of fixing it.

Tim lay back on the Naugahyde couch and, without anything else to think about, closed his eyes and thought about Gwyneth. The beautiful, luscious Gwyneth. He could almost taste her, the smooth pale skin, the fine flyaway hair, the curving wide mouth. There were paintings of women who looked just like her. Pre-Raephalites maybe? But the paintings that sprang to his mind were less innocent, more sinuous and decadent, slender, languorous women with parted lips and burning eyes, and though Tim struggled to dream up other images, the sinful ones persisted and suddenly made him lustful and horny. Quick, think of something else . . . Think of the young and beautiful Gwyneth with his father—that should put an end to any feelings of lust. But surprisingly, that only made things worse, because the thought of her with his father only made him angry and envious as well as jealous. Angry? Jealous? Yes, indeed. The idea of her with his own father was astonishingly Oedipal. He wanted to imagine her white arms and loosened hair and long legs bared just for himself. Jesus! He had an immediate, spontaneous, and disconcerting erection.

Sitting up quickly, Tim clutched his hands over the front of his shorts, hoping to God the embarrassing hard-on would go away soon, before the doctor caught sight of it and made more sarcastic comments. At least, thank heavens, he'd have no idea where Tim's mind had been straying. Or would he? Rhys Edwards seemed to have an unnerving capacity for seeing right through him.

At that very moment, the door opened and Rhys Edwards came in.

He wasn't wearing a white coat like a normal doctor, had just rolled up the sleeves of his shirt and tucked the striped tie into his shirt front. But his hooded eyes were dark and watchful and that secret sardonic smile was on his face.

"Now then," he said briskly. "We'll soon have that problem fixed for you." For one awful moment, Tim was certain he'd recognized the fast collapsing erection.

"Don't look so startled. I'm talking about your leg. A young fellow like you can't possibly have any other problems."

What did he know? He was so damned superior. Tim was annoyed and aggrieved. The fact that a moment ago he'd been lusting after Rhys Edwards's wife made him even more aggrieved.

"No?" He tried to sound sarcastic. "Only the problem of my future. Only the problem of the war in Vietnam and my low draft number. Then there's the problem of the murders of President Kennedy and Martin Luther King and now there's Bobby Kennedy, and the problem of what the hell is going to come of all of it."

Rhys raised his eyebrows, took Tim's ankle between his hands carefully. "I'm just a lowly Welsh GP. There's only so much I'm qualified to handle." He gazed into Tim's face. "Is there really a likelihood you'll have to go to Vietnam?"

"If I can't find a way to get out of it." And though Tim hadn't considered the possibility before, he had a sudden hope. "Perhaps you can fix my leg so I won't be fit enough to go."

Rhys smiled. "So the problem of your ankle could come down to a conflict between British doctoring and the politics of America?" He sighed. "That's a heavy burden you're placing on my shoulders, young man. I'm pretty sure I can fix your ankle but don't ask me about fixing your country or your war. War is a terribly blunt instrument. Whole peoples bleed to death from it all too easily. That's our problem in this country. We've almost bled to death from too many wars and now we've no more blood left to give. Whereas you Americans seem eager to give more."

He smiled at Tim again, no longer sarcastically, but ruefully, almost sadly. "It seems you're not so eager to shed your blood, eh? Well, I'd like to help you out, but the truth is that is something you'll have to work out for yourself. Your war, your country. You've got a lot on your plate, haven't you?"

Eight

Gwyneth waited in the car outside the surgery, facing into the wall and the sign that read "No Parking." She didn't need to look out at the square because she knew exactly what was there, the church on one corner, the Red Griffin on another, the dominating monument in the center. Knew it all too well, had seen it all too often.

How long before Rhys would be finished with the boy? Maybe she should have stayed in that dungeonlike room with him, but the room was claustrophobic, dim and depressing, like the rest of the surgery. And the truth was the pervasive smells of medicine, the disinfectants and bad breath and hints of blood and pain, unsettled Gwyneth. She had no stomach for any of it. Whenever she set foot in the surgery, which wasn't often, she wanted to brighten it up, at least give it a coat of fresh paint and find new furniture for that awful waiting room. Didn't Rhys notice? Or was he so engrossed in his work that he didn't see it? The surgery was Rhys's domain and she shouldn't interfere; if Rhys and Mavis didn't care what it looked like, then she supposed she shouldn't either. But it was no wonder Rhys liked getting out and about to visit the patients.

She could have stayed with the boy. Held his hand, given him moral support. He was so shaken up by this Kennedy thing, he needed some comfort and aid. Except she wasn't his caretaker, was she? He was, in spite of signs to the contrary, quite grown up enough to take care of himself. And the truth was that his physical presence made her edgy and anxious, as if he were about to expose her in some way, as if he threatened some kind of danger. It was the startling resemblance to his father, she supposed. God knew Carlton Bruce had proved dangerous, but those memories would have remained decently buried if the boy hadn't turned up out of the blue like that.

After a while, Gwyneth grew restless, just sitting in the car, gazing at the wall. She felt conspicuous, even though the streets were almost deserted, hardly any people around, only the pub and the doctor's surgery open at this time of the evening. Most of the inhabitants of Clarrach were home for supper by now. Turning to look away from the wall, she stared across the square and up High Street. Beyond the far corner of the square was the shop her mother had kept, and as she gazed in that direction, Gwyneth thought how long it was since she had so much as set eyes on the shop. These days, she never came into Clarrach, not unless she absolutely had to. Clarrach was a gray and stony place, not attractive; she'd thought that even when she lived here. Perhaps especially when she lived here.

After a few more minutes, Gwyneth had a sudden desire to see what the old shop looked like these days. She didn't question the reason for wanting to look at it because there was no real reason. The shop wouldn't have changed. She was the one who'd changed. Uncoiling from the cramped seat, she got out of the car, walked with determination past the dress shop with the papier-mâché mannequins, past the Red Griffin on the corner and up High Street a little way, to stand in front of the place where she'd spent so much of her early life.

The little shop was locked and silent at this time of evening, Venetian blinds pulled down over the glass entrance door, a "Closed" sign hanging from an inside hook. There was nothing much to see, only her own reflection in the dusty windows, and as Gwyneth stepped into the space between the door and windows to peer inside, her reflection angulated and triangulated in the opposing panes of glass, repeating endlessly, like those mirrors at a funfair. She stared at the repeated images and thought she didn't seem that much different from the days when she'd lived here. Now she had to put a hand to her face to reassure herself she was not merely a ghost from the past, not an image from a funfair. She had to put her hand on the cold glass of the door, too, to convince herself that the shop was real.

It hadn't changed since her mother's days, not at all. The windows were still decorated with empty mock-ups of fancy chocolate boxes tied with fading gold ribbons; the trim around the doorway was still painted bright pillar box red. The name above the door was different, of course. Now it read, "Proprietor, John Jenkins," instead of "Proprietress, Elizabeth Griffiths."

The day her mother took over the shop, the town handyman, Dai Jones, had meticulously stenciled her name up there. He was a bit "slow," Dai Jones, but very good with lettering. And patient. He'd stood for hours on the stepladder with a tiny tin of gold leaf and a special camel hair brush while her mother spent the whole day inside with old Mrs. Barrett, counting stock. In the evening, about this time, her mother took Gwyneth outside to admire the new name. Her mother, she remembered, had been wearing an old-fashioned blue flowered apron that covered her back and front and tied at the sides with strings, her light brown hair hidden under a scarf and wound into a turban. It was what all women wore in those days, what her mother had worn every day on the farm, but though she was dressed in the same clothes, she seemed different down here in Clarrach, younger, more energetic, more light-hearted. She'd looked at her name above the door and laughed aloud with delight.

"Never seen my name in lights before," her mother had said. "Makes me feel like someone important. And mark my words, Gwyneth. If there's one thing you can count on, it's that people will always want to read newspapers and eat chocolate. That's something you can count on, Gwyneth."

It was important to have something to count on. Times were very uncertain.

"You'll like it here, *cariad,*" she assured her, and she'd squeezed Gwyneth's hand and Gwyneth had noticed the roughness of her skin, the dry warmth of her fingers. "Soon you won't miss the old farm one bit. You'll have lots of friends now we're living in the town. Not like out in the country. So many days you could go without seeing another human being." She'd sighed melodramatically. "Maybe you didn't understand, Gwyneth, but it could be very lonely on the farm."

Gwyneth considered this new place much too tiny, the ceilings too low, the upstairs flat that would be their home now much too cramped and dark. She couldn't imagine what it was going to be like living there. At the farm, there were acres and acres of green fields, miles of hedgerows, cows to be brought home for milking and Shep, the black and white collie, to help bring them to the milking shed. There was no room in the flat for Shep, and anyway he was a farm dog, so he'd stayed behind with the farm's new owners. Gwyneth wished she could have stayed with him.

She didn't tell her mother any of that. She never told her mother that a girl at school whispered from behind her hand to say that "proprietress" was someone who ran a brothel. Gwyneth wasn't exactly sure what a brothel was, and certainly wasn't going to ask, but she recognized the remark was meant to be insulting. Her mother liked keeping a shop after the life on a farm. She wasn't born to be a farmer's wife. She was an Anglicised girl from south of the county who should have married a schoolteacher or a minister, not an impoverished dairy farmer in the Welsh-speaking uplands who may have done her a favor by dying young so she could leave the farm and come to live in the middle of a town instead of the middle of nowhere.

Coming closer to the door, Gwyneth rubbed a clear spot in the dusty glass and peered into the half-lit interior. She hadn't been inside there since before her mother died, but now, as she tried to peer past her own reflection, she felt almost as though she was still trapped there among the sweets and the chocolates and the sharp morning smell of newsprint. Everything looked exactly the same, even to the single light bulb burning dimly above the counter, casting shadows into the corners. She could almost see herself, Gwyneth Griffiths, from the age of eleven until the age of fifteen, a tall skinny girl perched on the high wooden stool behind that selfsame counter, dreaming of another life, a life more exciting, less confined. But even though she'd dreamed of another life, because who didn't at that age, she knew it hadn't been such a bad one, sheltered and warm and safe with her mother, a steady little income coming in, no worse off than many others whose husbands and fathers had gone off to the war. Her father, Meredith, had died of the tuberculosis at the age of thirty-nine before the war ever came along. "A sort of blessing," her mother said. "Now we don't have to lie awake at night worrying about him out there getting killed by the Germans." But Gwyneth knew even then that her father would never have had to go off to war. Sometimes she had trouble remembering him at all, and as the memories of farm life faded, it seemed as if she and her mother had lived forever in the stony center of Clarrach, had kept a shop forever, had never had greater horizons than the tinkling bell above the shop door.

She could remember the exact moment the smells of sugar and artificial flavorings began to overwhelm and nauseate her.

She'd been sitting as usual on the high wooden stool behind the counter, school books spread out on top of the magazines and newspapers. Latin. Trying to translate a passage from Ovid. What an awful waste of time it was to have to learn Latin, a language even more dead and gone than Welsh. It was warm and stuffy in the shop, nearly closing time, thank goodness, when she could escape, run down to the Gaer for a swim, and she kept glancing up at the clock above her head, counting the minutes until she could lock the door and turn the sign from "Open" to "Closed." The minutes before closing time dragged by endlessly, as they always did, those last minutes going as slowly as early mornings went fast, when the bell above the door tinkled and a soldier in khaki uniform came in. An ordinary soldier, neither young nor old, his hair cut in the ugly army way of short back and sides, his face in need of a shave, the shadow of beard very dark on his cheeks.

He rattled the change in his pocket. "Got an Express?"

Gwyneth had slipped off the stool to reach for the paper in the rack behind her, folded it and placed it on the counter, and the man stretched out his hand and grasped her wrist and kept holding on to it. "So, darling, what's your name?"

He was leaning nearer to her and running his tongue over his lips, his eyes glittery and somehow challenging, and she turned her head away, not wanting to look at him, trying to pull her hand from his. He clutched it tighter. "You're very pretty, darling," he said. "Did you know that?" But he wasn't looking into her face as she was used to people looking at her. He was looking at her dress, an old one of her mother's, thin and lightweight with tiny buttons down the front. She remembered the dress well. No one had ever looked at her in that way before, and as his eyes traveled up and down her body, Gwyneth was sure she must somehow have grown too tall, quite suddenly, like Alice, and was bursting out of her clothes. She glanced down involuntarily, to make certain she was covered up, but there was nothing wrong with the dress, and she held her other hand against her breast to shield herself from his bold gaze, the blood running hot in her cheeks and her heart thumping in her chest. Then she managed to tug her hand away from him, quickly and abruptly, and she retreated into the shadows behind the counter.

"Okay, darling, so you don't want be friendly to a poor bloody private in uniform. Isn't that just like all you girls? What do you want? Some officer?" He grinned at her, but not pleasantly, and she could smell the beer on his breath, the rankness of old sweat in the thick uniform, the male smells mingling with the chocolate bars and the liqorice all-sorts and the mints. She thought for a moment that he was going to come round the counter after her and she was alarmed and bewildered and the conflicting smells were making her feel sick. She thought she might actually throw up.

Then there was a quick rush of footsteps on the stairs leading from the flat upstairs, the brown velvet curtain separating the shop from the living quarters pulled aside with a rattling and clattering of wooden curtain rings. "Time to close up, Gwyneth," her mother announced loudly. Her mother was a stickler for promptness. Her heels went clacking across the floor as she hurried to the door and flipped the cardboard sign. "Sorry," she said to the man in khaki. "We're closed."

He grabbed the paper off the counter. "Just came in for an Express," he muttered and retreated quickly, ducking out through the door. Gwyneth's mother slammed it shut behind him, leaned against the glass.

"Was he bothering you?"

"Bothering me?" Had he been bothering her? He'd only been looking at her, hadn't he?

"He didn't pay for the paper."

Her mother clucked her tongue. "Honestly, Gwyneth, how do

you think we can we make a living if you let people get away without paying for things?"

At first Gwyneth avoided her mother's eyes, but she was sure it wasn't the clock or coincidence that brought her downstairs at that particular moment. She was grateful to have been rescued.

"Don't stand for any nonsense from the men," her mother said. "You have to be careful of them. You're getting to be a big girl now."

Going to her mother, Gwyneth put her arms around her, and for a moment her mother held her, patting her back and then pushing her away. "Almost a woman you're getting to be," she said. But fondly. "Look how tall you are. And too thin, Gwyneth. Much too thin."

But Gwyneth preferred being thin than being fat like some of the girls at school. She was finding it increasingly difficult to finish the food her mother cooked so religiously every day, and her appetite dwindled even more after that particular day. Every day she seemed to grow taller and taller, skinnier and skinnier, while her mother clucked her tongue ever more frequently. "Think of the starving children in China," she admonished. "You're like a bean pole, Gwyneth. I don't know what I'm going to do with you."

Gwyneth couldn't see it would make the slightest bit of difference to Chinese children whether she, Gwyneth Griffiths, here in Clarrach, Wales, did or did not finish the food on her plate. But despite growing so tall and thin, the men who came into the shop kept looking at her with hot secretive eyes and whispering things under their breath, so she began to dread being behind that counter for them to stare at.

Now, as she stood outside the shop, she thought she could remember every man who ever came into the shop, the RAF "boys" in their dusty blue uniforms, those clever scientists from Oxford and Cambridge in loose baggy trousers and long woollen scarves who were rumored to be inventing secret weapons in the south of the county, and because some of them spoke in strange foreign accents, were also rumoured to be spies, and for all anyone knew, they could well have been. So many rumors. So many men. In the war, there were a lot of men in Clarrach, farmers and mad scientists and brave air force boys, and all of them visited the shop and stared at Gwyneth.

She began to make excuses not to be there. "I've got too much homework to do. I've got a French exam tomorrow. I have to write an essay," and sometimes her mother would sigh and say, "All right, *cariad,* just for today."

But Gwyneth understood it was her duty to help keep food on the table and a roof above their heads. There wasn't anyone else. So more often than not, she'd come home from school in her white blouse and navy blue gym tunic, change into a dress, and go down the narrow steep staircase from the upstairs flat and spell her mother from four o'clock to five o'clock while supper was cooking, sit on the high stool behind the counter, study her schoolbooks or unravel old sweaters and knit them into something new, better than merely sitting idly, dreaming of some other life, dreading who might come in and stare at her.

Now, as Gwyneth hovered outside the shop, her reflection in the windows seemed dimmed and insubstantial, a ghostly reincarnation of the girl who'd once fled from here. A quiet girl. Modest. Shy, really. Retreating away from all those men who stared too boldly at her.

Retreating, that is, until the Americans arrived in the little town of Clarrach.

The Americans had come like gods, almost dropping from heaven, it seemed, out of nowhere, without warning, crowding the narrow streets with their odd-shaped Jeeps, strolling arrogantly along the pavements in their smooth, well-fitting uniforms, saluting casually, smiling with white perfect teeth, doling out gum and sweets to the children and whistling at the girls indiscriminately.

Even the weather seemed to smile for the Americans. With them came a long, sweet, warm spring and the promise of an end to the hard days of war and rationing and bombs. All the local girls wanted an American soldier as a trophy, as a feather in her cap. Gwyneth's mother said, "Keep away from those American soldiers, Gwyneth. Don't make yourself cheap. Not like the rest of the girls. Shameful, the way they carry on."

But when any American soldiers came into the shop, tall and healthy and clean and polite, and said things such as, "A charming little place you have here, ma'am. So quaint. There's nothing like this back home," Gwyneth saw her mother blushing and giggling just like one of those girls she'd been warning her about.

The local townspeople invited Americans into their homes, not only as a welcome change from the ordinary, but also because they brought luxuries with them, bottles of whisky and tins of ham and peaches. Uncle Emlyn, her father's brother, met some officers in the pub one evening and invited them for Sunday lunch and instructed Gwyneth and her mother to come, too. Gwyneth could help with the lunch, he said, and her mother could play the piano. Uncle Emlyn only had officers to his house because he'd been an officer himself, in the first war, and didn't mix with other ranks.

Gwyneth's mother was clever with a sewing machine, and she used precious clothing coupons to make new dresses for the occasion, one for herself and one for Gwyneth. Gwyneth had never had a brand-new dress before, only hand-me-downs, and she loved the feel of the dress against her skin, soft and silky and absolutely her own. The material clung to her hips and waist, and she admired her reflection in the long mirror in her mother's bedroom. She looked quite grown up, quite suddenly, and she pinned her hair up, gathering it off her neck and heaping it on top of her head. Though she didn't particularly want to go to lunch at her uncle's house. Uncle Emlyn was too fond of the whisky and too fond of the sound of his own voice and made too much of the fact that his brother's widow kept a shop. Keeping a shop was "a come down," he said. Nobody in the family had ever kept a shop before.

The invitation to her uncle's house changed her life. Gwyneth fell in love that day, instantaneously and precipitously, took one look at the American officer, taller than anyone else, his hair lighter, his smile wider, handsome beyond belief in his smooth olive green jacket with brass buttons, and was transformed in the space of one Sunday luncheon from an overgrown, awkward, and shy schoolgirl, to a shining-eyed seductress, skin creamy and soft, hair curling above her neck, melting and oozing with love inside her new homemade dress. She helped Aunt Ethel with the lunch, fumbling with the dishes, her hands shaking and clumsy, then she'd sat across the table from this extraordinary young man who was like no one she'd ever seen before and did her best not to stare at him. She could hardly speak when he spoke to her. "My name's Carlton," he said and smiled with his fine white teeth. "Carlton Bruce."

She managed to whisper, "My name is Gwyneth."

"Gwyneth?" he repeated. "Gwyneth. I like the sound of your name."

He didn't know, and Gwyneth never told him, that she was only fifteen years old.

Now, outside the shop, staring at the ghostly reflection of her younger self, Gwyneth didn't want to remember him. Had forgotten him, deliberately, buried him in the past where he belonged. If only that boy hadn't appeared, unbidden, dragging the memories to the surface.

Nine

Rhys Edwards had gentle hands. Tim knew they were not as rough as his tongue, but he flinched when the doctor first took hold of his tender ankle, then gradually relaxed under the delicate handling of his swollen flesh and sore bones. Draping a black lead apron over his striped shirt, Rhys shot X rays with the ancient machine, and disappeared to develop the films; this impressed Tim, who'd thought only real radiologists had those skills. Mavis, the nurse, wheeled in a cart piled high with rolls of plaster of Paris and stainless steel bowls of steaming water, covered Tim's leg with soft, clingy material, and then Rhys brought the dripping films back and held them up to a flickering box of lights.

He stabbed at the blur of bones with his index finger. "That's the tibia and that's the fibula, and there at the lower end you probably can distinguish a few separated ligaments." He peered more closely. "And that might just be a hairline crack in the tibia. But nothing to worry about. It'll mend easily enough with a good firm cast."

Tim, too, peered at the X rays, but he was unable to decipher either ligaments or a hairline fracture. He didn't doubt the diagnosis. He'd decided that Rhys Edwards seemed to know exactly what he was doing, and he watched with interest as Rhys dipped the rolls of plaster one by one into the water and slapped them fast around Tim's ankle and foot. Wet plaster flew around the room, the whole messy process taking only a few quick minutes. The end result was a large, comforting cast that encased his leg from toe to knee. Rhys smoothed the bright white plaster with his gloved hands, polished it into a gloss, made one final swoop to neaten the edges, and stepped back to assess his handiwork.

"It's most satisfying to have an end product. Other aspects of medicine aren't like that, unfortunately. Except for babies, of course. Sometimes, in my moments of triumph at a birth, I have to remind myself that the mother is due more credit for the baby than I am."

Pulling off his gloves, he tossed them aside. "I once seriously considered becoming an orthopedic surgeon, you know. Quite fun, orthopedics, hammering and sawing and straightening things. And if one doesn't get it quite right the first time, it's eminently possible to do it all over again." He tapped the cast and it made a hollow sound. "No weight on this for at least two weeks."

Tim flexed the disembodied toes protruding from the lower end of the cast. "Why didn't you? Become an orthopedic surgeon, I mean?"

Rhys shrugged and shed the apron. "Then I wouldn't have become a GP, would I? That was my destiny. Of course, I know Americans don't believe in destiny. They believe in remaking life anew at least once every generation."

Was that what Americans believed? Tim pondered the idea briefly. Could he change his destiny? And what was his destiny anyway?

"This isn't going to keep me out of the draft, is it?"

Rhys shook his head. "I fear not. Perhaps you should have broken your back instead."

"I'll try harder next time," Tim said.

"Give this ten minutes to dry, then you can go. With the crutches, don't forget. Where's my wife, by the way?" Rhys glanced around the bare room as if Gwyneth were hiding somewhere, as if he'd only just noticed she wasn't there. "Isn't she taking you back to the house?"

"She was going to wait in the car."

"Ah yes, well, Gwyneth doesn't much care for the sordid surroundings of my humble profession, nor for the suffering involved. Please go and inform her, Mavis, that it's now safe for her to return."

He rolled down his sleeves and straightened his tie. "See you later, *bach*," he said, and was gone before Tim had time to express his thanks. The rubber apron and the gloves lay in an untidy heap on the floor, blobs of white plaster were everywhere, and pools of water were dripping off the cart and the couch onto the floor. With an exaggerated sigh, Mavis scooped up the gloves and apron and mopped at the floor with a rag.

"He always leaves the dirty work for someone else," she complained, but Tim recognized a fondness in her voice, that mixture of reverence and tolerance people saved for their own physicians. Even if they worked for them.

"What's this *'bach'* everyone keeps calling me? Bach like the composer?"

Mavis clambered to her feet, awkwardly. She was not a young woman. "Yes, *bach*. Just like the composer. It's Welsh for little one."

Tim laughed. "Little? Me?"

"We use it for children all the time. You could say it's a term of affection."

For children? Tim resented that. But it would be nice if he'd somehow earned Rhys Edwards's affection, he thought, and realized he was in danger of falling into the same doctor worship syndrome. It wasn't as if this particular doctor had saved his life or anything; it was only a stupid cracked ankle, but still . . . His ankle felt warm and safe and secure and didn't hurt anymore and Tim was grateful.

Mavis tidied up the worst of the mess and went in search of Gwyneth, and Tim was left alone again in the oppressive little room. He fiddled with the height adjustment on the crutches, stood up to test them, sat down on the couch once more, and considered his options. What the hell should he do now? Where should he go? And how? He imagined the call to tell his parents what had happened, imagined the response, his father's exasperation, his mother's almost certain panic. She'd want to come and take him home like a baby. He didn't need that. He could skip Ireland all right, but he'd no intention of skipping Paris. Except how would he manage there? On a leg that couldn't bear weight for two weeks? All very well for the doctor to say it so casually, but now he, Tim, was in a hell of a fix. Nobody's fault but his own, of course. He knew he'd been showing off for Gwyneth when he'd climbed those rocks. But now what? He couldn't just dump himself at the doctor's house, relying on the kindness of strangers. He couldn't stay alone all day with the beautiful Gwyneth until he was able to walk again. Could he?

Tim waited. And waited. The cast grew warm and then cold and when he poked at it, the plaster seemed quite dry. He tested the ancient crutches again, at their highest point now, took a few experimental hops around the room, sat on the couch again, looked at his watch. Ten minutes past seven. Where was everyone? After more endless minutes, he edged on the crutches, cautiously, out of the room, along the corridor to the waiting area, and was amazed to find people still sitting in the uncomfortable wooden chairs, still thumbing through old magazines. For heaven's sake, what time did doctors quit around here? The waiting patients looked at him, at the cast on his leg, and then looked away again, as though it was none of their business.

There was no sign of Gwyneth or Mavis or the doctor himself.

Tim sidled out through the door, crabbed and awkward. Outside, Gwyneth's little car stood in the same spot, but there was no Gwyneth. Or anyone else. The square was deserted, only the carved stone soldiers on silent grieving duty in the center. The square had a different aspect from his first view of it this morning, a hushed breathless quality to it without the traffic racing around the monument. The morning mist was gone and the evening sun was high in the sky and beyond the steep slate roofs and tall chimney pots, green fields rose above the town. Through a gap between buildings, Tim could see a curve of the bay and a breakwater where painted boats rocked at anchor. In the sun's evening glow, the wandering narrow streets had a haphazard charm and the stone houses seemed mellow and brushed with age rather than harsh and stony. Even the war memorial appeared less stark and grim.

From the pub on the opposite corner of the square, he caught a faint murmur of voices and the distinct aroma of hops and malt. Boy, could he do with a beer!

Tim took a tentative step in the direction of the pub and then hesitated. Gwyneth must be waiting somewhere for him. He wondered where she'd disappeared to, and when he reached the corner he caught sight of her up the street on the other side of the square. She was standing before one of the small shops, oddly intent, as though the window held something of riveting interest, standing very still and poised, hands clasped behind her back, back very straight, head tilted slightly to one side. Then she swiveled her head slowly, as if she was aware she was being watched, and she gave a start of surprised recognition, as if until that moment she had forgotten Tim's existence. She turned away from the shop window, came walking towards him along the narrow sidewalk, tall and graceful, skirts swinging against her long legs, and her distinctive stride, spine arched, shoulders thrown back, seemed not to belong in this remote nowhere place. Gwyneth Edwards was unlike any other woman Tim had ever met, in this country or his own country, for that matter. It wasn't only that she herself was different, her clothes were different, too. And she wore them in a different way. Tim had never before bothered to think about the way women dressed, but now he compared the stiffly tailored tweeds and sweaters his mother wore and those ridiculous miniskirts and teetering high heels he'd seen on so many girls in this country, to Gwyneth's clothes. Her clothes flowed and eddied in soft waves around and about her, like liquid air.

She came closer, surveyed the cast. "That's a serious piece of plaster of Paris. I hope we can fit it in the Mini. Does it hurt?"

"Not at all. It all feels much better now. Your husband did a great job. He seems to enjoy his work. But whatever time does he get to quit?"

"Quit? Rhys never quits. But if you mean finish, probably not until seven-thirty. And then he might have to go and see someone at home." She shrugged. "But yes, Rhys does enjoy what he does, thank God. Think how awful it would be to work all and every day at something you absolutely hate. That'd be like slavery, wouldn't it? Suppose he had to work down a coal mine, for instance? Wales has such a terrible history with coal mines. It makes me shudder to think of men down there in the dark and danger all the time." She opened the car door. "Shall we go?"

Tim hesitated. "I don't know about you, but I could really use a beer. Could we make a quick visit to the pub?"

A sudden hectic flush of color ran into Gwyneth's cheeks. Her eyebrows arched and her eyes widened, as if he'd made some kind of indecent suggestion, and for a moment she seemed lost for words. Then she said, "Which pub were you thinking of exactly?"

"Oh, I don't know. That one there?" He waved towards the

Red Griffin on the corner, but he could tell she hadn't thought much of the suggestion. Perhaps she didn't drink. He said hastily, "Though that's okay. I don't really need it, you understand. British beer's pretty strange, anyway."

What he needed, he'd abruptly decided, was the company of other people. He was suddenly wary of more time alone with her in the cozy house in the hills. Not her problem, of course, but his, too aware of her, too fearful of his own fantasies. As she'd come walking across the square towards him, that lurid, obscene picture had leapt unbidden into his mind again, that vision of her body laid out for him. He must put such ideas out of his mind, for God's sake. If they could just go sit in a pub with a bunch of other people and discuss neutral matters, topics such as jobs and slavery now she'd brought those up, until the doctor was ready to go home, then perhaps he wouldn't be afraid of betraying himself in some way or betraying Rhys Edwards.

Gwyneth held the car door open for a few seconds, then slammed it shut with a thump. "Why not? I never go into a pub these days. I bet I haven't been in the Red Griffin for ten years."

But as she stepped through the front door of the Red Griffin with its beveled glass panes and crinkled layers of old paint, she was struck by the incredible familiarity of it all, the thick stale smell of beer and cigarettes, the low ceiling with the black oak beams, the gleaming horse brasses on leather strips on the cream walls, the creaky uneven floor underfoot. Even the carpet looked exactly the same, dark green and patterned, stretching across the public bar and up the few steps into the lounge bar overlooking the harbor. It felt as if she was in here only yesterday.

As her eyes adjusted to the dimness, Gwyneth was relieved to see there weren't many people inside, only a couple of men at the bar, a group who looked like tourists at a table by the window. No one she knew, thank heavens. Then, in the same second, she realized the woman behind the bar was the same Bethyn Harries who'd been tending bar in the Red Griffin forever. Forever. Bethyn hadn't changed either, still blonde, still short and plump and big-breasted, bright red lipstick, a permanent cheerful smile on her soft, powdery face. The stereotypical barmaid. Bethyn Harries had looked like a barmaid when she was in the fifth form at school.

Of course, Bethyn recognized Gwyneth immediately. Of course.

"Why, as I live and die, if it isn't Gwyneth Griffiths," she called out in her bright piercing voice. The men at the bar turned for a quick look. "How are you, Gwyneth, for heaven's sake? Don't see you in here very often." An understatement if ever there was one. "But we do see the good doctor now and then. Such a wonderful man, Gwyneth. It's lucky you are, that's for sure, to have such a wonderful husband."

Resting a proprietory hand on the beer pumps, Bethyn regarded Tim Bruce with sharp curious eyes. He teetered unsteadily on the beggarlike crutches, very tall under the beamed ceilings, ridiculously conspicuous in the cutoff jeans and the bright white cast.

"Do sit down," Gwyneth told him. "Before you fall down. I'll get you a beer. What would you like?"

He dropped with a sigh of relief into one of the wooden chairs, looking weary now, definitely in need of some sort of cheer. "What's good around here?"

"Sorry, I don't really know. I never drink beer. But I'll get you a half pint of something and you can tell me if it's any good."

Tim frowned. "It's not polite to make the lady buy the drinks. Especially when I dragged you in here. Back where I come from, you know, women aren't allowed to buy drinks at the bar. They have to sit down and wait for someone to come and serve them."

"Really? How old-fashioned. I thought America was a modern kind of place."

He grinned. "Not in the alcohol department. There's no alcohol for sale within a couple of miles of the campus back home, for instance. Which, of course, only means students have to drive their cars to get their beer instead of walking to it."

"They have cars?"

He looked surprised. "Of course. How else would they get around?"

"Buses? Bicycles?" And when he seemed astonished by the suggestion, Gwyneth said tartly, "Students in this country can hardly afford to eat, let alone drive cars."

But as she went up to the bar to order, she realized it did seem strange to be ordering the drinks herself. Now she came to think of it, she didn't believe she'd ever ordered at the bar in a pub, and felt as if she'd been living a strange sheltered existence, like some Victorian woman. "A half pint of some good beer for my young friend," she said to Bethyn. "Gin and tonic for me."

Bethyn looked impatient. "Bottled or draft? Welsh bitter? Worthington? Bass?"

"Welsh," Gwyneth said firmly, though she hadn't the faintest idea whether Welsh beer was any better than any of the others.

Bethyn filled a glass with dark foaming brew. "So, how've you been, Gwyneth? Still living up there on the mountain? Far from the madding crowd and all that?"

"Still on the mountain."

"Who's your young friend? Such a nice looking boy. What did he do to his leg?"

She hasn't changed a bit, Gwyneth thought. Still nosey. Or interested. Call it what you will. Still asking too many questions.

"A visitor."

"Did the doctor put that cast on for him? Such a wonderful man, our Dr. Edwards. So lucky we are to have him here in Clarrach.

You know he just delivered my Annie a couple of weeks ago? A six pound four ounce baby girl. Jennifer they're calling her. Jenny. That's quite a nice name, isn't it? Of course, if she'd been a boy, they'd probably have called him Rhys, after the doctor. There must be dozens of boys called Rhys around here, mustn't there?"

Gwyneth stood at the bar awkwardly. "Your Annie had a baby? Heavens, Bethyn. You surely can't be old enough to have a grandchild."

"Well, I'm the same age as you, Gwyneth. You know that. But I was married at eighteen and so was my Annie." Sliding the glass of beer across the counter, Bethyn snapped the top off a bottle of tonic, poured it into a stemmed glass. "That'll be six and six, please."

Gwyneth gazed at Bethyn's peroxided hair, at the pancake makeup congealing around her nose and below her eyes. A grandmother! A girl she'd gone to school with only the other day! Not a friend, just someone she'd known forever. Gwyneth didn't have friends in Clarrach. Didn't have many friends at all, now she came to think of it. Except for Rhys, of course. He was her friend. He'd rescued and nourished her. Saved her, you could say. But Bethyn Harries had become a grandmother while she, Gwyneth, had nothing to show for her life, not if children and grandchildren counted as something.

"Six and six, please," Bethyn repeated.

For a moment longer, Gwyneth was still lost for words, still stunned by the realization she might have been a grandmother herself. She shouldn't have come down off her mountain to be reminded of the passing years. She should have stayed up there where time couldn't touch her. Bethyn was waiting, plump hand spread open on the bar, ready for the money, and Gwyneth jerked to attention, looked around vaguely for her handbag. "Oh, Lord. I don't have any money on me. I'll go and get some from Rhys. In a minute. All right? Will you trust me till then?"

She caught the expression in Bethyn's blue eyes, quick and sly, gone as swiftly as it had come. But definitely there. Gwyneth knew she hadn't imagined it. No, Bethyn Harries didn't trust Gwyneth Griffiths. Never had, never would.

Gwyneth picked up the glasses and saw that her hand was trembling very slightly, gripped the glasses tighter, and carried them to the table where Tim sat with his legs stretched out. He was leaning back in the chair and gazing at the beams above his head, and she wished they'd found a seat further away from the counter, up there in the private lounge where they could look out over the harbor, away from the bar and Bethyn Harries.

"Thanks a million," Tim said. "Cheers." He took a long swig of the beer and immediately looked startled, his mouth pulled down at the corners, his eyes blinking. "Wow! That's certainly different."

"Best Welsh bitter. You don't like it?"

"Love it," he said gamely.

"Your face says you hate it."

Setting the glass down, Tim peered into it with caution. "I guess you could say it's an acquired taste. But if I work on it, I bet I can acquire the taste."

He shoved the beer to one side, leaned his elbows on the table and cupped his chin in one hand, looked into her face. Gwyneth slid her eyes away from his, gazed instead at his hand, at the fine blond hairs on the back, the knobby knuckles and the broad, flat, very clean fingernails. She thought how some men wore dirt in their fingernails as a virtue, as a sign of manual labor, men such as farmers and coal miners and garage mechanics, and how there were some men who just didn't care if their hands were dirty. Obviously, Tim Bruce cared. But Tim Bruce didn't work with his hands and he was also American. Americans were clean people, shining and buffed and deodorized, gleaming white teeth, clear innocent eyes. Even if, behind the eyes, they weren't innocent at all.

He pushed the hair away from his forehead and she saw that the sticking plaster was still there, the edges of the plaster pulling on the fragile skin. Gwyneth felt a sudden stab of something . . . what? Pity? Tenderness? Something unusual, maternal almost, something odd that grabbed at her insides. This boy touched her in some strange way and she had to turn her face away from him. She took a cautious sip of the gin.

"Tell me about this place," he said. "How old is it?"

Gwyneth gazed around the familiar space vaguely. "You know, I'm not entirely sure. A couple of hundred years or so, I suppose. A lot of pubs like this date from the seventeen hundreds or earlier. They were staging posts for . . . well, for stagecoaches." She laughed, a little uncomfortably. Being in a pub made her uncomfortable. Bethyn Harries watching from the other side of the bar made her uncomfortable. Tim Bruce looking at her so intently made her uncomfortable. "Clarrach isn't very old, really. It grew up around the middle of the last century, when the railway linked up with the boat to Ireland. Of course, there was farming around here long before then. And before there was farming, there was prehistoric man. There are standing stones and those burial chambers I was telling you about. They must be at least three thousand years old."

Tim Bruce seemed struck dumb by this statement, much as when she'd told him how old the house was. And as then, when she'd been telling him about the house, she thought she was talking far too much, the words running on, and somehow she seemed unable to stop.

"There's one burial chamber not too far from here I'm particularly fond of. Cefn Mabis, it's called, way up on a hill, among the skylarks . . ." She saw Tim's eyes wandering up to the beams in the ceiling again, and thought, how silly, what possible interest could a prehistoric burial chamber hold for a young American male? "But, of course, you couldn't manage it with that cast."

"In a couple of days, I'll be able to manage just fine. It's really easy to get around on crutches once you get the hang of it. Only a matter of practice. I tore the ligaments in this same knee skiing and had to spend weeks on the damned things and got pretty good at it." He took another swig of beer, pulled another face, set the glass down, and made small circles on the table with it. "But I was thinking . . ." He glanced up at her, the green in his eyes gone gray now, stared down into the glass again. "I'm supposed to be meeting friends in Paris next week. I realize I won't be able to do much hitchhiking but I can hang out for a few days, see Paris and all that. I'd really like to see it." He looked at her squarely. "I understand Ireland's out of the question but I thought I'd go back to London tomorrow. I can take the train. Are you quite sure it's okay to spend tonight at your house? I hate to impose."

"Go? Tomorrow?"

Gwyneth was taken aback. There was so much to show him, to tell him. She'd thought perhaps, after all, that she might show him her paintings. He'd seemed interested. Perhaps she'd even ask if she could paint him. She'd painted so many faces from memory, it would be an experiment to paint a real face, this one right in front of her, all those angles and planes, the way his fair hair caught the light, that high-bridged nose, those blond eyebrows thick and straight above, the subtle shading of the irises, that faint endearing stubble of a beard, that line of his jaw . . . Oh no, he couldn't possibly go tomorrow.

Gwyneth folded her hands carefully. "Of course. If you really want to go. If you think you have to . . . But you could stay for a few more days, if you like. I'm sure Rhys wouldn't want you to go off on that cast just yet. And didn't he say he'd take you on his rounds with him? I'm sure he'd appreciate some company. He spends a lot of time alone in the car, you know. I think he'd be disappointed not to be able to show you what the National Health Service is really like."

Tim was shaking his head from side to side. "It's very kind, but it's not as if you know me, is it?"

Without meaning to, almost thoughtlessly, Gwyneth said, "You've forgotten I knew your father," and then put her hand to her mouth so she wouldn't say anything more. She was getting careless with her words.

He smiled. His eyes were exactly like Carlton's.

"No, I hadn't forgotten. I was looking around this pub and thinking about him just now, wondering if he ever came in here. Into this very pub? You think that's possible?"

Gwyneth knew she'd opened the door herself. Like Pandora with her box. Opened the lid and now they'd surely come out, all those ills she'd tried to keep hidden for so long.

Ten

It was the pubs that were the catalyst for some of the trouble with the Americans in Clarrach. Not for all of it, of course. There was blame on both sides. Gwyneth wanted to try and explain to Tim Bruce how it was in those days, when young American men descended in foreign droves upon the tiny town, swamping it, driving the whole place crazy with their brashness and foolish optimism. And with their prejudices.

Of course, the local people had their own prejudices, too.

By the time the Americans arrived in Clarrach, the war had been going on for almost five years. No one of Gwyneth's age could remember life without rationing, food shortages, blackouts, and constant air raid warnings, couldn't recall simple everyday normalities such as lights shining in the streets or the ringing of church bells. For an older generation, this war was too soon after last one, the war that was supposed to end all wars. In that war, sons and husbands and sweethearts had died senselessly, uselessly, horribly, in the mud of France; now, only a few years later, bombs were dropping on the country and there was more menace from the other side of the English Channel. Clarrach might be too insignificant to have bombs dropped on it, but sometimes mines with sinister black spikes like deadly giant sea urchins washed up on their beaches. When the bomb squad came to blow up the mines, people watched from a safe distance and cheered, pleased to have something to cheer about. There was so little to cheer about in those days.

The church bells had been silent since the first day of the war and would only ring again for one of two things. For peace, when and if it came, or for invasion. Invasion was what everyone expected, holding a collective breath, arming themselves with foolish, hopeless defenses, pitchforks and old rifles and shotguns, waiting for Germans to come mushrooming out of the skies. After waiting for two years for an invasion that never came, boredom and restlessness were the main effects of war.

Until the Americans arrived.

The Americans arrived full of optimism and enthusiasm, something long exhausted in the inhabitants of Clarrach. The Americans believed that war wasn't a normal state of affairs and were convinced they would bring an end to it, very soon. Everyone believed in eventual victory, of course; they *had* to believe in victory, otherwise it would have been difficult to carry on from day to day, but only the Americans could foresee the end.

In Clarrach and all over Britain, a faint hope began to dawn that one day this would all be over. But they weren't optimistic. Optimism wasn't a national trait. Particularly among the Welsh.

The Welsh are by nature a melancholy people, with a tendency to depression; a people of music and song, but not happy song. They prefer songs of loss and yearning, especially hymns, their puritanical religion dire with foreboding and darkness, with threats of hellfire and eternal punishment. A state of war merely reinforced the pessimistic aspect of their nature. And although the

Welsh are firebrand socialists, they are also deeply conservative, adhering to strict social patterns, so they were suspicious of those young and informal gladiators who arrived in their country to save them. Such openness, such a lack of formality, such willingness to strike up instant superficial friendships with anyone who crossed their paths. In the opinion of the Welsh, Americans had too much money, laughed too easily about nothing in particular, had too many luxuries while everyone else had to make do on meager rations, used the cornucopia of their PX to win over children with candy and seduce girls with cigarettes and nylons. The older generation were shocked how easily their children and daughters succumbed to temptation.

The Welsh, in a continual state of social rebellion against the perfidious English and the rapacious owners of coal mines, were simply not prepared for American egalitarianism. The Welsh were used to addressing each other formally, by surname and title, even when they were married, so they couldn't be expected to be on first-name terms with complete strangers with odd nicknames, Chuck or Hank or Joe or some other odd versions of a real name. In a town like Clarrach, a place that rarely saw visitors, there was ambivalence about these conquering heroes. Welcomed on one hand because they'd help bring an end to the war, they were resented on another.

Perhaps most resentment came from British servicemen. Envious of the money their counterparts were being paid to fight the same war, British soldiers also considered Americans undisciplined and soft in the matters of combat; underpaid British soldiers watched American soldiers riding around in Jeeps and stealing the local girls and were consumed by impotent rage. If the two sides ended up in the same pub, fights inevitably broke out, alcohol-fueled fights between virile young males spoiling for battle with someone, anyone. The military powers of both sides decreed certain public houses off limits, British in some, Americans in others, but still the fights continued surreptiously, in back alleys and along remote lanes instead of in the pubs. Sometimes knives were used instead of fists, with distressing results.

The local townspeople didn't know which side to choose.

But it was when the Americans made public houses off limits to some of their own soldiers, the Negro soldiers, that the locals really became outraged. As far as they were concerned, an American soldier was an American soldier, as good or as bad as any other, same uniform, same careless manners, same low-class habit of chewing gum. Americans were Americans, weren't they? Everyone in Wales knew of Joe Louis, the world's greatest boxer, the sport of boxing worshipped almost as much as the game of rugby, and the great Joe Louis was now a G.I. Everyone in Wales knew of Paul Robeson, a hero for his singing and fine socialist principles, and would have been honored to have either of those two gentlemen in their pubs, no matter what their color. It offended the Welsh socialist ethic that men like Joe Louis and Paul Robeson should be denied entry to Welsh public houses. Public houses were exactly that, *public,* not private clubs from which someone could be excluded, and anyway, the pubs were Welsh, not American, so they felt they should be the ones to have the final say. But the military authorities pronounced it "an internal matter. A matter of military discipline. The local people don't understand the problems of mixing the races."

The local people accepted that officers and other ranks shouldn't drink together. It made some sort of sense that soldiers would pick fights with each other as a matter of national pride, but it was shocking that anyone would want to exclude their own comrades-in-arms. Clarrach was troubled to have its peaceful little town become a war zone of its own, with ugly little melees in the streets, not only between British and American soldiers, but between black and white Americans, and to have menacing military police patrolling with guns. No one had ever before walked the streets of Clarrach with a gun.

Inevitably it led to tragedy. Perhaps not a large tragedy compared to the many lives lost so shortly afterwards, but it was a tragedy in which Gwyneth Griffiths played a small part. She still blamed herself, even though she considered her part had been quite innocent, and she also knew that others still blamed her, and hadn't forgotten.

Forgiving and forgetting was not a Welsh trait.

It was all long ago but it was one more reason why Gwyneth came to Clarrach so rarely.

Eleven

.

Some of this Gwyneth wanted to explain to the son of Carlton Bruce so that he might have a better understanding of those times, how certain events had come to pass, how people had felt about things then. Surely what happened then wouldn't happen nowadays, not now the world had changed so much. Or had it? People were still as ignorant about each other as ever.

Perhaps the Red Griffin wasn't the appropriate setting for such a personal story, personal not only for her, but also for the boy. After all, it was his father's story as well as hers. And though Gwyneth understood that many confidences, too close to the heart to be spoken about at home, were often spilled out in places such as this, where the truth drug, alcohol, was freely available, she also understood you had to be careful where and how and to whom you confessed your secrets. Secrets could be a burden. Her secrets would be a burden for Tim Bruce. She also understood that if she didn't start right here and now, those secrets could be locked up inside her for the rest of her life. She was ready to be rid of them and to hell with the consequences.

No one was within eavesdropping distance in the smoky, malty space, only Bethyn polishing glasses at the bar, talking animatedly to a nearby man who didn't appear to be listening. Gwyneth leaned closer to Tim, looked directly into those eyes so like his father's, opened her mouth to begin the story. She wasn't entirely sure where to begin, and certainly not where to end because she'd never really known the end, but even as she fumbled for the first words, a loud voice called out from behind, interrupting her before she could begin.

"Dew! Isn't this the young lad I drove up to the doctor's house? You never caught the boat, then?"

The secrets died on Gwyneth's lips. Tim Bruce, looking up from the table, smiled his wide trusting smile, and she swiveled her head to see the black-painted front door swinging back and forth behind Billy Price, the baker. He grinned cheerfully, his flat tweed cap plastered to his head like an extra layer of hair. She might have guessed she wouldn't get out of here without running into someone who knew her, but she hadn't reckoned on anyone knowing Tim Bruce.

Billy Price tipped back the peak of his cap with one thumb and rested a proprietory elbow on the bar. "Trying a drop of our Welsh beer are you then, boyo? What d'you think of it?"

Tim gazed doubtfully into his glass. "It's . . . um . . . a bit strong and dark."

"Just like the Welsh. Isn't that right, Bethyn?" Billy Price laughed as if he'd made an original joke.

Bethyn smiled ingratiatingly. "Perhaps the young man would like to try some other kind of beer?"

"He's American, you understand," Billy informed her. "He should be trying lots of different beers. Draw him a half of Worthington,

Bethyn. I'll have the usual. And you, Mrs. Edwards? What would you like?"

"That's kind of you, Billy, but I won't have anything more, thanks."

Pulling at the porcelain pumps, frothing beer into one glass for Billy and another for Tim, Bethyn said, "American, are you? I didn't realize that. Visiting, are you?"

"His father knew Mrs. Edwards in the war." Billy Price was being helpful again. "An old friend of hers."

Gwyneth turned her head away and didn't need to be looking at Bethyn Harries to recognize the sharp knowing glance. She could feel it stabbing at the back of her neck. Billy Price delivered the beer to the table with a flourish, pulling out a chair, ready for a nice chat, and she got up slowly. "If you'll excuse me for a few minutes, I have to run over to the surgery. Take your time. Enjoy the beer, Tim."

She ignored his startled expression and escaped quickly, and as the door of the pub closed behind her, she took a deep breath. She hoped Rhys hadn't left the surgery yet. Perhaps he'd pick up the boy, so that she wouldn't have to go back into the Red Griffin. How foolish she was to have gone there in the first place, still so ridiculously aware of the stares and the whispers, her skin too thin, her nerve endings too near the surface, never learning not to pay attention to people like Bethyn Harries and Billy Price. They probably meant nothing by it; it was probably all in her own head, but if she didn't want to upset the calm tenor of her life, she should keep out of Clarrach, keep away from the gossip and the curiosity of people who'd known her for too long.

But she wasn't to escape quite so easily. Heading directly towards her, more or less in a straight line, and right into her pathway so it was impossible to avoid him or pretend she hadn't seen him, lurched the familiar figure of Hugh Williams. He was obviously on his way to the Red Griffin, which was hardly a surprise.

Gwyneth had known Hugh Williams, as she'd known Bethyn Harries, since early school days, and he'd been deteriorating into the quintessential small town drunk ever since, imperceptibly but inexorably. Not the fall-down, incapable type of drunk, merely the ingratiatingly polite, never quite sober, persistently annoying type of drunk. At eighteen, Hugh had been wildly good-looking, but now his once smooth and handsome features were coarsened and blurred, the pale blue eyes puffy round the edges and slightly bloodshot, the firm jawline slipping into jowls.

Hugh stopped dead in his tracks, pulled his hands from his pockets, and raised his eyebrows in exaggerated astonishment.

"Well, well, the lovely Gwyneth. Come down from your mountain to speak to the little people?"

"Hugh. It's been a while. How are you?"

Not that she needed to ask. Gwyneth knew exactly how he'd be, still full of himself, still an embarrassment. He wouldn't stop being an embarrassment until the drink destroyed what was left of his liver, and perhaps not even then. She tried to walk around him but he reached out a hand and clutched her arm above the elbow, his fingers digging into tender flesh. When she tried to pull away, he moved closer, breathing secondhand scotch over her. "How perfectly wonderful to see you, Gwyneth. How is it we never see you down here in Clarrach anymore?"

Hugh spoke with the vaguely upper-class English accent he'd always affected, even though he was nothing but an ordinary Clarrach boy. Sent to an English boarding school because his parents had ambitions for him and enough money to afford the school fees, the accent and sense of self-importance had only been reinforced.

Gwyneth put his drinking down to the fact that he sold houses for a living, not a job she considered appropriate for an able-bodied male. He spent every day sitting in his little office in High Street, waiting for the phone to ring or for a customer to walk through the door. He didn't build anything or grow anything or risk anything, just waited around for someone to drop in and provide him with a cushy living. At the same time, how could she not be sorry for someone who had seemed full of promise not so long ago and now seemed destined to be washed up by forty-five, if not sooner? It saddened her that someone with his advantages hadn't used his life to better purpose, and she recognized in herself the strong puritan streak of disapproval that ran through all Welsh hearts.

"As beautiful as ever," Hugh muttered. "Still driving me mad with desire."

"Oh, for heaven's sake, Hugh. Do act your age."

Now he had hold of both her arms and was pulling her towards him, leering at her, breathing over her. "Come on, Gwyneth. Be a bit friendly now. After all, we're old friends, aren't we?"

"Let go of me, Hugh," she ordered sharply. "Stop making an idiot of yourself."

His face crumpled ridiculously. "It's you who makes me an idiot, Gwyneth Griffiths. Always have and always will. If I occasionally overindulge in the booze department it's because of disappointment, Gwyneth. Because you spurned me when I was a vulnerable youth and I've never got over it. Look at me. A broken hulk."

She tried not to laugh, tried to be disapproving. "You certainly are a broken hulk, Hugh. And a married one, too, I'd remind you."

"Oh, Gwyneth, Gwyneth, you need hardly remind me of that sad fact. You may laugh but it's yet another of those minor tragedies from which the tapestry of our meager little lives are woven. Quite Chekovian, don't you think? I see the Russians and the Welsh as kindred lost spirits in an aching void of middle-class respectability."

For a moment, Gwyneth stopped trying to pull away. His words struck a sudden and absurd chord in her, as if he were not drunk, as if they were engaged in a rational conversation, not arm wrestling outside a public house.

"If only you didn't pretend to be so respectable, Gwyneth," Hugh said mournfully.

"I'm on my way to see Rhys," she said, snatched her arm away, stepped off the pavement, out of his reach, and headed across the square towards the surgery. She didn't look back.

"Oh, that's right," Hugh called after her. "Off to hide behind your respectable husband, the doctor. That's what you always do, isn't it, try to hide? But don't forget we know about you, Gwyneth Griffiths. We know."

His words shouldn't have upset her, but as she reached the surgery door, unexpected tears pricked at her eyes and throat. Angry at the betraying tears, not willing to accept that anything the idiotic Hugh Williams said could wound her, she pushed hastily at the door, relieved to find it wasn't locked, and slipped inside quickly. But she was well aware that Hugh was still standing outside the Red Griffin, watching her run away from him.

Inside the surgery, the waiting room was deserted, the chairs emptied of waiting patients, the scuffed tables still littered with old magazines and newspapers. Pausing, Gwyneth caught her breath, and was reassured to hear the voices of Rhys and Mavis somewhere in the back. She stopped for a moment to wipe her eyes, to rearrange the magazines in tidy piles and smooth one corner of the worn carpet.

Mavis appeared behind the desk. "Oh, it's you, Mrs. Edwards. I heard the door and was afraid it would be another patient. I thought we'd never finish this evening. I should have locked the door." She came into the waiting room, put the bolt on the door. "You don't have to tidy up, you know. Mattie Lewis comes in the morning to clean up."

"Mavis, don't you ever get sick and tired of looking at this room?"

Mavis stared at the ill-assorted chairs, at the ancient carpet, the walls streaked with black dust from the radiators. "What's wrong with it?"

"It's so . . . so depressing. We should get it painted at the very least, find some cheerful pictures. Surely there are more comfortable chairs than these? And another carpet, perhaps? What do you think?"

Folding her arms and pursing her lips, Mavis said, "Well, of course, it's up to the doctor, isn't it?"

"But you have to work here, too. I'd like to know what you think."

"Well, to tell the truth, Mrs. Edwards, I think it's just fine. It isn't as though anyone complains, is it?"

"I'll speak to Rhys about it. I don't think we should wait until someone complains." As Gwyneth went down the corridor to Rhys's room, she heard Mavis muttering, "We? Who's we?"

In his room, Rhys had his jacket on, which was a good sign, but he also had the battered black leather doctor's bag open on the desk and was sorting through it, as though he was about to need it. Glancing up as Gwyneth rapped her knuckles on the open door, he frowned, then smiled.

"Finished?" she asked.

"Just have to make one quick visit. Old Johnnie Watkins out at Tregwyn. His heart's a bit dicky." He fished in the bag. "Okay. Digoxin. Amyl nitrate. But then I'll be right home. I thought you'd be there yourself by now. Where's the boy?"

"In the Red Griffin. Drinking beer with Billy Price. It was Billy who brought him up to the house this morning, as a matter of fact. Now they're old friends."

Rhys snapped the bag together, picked it up, and swung it heavily in his hand. The bag, like the practice, was inherited from his father. "I meant to ask you about that. How did Billy Price know where to bring him? Did the boy have our address or something?"

It was something Gwyneth hadn't questioned. She said slowly, "Now I come to think of it, I'm not sure. It was all such a surprise.

I never gave it a thought. How could he possibly have our address?"

"You hadn't kept in touch with the father?"

"Oh, Rhys, of course not." She felt her cheeks grow hot. "I hardly even remember who he was."

"Odd then, isn't it? Well, it looks like we're lumbered with the boy. For the time being, anyway. He can't put any weight on that leg for a week or so." Flicking the light off at the door, Rhys took Gwyneth's arm. "You don't mind, do you? I did rather jump the gun, telling him he could stay just like that."

"He says he's going to leave tomorrow, but I suggested he should stay a few more days."

"Good, good. Seems like a nice enough young fellow. For an American."

Gwyneth thought, he could show a bit of curiosity. He could at least ask about the father. Not that she knew what she'd say if he did ask, but at least he could ask. But Rhys had never been curious about her past, accepting her into his life as though they'd always known each other, as though she'd never had an existence without him. She'd always been grateful for it except that just now it didn't seem entirely natural. If someone turned up suddenly from Rhys's past, wouldn't she have a few questions? Who, when, what? But when she stopped to think about it, she'd never wanted to know who'd been in his past either. There must have been someone, of course. No healthy young male went through medical school and the army without some involvement of some kind. She'd never needed to know. She had Rhys and he had her. That was what was important. Which was exactly how Rhys must feel. Why did she think either of them should change now?

Rhys shouted "Good night" to Mavis and walked with Gwyneth out to the back of the building where his car was waiting. The sun was still high in the sky towards the west and Gwyneth said, "Why don't you take the boy with you to see Johnnie Watkins? It'll be a nice ride out there this evening. You said you were going to show him how the NHS worked. It'll be a different experience for him. Take his mind off this terrible Robert Kennedy thing."

Rhys paused halfway into the car. "You think he's upset over Robert Kennedy?"

"Oh, Rhys, of course he is. Can't you see that?"

"He's just a youngster. Young people get over that kind of thing quickly enough. I don't think you need to worry about him."

"Well, it upsets me. How would you feel if one of your political heroes got gunned down?"

"Gwyneth, *cariad*. This is the United Kingdom of England and Wales, not the United States of America. We don't go around shooting people here. Don't get so worked up about it."

Robert Kennedy was only a name to her, a cipher in the political chaos that was America, but she'd seen the look in Tim Bruce's eyes and knew it meant much more to him.

"Please, Rhys. Just take him with you." She paused. "I don't ask many favors."

"You don't. Why is that, Gwyneth? Why don't you ask more favors?" Rhys held the car door for a few more moments. "But all right, I'll take the boy with me. Why not? Where did you say he was? The Red Griffin?"

"Yes. And would you pay for our drinks? I didn't have my bag with me."

Rhys raised his eyebrows. "Not like you, Gwyneth. Going into pubs, leaving without paying. Well, I'll go and settle your debts for you. Maybe I'll even have a pint myself before the house call. All work and no play can make a dull life, can't it?"

Yes, it can, Gwyneth thought. She watched as he backed the car fast down the street, its body rattling and shaking on the rough cobbles. You work too hard, Rhys. You don't play enough. When do you ever get time to play, chained to the practice all day, every evening and weekend? Single-handed practice was an enslaving occupation. But she understood that Rhys loved his life and wouldn't contemplate it any other way. He didn't think of himself as a martyr or even as particularly dedicated, just as an ordinary doctor who had too much work. No wonder everyone thought of him as a kind of saint. Sometimes she did herself, come to that.

Gwyneth knew she was inadequate as a GP's wife. The wife of a GP should be like a vicar's wife, as involved with the congregation, or the patients, as he was, as dedicated to the cause. It wasn't that she didn't sympathize or empathize with Rhys, but she was detached from his cause, apart, as though it had little to do with her, a mere bystander as opposed to a wholehearted partner, dreaming her life away on the top of a mountain, playing with her painting, when she should be down here with her saintly doctor husband, laboring in the trenches.

She'd forgotten to bring up the subject of redecorating the surgery.

Tim was enjoying himself in the Red Griffin. Not that anything exciting was happening, not by a long chalk; the Red Griffin wasn't like one of the crowded taverns around campus with huge pitchers of beer and a crush of students and an overwhelming din; there wasn't even any music here, not even a jukebox. It was all very sedate and genteel, and now that Gwyneth had gone, rather boring. But boring in a different way, the warm flat beer sliding down his throat easily, giving him a definite buzz, listening to the rise and fall of the voices, the lapses into Welsh. They certainly put away plenty of this strong beer. Billy Price the baker, and the raddled guy who just walked in, even the barmaid, they were all sipping something that looked like the same brew. They knew each other, that was obvious, talking to each other in the way of familiars about things a stranger wouldn't know about, even if he could understand what they were saying. After a few minutes, they stopped speaking Welsh and turned to Tim.

"So what happened to your leg?" Billy Price wanted to know. "Is it broken?"

Tim stretched his leg out for them to admire the workmanship of the cast. It shone pristine white and smooth. He admired it himself. "Just a few torn ligaments in my ankle. Dr. Edwards put this on to keep the weight off it for a while."

"Looks like he did a good job. But that's Dr. Edwards for you. He always does a good job. So you won't be going to Ireland, then?"

"Doesn't look like it."

"You'll be staying up at Llanberis with the doctor and his wife, then?"

"Maybe a day or two. They've been nice enough to invite me."

The new guy, Hugh, said, "You're honored. Not many people get to stay with the elusive Gwyneth."

"He's a friend of the family," Billy Price explained. "His dad knew Mrs. Edwards from the war."

The three of them looked at each other, quick sideways glances passing between them. The barmaid said something in Welsh and smiled slyly.

"I'm sorry? What was that you just said?"

"Oh, I just said it would be nice for her to have some company. It must be a bit lonely for her up there on the mountain."

But Tim, who hadn't understood a word of the Welsh, knew she hadn't said that much. She'd used just a couple of short words. She was talking about Gwyneth and it was annoying, upsetting even, that he couldn't break the barrier of the language. He was equally sure they were all using it deliberately in order that he wouldn't understand. He wished Gwyneth would come back.

But when the door opened again, it was Rhys Edwards, not

Gwyneth, who came in. The atmosphere at the bar changed immediately, as though someone of significance had arrived in their midst. The blonde barmaid straightened up and smiled radiantly and Billy Price touched his cap. "Good evening, doctor," he said. "How are you this fine evening?"

"Well, Billy, very well. And how's your pretty daughter?"

"Oh, bonny, thank you, doctor. This lad met her this morning, didn't you?"

"Yes," Tim agreed. "Eirwen. I'd never heard that name before."

"You'll have to teach him a bit of Welsh, doctor, before he goes back to America."

Rhys smiled his dark sardonic smile. "Oh, I think it would take more than just a few days to learn Welsh, don't you? I'll have a pint, Bethyn, then I'm taking the young man with me to begin his first lesson in the National Health Service."

"A house call?" The barmaid leaned forward on the counter. "Someone I know?"

"I expect so, Bethyn. You know everyone, don't you? Forget the beer. Come on, Tim, let's see how you do on these crutches." Picking them up, Rhys held them out to Tim. "You can learn to say *nos da*. It means good night."

Twelve

It was almost as difficult to squeeze himself into Rhys's car as into Gwyneth's, especially now with the cast and the crutches. These puny little cars had to fit the puny little roads, Tim supposed, but neither the width of the roads nor the size of the cars seemed to inhibit the racing-car mentality; he'd barely closed the door before Rhys shot away from the curb, hurtling out of the square in the opposite direction from his house, keeping his foot firmly on the accelerator until he swung abruptly off the main road into a winding, narrow lane. Tim was convinced everyone in this country came hot-wired with Formula One genes.

They raced through an intersection by an ancient square-towered church, past soft-eyed cows crowding against a five-barred gate, past barns bursting with hay, more small whitewashed cottages and rolling fields scattered with black-faced sheep. Gorse flared in yellow bloom and the air smelled of salt and Tim caught occasional flashing glimpses of the ocean, its metallic blue water darkened and dappled by cumulus clouds. From the direction of the sun, he guessed they were heading roughly west by southwest, in exactly the opposite direction from the house, and he waited for Rhys to tell him where they were going. But Rhys hadn't spoken a word since leaving the Red Griffin. It wasn't an unfriendly silence, merely as if his mind was occupied elsewhere, and Tim certainly didn't want to distract his attention from the road. Not that he seemed to be paying too much attention to the road, tapping his fingers on the steering wheel and humming a tune Tim didn't recognize, a cheerful enough melody, as though he was pleased with life.

"So where are we heading?" Tim asked at last, as Clarrach was left further and further behind. Rhys swiveled his head to glance at Tim as if he'd forgotten anyone was in the car with him.

"Didn't I say? To make a call on old Johnnie Watkins. His heart's a bit dicky. I thought it might be interesting for you to come along and see how an ordinary Welsh farmer lives. And let you glimpse a bit more of the countryside."

The countryside was rushing by so fast, a glimpse was all Tim could manage. "You usually go so far to visit your patients? This late in the day?"

"Just part of the routine. Morning surgery nine to ten, house calls till lunchtime, more calls after lunch if any are left over from the morning. Evening surgery from five until about seven, then late calls if necessary. But I don't have to go out in the evenings too often. Only if it's an emergency."

"This is an emergency?" Tim wasn't sure how he felt about being involved in an emergency.

"Johnnie Watkins is old and his heart's not so good and his wife's worried about his breathing. I probably only need to adjust the dose of digoxin, maybe up his diuretic a little, but I don't like to leave someone as old as he is, in his condition, overnight. They'll both get anxious and then his breathing will only get worse."

"Why didn't they come and see you in your office? Why do you have to go to see them?"

"Well, if they lived nearby and it wasn't difficult to get there, they'd probably have come to my office, as you call it. But Johnnie Watkins must be eighty-five if he's a day and his wife doesn't drive. Neither of them is in any shape to come traipsing all the way into Clarrach."

Tim thought about this odd way of practising medicine. "And all this is for free?"

"If you mean the patients don't pay a direct fee for my services, yes. But we all pay for it out of our taxes. It's known as insurance, young man. A whole lot of people contributing a little bit every month so that when something bad happens, they're taken care of. Like fire or flood or other disasters. Surely even in the United States you must believe in some kinds of insurance?"

"Yes, but . . ."

"But what?"

It wasn't a totally polite question but Tim was curious. "Well, how do you get paid, for instance? Do you get a salary?"

"I get a per capita fee for every patient on my list. Nice and tidy."

"And what about a call like this? Is this extra? What if you don't have regular patients? What if you're a surgeon, for example?"

Rhys changed gears rapidly up a steep hairpin bend through a grove of pine trees, and quite suddenly they were on top of a hill, the glittering empty ocean in front of them, the dramatic headlands unfolding and disappearing into the distance. "Ah, well, surgeons are another kettle of fish. They have to have an operating theater and a hospital to work in so it's a different game for them. Surgeons are either employed full-time by the Health Service or part-time so they can also take private patients. You know, the kind of people who pay cash on the barrel. And if you want to know, I don't particularly approve of private practice. I happen to think the profit motive doesn't have a whole lot to do with good medical care. Medicine isn't a commodity like soap."

Tim had never heard a good word for a national medical insurance scheme back home. Back home, he'd heard that physicians in such a system were nothing but slaves of the state and that they all wanted out. Rhys Edwards didn't seem to want out. Back home, everyone, even in Berkeley, believed nationalized medicine was a communist idea and would surely consider Rhys Edwards nothing but a pinko socialist commie. Perhaps he was. Perhaps that's why he didn't approve of Americans or the war in Vietnam. Not that he, Tim, approved of the war in Vietnam, but he found a tiny illicit thrill in hearing such radically different opinions from the ones he was accustomed to hearing. Especially from someone of Rhys's generation.

The car took another fast swerve through a narrow gateway, lurched down a rutted lane, and came to a safe halt in a cobblestoned courtyard.

"So here we are," Rhys announced. "Tregwn."

The courtyard sloped down towards a clump of dark trees and a distant view of the ocean; on the right-hand side a whitewashed cottage had a dark slate roof and tiny windows like eyes and boxes of brilliantly red geraniums on the sills and on the left was a cluster of buildings in various states of repair, some with slate roofs, some with no roof at all. When Tim wound down his window, he could smell a strong odor of cows and pigs and old straw and the sweet, heavy scent of freshly cut hay. Rhys leapt out of the car, and at the same moment a black and white dog with one light blue eye and one brown eye came rushing out of the nearest building, barking furiously, the hair rigid on the back of its neck. Extending a hand, Rhys said something to it in Welsh, and the dog crouched low to the ground, wagged its tail and rolled over, exposing a pale naked belly. In the doorway of the cottage, an elderly woman in a flowered coverall waved and called out to Rhys.

He reached into the backseat of the car for his battered black bag. "I'll be fifteen minutes or so. If you get out of the car, just be careful on these cobbles. We don't need you falling and wrecking anything else." Then he disappeared into the house with the woman, the dog loping after them.

Everywhere it grew very quiet, just a faint cawing of crows in the trees at the bottom end of the yard. The front door to the house remained open. It seemed as though doors around here were left open all the time; the blue-painted door to Gwyneth's house had been open when the baker guy took him up there this morning. Tim stayed in the car for a while, thinking how long ago this morning was, then he slid out of the seat and stood upright, stretching himself. God, it felt good to stretch! His whole body was cramped, squeezed all day long into spaces too small for it. The cast weighed heavily on his leg, but he didn't doubt that Rhys Edwards had done the right thing. Something about Rhys Edwards gave Tim confidence that he knew exactly what he was doing.

Under his feet, the cobblestones were covered with a fine layer of moss and Tim decided not to risk the crutches on it; he'd no desire to make any more of a fool of himself than he had already. But he'd have liked to look around because he'd never been on a real farm before, only that show place his mother had taken them to as kids, years and years ago. To learn about "real life," she'd said. On that visit, his sister Annette had been disgusted to discover that milk not only came from a big old cow, but from a bag between its back legs. "Yuk!" she'd yelled, screwing up her face and making throwing-up noises. Tim hadn't thought through the business of udders and teats before then either; he didn't let on, of course, but the truth was that he, too, considered it pretty revolting, and neither he nor Annette would touch milk for weeks, which wasn't quite the effect of real life their mother had in mind. Tim grinned at the memory. Much of their mother's educational efforts didn't work out quite right; the swimming lessons when they'd balked at going into the water, the trip to the aquarium where Annette had hysterics over a captive killer whale, the hike in the woods when Mark ran ahead of the party and was lost for hours. If their father had been on any of these outings, it would have been a different story, of course. Carlton brooked little nonsense from any of them. But he was always at the university or off somewhere, consulting, organizing other people's lives, leaving the raising of his three children to their mother. The children took full advantage.

Tim had caved in over the milk boycott long before Annette. Annette was capable of hanging on to a principle far longer than either of her brothers. It was surely a big mistake to let her go off to Berkeley, too. Now she'd be marching and protesting with no holds barred. Though when Tim thought about it, the radical politics of Berkeley, where marching and protesting were normal, might well persuade Annette to try something else. Go-go dancing or something. His sister could be a royal pain in the neck. A carbon copy of her mother, blonde straight hair, turned up nose, small breasts and tiny waist, she worked hard to do everything and anything in a completely different way from her mother. Certainly not to be dutiful and correct and polite, which their mother was to a fault. At least, these days, it was considered a fault. Poor Mom. She'd almost certainly vote for Nixon.

Which reminded Tim about Bobby Kennedy. He hadn't thought about the whole wretched business for a couple of hours and now it hit him with a sudden thump in his chest, sickening him all over again. Forgetting was shocking in itself, as if he were incapable of keeping any sort of faith. Everyone at home must be traumatized all over again, even his father, who considered the Kennedys cheapskate politicians in bed with the Mafia. He'd like to call home right now and talk about it. Perhaps he would, later. What was the time there now? But if he called, he'd have trouble not telling his mother about the stupid accident. She managed to get things out of him he'd prefer she didn't know. Perhaps he'd just write a letter. To Annette. Ask her about Kennedy. Tell her about Wales. Not that he knew too much about Wales, but it was certainly more than Annette knew. He'd describe this farm, for instance, this feeling of remoteness, of otherwordliness, as though he was somewhere on the edge of the universe. Which he was. He'd describe the stink of cows and pigs, the black and white dog scratching itself now by the open front door, the sound of doves and crows in the pine trees, this sense of tranquillity and stability. He'd tell her about the people he'd met so far, people who surely never went off marching anywhere in any sort of protest. And certainly didn't shoot their politicians.

He might not say anything about the socialist views of Rhys Edwards, even though that was almost the most interesting thing about him. Apart from being married to the beautiful Gwyneth, of course. He might not say anything about the beautiful, mysterious Gwyneth, either. He could imagine what his father would say if he knew he'd gone looking for her.

He heard Rhys calling his name. "Hey, Tim. You're invited in for a cup of tea."

Jerking to attention, Tim took one step forward, remembered about the crutches just in time, and reached for them from the backseat. Rhys came across the courtyard, put a hand out to steady him.

"Tea's a ritual, you understand. It's not polite to refuse. God knows how many gallons of tea I've drunk over the years."

The cobblestones were slippery and uneven, but Tim managed to get across them in some sort of dignity, even remembered to duck his head as he went through the front door. The hallway of the cottage was dark and narrow with colored tiles on the floor, and once again he felt gigantic, out of proportion, like Gulliver in Lilliput. Rhys steered him under an even lower lintel, into a dim room where a table was set with an embroidered cloth and cups and saucers, a round cake on a round glass plate stand. Beyond the table, red coals glowed through the black bars of a range and sent waves of heat into the overheated room. The woman from the front door bustled in with a teapot in her hand, set it down on a brass trivet, and Rhys said, "Mrs. Watkins, this is Tim Bruce. All the way from America."

Balancing on one crutch, Tim stuck out a hand but she didn't take it, only smiled sweetly. Her curly hair was faded and gray, her eyes faded and gray like her hair.

"There's sorry I am to hear about your poor leg," she said, clucking her tongue. "Come and sit down here by the fire and I'll give you a nice cup of tea." Though she spoke in English, it didn't seem to come naturally to her, her Welsh accent so thick that for a moment Tim had trouble understanding what she was saying.

"I'm fine, really," he assured her. "Not to worry."

"Go and sit down like you're told," Rhys ordered. "You take up far too much damned space when you're upright."

Limping on the crutches to the fireplace, Tim settled into a plush covered armchair with a high back and winged arms and was immediately far too hot, then realized there was someone sitting in the chair opposite, collapsed into it, an old man with a thin fringe of white hair around a bald pate. His cheeks were sunken, his lips a dusky blue color, his chest heaving and wheezing. To Tim, he looked far too sick to be sitting in a chair rather than lying in bed, too sick for everyone in the room to be ignoring him, drinking tea and making polite conversation.

Tim cleared his throat. "Hi, there. I'm Tim Bruce. Are you Mr. Watkins?"

The old man regarded Tim warily. He gasped for breath and Tim thought he shouldn't even try to talk, the effort of speech too much for him, but when he spoke, his voice was strong enough. "Yes, boyo, I'm Johnnie Watkins. Who did you say you were?"

"Tim Bruce. I came with the doctor."

Mrs. Watkins placed a cup and saucer and a plate with a slice of cake into Tim's hand. "He's with the doctor, Da. From America he is. Can't you tell just by looking at him, so tall and strong with those fine teeth." As if she were talking about a horse.

"America?" The old man stared at Tim. "Haven't seen many of them Americans round here since the war. Up on the camp above Nantcarew, they were. You remember, Mam?"

"Do I remember? Who'll ever forget them? Big fine boys, most of them. Like this young one. So smart in their uniforms. So nice they were to everyone."

"Nice?" The old man snorted and coughed. "Not everyone thought that. No, not by a long chalk. A lot of trouble they were, one way and another. There's stories some can tell and there's some stories that have never been told."

"Yes, yes, but not now, Da. This young fellow's a guest of the doctor's."

"Perhaps he'd like to hear what them Americans got up to." The old man's face set stubbornly and he leaned closer to Tim, his breath laboring. "I'm sure a young lad like you is interested in war stories. All young lads like war stories, don't they?"

"Yes, of course," Tim said, just to be accommodating, but he didn't really want to hear any war stories, even if that war was a different kind of war, a cleaner one, one from which heroes came home. There weren't any heroes coming home from Vietnam. Dead or alive.

The heat from the fire was making him sweat and the last thing he needed was hot tea, but he took a polite sip. The old man picked up his own cup and saucer with a shaking hand, the cup rattling in the saucer, and he slurped at the tea and seemed to forget about war stories. Tim could see he didn't have enough breath for drinking tea and talking as well, and tried not to stare in morbid fascination at the engorged neck veins, the struggle for breath. It was amazing how everyone remembered the Americans who'd been here so long ago; anything that had happened twenty odd years ago back home would be well and truly forgotten by now. Or perhaps it was just that he, Tim, hadn't yet lived long enough to remember so far back, like the girl in the café, Eirwen. She didn't remember. But if this old man was eighty-five now, as Rhys said, he'd have been about sixty then. Old enough to remember but too old to go off to war himself. He'd have stayed behind to farm anyway. Gwyneth had said, "Farmers don't go to war."

What age would Rhys Edwards have been then? What age was he now? Tim glanced over to Rhys at the table, teacup between two hands, elbows resting on the embroidered cloth, nodding silently as the old lady chattered away in Welsh. Was Rhys Edwards the same age as Carlton? Carlton Bruce was big and tall with fair hair so it wasn't easy to spot the gray in it, while Rhys was thin and dark with those wings of gray springing from his temples and dusting across the crown, but in many ways he appeared more youthful than Carlton, more supple, altogether less ponderous. If Rhys Edwards was the same age as Carlton, then he'd have been in the war as well, but somehow Tim couldn't imagine Rhys Edwards as a soldier. Much easier to imagine his own father as a soldier than this doctor, whose tongue was sharp but whose hands were gentle.

The old man leaned even nearer and said something incomprehensible in Welsh, and Tim apologized. "Sorry, sir, but I don't speak the language," and the old man said, "No, that's right, American, isn't it? I remember the Americans. Trouble they were. Lots of trouble."

Mrs. Watkins broke off her conversation with Rhys. "Not now, Da," she said in a warning tone. "Let the boy drink his tea in peace. Look at his poor leg and that great cast the doctor had to put on for him."

The old man's rheumy eyes focused on Tim's cast. He put out one finger and tapped the plaster. It made a faint hollow sound. "If the doctor took care of it for you, then you'll be all right, *bach*. He always does me the world of good, that's the truth." He gripped the arms of the chair, made as if to stand, sank back again. "I'd show you my cows if I could. Maybe not tonight. A bit short of breath tonight. Come back again another day. First-rate milking herd I've got. You know anything about cows?"

Tim shook his head.

"Twice a day they've got to be milked. Seven days a week. Summer and winter. Never a break. The wife, now, she'd like a little holiday now and then, but you can't go away and leave your cows, can you? And it's getting harder, that's the truth. When I'm gone, who's going to look after them? So it's glad I am the doctor comes round and gives me a bit of the medicine so I can get out there and take care of them myself."

"You have to take care of your cows?" Tim could hardly credit it. The old man didn't have enough strength to get out of the chair. "Don't you have any help?"

"Oh, yes. There's a fellow comes in for the afternoon milking. Idris Davies. But you can't get anyone for the mornings. Four A.M.? You think anyone will come at four A.M.? Not these days, *bach*. Life's too easy these days. Once upon a time the hired hand would sleep out there with the animals and be glad of three square meals a day. Yes, indeed. So now we have it to do, the wife and me. As long as we can. I don't like to think what's going to happen when we can't do it anymore. I suppose we'll walk the herd over to my daughter's place one day. She's married to Dai Thomas over at Ty Clwd, and they'll have the best of them. Some great milkers among them. But who'll have Tregwyn? Born I was, here on Tregwyn. My father before me and his father before that. Yes, *bach*, there's been Watkinses at Tregwyn since more than two hundred years. But there's no one to follow, more's the pity. Our boy, you know, he went in the war. At Dunkirk. Bad things, wars." The old man paused for breath and peered at Tim. "Hope you never have to go in a war, *bach*."

Mrs. Watkins came to offer Tim more tea. He shook his head wordlessly.

"Now then, Da, don't trouble the boy with your complaining. Lucky it is that he'll sit there and listen to you going on like that."

"No, really," Tim said. "I'm interested. I'd no real idea, you see, what it's like to keep a dairy herd. I've never thought about it before, you see. If you live in a city . . ." His voice trailed away.

"Oh, there's plenty of people don't understand about these things," Mrs. Watkins said cheerfully. "But we've always been on the farm so we've never known any different, have we? Someone's got to keep cows now, haven't they? Lovely creatures they are, too. You can get very fond of them. Very gentle they are. And affectionate, too. You come back with the doctor when he comes to see Johnnie again and we'll take you out to meet them. He's coming back the day after tomorrow, he says. Isn't that right, Dr. Edwards? You'll bring the young man with you?"

"If you like, Mrs. Watkins," Rhys said.

"If you'd like to," she said to Tim.

"Yes, of course I'd like to. I'd be honored. I've never actually met a cow before."

"There you are, then. Sure you won't have another cup of tea now, *bach?*"

Thirteen

The next morning, Tim woke slowly and painfully. He was lying flat on his back as though poleaxed, his mouth open and dry, his legs pinned down by a great weight. When he tried to move, his legs wouldn't respond and a swift lurching alarm flooded him awake.

For a moment, he couldn't think where on earth he was. Staring down, he saw a thick nubbed counterpane on top of him, saw the bright edges of daylight seeping around unfamiliar drapes at an unfamiliar window, a window set into a sloping ceiling papered with a pattern of tiny red flowers. He thought he'd never seen any of it before. Then suddenly it came to him, Wales, Gwyneth, the rocks, his leg! It was a huge relief to remember. He pushed the bedclothes aside and peered at his watch. Past ten o'clock. In the morning, he supposed.

He reckoned he must have slept for more than ten hours straight and not moved an inch in all those hours. All his muscles were stiff and sore and his leg ached under the cast, and when he sat up and swung his legs over the side of the narrow bed, the room swayed gently around him, like a boat at sea. The previous evening came back slowly, a vague recollection of driving back to the house, a slightly clearer recollection of drinking whisky with Rhys in the living room until the clock in the hallway struck midnight, but he had no memory of climbing the stairs or getting into this bed. It must have been the scotch. He wasn't used to scotch.

Eventually Tim stood up gingerly, lowering his head to avoid the slope of the ceiling, reckoned he'd absorbed the hard lesson of his height compared to everything else. He pulled aside the curtains at the window. The window overlooked the walled garden and the mountain; sheep were still nibbling at the cropped turf on the hillside and up at the top were those damned rocks he'd fallen from yesterday. In the hazy bright morning sun, the rocks appeared very near now, but Tim remembered the painful journey down that had made them seem miles away. Heaving the sash up, he stuck his head out of the window and took deep breaths of air, then stretched further to look into the garden to see if Gwyneth was out there tending her flowers. There wasn't any sign of her, and when he drew back inside to listen for some sound from the house, he couldn't hear a thing.

Last evening, too, she'd been very quiet. When Tim and Rhys finally got back to the house, there was cold meat pie and salad waiting on the table in the dining room, but though Gwyneth sat with them while they ate, she was silent, apparently not curious about where they'd been or what they'd been doing. Tim thought it odd she showed so little interest in Rhys's activities, as if where he'd been or what he'd been doing hadn't much connection with her, as if her life was totally separate from his. At home, his mother's life revolved around his father, his days, his cases, his students, and she always wanted to know what he'd been doing and where he'd been.

He'd wondered what Gwyneth did while Rhys was gone.

Rhys didn't seem to find her silence odd in any way. "Poor old Johnnie Watkins," he'd said. "I fear he's not much longer for this world, Gwyneth," and she'd shrugged somewhat dismissively.

"Oh, those Watkinses live forever, Rhys. His father didn't die until he was well into his nineties and then only because he fell off a horse."

"He took a fancy to our American friend, though. Tim's been invited back to see his cows."

Gwyneth seemed surprised. "You're honored," she'd said, and then lapsed once more into the preoccupied silence.

Now Tim had to get to the bathroom, and he hopped along the long narrow landing, white painted banisters on one side, closed doors on the other; on the way he leaned over the banister rails and listened again. No sound, except for the ticking of the big clock in the hallway, the only thing that seemed alive in the whole house. As he opened the door at the end of the landing, bright sunshine came flooding through an opaque glass window, fracturing into a thousand points of light that blinded him for a moment. He lurched over to the toilet bowl and emptied his aching bladder, which made him feel minimally better. He ran cold water at the sink, sloshed it over his face and groped for a towel, and in the thick soft terry cloth, he caught an echo of Gwyneth's scent. He held the towel against his face for a moment.

Last evening, in the sitting room, she'd been working on a piece of embroidery in a wooden hoop. Tim had never seen anyone embroidering before. The room was cozy and soporific and after the long day and his wrecked ankle, the bruising and battering of his body and the indoctrination into the National Health Service, Tim ached with weariness. But he couldn't bear to leave the room to go to bed, didn't want to stop watching Gwyneth as she bent over the circle of cloth, her profile lit by the lamp at her shoulder. Rhys was reading the newspaper, classical music was playing on the radio, and Tim was having trouble keeping his eyes open. Gwyneth glanced over at him. "Aren't you tired? Isn't this very boring for you?"

"Boring?" He pulled himself upright in the too comfortable chair. "This may just have been the most eventful day of my life. So far."

Rhys snorted from behind the paper. "And who knows what tomorrow will bring? It's always incredibly exciting around here." It was then that Rhys had gone to the cupboard and poured the scotch. "Have a drop," he'd said. "It'll help you sleep, then you'll be in fine fettle for further excitement tomorrow."

One drop might have been okay. The second had finished him. He didn't even care for scotch and today he certainly wasn't in fine fettle. Why on earth had he drunk it? Staring into the bathroom mirror, Tim saw the white plaster still sticking absurdly above his right eye, his forehead stained by a livid purple bruise as if he had an unpleasant skin disease, a thick stubble of unshaven beard sprouting like fungus on his cheeks and chin. He looked like a bum. A bum with a hangover.

His razor was in his backpack. Where was his backpack?

He could do with some more of that codeine Gwyneth had given him yesterday.

Behind the mirror was a medicine cabinet. Tim opened the door cautiously and peered inside. The shelves were crowded with an assortment of pills and liquids, exactly like any other medicine cabinet, except these were all labeled "By prescription of Dr. Rhys Edwards," with that impressive string of letters after the name. But the labels didn't say what the contents were and a quick glance didn't reveal anything resembling codeine. Tim was well aware that he shouldn't root around in other people's medicine cabinets, that some things in life were private, but he also was aware they could reveal a great deal about people's weaknesses and infirmities, their sexual habits, their sleeping habits. Pretty well everything about them. Curious enough to take a closer look, he picked up the containers and turned them over in his fingers, but he still couldn't tell what the contents were, and soon he felt nosey and furtive, and shut the door guiltily. Gwyneth would surely give him more codeine if he asked.

On the way back to his room, he stopped to call over the banisters, "Gwyneth, are you there?" No answer. He couldn't resist trying the other doors as he passed, rapping first with his knuckles and then turning the cool brass knobs to stare inside. The rooms, like the medicine cabinet, revealed nothing startling, just an old-fashioned sewing machine with a treadle in one room, a desk, an easy chair, and a single bed in another. The final room was obviously Gwyneth's and Rhys's, a big double bed with a brass headstand, a silky cover on the bed, the windows facing down to the ocean. Lingering at the door for a few minutes, Tim gazed at the bed, imagined Gwyneth lying there, her light brown hair spread on the pillow, her amber eyes closed. The image made his heart thump.

The easiest way to get downstairs was on his backside. He clattered the crutches behind him and made a lot of noise, but still Gwyneth didn't appear. In the kitchen, he found the pine table set with a loaf of bread on a wooden board, a crock of butter, a pot of thick orange marmalade, a pitcher of milk, and boxes of unfamiliar cereals. And a note that read: "Coffee on the counter. Eggs and bacon in the fridge. Help yourself. I'll be back about eleven. Gwyneth."

The note itself was a thing of beauty, thick, creamy paper, neat handwriting, upright and legible and almost certainly written with a fountain pen. He gazed at the piece of paper far longer than was necessary to read the few words, then folded it and slid it into the pocket of his shorts. As a keepsake. He wondered where Gwyneth had gone. It was a fatuous thing to wonder about, she must have a hundred places to go, a hundred things to do, but he wanted to know where she was and what she was doing, right now. Tim was unsettled by such unreasonable possessiveness. He'd never thought of himself as possessive. He thought of himself, if he ever thought of it, as undemanding, incurious, careless almost, not needing to know where people were when they weren't with him. Even girl-friends. Now, as Tim considered those girls, pretty golden girls with perfect teeth and slender bodies, they seemed dim, unformed, unfinished, unexciting. Not with wisdom in their eyes or an undu-lating grace in their walk, not with a secret smile lurking around their mouths, as though they knew something he didn't know. Not like Gwyneth Edwards.

He didn't feel like eating but the food was in front of him, so he sat at the table and filled the bowl with cornflakes and milk. The milk was rich and creamy and not cold enough. He'd have liked some fresh squeezed orange juice but had given up hope of finding such a luxury. A newspaper lay on the adjacent chair and when he picked it up, the headlines were huge and black: ANOTHER KENNEDY TRAGEDY.

Tim pushed the cereal away.

In the newspaper were photographs of Robert Kennedy lying on his back, staring vacantly, not appearing badly injured. Quickly, Tim scanned the reams and reams of print that hashed over the legend of the Kennedy family, Martin Luther King's murder, the war in Vietnam, the cult of guns in the U.S. A person had been taken into custody, the paper reported, a person with a bizarre name, Sirhan Sirhan. A joke name. As though it was all a cruel joke invented by some sick storyteller, something that couldn't possibly have happened again and yet had. Robert Kennedy, the paper said, was fighting for his life.

The paper had been printed last night. There must be more news by now. Tim got up from the table slowly, reluctantly, hopped over to the window and fiddled with the switches on the small radio on the sill, and before he had time to prepare himself, the same portentous British voice he'd heard yesterday was spewing solemn words into the kitchen. "Here is a special bulletin. It has been announced from Los Angeles that Robert Kennedy, brother of the late President Kennedy, was pronounced dead at one forty A.M. Pacific Daylight Time."

Tim turned the radio off quickly, as though the words had burned him, stared around the silent kitchen, sat down at the table again, cradled his aching head in his hands, and wanted to weep and couldn't. Dead? Dead. For God's sake, why? The flickering hope of Bobby Kennedy had been extinguished, brutally, senselessly. Nothing seemed to make sense anymore.

He'd never fight in their stupid fucking war. Never. He wanted out of it all, the violence, the idiocy, the hypocrisy, the lies.

Tim had no idea how long he sat there. Long enough for the silence to get to him. Long enough for the pain in his breast to force him to move, abandon the table, and limp to the front door. It stood open, of course; he took it for granted now that doors always stood open around here. Outside in the bright daylight, he could see all the way down to the town of Clarrach, could even see the boat for Ireland nestling in the lee of the breakwater. He'd never get to Ireland. He might not even get as far as Paris because after all he'd no desire to go anywhere anymore, to see or do anything. A terrible lassitude seemed to grip him, a total lack of initiative and energy. He might just go back to bed and sleep some more.

Somewhere past the town of Clarrach was where he'd been yesterday evening with Rhys Edwards. Tim pictured the old man in his chair, too weak to get out of it, yet who somehow got out of his bed at four A.M. to milk his cows. How long would Rhys be able to keep that old man alive? How sad it would be when he had to give his cows away. Maybe he'd be better off dead. But everyone got too old for something, sooner or later, if they were lucky enough to live that long. It was beginning to seem like luck, pure chance, to live long enough, not be mown down halfway through life by a bullet, in Vietnam, in a hotel kitchen in Los Angeles, on a street in Dallas, at a motel in Memphis, lucky to survive to be old enough to give up anything.

Tim tried to imagine himself at the end of a long and productive life and simply couldn't see that far into the future, couldn't even envisage what he meant by a productive life. Except it didn't include going off to war and shooting people. Or being shot at himself. Vietnam made any plans for his own future irrelevant and almost frivolous, because there was absolutely no guarantee of any future whatsoever.

Last evening, he'd asked Rhys about his war. Which was how they got round to drinking too much scotch. Rhys had said, almost apologetically. "Frankly, I had rather a good time. Wars give new doctors wonderful training, you know. As soon as I qualified, they packed me off to Italy to learn about gunshot wounds and battle fatigue and other things I'd never need to know about again, and it was all rather exciting and dramatic and stimulating. For me, at least. Not for the poor buggers who'd stepped on mines or had grenades thrown at them. When it came time to return home, I thought general practice would be dull and unrewarding but instead I found it comfortable and reassuring. I'd got all the sturm and drang out of my system, you see. Perhaps all young men need to be in a war to rid themselves of their natural aggressions."

Tim remembered saying, "But you weren't doing the fighting, were you? Not actually pulling the triggers or throwing the grenades. Anyway, doesn't it have to be the right sort of war? To be fighting for the right reasons?"

Rhys had shrugged casually. "Young men have always marched off to war for the most ridiculous reasons. It seems they just need a good old-fashioned bloodbath now and then."

Tim knew he didn't need a bloodbath. But what did he need?

He sat on the bench outside the blue front door and tried to contemplate the future. He *had* to come to grips with it. He couldn't keep stalling like this. What was he going to do? He *had* to think about it.

The breeze blew up the hillside off the ocean and smelled of salt and distant places, and Tim vowed he'd never, never go off to war to kill anyone. Somehow or other, by hook or by crook, by fair means or foul, he'd keep out of it. It was the only conclusion he could come to, and though he wasn't sure whether it was principle or fear or inertia that made him arrive at that conclusion, somehow he felt calmer now, because it was the only possible conclusion.

A cloud came racing over the high thin sun. He couldn't just sit here, mourning Robert Kennedy, waiting for Gwyneth to rescue him. He had to make some sort of effort. Picking up the crutches, he went slowly down the graveled driveway to the gate leading to the lane, just to go somewhere, but there was nothing at the gate, only the pine trees sighing overhead and the road down the hill, so he turned around and set off along the left-hand side of the house where another gate was set in the side wall. Tim assumed the gate would lead into the backyard, but it opened instead onto the hillside and the path outside the garden, up the grassy slope between the skittering sheep, past the building that was Gwyneth's studio.

Yesterday, he hadn't looked too closely at the building. Yesterday he'd been much too taken with looking at Gwyneth. He could see the two large skylights in the slate roof and the windows set high in the walls, and tried to imagine what might be inside. What she might be painting. There had to be an entrance into the studio somewhere. Swinging on the crutches, covering the ground in huge strides, with finally some sort of goal in mind, Tim followed the path around the corner of the building and found a door at the other end. The door was in two halves, with big iron latches, and unlike the front door to the house, it was closed. He tried the latch.

The top half opened creakily, the planked wood swinging outwards on black hinges. Leaning against the lower half, Tim peered inside. Inside was a surprisingly large and high space with no ceiling, only bare beams exposed under the slate roof, the windows and skylights flooding a pale even light onto a bare concrete floor. He could see a workbench covered with painting paraphernalia, a couple of chairs and a slip-covered sofa, an easel with a canvas, a stack of canvases propped against the rough, white-painted plaster walls.

"Gwyneth?" he called out. "Are you here?" Though he'd have known immediately if she was there, of course. He desperately needed someone to talk to.

The easel faced away from the door, toward the light from the windows and skylights. A light blue painting smock, smeared with streaks of oil paint, hung on a hook on the bench, bearing her shape. He could imagine Gwyneth wearing it, her hair in a wild cloud, her face pale and concentrated, a frown line between the amber-colored eyes. He wanted to see her paintings. He wanted to know all about her. But he didn't quite have the nerve to cross the barrier into her inner sanctum. She'd made it clear enough. "I don't show anyone my paintings," she'd said. Except if he did see them, he might learn her secret. If she really had a secret. Her mystery might only be a mystery he'd invented for himself, wishing her to be a mystery, an enigma.

Tim dithered on the threshold, his hand on the lower half of the door, a small sense of decency keeping him back. Then he heard, faintly, the sound of a car coming up the hill, the thrumming of an engine borne on the ocean breeze, and though he couldn't know whose car it was, he guessed it was Gwyneth's, and thought he might never get another chance to see her paintings. That he *had* to see them, for some reason. There would only be a few moments before the car arrived at the house, and he hastily lifted the lower latch and scooted with the crutches across the concrete floor.

The air was curiously cool and still, redolent with the smell of turpentine and oil paint and the scent of Gwyneth's hair. He wanted just a quick look, a peek, a once-over and then out of there quickly, before he was caught red-handed. Except when he saw what was on the canvas, he froze into place, stock-still, almost dropping the crutches in amazement. Because the painting was not just any painting, not just a nice little landscape, which he'd half expected, or some wild abstract, which he hadn't. The painting on the easel was an almost completed portrait of someone he knew quite well. Himself.

The painting made him forget Robert Kennedy for a moment. He stared at the face on the canvas for a long time, trying to understand when she could have done it. And why. But he didn't want to know why. It was enough that she'd been painting his face, an astonishing, flattering, exciting idea. Then it came to Tim gradually that this could equally well be a painting of his father. It could even be his brother Mark. It could be any one of them, a strangely elusive slant to the eyes and cheekbones, as though all the male Bruces were somehow embodied within this one portrait, each one of their features superimposed upon the other. Tim couldn't tear his eyes away. Until that moment, he hadn't realized how much he looked like his father or how much his brother looked like him. It had taken someone else's eye to make him aware of that.

But it wasn't only the subject of the painting that held him in thrall; it was the skill of it, the quick and sure lines of the brush, as if the artist hadn't needed time to think, hadn't been hesitant or unsure, but had merely picked up a brush and allowed the portrait to emerge on the canvas, a spontaneity to it, a freshness, an unstudied ease. Tim didn't know whether to be more amazed by the subject Gwyneth had chosen or by the fact she was so good at it. He was blown away by the art of the artist. He was blown away by the artist herself. And by the idea that she should have painted his face.

Surely this had to be his face. He wanted it to be his. His, Tim Bruce's.

Fourteen

Gwyneth was disconcerted not to find Tim either in the house or out in the garden. He couldn't have gone far, not on those crutches, and she stood in the garden for a while, gazing up the hillside, as though she might catch sight of him on the path.

"Tim?" she called out. "Where are you? Tim Bruce?"

The sound of his name was strange on her lips, and it occurred to Gwyneth that she never had reason to call to anyone from here in the garden, or from the house. Or from anywhere else for that matter. "Tim?" she repeated, just to hear the sound of it again. "Tim Bruce?"

The breeze snatched away the echo of her voice, blowing it up the mountainside until it scattered on the wind like chaff, going, going, gone. Almost a wail, a lament. Only the sheep on the hill took any notice, lifting their narrow heads for a moment, then bending back down to the grass as though the air hadn't been disturbed. At that moment, a dark cloud slid over the sun and cast a cool shadow, and Gwyneth shivered. But it wasn't the sudden cooling of the air that made her flesh creep. Until that instant, as her voice faded and disappeared between the sheep, she hadn't realized how much she'd wanted Tim Bruce to be waiting for her; until that instant, she hadn't acknowledged how solitary and alone her life was here on the mountain. Not, after all, so content to let her days simply drift away, not so self-sufficient, not so absorbed in her garden or her house or in the painting of faces. Not, after all, past the need for another human being. She'd wanted him to be here to smile at her with those green eyes, that endearing puppy-dog expression, the panting eagerness to please.

It was something she must not want. She was all too aware of the way Tim Bruce looked at her, recognizing the effect she had on him because once she had that effect on many men. She must not let Tim Bruce come close to her in any way. Must not. Could not. It was important to keep herself safe because she couldn't afford to repeat the mistakes that had blighted her life. She muttered the mantra over and over, "Keep safe. Keep yourself safe," and went wandering, distracted, along the grassy paths between the lavender and the roses. But in the scented oasis of garden hidden from the world by high stone walls, there was no sound of another human voice, only the ubiquitous bees droning among the flowers, the birds singing in the trees. The walls loomed over her like prison walls, as though she'd been shut away, confined. From here she couldn't see anything of the rest of the world. Which was what she'd wanted, hadn't she? Hadn't she welcomed the walls because they trapped the sun and excluded the wind and the rest of the world?

At the bottom end of the garden, below a rustling ash tree, Gwyneth sank down on the old wooden bench, crackled and mossy and silvery gray, where she often sat to contemplate the flowers. Now she didn't look at the flowers but covered her face with her hands and contemplated her life instead, how she was drying up like an old, old woman, setting her mind against people, avoiding them, hiding up here on her mountain, among the rasp-berry canes and lavender bushes and stupid sheep, as if that was all that life was about, as if tending a garden and playing with paints could be a whole life. She didn't even care that much about her painting. Not really. It wasn't as though she was any good at it. If it was taken away from her, if someone said, today, you'll never paint again, how much would she care? It might be a relief in a way. She could stop seeking perfection, striving to get the faces just right. It wasn't as if she'd ever know when a face was just right.

Pressing her fingers deep into her eye sockets, she saw a kalei-doscope of colored lights flashing in the inner darkness; the colors reminded her of her paintings, and suddenly Gwyneth wanted to weep, for the faces she'd been striving to perfect so obsessively, for the silence on the mountain, for the emptiness at the center of her life. For being caught in a despair she usually managed to keep at bay. Usually she recognized when the shadows were creeping up on her and could take steps to fend them off. Go for a walk. Scrub the kitchen floor. Polish the furniture. Paint another face. Usually the dark shadows didn't catch her unawares like this, not out in the garden on a hazy sunny day.

These sudden attacks of melancholy, these abrupt descents into the stygian depths of gloom, were not unfamiliar to Gwyneth. She'd almost learned to cope with them. But not totally. When they threatened to overwhelm her, she had to turn to Rhys for help. Rhys had recognized the problem when they very first met, when her mother was dying and Gwyneth was overcome with guilt and shame and panic. He'd been pragmatic about it. "A very Welsh affliction, this genetic tendency to depression. God knows I see enough of it. Half the people I see are suffering from some sort of depression. They just don't recognize it." Rhys had pills he prescribed for his patients and he prescribed them for Gwyneth. "It'll pass, never fear," he reassured her. "And there are always new pills."

There were generations of Welsh blood in Gwyneth's veins, but she wasn't entirely convinced the melancholy was genetic, no matter how often Rhys reassured her. She believed people like Rhys didn't suffer from it because they had the sort of jobs which kept their minds occupied, their emotions intact; if she hadn't left school at the age of fifteen, she too might have found some worthy and productive work. Because she was Welsh, she accepted the theory of retribution and believed it was guilt she suffered from, plain and simple. Though she'd given up reading the Bible long ago or believing in a God, embedded somewhere deep in her soul was the concept of sin. The downfall of Eve, for example. Myth with a real foundation. When women tempted men, trouble was the inevitable result, and someone had to pay for it. She'd tempted Carlton Bruce when she was fifteen years old and she'd paid for it. Over the years, she'd tempted other men and so she had to pay for that, too. One of the curses of beauty was the ease with which men could be tempted by it.

She would not tempt Tim Bruce.

Gwyneth thought about Tim and his bumbling efforts to please her, the eager way he hung on her words, and she was thankful to have been interrupted before spilling out his father's story. The boy already had enough trouble deciding what to do with his life. Now he'd have to cope with the awful news of Robert Kennedy. As Gwyneth thought about Tim, about the tragedy of the Kennedys, about someone other than herself, her own darkness became less dark. What she needed was to do something worthwhile with her life, to stop moping on her mountain. She'd have to think of something, something . . . If only she could start again, if only she had all her life ahead of her, as Tim Bruce had.

Where was he now? Where could he have gone? Suddenly, Gwyneth knew he'd gone to the studio. She dropped her hands and was blinded by the sunlight for a second. He must be in there now, looking at her paintings. My God! Jumping to her feet, she hurried on silent feet across the garden to the gate in the wall, along the grass path to the door to her studio. The door was standing ajar, as she knew it would be.

He was leaning on the crutches in the middle of the room, right in front of the easel with the painting, staring at it, and as she came slowly through the open door, he turned his head and showed no signs of apology for being caught in her private space, for invading it.

He said, "I didn't know where you were so I came looking for you. I knocked on the door and when you didn't answer, I came inside."

Closing the door, Gwyneth walked carefully and deliberately across the concrete floor, came close to him and looked into his face. His eyes crinkled and his mouth stretched into the beguiling smile, and even as she looked at him, she forgot what she was going to say, distracted by his cheekbones, by the way the light caught his hair. She wanted to be angry with him for being here. She *was* angry, and at the same time, it was some sort of relief, one secret she didn't need to keep any longer.

"I had to go into town. To Newlyn. Not to Clarrach," she said, though where she'd been had nothing to do with anything. "You were still asleep when I left so I wrote a note. Didn't you see it?"

"Oh, yes. But then I read those damn newspapers and I turned on the radio and heard the news and I felt . . . Oh, I don't know how I felt. I just hoped you might be here. I needed some company." He pulled his mouth down. "I wanted to sit and cry, but that wouldn't have been any use, would it? So I came looking for you." He smiled again, disarmingly. "Then I saw this painting and it made me forget about the news for a moment. It's a wonderful painting," he said, and waved a hand towards the canvases piled against the wall. "You did all those, too?"

"Have you been looking at them?" she asked quickly and heard the sharpness in her voice.

"No. Only this one. But now I want to see the others."

"I told you. I don't show my paintings to people."

There was a small silence. "I know I shouldn't have come in here," Tim said. "I apologize." But he didn't appear apologetic. "Now I've seen it, won't you tell me about it?"

"There's nothing to tell," she said, and tried to turn away, but Tim reached out and grabbed hold of her hand, startling her.

"It's the most wonderful painting, Gwyneth. You're wonderful, too. And beautiful. You're absolutely the most beautiful woman I ever laid eyes on."

Regarding him gravely for a moment, she loosed her hand from his. "You can't possibly think that. I'm old enough to be your mother, Tim. One doesn't think that sort of thing about someone who's old enough to be your mother."

"No? How can I not think you're beautiful when you are?"

Gwyneth knew she ought to make him stop looking at her in that way, adoring, lovesick, but in spite of herself, she found his words reassuring, as though she needed him to think her beautiful. She sighed. "Beauty is nothing but a curse, Tim. It isn't something to be admired. It's not an achievement, only a mere accident of birth. Like being born royal. And it hasn't done me any good. On the contrary."

He didn't seem to be listening. "I've wanted to tell you from the first moment I set eyes on you," he said, and stared at her boldly for another moment, then at last he looked away from her to the painting on the easel. "Please tell me about this painting. Why you did it. And when? You're very talented. You've obviously had proper training."

Gwyneth thought she was much too easily flattered and gratified, too easily diverted. "As a matter of fact, I studied at the Slade for a couple of years."

"The Slade? What's that?"

"Quite a famous painting school. In London."

"So why pretend you just dabble at it? And why don't you want anyone else to see your work?"

He wouldn't understand. She didn't really understand herself. She struggled to explain. "Because it's for myself, not for anyone else. Anyway, I wouldn't want to go around galleries, begging them to show my work. I've seen what happens to artists, always scratching and hassling and being rejected." Now she wanted this conversation over and done with. "I just have this need to paint faces. Not any face in particular, you understand. Just . . . faces."

Frowning, as though he didn't believe her, Tim touched the painting with one finger. "What I don't understand is when you did this. I mean, I only got here yesterday and it's nearly finished. I may not know too much about paint and paintings but enough to know oil paints take days and days to dry."

Gwyneth narrowed her eyes to get a perspective on the painting to see what he was seeing, sat on the stool in front of the easel and studied the shape of the head, the eyes, the mouth, the planes of the cheekbones, tilting her head first one way, then the other, trying to see it from his eyes. And suddenly she understood. It looked exactly like him! Of course! How stupid not to have recognized it before! She always stood so close to the faces while she was painting them that she was conscious only of the small details, not the end result. She never looked at them when they were finished, never stood back and said, yes, that's right, that's the face. I've got it right at last. Because of course she'd never know if it was right. Now it came as a shock to understand she'd painted an actual living face. Tim's face. She thought she'd been creating the faces from the deepest recesses of her mind, from her imagination, not from some distant memory. She was wrong.

After a moment, she asked, "So who do you think it is?"

The color ran up into Tim's eyes. "I thought . . . it was me?"

"Yes. Yes, I can see that now. It does look a lot like you, doesn't it?" She laughed nervously. "I told you I wasn't very good. Because the remarkable thing about faces is that although we all have two eyes, one nose, and one mouth, each and every face is quite different. Isn't that so? Every single face in the world quite distinct from another? Isn't that extraordinary? So it shouldn't be so easy to get one muddled with another one." She was talking too much again. "The reason I didn't recognize this face is because I believed I was painting an imaginary one. It wasn't possible for me to recognize anyone real in it."

They examined the painting together. Tim said slowly, "I really don't believe you. The features are too well-defined. You handle the paint too well. It looks as if you knew exactly who you were painting." He shifted on the crutches, awkwardly. "If this isn't me, it could easily be my father. Or even my brother. But you don't know my brother. So it must be my father. Have you been painting my father's picture?"

"A brother? You have a brother?"

"Yes, I have a brother. And I have a sister, too. But this is the male face in our family."

Gwyneth clasped her hands together tightly. "It's not meant to be your father. Or you. It's an imaginary face." Screwing her eyes up, she squinted at the painting some more, then looked down at her hands. "No, that's not quite right, either. It isn't totally imaginary. It's a real face, but I've never seen it. I've been trying to re-create it. Do you understand the difference?"

Tim shook his head. "No. And to tell the truth, I'm not sure I care. I mean, if it's not me, I don't really care who the hell it is. I wanted it to be me. I wanted you to be painting my picture. I liked that idea."

She couldn't explain any further. "All right, then let's say it's you."

"Gwyneth, please don't be patronizing."

The sharpness of his tone surprised her. "You know, you're the second person in as many days to accuse me of being patronizing. I apologize. Obviously I need to change my attitude."

Tottering on the crutches, Tim reached out again and pulled her hand close against his chest. She could feel the thudding of his heart under her fingers. "No. Please don't change a thing. You're perfect the way you are. Perfect. Perfect and beautiful. The perfect beautiful Gwyneth."

For a moment, it was almost impossible to resist the warmth of his hand, the beating of his heart, and Gwyneth sensed the air around her growing thick with half-forgotten desire. All of a sudden she longed to put her hands on him, all around him, ached to be folded into his arms, and it was as though she was being sucked into an old vortex of foolish longings and sinful pleasures that she'd vowed to leave far behind. For one moment, one brief second, she wanted anything to be possible, anything, everything, to hell with all the damnation and guilt and duty and conscience. To hell with it all.

For one moment . . .

Abruptly, Gwyneth pulled her hand away. Tim's crutches clattered to the concrete floor with a loud fracturing sound and they both stared down at them, wordlessly. An elongated silence spun around the studio and seemed to last forever, a stretching and cracking of the spaces between the two of them. The silence was choking and stifling her and she put her hand over her mouth, and at last, in the silence, bent down and picked up the crutches and handed them to him.

The moment had passed. Saved, she thought, saved. Both of them saved.

Tim attempted a laugh. "Such ridiculous objects, these damned crutches. They make me look such a fool."

"Oh, no," Gwyneth said quickly. "You don't look like a fool, Tim. Not at all."

She was the one who was a fool. She recognized it, even if he didn't.

"You want to see those other paintings? I'll show them to you. You don't have to say anything."

She'd never let anyone else look at them, had never looked at them herself once they were finished, had no real way of knowing if they were really ever finished. He wouldn't know what to make of them, and yet, if anyone was to see them, perhaps it should be him. He looked suddenly fearful and collapsed on the stool, stretching his long legs out and staring down at his cast and Gwyneth wanted to reassure him somehow, but instead she just began turning the canvases, one by one, and then she was interested to see them, too, because it was a long time since she'd done them, or looked at any of them. Now, as she exposed the paintings, she could see them with new eyes and was almost as surprised by them as he was. She heard the sound of her own breathing, his breathing.

"But I don't understand," Tim said at last, puzzlement in his voice. "They're all the same. Exactly the same face."

Gwyneth stepped back to get more perspective on the paintings, then heard the sound of a car engine coming up the hill and quickly began turning the canvases against the wall. "That'll be Rhys," she said. "Home for lunch."

The light was catching Tim's hair, and before she thought too carefully about it, she said, "Will you sit for me? So I can paint a real face for once? Not just the one that I've been imagining all these years. Please, Tim."

Fifteen

Rhys thought the boy particularly quiet today. Not that he was the talkative type at the best of times, rather an unusual youth who appeared to think his words over before spilling them out, a trait Rhys liked in him. But now he was completely silent, sitting at the table and picking at his food as though not interested in it. A damn fine lunch it was, too. Gwyneth had been to Newlyn to buy fresh lobster from the fishermen on the quay, a real treat at lunchtime, if somewhat messy. Perhaps their guest didn't care for lobster or the mess. Rhys loved the whole process. He dug the thick white meat from the bright red shell, slathered it with melted butter, rinsed his fingers in the silver bowls, wiped his face and hands with his napkin. Yes, a real treat.

"Ankle all right?" he asked Tim. "Not swelling or anything?"

Tim shook his head vaguely. "It's okay, thanks."

"I'll take a look at it after lunch. When I've got myself cleaned up. By the way, I'm off to see old Johnnie Watkins again this afternoon. Want to come along?"

It appeared to be a difficult decision. Tim wrinkled his forehead and glanced uneasily across the table to Gwyneth, as though seeking her permission, and she frowned, a small creasing between the thin curving eyebrows.

"I was thinking of showing him Cefn Mabis."

Rhys felt quite put out. "A burial chamber? You think that'd interest him?"

"Why not? It's impressive, all alone there on the mountain, so quiet and still, as though one has stepped back a thousand years."

"Four thousand actually."

"All right. Four thousand, then. All the more reason Tim should see it. Something really prehistoric."

"Which is exactly why he should come with me to see Johnnie Watkins. You could definitely say he's prehistoric." Rhys searched a lobster claw for stray tidbits. He'd been counting on the boy coming with him, a bit of company in the car, someone to sharpen his wits on. How was he supposed to know that Gwyneth wanted to take him to Cefn Mabis? She rarely announced what she was doing with her days, perhaps because she did so little with her days. Did she really imagine a healthy young American would want to see a burial chamber, a heap of stones that hadn't changed in four thousand years? Hardly a lively topic for conversation. Not like medicine now, an endlessly fascinating subject.

"So which do you think you'd prefer, Mr. Bruce? The mysteries of present-day medicine or the mysteries of ancient Cymru?"

Tim seemed startled to be addressed directly. "Cymru?"

"That's Welsh for Wales," Gwyneth explained. "He's just trying to confuse you again."

"No, Gwyneth, you've got it wrong. Cymru is Cymru. Wales is what the English choose to call it. As you may be aware, Tim Bruce, the English have a predilection for changing native names. They did it all over the world. No doubt they did it in America, too."

Gwyneth sighed, her eyes glinting at Rhys, sparking fire, and he understood he'd irritated her in some way. She said, "He's been to Tregwyn. He hasn't seen a prehistoric burial chamber."

"Well, he can make up his own mind." Rhys peered at Tim. "You're capable of making up your own mind, aren't you?"

Fiddling with the lobster pick, Tim examined a piece of shell, swiped his mouth with his napkin. "I can't decide. Couldn't I do both?"

Rhys was amused. "Spoken in the true spirit of greedy youth. The burial chamber will still be there tomorrow but part of my plan for your afternoon won't be there tomorrow." He paused dramatically. "Actually, I was going to take you to see a delivery."

"A delivery? Of what?"

"A baby, of course."

Tim dropped the pick on the edge of his plate with a clatter. His face grew pale, the indistinct freckles across his cheeks suddenly livid. "Are you suggesting . . . ? I've never been anywhere near a delivery room."

"This won't be in a delivery room. Normal babies are born at home around here. Same way they've been for centuries."

The expression of dismay on Tim's face made both Gwyneth and Rhys laugh. Stammering, he said, "I don't believe I have the guts to watch a baby being born."

"Then it's high time you experienced it. It's a passage of life, after all. All men should see how babies come into this world."

Gwyneth gazed at Rhys with surprised approval. "Why, how very progressive of you, Rhys. I thought fathers were always thrown out of the room."

"They don't need to be thrown out. Keeping them in is the problem. Most men are gone as fast as possible. And I do believe farmers are the worst of all. You'd be amazed at the excuses they come up with, cows to milk, hay to bring in. Et cetera, et cetera. Beats me. They can deliver calves and lambs and foals with their bare hands but seem unable to stomach the sight of their own kind emerging from the very womb they've fertilized. And it isn't only farmers. All men run as far from the scene of the crime as they can get. Cowards, all of them."

"Perhaps they are just afraid something terrible might happen and they'll be responsible for it? It isn't so long since women died everyday in childbirth." Gwyneth asked Tim, "What happens in America?"

He looked totally blank. "I haven't the least idea. But I do know everyone goes to the hospital."

Rhys flexed his sticky fingers. "So it'll be something new for you, won't it? I'm going to wash and brush up and then I'll be off. Are you coming or not?"

"Go on, Tim," Gwyneth said. "Why don't you? It'll be something to tell your friends back home. What I did on my summer holidays. Helped deliver a baby in a Welsh farmhouse."

Once more, he seemed horrified. "Surely you don't mean I'd be expected to help?"

"Oh, don't worry," Rhys said reassuringly. "I wouldn't dream of letting you put your grubby hands anywhere near one of my mothers. The midwife delivers the babies. Even I just have to put in an appearance to satisfy the powers that be and make sure everything's going according to plan. It's Megan Caldecott, Gwyneth, out at Llantrynt. Her second. Should go just fine. We can stop in on our way to Tregwyn and be back here in time for tea. There'll even be time to go to Cefn Mabis afterwards, if you like." He looked Tim up and down. "You'll need to shave first. And put on some decent trousers. You can't turn up looking like a ragamuffin. You've got five minutes."

Rhys watched Tim Bruce get up from the table, his eyes still pale and troubled, and then he remembered, quite suddenly, about Robert Kennedy, and realized what was wrong with the boy. Damn them all, damn all the guns and all the madmen in America.

Tim wondered what on earth he was getting into. Watch a baby come into the world? Jesus! He could refuse, of course, but that would definitely be cowardly. And now he came to think of it, perhaps he'd rather go off with Rhys and have a chance to think through this business of Gwyneth's paintings. Going off with Rhys would give him time to try and work out why she was painting the same face, a face that looked just like his, over and over. Very odd. Obviously some sort of obsession. Of course, all painters were a bit mad, he knew that. He'd known someone who painted Canada geese over and over again, as though one Canada goose didn't look exactly like any other. Except Gwyneth didn't seem the least bit mad. Or did he just prefer not to think of her as mad? Someone as beautiful as her couldn't possibly be nuts. Could she?

In the upstairs bathroom, Tim shaved and stared at his face in the mirror. He might grow a beard. Two or three days would just about do it. Perhaps when he got to France. If he ever got there. He should be able to make it as far as France. He might get further, sleeping on trains overnight, schlepping around the cities during the day. Surely he could manage that. If nothing else, he could hang out at corner cafés all day, watching the girls go by. He wondered if any of them would be as good-looking as Gwyneth.

There was still the thorny issue of how much to tell the family about this whole Welsh episode. While he scraped at his chin, he composed a letter in his head: Hi Mom and Dad. *Spent a few days in Wales on my way to Ireland. Liked it enough that I never got to Ireland, after all. I didn't know anything about Wales before. Did you know they speak a different language? Ran into an old friend of yours, Dad. Knew you in the war, apparently. Everyone round here remembers the Americans. Thought you'd like to know that. Off to France soon. Will write from there. Love, Tim.*

A postcard would suffice. Yes, a postcard would be a better

idea, no room to fill in any more details, no need to say anything about torn ligaments and a humongous cast. It would be all healed by the time he got home again.

But he wasn't sure he could manage this baby stuff. What in God's name was he thinking of, letting himself be talked into such a thing? Still, it might impress his father. Or not, of course. Sometimes it was difficult to know what might impress his father. But what was Rhys Edwards thinking of, bringing along a complete neophyte to watch someone's baby being born? Weren't there any privacy laws in this country? Weren't they afraid of being sued? Every doctor back home was scared shitless of a malpractice suit, a war of sorts going on, lawyers and doctors duking it out in the courts.

He'd have to ask Rhys about malpractice suits.

Later on, in the car, he did ask Rhys. "Do you ever get sued?"

Rhys turned to Tim, taking his eyes off the road for long terrifying seconds, and appeared incredibly offended by the suggestion. "Sue your doctor? What an outrageous notion! It comes to something when the people you're doing your damnedest for would turn around and try and get money out of you." He shook his head in disbelief, then thankfully returned his attention to the road. "I've heard about the malpractice problem in the United States. Shameful, I'd say. But then many things in the United States are shameful, if you'll forgive me for saying so, young man. Allowing any nincompoop to carry a gun, for instance. Treating your Negro population so disgracefully. Propping up tin pot dictators like that fellow in Vietnam. Letting that appalling McCarthy put the fear of God into free-thinking people. Your country has become a good deal less than progressive, Tim Bruce. Such a pity. A noble social experiment gone off the rails. Started out so well, too, throwing the English out, something we should have done in Wales centuries ago. But you've allowed it to slide into a catch as catch can society, winner take all and devil to the hindmost. Why, you can't even manage to have a universal health care system."

Mulling over the points in his mind, Tim opened his mouth to argue and could only think of one rebuttal. "McCarthy died. Years ago."

"Shouldn't have been born at all. Certainly shouldn't have been allowed to get away with what he got away with. Now, if someone had shot *him,* there may have been some reason to it." Rhys swung the wheel hard. "Not that I hold with shooting people, you understand."

Tim's heart lurched inside his chest. He didn't seem capable of remembering about Bobby Kennedy, as though he was trapped in a sort of time warp in this ancient, old-fashioned land, in a kind of Brigadoon. If Rhys hadn't brought the news back to the house on the hill, it was quite possible he might not have heard about Robert Kennedy at all. They didn't even have a TV, for God's sake. Would Gwyneth have known? She lived in her own little dream world, painting those strange paintings in the studio at the bottom of the garden. And even if she'd known about Robert Kennedy, would she have cared? Did any one here care about what went on in America?

Tim decided that perhaps Rhys Edwards cared. He seemed anchored enough to reality, what with his doctoring and his political views and his social concerns. Rhys Edwards cared more about what was going on around him than his own father did, for example. Now that Tim came to think of it, his father didn't seem to care too deeply about anything very much. He might be the teacher of students, the arguer of cases, but he wasn't *engaged* with the rest of the world, no antenna waving around to find out how anybody else felt about anything. Teachers shouldn't become too involved, his father insisted, but perhaps he didn't *want* to get involved. Perhaps he wanted to keep the world at arm's length. Perhaps he preferred it that way.

By now, Tim had quite forgotten where they were headed until the car lurched through a gate and bounced across another cobblestoned courtyard, just like the one at Tregwyn. At first, he assumed they'd arrived back at Tregwyn, a similar whitewashed cottage on the right-hand side and stone barns on the left, even a black and white dog rushing out to bark at the car, but then a young man in brown corduroy breeches and long rubber boots followed the dog out of the barn and waved at Rhys.

"Here you are then, doctor. Good, good. I don't think it'll be long now. The midwife's with her, says it shouldn't be more than another hour."

"Why aren't you with her?" Jumping out of the car, Rhys reached for his bag and pointed to Tim carelessly. "Gareth, this is Tim Bruce. He's a student, here to observe."

The man took no notice of Tim. "Megan doesn't want me there. The women like to get on with it by themselves, don't they?"

"Unfortunately, Gareth, you might have to give a bit of a hand because Tim here has wrecked his ankle and is on crutches, so he can't be running up and down the stairs for me. I suppose she's upstairs?"

"That's where all the babies have been born in this house, doctor. In the same room as my mother and her mother before her—"

"Yes, well," Rhys interrupted, "I've explained to Megan that it'd be a lot easier for everyone if she and all the other women around here had their babies downstairs. I'm not getting any younger and I don't want to have to be carrying some poor bleeding female downstairs in an emergency."

Tim felt his hands go cold and sweaty but the father-to-be didn't blink. "Of course not, Doctor."

Rhys let out an exaggerated sigh. "But nobody does anything about it, do they? Can't get anyone to change their habits. Come on, Tim, let's be taking a look."

No, let's not be, Tim pleaded silently. He sympathized with anyone, even a husband, perhaps especially a husband, who wanted to keep as far away as possible. But he was damned if he was going to be labeled a coward by Rhys Edwards, so he hauled the crutches out of the car and struggled across the courtyard after Rhys.

Rhys was already running up the narrow steep stairs at the end of the hallway by the time Tim made it to the foot of the staircase. Gareth took off his cap and turned it over in his hands repetitively, nervously. He had black hair that lay in flat curls close against his head, dark brown eyes, and weathered skin, but without the cap, Tim could see that he was quite young, maybe not much older than he was himself. It occurred to Tim, with a slight shock, that he was old enough to be a father himself.

Gareth looked at Tim's crutches and chewed his lower lip. "It's not going to be easy to get up there with those. And I'll tell you something else. There's not going to be much room up there in that bedroom with all of us. Especially a big tall fellow like you. Break your leg, did you?"

"Just tore the ligaments. But I can't put any weight on it for a couple of weeks."

Gareth looked skeptical, as though torn ligaments couldn't possibly be enough of an excuse for a cast and a pair of crutches. "Tell you what. Why don't I just go in the kitchen and make a nice cup of tea? I'm sure everyone's ready for a cup of tea. My Megan always likes one about this time."

"Good idea," Tim said. "I'll come with you," but at that moment, Rhys called from overhead. "Okay, Tim Bruce, get your bones up here if you want to see this baby coming out."

Which was just what he didn't want. If he went up the stairs very, very slowly, he might miss the worst of it. He had no idea how long it took a baby to come out, as Rhys put it. Five minutes? Two minutes? An hour?

"Are you sure this is okay with you?" he asked Gareth and Gareth grinned sheepishly. "Bit late now to worry about that, isn't it?" Tim realized he'd misunderstood the question. Whether a stranger was there or not was of no consequence to Gareth. He had more important things to worry about.

Tim started to edge slowly up the stairs, gripping the banister rail with his right hand, the crutches with the left, and then suddenly thought that he might, after all, like to see a baby being born. He hopped up faster, crashing on the treads, shaking the whole house, and there was something oddly triumphant in the noisy progress, as though he was overcoming fear, facing the unknown. When he arrived at the top, he turned into the bedroom almost eagerly.

The scene in the dim bedroom was at once chaotic and yet oddly calm. Rhys was clad in a white gown and mask and was leaning over the head of a large double bed, while a nurse in a similar white gown bent down among the sheets. The nurse was calling out, "Come on, Megan, come on now, there's a good girl, nearly there, nearly done. We can see the head now. Yes, yes, lots of lovely black hair."

Tim hovered in the doorway, filling it, and though he couldn't make out the shape in the bed or see what was going on, he could smell disinfectant and hot blood and unpleasant unfamiliar odors, could hear hard stertorous breathing, not a moaning exactly, but a loud dragging of air in and out of laboring lungs, and then almost immediately the sound changed to a straining and a grunting. The cries from the nurse grew louder and more encouraging, and Rhys joined in, "Good girl, Megan, well done. Marvelous, wonderful," until it seemed as if everyone was together in this venture, cheering and breathing heavily in unison. Suddenly there was a piercing shriek, a nerve-tingling scream that forced Tim backwards out of the room, and he heard Rhys shout, "Oh, well done," and the nurse cried triumphantly, "There, Megan, there, a beautiful little girl. Just what you wanted."

A different sound rose in the crowded room, a faint wail, a hiccupping small cry that grew gradually louder and stronger.

Unexpected tears sprang in Tim's eyes. He wanted to cheer, too. He watched as the nurse wrapped something in a white blanket, plucked it out of the bed, and walked it round to the other side, saw two arms reach out and take the bundle, and then Gareth came thumping up the stairs, two at a time, brushing past Tim as though he wasn't there.

"A girl," Rhys announced.

"A beautiful little girl," the nurse said.

Gareth kneeled down by the head of the bed. "My beauty. My Megan," he crooned, and laid his dark head on the pillow. "My *cariad*." A disembodied hand came out from the sheets and stroked his curly hair, and a voice breathed, "There's lucky we are, Gareth."

Gareth looked up to the assembled bystanders. Tim saw tears in his eyes. "We give thanks to God," he announced. "Thanks to you, Dr. Edwards. And to you, Nurse Webber." He even seemed to include Tim. "We give thanks to everyone."

Tim, who'd seen nothing but felt as though he'd seen everything, wanted to kneel down and thank everyone, too.

Sixteen

.

The little house grew suddenly raucous with a host of women in flowered dresses, all of them carrying baskets of homemade cakes and pies, as if some secret food signal had rung out across the countryside. Shrieking with delight over the baby, the women chattered in Welsh and brought endless cups of tea up to the bedroom, and the new mother sat smug and bright-eyed in the big bed, new baby clutched in one arm, new father grinning by her side. Everyone drank tea and ate sponge cake with icing and agreed, sometimes in English, more often in Welsh, how fortunate Megan and Gareth were to have a daughter, a *merch* to look after them in their old age, how beautiful a *babi* she was, what a joy, and didn't she have her mam's eyes and her dada's hands, and perhaps they should name her Tegwyn after her Auntie Tegwyn, or perhaps Dilys after Megan's mam.

Out of the bewildering mixture of Welsh and English, Tim picked out the odd word here and there. He recognized *diolch*, which he now knew meant thank you. *"Diolch en fawr,"* Megan said over and over to Rhys and to the nurse. Even Tim came in for a few *diolchs,* which was embarrassing in his role of useless by-stander. "If she'd been a boy, we'd have named him Rhys after you, Doctor, wouldn't we, Gareth?" and Gareth nodded in happy agreement, obviously ready to agree with anything at that point.

The doctor didn't appear the least bit pleased by the sugges-tion. "Good God, no! Let a child have its own name, for pity's sake. We were just doing a job. Isn't that right, Tim?"

Smiling and blushing, Tim tried to pretend it was all in a day's work, and when he and Rhys finally got on their way to Tregwyn, he was still basking in the afterglow of the momumental event. "How great people should want to name their babies after you. How fantastic!"

Rhys snorted. "For some reason people always want to name a child after someone else. If it's a boy and they can't decide which father or grandfather to choose, they'll pick on the nearest male. Who's usually the doctor, of course. It's a long-standing ritual. It doesn't do to get a swelled head about these things, Tim *bach.* It's just the way things are around here."

"I like the way things are around here." Tim struggled to find the appropriate words. "Thanks for taking me with you. I'd no idea how . . . how profound it'd be. One moment nothing, and then suddenly, a whole new human being. Extraordinary. Really a miracle!"

Rhys gave a cynical little laugh. "A miracle that happens far too many times a day, I'd say. How many times a day, do you suppose? Our world's in dire peril of being swamped by new human beings now we've learned how to keep them alive. Look at India, at China. Though as a matter of interest, the population of Europe is more or less at a standstill. For every child born in these parts, someone's waiting to bite the dust. Take Johnnie Watkins, for ex-ample. He's not going to last much longer. Maybe a couple of weeks or so, and then we're back to zero population growth again. Megan and Gareth's baby girl for one old farmer. Hope it turns out to be a good swap."

Tim pictured the old man in the deep, winged armchair, struggling for breath, his chest heaving painfully. "So soon? A couple of weeks?" He was shocked that Rhys could shrug it off so casually.

"I'd have thought you'd have known just by looking at him. Does it bother you? It shouldn't. If you're going to be a doctor, you'll have to acknowledge when it's time for people to go. Everyone has to go sometime, you know. Johnnie Watkins has had a good long life. Hard, maybe, and maybe not the sort of life you might want, but I believe he's content enough."

"He was going to show me his cows."

"Oh, don't worry. While Johnnie's still got breath in his body, he'll take you to see his cows. If he had his choice, he'd probably sleep in the byre with them. He's like a lot of the farmers round here, loves his animals as much as his wife. Perhaps more. Though love isn't a word they ever use, of course. Not to their wives or even to their animals."

Tim wondered if Rhys ever used the word, love, to his own wife. He stared at Rhys's profile, the shadow of beard on his cheeks, the droop of skin at the edge of his eyes, those black eyebrows with the satanic tilt. He understood now that Rhys Edwards wasn't satanic at all. He was kind, and concerned for the welfare of his patients even if he didn't express it in so many words, as if he preferred to maintain a coolness, a distance, as if he didn't want anyone to become too close. Was he that way with Gwyneth? Did he speak of love to her? Rhys and Gwyneth seemed to drift along in separate worlds, not exactly apart, but not exactly together either. Not in a cohesive state of oneness.

Tim wondered what made two separate people bond in a special way and present a solid front against the rest of the world. His parents, for example. They weren't just Carlton and Janice Bruce, they were *The Bruces,* a wall, an institution. He'd hardly ever heard them use the word love, either, now he came to think of it. Maybe his mother, when they were little, but his father? Had Carlton ever used the word love to any one of them? Was love something to take for granted, never to be questioned or spoken about? In that regard, he guessed his own family was no different from those of Welsh farmers.

Love was a curious concept. What was it, for instance, that he felt for the beautiful wife of Rhys Edwards? Could it be called love, that extraordinary melting of his senses when he'd first set eyes on her, the dizziness when she came close, the pounding in his chest? Why did he get a panicky feeling of danger when she was near? Already, it seemed he'd been sighing after her all his life, lusting for her white flesh and her soft hair and her glowing amber eyes.

Love was one thing. Lust was another. He understood perfectly well that whatever it was he felt for Gwyneth was quite different from love of family. Or country. Love of one's country was automatic, imprinted, like love of one's parents. The first thing you saw in a new world, that's what you loved, whether you were a human or a bird or an animal. That baby who'd arrived in this world an hour ago had opened and closed her unfocused eyes, blinking up at Megan and Gareth, learning to love those particular people. No matter what they did, no matter what sort of parents they turned out to be, she'd never be able to help but love them. Whether they deserved it or not. It wasn't a matter of deserving. Love was love. It just happened, no rhyme or reason.

Tim had never tried to sort out different forms of love before. Never had to. Perhaps it was this distance from country and home that was making him dwell on it. Maybe that was what people meant about travel broadening the mind. But whatever it was he felt for Gwyneth Edwards, love or lust, Tim knew it was wrong. He hadn't been brought up to dwell on sin, but he could sure recognize it when he saw it. Gwyneth was Rhys Edwards's wife and Rhys Edwards was someone to respect and admire. Someone to emulate. This business of becoming a doctor just to get out of the draft didn't seem such a ridiculous idea after all. Becoming a doctor was a lot more useful than becoming a soldier in a stupid war. Delivering babies, having them named after you, could be a wonderfully satisfying way to spend a life.

Fixing his eyes on the road unwinding in front of him, Tim tried to concentrate on Rhys's explanation of congestive heart disease, apparently what old Mr. Watkins suffered from, but despite his best intentions, his mind kept wandering back to Gwyneth and to the idea of being alone in the studio with her while she painted his picture. An idea that made his blood run hot again.

It was a relief to finally arrive at Tregwyn and put Gwyneth out of his mind. Tregwyn looked exactly the same as the day before, the pine trees still rustling at the far end of the courtyard, the crows still cawing, even the black and white dog running out of the barn and barking. When Mrs. Watkins appeared at the door of the cottage in her apron and waved to Rhys and called out to him in Welsh, Tim felt as if he'd been coming to this same house, at this same time of day, for years and years. As though he almost belonged here, as though he wasn't just a stranger in a strange land who couldn't speak the language.

Old Mr. Watkins, too, looked exactly the same as yesterday, collapsed in the chair before the fire, panting for breath. Rhys pressed his stethoscope to the pale, heaving chest and Tim searched the old man's face for signs of impending death, but he saw nothing any different from yesterday, though he was prepared to acknowledge the doctor might be more capable of recognizing approaching death than he was, as he'd never actually seen anyone die. Or being born, for that matter. Not until today.

The old man buttoned up his shirt and Rhys went to write a prescription and Tim said, "How are you, Mr. Watkins? Remember me, I was here yesterday?"

Johnnie Watkins looked up from the chair. "Of course I remember you. You think I'm gaga? You come back to see my cows?"

"Yes, sir. That's exactly what I've come for."

"Well, it's a good time of day for that. They're all in the barn for milking now. Hand me my stick." An odd-shaped cane, bent and worn smooth, was leaning near the fireplace, and Tim handed it over. The old man grasped the arms of the chair, the veins on the back of his hands blue and ropy, took a few laborious breaths, and rose painfully to his feet. He almost straightened up, but not quite. "There you are then, boyo," he gasped. "We make a fine pair, don't we, two cripples together? If you fall down, I can't help you up, and it don't look like you'll be much more of a help to me."

Tim was immediately concerned. "Maybe someone should come with us."

"No, no." The old man waved his stick. "Idris is already there milking now. Too many people just unsettle the cows, sensitive creatures that they are. They don't like people staring at them when they are letting down their milk."

As they proceeded slowly out of the house and across the courtyard, Tim imagined they must make a ridiculous picture, the old man with his cane, he with his crutches, like two relics of some crippled ancient army, but as he swung easily across the cobblestones, he was aware how he towered above the old man. His own back was straight, his arms muscled and strong, not like the thin, wasted hand on the cane, and Tim was suddenly filled with a heady sense of youth and health, was almost overcome by a treacherous sense of well-being and gladness that he had his whole life in front of him. Anything seemed possible. Anything and everything. He wanted to whoop and holler with delight. And restrained himself.

The black and white dog came out of the barn as if operating on a conditioned reflex, but it didn't bark this time, only crouched low to the ground and sniffed suspiciously at the cast. Tim stooped to pat its head and then followed the old man into the cowshed through a door in two halves like the one into Gwyneth's studio. But inside, unlike the studio, the cowshed was dim, only a hint of daylight creeping through tiny, dusty windows set high in thick stone walls, a couple of bare electric bulbs casting a paltry glow. The atmosphere was thick and warm and heavily aromatic with hay and cow dung and punctuated by the sounds of breathing and chewing and sighing and the faintly sinister rattling of metal chains. There was an odd thumping of a steady mechanical suspiration, like the beat of blood through a stethoscope, and from somewhere deep in the darkness, the unlikely sound of a male voice singing, low and soft and soothing.

Johnnie Watkins called out, "Brought you a visitor, Idris."

The singing stopped. "Too bloody busy for visitors."

"Well, he hasn't come to see you anyway. It's the cows he's come to see."

Gradually, as his eyes adjusted, Tim could make out two lines of cows' heads facing toward the middle, their necks loosely chained to feeding bowls in an elaborate maze of metal railings. At the sound of Johnnie Watkins's voice, the cows raised their muzzles from the bowls and swiveled their heads, and the old man went limping with his cane down between them, touching a head here and there. "There, there, my beauties," he crooned softly. "There, there. Daisy. Betsy. Cherry. Beautiful you are, my *cariads*." Then he spoke to them in Welsh and they appeared to be listening, twitching their ears and following with their melting eyes. Some of them began lowing softly, almost like cats purring.

Waving at Tim to follow him, Johnnie Watkins gestured with the cane. "Devon mix, most of them," he said. "Good steady milkers, Devons. Nice high fat content in the milk, not like them foreign Friesians, gallons and gallons of watery stuff, no substance to it. A bit of Angus in most of them, too, and a bit of Hereford, and see here, see these two little ones?" He scratched between the ears of a couple of smaller cows at the end of the row. "Guernseys, of course. Prettiest damn cows in the whole damn world. Wonderful milk. Wonderful. We keep their milk for ourselves, to make butter, you know. Churns up a treat, nice and thick and yellow."

"You make your own butter?" Tim wasn't sure why that should so surprise him, but he'd never known anyone who made his own butter before. As far as he was concerned, butter, like peas, came in packages. He'd never been so close to a live cow before, either.

"You think we'd go down to the shops in Clarrach and pay for something wrapped in tinfoil? Why, we wouldn't even know which animal it came from."

"Of course not," Tim said and laughed.

He didn't know what comment to make about the cows without sounding stupid. They all looked exactly alike to him, large rawboned creatures with kindly eyes that regarded him wisely, as if they knew something about him. Their size and their wise eyes made him a little uncomfortable.

"What's the Welsh for cow?" he asked, for something to say.

"*Buwch.*" Johnnie Watkins seemed pleased to have been asked.

Tim tried to imitate the softness of the word. "*Buwch.*" He repeated it a couple of times. "*Buwch.*" He liked the sound of it.

Gradually, Tim became aware the cowshed was a little less primitive than at first sight. Overhead, running the whole length of it, was a complicated track with tubes and wires, apparently the source of the sighing, pulsing sound, and he could see that some of the animals were attached by their udders to the black tubing looping down from the track. Obviously it was some sort of milking device. Somehow he'd assumed cows around here would be milked by hand, and as if reading his thoughts, Johnnie Watkins said, "It's not like the old days when it took hours and hours to do the milking. Now it's over and done with in a jiffy.

An hour or two at most. Though sometimes we have to strip them out by hand, of course. Some of my girls don't do all that well with the machine. They're funny that way. Temperamental, you might say. And it doesn't do to leave milk in them because that can lead to mastitis. But you must know about these things, you being a doctor and all. These two Guernseys, now, we milk them by hand to keep their milk separate."

He paused. "Ever milked a cow?"

"Good heavens, no." Tim wanted to explain he wasn't a doctor, not by a long shot, but then the old man said, almost slyly, "Like to have a go?"

"What, me? Milk a cow?" At first Tim was astounded by the suggestion, then repelled, then intrigued. Why not? After all, he'd almost seen a baby being born. Milk from a cow was just one more aspect of the reproductive process. "Sure. Why not?"

"That's the boy." Johnnie Watkins grinned and nodded. Tim noticed, for the first time, his ill-fitting false teeth. "I'll watch. And give advice. That's all I'm good for these days." He called out, "Idris, find the boy a stool, can you, so he can have a go at milking Heather."

At the distant end of the barn, a head popped up from behind a cow's hindquarters, and though there wasn't quite enough light to make out the man's features, Tim could see he wore a tan-colored lab-type coat and one of those flat tweed caps all the men around here seemed to wear. Saying something to Johnnie in Welsh, Idris bent down again behind the cow. Welsh words flew around the barn. Tim was pretty sure he was protesting the idea of anyone practicing on one of his animals.

"It's all right really," Tim said. "It's probably time to be getting back to Dr. Edwards anyway."

"Oh, Dr. Rhys will be drinking tea with the missus and they'll be having a good old chat. Does her good to have someone else to talk to now and then. Don't you worry about them. And don't worry about Heather. She won't mind. And take no notice of Idris."

The head popped up once more. "You want to ruin her? You want to let strangers mess about with one of your prize beasts?" He stared resentfully at Tim over the back of the cow. "Who is he anyway?"

"He's with Dr. Edwards. He's an American."

"An American?" A hawking noise came from the back of Idris's throat, as though he was about to spit, and he glowered at Tim. "Oh well, dew," he said at last reluctantly. "If he's with Dr. Edwards, I suppose he might be all right."

Vanishing for a moment, he reappeared suddenly at Tim's elbow, a small, dark-skinned man with a deeply lined face and beady brown eyes. His long rubber boots made no sound on the concrete floor. He handed over, without enthusiasm, a tiny three-legged wooden stool, a grubby-looking towel, one empty galvanized steel bucket, and another with water and a sponge.

"Wash her off good first, mind you. And no pulling too hard. Let's see your hands."

Tim spread his hands obediently and Idris peered at them. "All right, they'll do. But make sure you dip them in the bucket first. Don't want our Heather to catch some nasty disease."

The water in the bucket smelled strongly of disinfectant and Tim dipped his hands in cautiously, wiped them off with the towel, and maneuvered himself onto the small stool awkwardly. It was too low to the ground, and uncomfortable, and the bright white cast stuck out beneath the animal's belly. She skittered sideways with a rattling of chains.

"Get closer to her," Johnnie instructed. "You've got to be close enough to rest your head against her side. That'll calm her. And it'll be easier to get hold of the teats."

Shifting the stool nearer, Tim wondered why the hell he was doing this. From his lowly position, the small cow loomed extremely large, brown flank heaving, huge pale udder hanging below.

"Right, boyo, wash her off good now," Johnnie ordered, and Tim took the sponge and mopped around the teats. "Wipe her nice and dry. That's right. Now place the milk bucket right below the udder, take two teats in both hands, and squeeze and pull. Squeeze and pull. Gently but firmly."

Gripping two of the teats between his hands, Tim obediently squeezed and pulled. Gently but firmly. Squeezed and pulled. Nothing happened. The teats were like hard, warm, unyielding rubber and the cow turned her head to stare at him. She had long straight lashes, like a cartoon animal, and she sighed and shifted on her four cloven hooves and farted loudly. Tim kept squeezing and pulling and soon his hands were aching and still no milk had appeared. He pressed his forehead against the flank of the animal, her hide warm and firm and prickly, like upholstered furniture, and he thought this shouldn't be so difficult. Milking a cow was surely one of the more primitive of human skills. He kept kneading the huge rubbery teats until his hands hurt, and then all of a sudden milk began squirting out, a thin white stream that pinged against the side of the metal bucket and frothed and grew creamy yellow. Tim was triumphant.

"Good, very good, boyo," Johnnie Watkins said, and even Idris nodded his head and commented, "Not bad. For an American."

The milk continued to flow, the stream thicker and richer, until the bucket was more than half full. Tim began to wonder how much milk the cow had inside her. More than this bucketful? If he stopped to rest his hands, would it be difficult to start again? Glancing up to ask Johnnie Watkins, he realized the old man was no longer standing over him, and when he looked around the barn from his disadvantaged position on the stool, he could see only Idris leaning against the rails, cap shading his eyes, still unfriendly, still suspicious. Tim wondered where the old man had gone, why he'd left without a word. Remembering what Rhys had forecast about him, he hoped he was okay.

"Don't stop now," Idris commanded. "Got to get all the milk out in one go. If you can manage it, mind. Those hands of yours look a bit lily white, if you ask me. Not as if they're used to hard work." His accent was thick and very Welsh. "Of course, Americans don't have to work hard, do they? Got machines to do everything for them, haven't they? Must be nice being an American," and he cleared his throat again in that disparaging way.

Tim gripped the teats harder, determined not to stop until every drop of milk was extracted. Now that he'd got a rhythm going, the milk was flowing more easily and the cow seemed content, her belly rumbling beneath his forehead. He began to feel as though he really was in tune with some force of nature. If it hadn't been for the disapproval emanating from Idris, he'd have been halfway enjoying himself. He could understand now why someone would love a cow; there was something infinitely generous in the way she gave up her milk like a gift, like a kindness to mankind. The simple but challenging act of milking a cow seemed almost profound, just as witnessing a perfectly normal birth had felt so profound.

At last, when the bucket was nearly completely full, the flow of milk slowed to a trickle. Tim could feel the udder emptying, slack now where it had been taut and full when he'd first started, and Idris said, "All right, Yankee, move over. Leave the rest to me. Got to get the last drop out. That takes a professional."

Tim was glad to stop. His hands were burning and sore and he climbed off the stool with difficulty, watched as the little man squatted down, caressed the cow's teats, and spoke soothingly to her in Welsh, as though he was reassuring her, comforting her, after the rough handling Tim had given her. It looked easy when Idris did it.

"That's the first time I ever milked a cow."

Idris snorted. "Any fool could see that. Johnnie gets some weird ideas sometimes, if you ask me." He looked up from under cow's belly. "He knows I don't like Americans anyway."

Taken aback, Tim laughed uneasily. "I guess any fool could see that, too."

"You want to know why I don't like them?"

"No. Not really."

Idris got slowly to his feet. His head only came up to Tim's shoulder. His dark face under the cap grew darker, the thick black brows drawn down, the small eyes gleaming with some sort of malevolence. "They were here in the war, you know. Stationed up there on the hill outside Clarrach. Before D-Day. Thought they owned the world. Acted like it, too. You know what people used to say about American soldiers? Overpaid, oversexed, and over here. Bad enough it was when they ran around after the girls all the time, girls who should have known better, damn fools, but the way they carried on with their own comrades, that was something to be ashamed of. Yes it was, indeed. Shocking it was, that's the truth. Fighting all the time. Killing each other. In the streets of Clarrach. Disgraceful it was. What they got away with was a sin and a crime. Yes, indeed. I wouldn't be so proud to call myself an American if I was one of them."

Tim backed away. "I don't know what you're talking about."

"No?" Idris picked up the bucket of milk, swung it in his gnarled hand, the precious contents sloshing over the edges. "Why don't you ask Dr. Edwards? Or better still, ask Mrs. Edwards. Gwyneth Griffiths, that was. Ask her, why don't you? She's the one who knows about it all. She could tell you everything. If she chose to. Of course, she probably won't. Why should she? She was the cause of it all, they say, and some things are better kept quiet, aren't they, even if they did happen twenty or more years ago. But ask her, why don't you? She's the one that fancies Americans, after all."

Tim was shocked by the venom in the little man's voice, the way his shoulders hunched tightly around his short neck, the obvious dislike in the small brown eyes. As though he had something personal against Gwyneth. Against Tim himself.

"I'm not going to ask her anything." Picking the crutches off the concrete floor, he tucked them under his armpits. "Dr. and Mrs. Edwards have been very kind to me. Everyone here has been kind to me, as a matter of fact." Though it wasn't particularly kind of Johnnie Watkins to have left him with this vindictive little man.

Turning, Tim made his way carefully out of the cowshed, trying not to look as though he was running away.

"That's right," Idris called after him. "Run away, why don't you? Just like all them others did after the trouble."

Emerging into the thin sunshine, Tim was relieved to be out of the claustrophobic atmosphere of the cowshed. He found it difficult to understand how someone could sound so benevolent when speaking to a cow and so unpleasant when speaking to another human being. He wasn't used to people being unpleasant to him.

He wasn't going to ask Rhys or Gwyneth anything. Of course not.

But he had to wonder what the little man was talking about. It made him curious, he had to admit.

Seventeen

.

Tim had been dreaming of cows and overflowing buckets of milk, and he instantly recognized where he was when he awoke, immediately aware how much better he felt this morning. His body was less sore, his mind less drugged. He lay for a moment, luxuriating in the warmth of the bed, a deep silence surrounding him, everything and everywhere quiet, even the birds silent, even the sheep, as though the world had gone away. When he pulled the curtains aside, he saw the sky was filled with a soft thick mist that obscured the ramparts of rocks at the top of the mountain, deadening all sound. A morning just like the one when he'd first arrived in Clarrach. Two days ago. A lifetime ago.

He clattered down to the kitchen, embarrassed again by the lateness of the hour, already past ten o'clock, and just as on the previous morning, breakfast was set on the pine table, plates and cups and saucers laid on a cloth. But today Gwyneth was at the table waiting for him. He stammered his apologies.

Pouring him a cup of coffee, she pushed it across the table, rested her chin in one hand. "That's real coffee. No more of that instant stuff. And don't apologize about sleeping late. It's easy on a day like this. A typical June day in Wales. The perfect kind of day to start on your portrait."

Tim gulped at the coffee. It was hot and black and strong and jolted the last shreds of sleep out of him. "Great coffee."

Gwyneth looked more radiant than ever this morning, her face pale and smooth, the amber eyes clear and untroubled as though she'd spent a peaceful and dreamless night. The unruly hair was pulled away from her white forehead and tied at the back of her neck with a ribbon, like a schoolgirl. She took his breath away.

"I was planning to take you to Cefn Mabis. You know, the burial chamber I keep promising to show you, but on a day like this, we wouldn't be able to see anything from up there. It's partly the view that's so wonderful. Which is silly when you come to think of it, isn't it, a burial chamber with a wonderful view? So I thought, if it's all right with you, we'd spend an hour or two in the studio. If you don't mind, that is. It's a bit of an imposition, really, to make someone who's come so far have to sit for hours in an old *twlc mochyn*."

"A what?"

"Oh, sorry. *Twlc mochyn*. Pigsty. That's what Rhys insists on calling it. Would you like some bacon and eggs? Toast?"

To label her studio a pigsty seemed some sort of insult. Rhys had an odd sense of humor. "Toast. If it's not too much trouble."

"No trouble." Gwyneth smiled and sliced a couple of pieces of bread from the loaf on the round wooden board, stuck them in the toaster over by the window, folded her arms, and leaned back against the counter. The gray light from outside threw a nimbus around her head. She seemed in good humor this morning.

Tim said, "I've never heard you using Welsh before. I thought you didn't speak it."

"I don't. I know lots of words, of course, but I didn't learn it as a child. Rhys speaks it because his mother's family came from the middle of the country where they still use it every day, but for those of us who lived on the fringes, well, we were thoroughly Anglicized. My father spoke Welsh but my mother didn't, and I suppose language is another of the things one learns at one's mother's knee, isn't it? Welsh nearly died out as a language, you know, but it's coming back now. There's a big push to save all things Welsh."

"Lots of people round here seem to speak it." Tim thought of Eirwen Price and her father, the women in the house with the baby, the people in the pub, Mrs. Watkins at Tregwyn. It came as a small surprise to realize how many people he'd met.

"Out on the farms particularly. Were they speaking Welsh around you yesterday?"

Tim suddenly recalled Idris. "Yes. Yes, they were." But he was remembering what Idris had said in English. About Gwyneth.

She smiled again. "The locals really like to use it when there's a foreigner in their midst. They know it confuses them. It doesn't work quite so well with someone like me who understands enough."

Tim had never thought of himself as a foreigner before. The rest of the world were the foreigners.

Gwyneth placed the toast in a silver rack and carried it to the table. "So, how do you feel about sitting for me?"

"Well, of course . . . If that's what you want." How could he refuse her anything? Though he couldn't imagine why she'd want to paint another picture, because now he'd seen all the others, his face would surely turn out just exactly the same. But maybe he'd discover what it was she was trying to do out there in the . . . whatever it was called. The idea of being alone with her for hours was exciting. He wondered what it would entail, this "sitting." What if she suggested painting him in the nude? Wasn't that what artists always wanted to do with their models? The idea was ridiculous, of course. It made him want to laugh. But his face flushed at the thought.

"Come on then. No time like the present. We'll take the coffee with us," and she picked up a tray holding a pot of coffee and two mugs as though she'd planned this all along.

The path from the house to the studio was slick from the rain and Tim had to go carefully on the crutches. There was no discomfort under the cast anymore and soon he'd have no excuse not to move on. Except he'd lost interest in moving on. Not to Paris or Versailles or all those other places he'd planned to visit. He'd much prefer to stay here, being painted by Gwyneth, going off with Rhys on his rounds, learning what the life of a country GP was about. Forgetting about the mess in America. If he went through with the medical school stuff, perhaps he could become a country doctor, too. Even in the States there were still country doctors, even if they didn't visit people in their homes anymore. Maybe he could become an obstetrician. Delivering babies seemed kind of cool, now he'd almost seen it happening, rewarding, thrilling even, better than being a surgeon and cutting people up, or watching them die like an internist. Yes, that's what he might do. Become an obstetrician.

Tim stopped to consider this idea, pausing on the path in the misty rain, staring at Gwyneth's erect spine as she walked ahead of him. For a moment, he neglected to watch the sway of her skirts, the shape of her ankles, was instead focused on his future. Not as a mere draft dodger, but as someone with a proper aim in life, a correct and concrete reason to go to medical school. Not just to get out of going to Vietnam. Until this very moment, Tim hadn't realized quite how bad wriggling out of the draft made him feel. He'd taken the easy way, joining a few futile protest rallies, signing up on Bobby Kennedy's campaign, applying for medical school, flirting with the idea of never coming back from Europe. Now, to understand that he might really *want* to become a doctor, *want* to be someone like Rhys Edwards, made him feel as if a great weight had been lifted from his heart. He could, after all, be someone with a future.

Pausing at the corner of the studio, Gwyneth looked back over her shoulder. The soft rain clung to her hair, curling it into ringlets on her forehead. "Are you all right? Can you manage?"

Tim laughed. He felt as he'd felt going across the cobblestones with old Johnnie Watkins, young, strong, healthy. Immortal. "I'm fine. I think I'm going to manage just fine from now on."

It wasn't nearly as bright inside the studio as the day before, the light muted and gray, the skylights in the roof misted now with fine beads of rain. The day before, he'd noticed the workbench and the painting on the easel and the canvases with their faces turned to the wall, but now he realized the space held quite a lot more stuff than that. There were a pair of overstuffed chairs, a sofa with a slipcover, a couple of small tables, a radio on the bench, a mirror on the wall. It was really quite cozy.

Gwyneth glanced up at the skylights. "This light's almost perfect. When it rains in the summer like this, the light is still bright enough to paint by but it's gentle and diffused. I prefer it that way. It suits the process better. In the winter the clouds get too dark and I have to use the electricity, which utterly changes the look of the paint. So I have my summer paintings and my winter paintings."

Placing the tray on one of the small tables, she removed the painting from the easel, the one he thought of as his portrait, turned it against the wall alongside the others as though discarding it. Then she picked out a blank canvas and fastened it to the easel. She stood back and folded her arms. "Now, let's see. Where shall you sit? Could you manage on this?" She dragged forward the tall wooden stool. "I don't have a real model's stand because of course I don't usually have a real model." She smiled happily, was almost brisk and decisive, not nearly so dreamy and distant. "Would you be too uncomfortable on this?"

The stool was a piece of furniture that was just the right height for Tim, like a bar stool. Perching on it, he stretched his legs out. "Perfect," he said.

"Yes, but now we have to position it so the light falls at the correct angle on your face." Waving him off the stool, she moved it a couple of feet until it was directly below a skylight. "Now," she said, and he sat down again obediently. She took his chin between the fingers of one hand and turned his head gently, this way and that, frowning intently, and Tim thought he might expire with excitement at the touch of her hand, at the nearness of her breath.

"Yes," she said and smiled into his eyes. "That'll do fine. Just relax now while I get my stuff ready."

Just relax! Easier said than done. He was already getting an erection.

Gwyneth couldn't believe he was so amenable to this crazy notion of painting him. Perhaps he didn't realize how crazy it was. She'd always painted from her imagination before, and now that there was a real live face in front of her, she was suddenly fearful of freezing up, of making a total mess of it. But she could hardly wait to get started on the planes of his cheekbones, the wide firm mouth, and the thick blond eyebrows that almost met in a straight line above his nose. Something so open and endearing about his face. She was growing accustomed to it and it was beginning to replace the one that had intruded on her imagination for so long. If she could concentrate on this face, this living, breathing face right in front of her, she might be able to drive the other one out of her mind, once and for all.

But the reality of him was making her nervous and unsure of herself. Putting on her smock, she fiddled with the height of the easel, picked up and put down the palette and brushes too many times, uncertain where to start and how. Normally she started in immediately, sketching an outline in light bold strokes, confident of what she was doing. Perhaps if he wasn't watching her so intently with those green eyes, she might be able to get started.

"Your leg. It should rest on something." She gazed around the studio for something suitable.

"It's okay," Tim assured her. "I'm okay, really."

"You have to be comfortable. This will take a while."

"I've got all day," he said.

Gwyneth moved the tray with the coffee from one of the small tables and was alarmed to see how shaky her hands were. She grasped his leg in the cast with both hands and placed it on the table, pulled the table further away until his leg seemed at a comfortable angle. "There, is that better?"

"Gwyneth, it's fine. Everything is just fine."

She liked the sound of her name when he said it with the American accent. Carlton Bruce had spoken her name like that, repeating it over and over. Gwyneth, he'd said, Gwyneth, Gwyneth, as if he were inventing her, as if she'd not existed before he'd come along to speak her name. No one ever said it quite that way again. Until now. But it didn't do to think of Carlton Bruce. Except this boy was so like him, as if he'd been sent to remind her of that time when she was so young and so infatuated. As if she were being given a second chance.

Picking up a pencil, gripping it too hard, Gwyneth poised her hand over the canvas, hesitated, closed her eyes for a moment, opened them, didn't look at Tim, finally started sketching the outline of his face. Then everything became easier because the shape of his face was the shape of all those others she'd been drawing for so many years. She sketched in silence for a few minutes, concentrating and yet not concentrating, and after a while, the silence became intrusive.

"Perhaps I should turn on the radio? It might make this less boring for you."

"I'm not bored," Tim said. "Far from it."

"Talk to me then. Tell me all about yourself."

He didn't answer and when she looked over at him, he was looking back at her, challenging her in some way. "No," he said. "You talk to *me*. You tell *me* about yourself. Tell me, for instance, about these other paintings. Who are they? Why do you keep painting the same face over and over again? I'm not so stupid, Gwyneth, even if I appear that way at times. I'm not usually so clumsy and accident prone, you know. It's you who has that effect on me. You addle my brain." Pausing, he pointed to the canvases piled against the wall. "Those paintings aren't just me. They're my father. And my brother. What exactly are you trying to do here?"

Putting down the pencil, Gwyneth picked up a brush, dabbled it in a pool of burnt sienna, gazed blankly at the outline on the canvas. "I thought he must be dead. Your father. I thought he'd gone off to France and been killed. In a way I wanted to believe that was why I never heard from him again. But deep inside, I guessed he'd probably been married all along. Girls in this country were always falling in love with American soldiers who promised them the earth and then found out later that they had wives back in America all along."

She didn't look at Tim but she could feel his eyes on her. He didn't move on the stool. At last he said, "My father didn't marry my mother until after the war was over. I don't know why he didn't come back for you, but it wasn't because he was already married."

Gwyneth made a stab at the canvas. "What's she like, your mother?"

"My mother?" Tim cleared his throat. "Are you sure you want to hear about her?"

"I'm sure." Though of course she wasn't sure.

"Well, for a start, she's not at all like you." Tim's voice trailed off for a moment. "My mother is always frantically busy. I'm not sure what she does all the time, but she's forever running off to meetings, fund-raisers and committees, women's organizations, bridge club, so on and so forth. She scurries here there and everywhere and then gets stressed because she's over-committed. Of course, she has to host quite a lot of functions for my father, visiting lecturers, student gatherings, that sort of thing. He's a dean, so it's expected of him. You know the sort of thing."

No, she didn't know. It all sounded foreign to Gwyneth's ears, an entirely different world.

"I'm sure you wouldn't like the kind of life my mother leads," Tim said almost apologetically. "But I think she does. I think she likes being the wife of a university professor, even though she complains about it all the time. She's very good at those social things. She's a good organizer." He paused again. "But sometimes I wonder if she does all those things just to fill her time because my father's never home. He's always busy, too, lecturing, teaching, going to meetings. But it isn't as though she wouldn't have understood that about him. They'd known each other for ages. They were pinned, before he went off to the army."

"Pinned?"

"You know, sort of engaged. While they were in college. Then the war came and so I suppose it didn't seem such a good idea to get married right then."

She shouldn't have asked the questions, because, after all, she didn't want to hear about his mother. Or about Carlton. Or about the life they led.

Tim said fondly, "They're very respectable people, my mother and father. Pillars of society, I suppose you'd call them."

Gwyneth stared at the painting, a painting that was going to look like all the others she had been painting for so may years. Quite suddenly, anger and hurt brought tears to her eyes, clouding her perception, her judgment, and the damaging words spilled out of her mouth recklessly.

"Respectable? So perhaps you'd be surprised to know you have another brother. Somewhere. I don't know where. My child. And your father's."

The room filled with a crackling, laden silence that sent the shocking words around the high spaces, and instantly Gwyneth wished to God she hadn't spoken them, and instantly it was too late to take them back. And then, instead of being sorry, she found it was a nothing but a relief to have at last told Carlton Bruce's son what she'd been afraid of telling him the first moment she set eyes on him.

Lifting her eyes from the canvas, she looked at Tim. His mouth was open, gaping, his eyes wide. At last he asked, stupified, "Are you sure?"

She almost wanted to laugh. "Of course I'm sure. It isn't something one makes a mistake about."

"Does he know? My father?"

She recognized the dismay in Tim's eyes, the disbelief, and then she wasn't angry or relieved anymore, but regretful and mournful. And once again, guilty. "Nobody knows. That's awful, isn't it? That he doesn't know and that his son, whoever he is, wherever he is, doesn't know either. I thought I'd forget about him, the child I mean, because you have to come to terms with these things, you have to, don't you, because otherwise how could you get on with your life? And then you came walking into my life, looking exactly like your father, looking much as I suppose the child would have looked, and it's as if they're both here with me, your father and the son I never knew and now I'm confused, because God knows whether I did the right thing or not and how can one ever know what is the right thing? How can one ever know?"

She hadn't cried about it for years. For years and years. But as she stood with the foolish dripping brush in her hand, the sketch on the canvas in front of her, the boy frozen on the stool, stricken as if she'd dealt him a mortal blow, the tears began to run down her face. The words had spilled out and released her tears and now they poured out of her as though there was no stopping them, down her cheeks and into her mouth, threatening to drown her. She knew she'd fractured her careful life, broken it, broken her life and perhaps this boy's. That's what happened when your sins came back to haunt you. Because you were never rid of them.

"Please. Please don't cry," Tim cried out, and it sounded as if he wanted to cry himself. He came thumping across the concrete floor and put his arms around her and she let her head fall on his shoulder. "Please, Gwyneth," he said, his mouth in her hair. "How can I make it better?"

She gulped for air, her voice muffled against his shirt. "I'm so very sorry. I should never have said anything. I've never told any-one and I should never have told you, of all people."

His arms tightened around her, warm and reassuring, as though he'd forgiven her. "You've never told anyone? Not even Rhys?"

Wordlessly, Gwyneth shook her head, and after a while the tears began to dry up, as though there were none left, as though they'd all drained out her. She pulled away, fumbled in the pocket of the smock for a handkerchief, blew her nose. "I hate to cry," she said and tried to smile.

"But now you have to tell me about it. You can't not tell me. Not now." He waited for a moment. "How can Rhys not know? Doctors know about these things. He must know you had a child."

She wiped at her eyes. "He knows I had a baby and that I gave it up for adoption and that I never wanted to talk about it. Rhys understands there are certain things that are too difficult to speak about."

"I wouldn't feel that way about someone I was married to."

"But then you're not Rhys, are you? I wanted to forget and start my life over again. You don't know how unhappy I was when

I first met Rhys. He saved me from a life I didn't like when he married me and he brought me back here to Wales where I belonged."

Tim stood looking down at her, silent for a long while, then he said, "But even if you never talked about it, you didn't forget, did you? Of course you didn't. That's who you've been painting all this time, isn't it? The child. As he might look growing up. Wouldn't it be better to talk about it?"

Eighteen

.

The memories were difficult. Even now. The train pulling slowly away from the platform, her mother raising one white-gloved hand in farewell. Herself at sixteen, leaning out of the window, watching her mother grow smaller and smaller, hand held high and still, not waving, not smiling, then the river sliding by under the iron bridge, the backs of houses and the green fields beyond the town moving away faster and faster, disappearing, then closing the window and pressing her forehead against it to watch Clarrach vanish into the distance.

It was the very first time Gwyneth had been on a train by herself.

She hadn't wanted to move from the window, just wanted to stand there and watch the Welsh countryside passing her by, but the journey was long, so at last she went to search for a seat, found one in a crowded carriage and struggled in with her suitcase. A young soldier jumped up to lift the case on to the overhead rack and offered his place in the corner, and though at first she shook her head silently, he smiled at her cajolingly.

"Come on, luv, take it. It's free." He sat down next to her and she was afraid he'd talk to her, but he fell asleep almost immediately, his head sliding towards her shoulder. There were no other women in the carriage, only men in uniform, all of them sleeping, their faces gray and exhausted, khaki bodies collapsed against one another. Those days, the trains were always crowded with troops; travel for civilians wasn't encouraged, posters in the stations asking the question, "Is your journey really necessary?" Gwyneth supposed her journey was really necessary.

Huddled into the corner, Gwyneth peered at the dim reflection of her face in the dusty window, clasped her hands tightly in the gloves her mother had crocheted, and pretended this was an adventure. The nursery rhyme kept running through her head, "Pussy cat, pussy cat, where have you been? I've been up to London to look at the queen." She was going up to London but she doubted she'd get a chance to look at the queen or the king.

Her head rested against the prickly upholstery and she was already weary. "Don't lean your head against the seats," her mother had warned. "That's the way you can catch lice. Don't sit on the lavatory seats. You can catch venereal diseases that way." Pity her mother hadn't warned her about catching babies. It was terrible to have been so ignorant, to be so ignorant still, not capable of imagining what was going to happen to her body over the coming months, only hoping they'd explain that sort of thing at the place she was going to, thinking she was glad to be going there, glad to be getting away from Clarrach and the gossip. Glad to be getting away from her mother and her angry, disappointed disapproval.

"Shame you've brought on us, Gwyneth Griffiths. Shame and degradation. How will we ever hold our heads up in this town if people find out? How could you? After all my warnings. How could you let a man make free of you? An American soldier, here today and gone tomorrow."

Her mother didn't know which American it was and didn't

seem to care. The Americans were gone, vanished overnight, off to France, and everyone knew they'd never be seen in Clarrach again. Her mother wanted Gwyneth out of Clarrach before anyone noticed her condition, so she'd packed a suitcase and put her on the train to London. To a home for unwed mothers. Gwyneth couldn't imagine how her mother found out about such a place, but knew everyone in Clarrach had been told she was "off to secretarial college in London. When she comes back, she'll get a nice job in the bank."

Her mother would have traveled with her, she said, but she couldn't leave the shop. "Anyway, it would look funny if I went with you, wouldn't it? If you're old enough to be going to secretarial college, you're old enough to be traveling by yourself." Gwyneth guessed her mother didn't come because she didn't want to be seen with her, even though there were no signs of her pregnancy yet. She didn't feel pregnant, though she didn't really know how it would feel to be pregnant. But the wretched morning sickness had passed and her clothes still fitted.

The journey to London was long and tediously slow, the train stopping at all the stations, Carmarthen and Swansea and Cardiff and Newport, and also coming to a halt between stations, for no reason anyone could tell, just sitting in the middle of nowhere for protracted and interminable minutes and then slowly getting up steam again, chugging deliberately through the green, lush countryside as though it had no real destination. Without warning, alarmingly, they descended into the inky rushing blackness of the Severn Tunnel and one of the soldiers leapt up to close the window and keep out the noise and the smoke from the engine. But the grit and grime penetrated Gwyneth's clothes immediately and she peeled off the crocheted gloves because they were already dirty.

Her mother had packed a sandwich and an apple and a thermos of tea for the journey. Gwyneth drank most of the musty, milky tea before the train reached Cardiff, and though she saved the sandwich until after the Severn Tunnel, it couldn't assuage her hunger. She was hungry all the time nowadays. Her mother said she might find something to eat at Paddington Station if the café wasn't closed by that time. No one ever knew what time trains would arrive in those days.

Her mother had given her two pounds. "Don't lose it, Gwyneth. You'll need it for emergencies." The two pound notes and directions to the home were in the black leather handbag, an old one of her mother's, and Gwyneth checked frequently to see that the precious notes were still safe, examining for about the tenth time the directions written on the scrap of paper. "Take the Northern Line to Whitechapel, turn left out of the station and go about a quarter of a mile along the Mile End Road. The sign for the home is on the left-hand side."

She hoped the place wouldn't be too difficult to find because if it was, what would she do then? It was a relief that it was still daylight when the train finally drew into Paddington Station, two hours late, and Gwyneth was swept along behind the hurrying crowds of soldiers and sailors to the ticket taker at the metal gate. Handing over her ticket, her last link to Clarrach, she looked around for a sign for the entrance to the underground and tried not to panic. Paddington Station was like nowhere she'd ever seen before, huge and cavernous and echoing, the high-arched glass roof disappearing into a sooty blackness, everything, everywhere black and overwhelming. "You've got a tongue in your head," her mother had said. "You can always ask someone." But Gwyneth didn't want to ask anyone anything. She wanted to find her way to the home that wouldn't be a home, and hide.

She had no conception of an underground railway system and couldn't imagine how it worked, but it was, after all, much easier to make her way through the maze than she'd feared. She purchased a ticket to Whitechapel at the glass-fronted booth, traced with her finger the black line of the Northern Line on the diagrammed map, and followed the signs down the escalators and along white, tiled tunnels, her heels echoing loudly. Her suitcase grew heavy and the hot stale air blew her hair into disorder and the roaring rushing sound of trains was like thunder in the distance, and when she finally arrived at what she hoped was the correct platform, she had to wait. And wait. When a round red train at last hurtled out of the tunnel, headlight gleaming like a Cyclops eye in the darkness, Gwyneth asked a woman standing nearby if this was the right train for Whitechapel and realized these were the first words she'd spoken since leaving Clarrach.

By the time she emerged from the underground station at Whitechapel, she was a little less fearful, the worst of the journey surely behind her, but as she turned left outside the entrance as the instructions said, she caught her first glimpse of the Mile End Road. Such courage as she had immediately failed her. The Mile End Road was a long and wide and dispiritingly straight street that faded into a gray and gloomy distance; on the opposite side of the road from the tube station loomed a dark, massive building that had a sign for a hospital. Ugly rectangular tenement blocks stretched in either direction. Gwyneth knew this part of London was badly bombed in the blitz, but it was a shock to see the gaping holes in the buildings, the walls sheared off to expose torn wallpaper and broken fireplaces, the walls propped up by leaning timbers, heaps of burned rubble and purple weeds growing where people once had lived. Apart from the weeds, nothing green or growing was to be seen anywhere. A pall of low cloud hung over the whole dismal area and the air was thick with the smoke of coal fires and the smell of river mud.

But it was too late to turn back. There was nowhere to turn back to.

She lugged the suitcase along the uneven pavements for what seemed like miles, trying to ignore the men who stood on the street corners and whistled at her, calling out unintelligible words as if speaking in a foreign language. Her face grew hot, and sweat broke out under her arms, and though she needed to stop and put down the suitcase that was making her arm ache, she didn't dare. Finally, with relief, she saw the sign, faded gold letters painted on a swinging wooden board: "Christian Haven for UnMarried Mothers." She paused for a brief moment to stare up at the tall, narrow building, lace curtains shrouding the windows, stone steps leading up to pillars beside the front door. She climbed the steps in an anxious rush to get in off the street, pressed the white porcelain doorbell, and after a long and nervous wait, the door opened a few inches. A woman with gray hair and a gray dress gazed unsmiling through the crack.

"Yes?"

Gwyneth's voice vanished. Her knees began to tremble and she dropped the suitcase, gazed speechlessly at the woman, and finally managed to stammer, "My name is Gwyneth. Gwyneth Griffiths. I've come on the train from Wales. To have a baby." She couldn't stop shaking and she started to cry.

"No use crying over spilt milk," the woman said, but she opened the door wider and let Gwyneth in.

The interior of the house was almost as dismal as the exterior, cold and damp even though it was summertime, long dark hallways and steep narrow staircases stretching into the distance. But it was a roof over her head and the street was shut away and when the woman took her up the staircase to a room in the attic, there was a bed she could lie down on. The room held six beds altogether, three on each side of the room, with black iron headboards like prison bars.

She would be spending six months in the home that was not a home. She was not ungrateful.

The girls who shared the attic room were unlike any girls Gwyneth had known before. They were sharp-tongued and years older than her and they all had bad teeth. They smoked cigarettes, although smoking was forbidden, lying on the cold linoleum beside an unused fireplace, blowing the smoke up the chimney, and they drank cheap gin they had somehow smuggled in, out of tooth mugs, though drinking was strictly forbidden. They told jokes that Gwyneth didn't quite understand, and screeched with laughter, and shrugged their skinny shoulders about their condition. They weren't the least bit ashamed of their condition. "Bit of bad luck, that's all. Can happen to the best of us. Isn't that right, Queenie?"

"Queenie" was what the other girls call Gwyneth, because she was tall and didn't speak like them. They weren't unkind to her, but treated her as a kind of pet, an innocent abroad, from a strange and distant part of the British Isles that none of them had ever been to or hardly even heard of. Not one of them had been anywhere outside the East End of London and had absolutely no desire to go anywhere else. They complained bitterly about the steely-eyed women who were the keepers of the home and led the prayers every morning and evening and set up the work schedules and enforced the rules. There were lots of rules. No smoking. No drinking. No male visitors. Compulsory attendance at prayer. Compulsory attendance at church on Sunday. Two passes granted each week to leave the home. No staying out after nine o'clock in the evening.

"Bloody gaolers," the girls complained. "Bitter twisted old maids. Not a chance of any of them ever getting in the family way. What a bloody hope! Can you imagine anyone doing it with them?" And they'd roll around on their beds, screeching with laughter at the very idea.

There were other girls in the home, twenty of them altogether. They scrubbed the floors, polished the floors and the furniture, cleaned the windows, did the cooking and the laundry. The laundry was the hardest of all, sheets and tablecloths and clothes boiled in steaming copper boilers in the cold basement, then wrung through huge wooden mangles and draped over lines stretched across the basement ceiling so the whole building always smelled of damp clothes. Gwyneth didn't complain like the other girls about the work. She was glad of something to occupy the time. She drifted into a dreamy withdrawal from the real world, didn't listen to the news of the war on the radio in the common room, hardly ever read a book, was only vaguely interested in the changes in her body. She thought of the other girls as sisters, in a way. She'd never had a sister. Some of them sometimes took her with them on small excursions, up to the West End to look at Buckingham Palace, or to the Tower, or to walk down the mean streets to stare at the muddy brown Thames. She hardly noticed the bomb damage anymore and she never saw the king or queen.

Life took on a different meaning when art classes began.

All the classes were compulsory, home economics and child care, shorthand and typing, classes which were meant to prepare them for a job. No one pretended that art prepared anyone for anything; it was only another way to keep the girls from being idle. Most of them considered drawing glass jars and bowls of apples a complete waste of time, and were suspicious of the instructor. The instructor's name was Mrs. Rubinstein, an elderly lady with a foreign accent whose hairpins constantly escaped from a gray frizzled bun low on the back of her neck. "Sounds exactly like a bloody Hun," the girls whispered among themselves.

Mrs. Rubinstein, too, seemed to consider the art class an entire waste of time until she caught sight of Gwyneth trying to capture the ephemeral translucency of a glass jar and the way the light glanced off it. She stood watching over Gwyneth's shoulder.

"Ah, *liebchen*. That is quite good. You had lessons before?"

Picking up the drawing, Mrs. Rubinstein looked it over carefully, peered into Gwyneth's eyes and touched her head with her fingers lightly, gently. "Your hair, it is *schon*. And your face. I would like very much to draw your face. You would permit it?"

Gwyneth glanced around the room to see what the others might make of this startling suggestion, but as usual everyone was talking to one another, pointedly ignoring the teacher and the task at hand. Mrs. Rubinstein smiled at Gwyneth, her face cracking into a thousand wrinkles. "After class," she murmured. "When these philistines are gone. Perhaps you also could learn to draw faces?"

After that, until the day Gwyneth had to go to the hospital to bring her baby into the world, she and Mrs. Rubinstein spent many hours together in the chilly room. Gwyneth was astonished by the ease with which Mrs. Rubinstein transferred her face to paper, by the innate skill of the artist. Mrs. Rubinstein taught her how to make quick strokes with the fickle watercolors. "But watercolors are difficult," she lamented. "Only the English are really good at them because it is always so wet and rainy in this country." As the days grew shorter and darker, she brought in oil paints and showed Gwyneth how to use them instead of watercolors. Gwyneth was a quick learner.

She was almost happy.

Mrs. Rubinstein told her how she'd left Berlin before the war, after her husband died. "Now I live with my daughter," she explained. "Here in this dark sooty London. Her husband is a good Jewish boy, even though he is English. A kind man, so it's not too hard for me. But now he is away fighting the Nazis with the British Army and I must make a little money to help. I was artist in Berlin so now I teach art. And I am pleased not to be living in Germany anymore. Except, *liebchen,* you understand, I would not be living in Germany because I am Juden. You know what is happening to the Jews in Germany?"

Gwyneth didn't know, but she liked listening to Mrs. Rubinstein. She'd never known anyone foreign before, unless she counted Americans. Americans spoke English, so they didn't seem like real foreigners, not like French or German or Italians who didn't speak English. When Gwyneth was with Mrs. Rubinstein, she forgot her swelling body and her increasing physical discomfort and the alarming unknown future, forgot the chill in the room and the dinginess of the surroundings, and was only absorbed in the intricacies of painting. She learned to use pastels and to draw with charcoal, and the week before she went to the hospital, she finished a portrait of Mrs. Rubinstein, oil on board, and presented it to her.

The old lady's eyes filled with tears. "You have learned your lessons well, *liebchen*. You are my star pupil. I am most gratified. I will come and visit you in the hospital."

And she did. She was Gwyneth's only visitor apart from a couple of girls who came to look the baby over. Mrs. Rubinstein brought her flowers and books and kissed the baby, as though she was pleased to see him. "He is beautiful, but not as beautiful as his mother," she said, and rocked him in her arms. "And it is best, *ja,* that he goes to a nice home. You must not mourn for him. His life and yours would be much too hard if you try to keep him. You will have other babies."

Gwyneth didn't want to acknowledge that the baby was beautiful. "He doesn't look like anyone," she said.

She tried not to love him. At first it was surprisingly easy, just as it had been surprisingly easy to bring him into the world; he seemed to have no connection to her, a rumpled dark-haired little thing with pretty hands and feet who slept most of the time in the nursery. She saw him only when the nurses brought him in for feeding. But it wasn't quite so easy not to love him when they went together to the home in Kent where she had to keep him for the required six weeks before he could be adopted. It was the rule: a baby had to stay with its mother to give him a good start in life, to give the mother a chance to change her mind. Gwyneth had no intention of changing her mind. She knew she couldn't possibly manage life with a baby. She wasn't even sure she could manage life at all.

She had to give him a name for the birth certificate, and once he had a name, Michael, because she didn't know anyone else with that particular name, he became a person in his own right. His newborn face filled out and the dark hair fell away and a light blond fuzz covered his small head, and as his eyes grew lighter, at last she recognized a resemblance to the man who was his father, whom she had loved so much. The touch of the baby's skin was like velvet and she would stroke it, and when he opened his eyes and gazed up at her and reached out with his tiny perfect hands, her treacherous heart crumbled within her. At the end of the six weeks, it was very hard to pass him over to the nurses and leave him in the home so she could start her life over again.

Somehow, though she tried, she couldn't ever quite forget the shape of his face or the softness of his skin. Sometimes at night, before she fell asleep, she imagined she could feel the touch of his skin against hers and see his eyes looking up at her.

Nineteen

Tim believed her story, of course. Every word of it. It would have been impossible for him not to believe her. But he could hardly believe that his father, the man of high-minded, strict moral principles, would desert her so thoughtlessly, would never have come back to see her. If he'd known about a child, surely he'd have accepted responsibility, war or no war. It wasn't as though he'd forgotten her. More than twenty years later, he'd still not forgotten her.

Tim had to know. "Did you tell him about the baby?"

"I didn't know myself before he went away. And then I was sure he'd come back when he could. He promised he'd come back. He knew where I was, didn't he?"

Why *hadn't* Carlton gone back for her? Even if he'd been wounded in the invasion and shipped back home to the States, which happened to so many in that first deadly wave, he could have written. But as far as Tim knew, his father had never been wounded. Though what did he know about his father's war? He'd never spoken about it.

"The baby? What happened to him? You didn't go looking for him afterwards?"

Gwyneth kept her head turned away. "I tried never to think of the baby. When he was six months old, I signed the final papers for his adoption and lost any right to look for him. It was the only thing I could do. I didn't have any doubts." She sighed. "But I had regrets, of course. How can one not?"

Regrets, Tim thought. She'd been painting his face. As it might have been. Over and over and over again. And she'd captured it so perfectly. A child's face that would become just like his father's. Like Tim's face. Like his brother's face. The truth was that child was his brother, too. Where was he? Could he find him?

Gradually, Tim noticed the skylights overhead were now bright with sun, with blue sky instead of gray. He wanted to leap up, escape into the fresh air, take deep breaths, think through this new and overwhelming knowledge. If he didn't have the damned cast, he'd go running up the path to the top of the hill to clear his head. Except his head would never be clear of this. Never. Gwyneth had borne his father's child and had to give it away while Carlton had gone blithely about his life, marrying, having children, making an important career.

Gwyneth's hands were relaxed in her lap, fingers curled upwards, as though the telling her story had given her peace. Tim didn't want to move and disturb that peace, understanding how fragile and vulnerable it was. If only there were something he could do to make it up to her. If only he could do penance for his father.

At last he asked, "So you came back to Clarrach afterwards?"

"Oh no. I didn't come back for a very long time." She pulled away from him with a sudden jerk, jumping up from the sofa as though unable to sit still for another moment. "Look, the sun is shining. Let's get out of here. I need to get out of here. I'll take you to that burial chamber I keep telling you about." She laughed, as though at a private joke. "A burial chamber is a suitable place to lay these kinds of memories to rest, don't you think?"

She's like the weather, Tim thought, changeable, clouds shadowing her eyes one moment, laughter chasing them away the next. Now her eyes were glowing again, alive and expectant, and she held out her hand. "Come on. We have to drive there but after that it's an easy walk from the car. You'll like it."

He'd like it wherever she took him, and he was pretty sure she'd tell him the rest of the story, how she went from the awful moment of parting with her baby to living here on the mountain with Rhys. He wanted to know the rest of it and guessed she needed to tell it.

Gwyneth drove very fast, up the mountain rather than down, on a road that appeared to be leading straight towards the rocks at the summit. Then it veered away round the side of the hill and they rattled over a metal cattle grid. The blacktop road turned into a dirt track snaking across dark and boggy heath, the hilltops beyond mounding into a blue-heaped distance, and further along they came close to a group of large animals cropping the sparse grass at the side of the track. At a distance, Tim assumed they were cows, but as the car came closer, he was surprised to realize they were thick-legged, long-maned ponies. Gwyneth slowed the car, rolled down her window. "Welsh ponies," she said. "They run wild up here." The ponies raised their heads and tossed their manes and shied away from the car with rolling, cautious eyes. Tim was amazed such big creatures would be running wild in such a small country.

"They're rounded up once a year and sold off as pets. Once upon a time, they were sold as pit ponies. Can you imagine that, a wild pony down a pit, never to see the daylight again?"

Up and up they drove, as though alone at the top of the world, no houses or farm buildings around and about, only the open heath and the odd piled rocks appearing and disappearing above their heads. Then the track curved round the other side of the hill and the crags disappeared. The car rattled over another cattle grid and Tim saw an electrified wire fence running away from the grid. "To keep the ponies from wandering," Gwyneth explained.

Dropping downward, the track became a blacktopped road again. A few windswept trees and sparse hedges began to fill in at the sides of the road, but the road was still steep, far up on the hillside, and when Gwyneth finally pulled to a halt against a hedgerow, the neat farmland fields and hedgerows were still a long way below, the coastline a hazy pastel painting.

"So," she announced. "We've arrived."

They seemed to have arrived nowhere. There was no sign of habitation, not even the sound of sheep, and as Tim climbed out of the car, he could hear only the faintest song of birds somewhere high in the milky blue sky. Skylarks, he remembered she'd told him. He was pretty sure he'd never heard the song of skylarks before. Otherwise, everywhere was deeply quiet, a hush in the air, a stillness, a breathlessness.

Gwyneth walked a few yards down the hill by the side of a hedge, paused, and waited for him. Tim, slower, ungainly on the crutches, caught up to her and saw she was waiting beside an old-fashioned wooden stile almost buried among the hawthorn. She said, "Can you make it over this? After this, it's not far," and she gathered her skirt together, clambered over the stile, and held out her hand to him. If he didn't have the cast, he could have leapt the barrier easily, no problem, but now he had to climb over gracelessly, a gigantic bumbling idiot once again, but once on the other side of the stile, he held on to her hand for a moment and liked to think that she didn't draw away too quickly.

On the other side of the stile, a grassy path ran alongside the hedgerow and meandered across a sloping field. Yellow primroses and purple campion were scattered on the bank below the hedge, hawthorn and honeysuckle perfumed the air, and bees hummed among the blossoms. Tim's crutches made no sound on the path and Gwyneth seemed to float silently in front of him, her feet skimming over the flowered grass, sunlight caught in her hair, and it was as if they'd entered into a different world, as if crossing the stile had taken them into another time, into some enchanted place where sound was nonexistent. The path went on and on, how far Tim had no idea. "Not far," Gwyneth had said, and it wasn't so much that the path was long, only that it seemed to have no beginning and no end, as though time had lost its meaning. But the path did come to an end, suddenly, around a bend in the hedge, just as Tim decided that he'd be following Gwyneth forever and ever, caught in her familiar spell.

The path took a right-angled turn behind the hedge and broadened into a wide depression in the hillside, the grass very green, a brilliant emerald green, and in the green, green grass there rose an improbable circle of huge stones, enormous towering stones that reached into the sky. Some of the stones were upright, some lay on the grass, but all of them were powerful and dominating, the expression of some primitive world completely different from the one Tim knew. The unexpected sight of the monoliths and their overwhelming size took his breath away. He stood stock-still, staring in disbelief. In awe.

Gwyneth said triumphantly, "I knew you'd be impressed. I knew you'd love it. It's my favorite place." She took his hand again and led him to the nearest stone, much taller than both of them, and held his hand against the rough pitted surface. "Feel how warm the stone is. As though it lives and breathes."

Tim could feel the warmth of the stone, but he was much more conscious of the warmth of her hand against his. "Think of it," Gwyneth said. "Man was here thousands of years before Christ. Here, in this very place, high on this Welsh hillside. Prehistoric man. Isn't that an extraordinary thought?"

She didn't seem to expect a reply, just pressed his hand against the stone for a while longer. Then she pulled it away and walked him slowly around the perimeter of the standing stones. The circle wasn't enormous, but the remoteness and loneliness on the hillside made it seem profound, a secretiveness to it, an intimacy, as though it was their own private place of worship.

Gwyneth said, "Somewhere like this makes one realize how short a space of time we occupy in the long history of mankind, doesn't it? Gives perspective to the kinds of problems we have here today on this same earth." She glanced at Tim and smiled dreamily. "Don't you feel that way?"

Did he feel that way? He wasn't sure what he felt about anything anymore. Except that he was here with her.

In the center of the circle one flat stone lay on top of others like an altar, and beneath it was a yawning space where the sunlight didn't reach. "People say that's the original burial place. A *cromlech,* it's called in Welsh."

Tim bent to peer into the space as though it might reveal prehistoric bones, but there was nothing to see except dark earth. Gwyneth let go of his hand, wandered away from the center of the circle, climbed up the high grassy bank surrounding the stones, sat down, and pulled her skirts around her knees. "I was going to tell you the rest of the story, but are you sure you really want to hear it? In the context of these eons of time, it isn't, after all, so important. Nothing is, is it?"

Tim clambered up the bank to sit beside her on the damp grass. "It's important to me. Everything about you is important to me."

From up here, he could see past the stones down to the etched cliffs and the shining, empty curve of the ocean. From here, it was even possible to recognize the curvature of the earth. On the far horizon, he could make out a dark smudge that might be land. He pointed. "Ireland?"

"Ireland," Gwyneth agreed.

Where he would never go now. Gazing at the smudge on the

arc of horizon, Tim looked back at the circle of stones. An odd hallowed quality pervaded the whole area, but the ring of sentinel stones and the flat altarlike one in the middle was more like a scene of sacrifice than a simple burial ground. He was curious about the ancient people who'd erected such vast stones in such an unlikely place, and he felt small and diminished here, as if life, after all, was not of any great consequence. Tim considered that a dangerous and seditious, un-American idea. Americans cared about their own lives. Perhaps not so much about other people's lives, but certainly about their own.

"They really wanted to give the dead a great view, didn't they? Otherwise why come all the way up here just to bury people? Why here? And how did they get these huge stones up here?"

Gwyneth lay back and closed her eyes. "Who knows why they did it. Or how. There are all sorts of theories. In a way, I don't want it explained. I like the mystery of it."

As he stared at her face, the shape of her cheekbones, the curve of her mouth, Tim longed to trace his fingers across the arch of her eyebrows and the place where the light hair sprung away from her temples. The skin was almost transparent at her temple, a tiny artery beating steadily under the thin skin. She didn't open her eyes, but her eyelashes fluttered as though she was aware he was watching her, and he had to hold back from bending closer, from pressing his mouth against hers, from throwing himself on her.

Sinking backwards until he, too, was lying on his back, he gazed up at the sky. "Tell me the rest of your story."

She was silent for a long moment. "Perhaps, after all, it's not so interesting."

"I'm interested. I'm interested in everything about you. And I'd do anything to make it up to you, Gwyneth. If I could."

She opened her eyes. "Would you really? That's very sweet of you, Tim. If only that were possible."

"Anything's possible," he said and thought, Now I could kiss her, now.

"I'll tell you the rest. If you really want to hear it."

He'd rather have kissed her.

She closed her eyes once more, and began, slowly and dreamily, as if watching a silver screen unrolling behind the papery, fragile eyelids. "Mrs. Rubinstein came to my rescue. The art teacher, you remember? Mrs. Rubinstein changed my life. Perhaps not all for the good, after all, but God knows what would have happened to me if it hadn't been for her."

Twenty

Gwyneth often wondered what would have happened if Mrs. Rubinstein hadn't suggested, just days before she was due to leave the place in Kent, "How wonderful if you could come to my daughter's home and help look after her children. Just for a while, perhaps, until you find some other work."

What other work? Gwyneth hadn't the faintest idea where to start looking or what to look for and certainly not where to live. Her mother took it for granted she'd return to Clarrach with the painfully acquired shorthand and typing skills, but Clarrach was the last place on earth to mend her bruised body and heart. The thought of the cramped, tiny flat above the shop, the tight proximity to her mother's disapproval, the small town full of memories and whispering people, made her even more anxious and tearful, so she clutched at Mrs. Rubinstein's offer as a drowning person clutches at a life belt. The day she handed over the baby, Mrs. Rubinstein came to fetch her and together they rode the train back to the East End of London.

The Jacobs family lived in a terraced house in Hackney, not far from the Christian Home for Unmarried Women. From the outside it looked much like the Home, a tall, narrow house blackened by soot, dirty white pillars at the front door, but inside there were thick carpets and soft upholstered furniture, oil paintings on the walls, a coal fire burning in the living room, a dining room table adorned with an embroidered cloth. The beds were covered with silky eiderdowns and there were velvet curtains at the windows to keep out the night. Gwyneth carried her suitcase up the hushed carpeted staircase to her very own bedroom, and knew she'd found a warm luxurious cocoon that would keep her safe from the outside world.

Mrs. Rubinstein's daughter, Esther Jacobs, had soft white skin and dark wavy hair. She spoke in an accented English, more fluently than her mother, but still not as a native-born Londoner. She sat on the edge of the bed in Gwyneth's room, put her hand on Gwyneth's arm. "My mother and I hope you will be happy here. We are not Orthodox, you understand, we do not keep Kosher, but we observe the Sabbath, of course."

Gwyneth gazed into the warm brown eyes and had no idea what she was talking about. She supposed she'd find out in due course. The children, Hannah and David, seemed ordinary enough little cockney children, dropping their aitches and mangling their vowels, and they were already cheeky and willful, like other cockneys. It was Gwyneth's responsibility to make breakfast for Hannah and David, walk them to school, wash and iron their clothes, clean and tidy their rooms, as well as help with general household tasks. It wasn't particularly demanding work. The children regarded her as some kind of servant, which she was, she supposed, but Mrs. Rubinstein and Mrs. Jacobs treated her more like a guest. They insisted, for example, that Gwyneth rest after lunch. "To get your strength back," they said in their funny accented English. She ate her meals with them at the elaborate table, strangely different food, little sweet pancakes and smoked fish and dark bread and strong tasting liver paté, watched as they lit candles at dusk on Friday evenings and listened to their incomprehensible prayers. On Saturdays, they all disappeared to the synagogue. Many people came to the house and spoke German with Mrs. Rubinstein, and it felt to Gwyneth that she'd landed in a foreign country. The memories of the last nine months began to fade, as though they were nothing but a bad dream. During the daytime, she usually managed to forget about the baby whose name was Michael, but sometimes at night she dreamed of his velvet skin and his pretty hands.

Then the month of May arrived and suddenly the war in Europe was over. Quite suddenly it seemed to Gwyneth, who hadn't been paying attention to the news. The end of the war meant the head of the house would be coming home. No one knew exactly when but they all knew it must be soon. Mrs. Rubinstein and Mrs. Jacobs threw themselves, and Gwyneth, into a frenzy of scouring and polishing, everything in the house scrubbed and washed until there wasn't a carpet left unbeaten, a corner of a room unscoured, a dish or curtain or chair cover left unwashed or unironed, and they all grew jittery with anticipation, leaping to their feet whenever the phone rang, running to answer the doorbell, hovering on the front steps by the pillars to wait for the postman. Only Gwyneth dreaded the arrival of the head of the house, for his arrival would surely disrupt the unthreatening female rhythm she was safe and comfortable with. She didn't allow herself to imagine that Carlton Bruce might also get back safely from the war and come looking for her, but she, too, began to wait for the postman.

It was August, after the surrender of the Japanese, before Samuel Jacobs, in his shabby khaki uniform, finally arrived home to kisses and tears and shrill cries of welcome. He did indeed bring disruption to the sedate female household in Hackney, but he also brought an air of festivity, loud male voices and hearty laughter, the unfamiliar aroma of cigarettes and whisky lingering in the rooms. Late night dinner parties were concocted like biblical miracles from hoarded food and wine from the cellar, and the dining room filled with men just like him, noisy, exuberant, talkative. Samuel Jacobs was a thickset jovial man with black snapping eyes, a fine head of hair, and an aura of authority. As soon as he appeared in the house, Hannah and David began behaving in a more civilized manner, even towards Gwyneth.

He chastised his children. "You must listen to Miss Gwyneth," he said, sweeping one arm around her in an encompassing gesture, smiling at her as though she were a real member of the family.

The household took on a new and different tempo, Samuel Jacobs's tempo, a rush and excitement, a buzz, the dinner table enlivened by optimistic discussions of the future of his business. Samuel Jacobs's business was making clothes. During the long years of war, while he'd been away, the company kept going by producing uniforms, but now the war was over and so was the need for uniforms. Clothing, like most other things, was still rationed, but Samuel Jacobs was certain women would very soon be wanting pretty dresses again. Dinner table talk was mainly about a new fashion line.

"Oh, Sammy," Esther lamented. "It's much too soon for that. You'll go broke for sure."

But Mrs. Rubinstein encouraged him. "Beautiful clothes are just another form of art and art is one of the things we fought the war for. Make something beautiful for me, Sammy, something to make me feel young again," and though Samuel laughed when she said it, somehow he found materials not seen since before the war, silks and cottons and fine wools, and made his mother-in-law a blue silk dress with a swish to the skirt and a cling to the bodice that took years off her age. It was the beginning of his new line.

One morning, across the breakfast table, Samuel stared with narrowed eyes at Gwyneth, as though seeing her for the first time, and said to his wife, "You know, Esther, I've been looking for someone just like Miss Gwyneth, tall and skinny like that, to model my line. And here she is, all the time, right under our noses. The perfect clotheshorse." Samuel's bold black eyes appraised Gwyneth's body until she blushed and turned away. "Can I borrow her for a day or two?"

Raising her eyebrows, Esther, too, stared at Gwyneth as if she'd never seen her before. "What do you think about that, Gwyneth? A model has to take her own clothes off."

The thought of taking her clothes off in front of anyone, let alone Samuel Jacobs whom she saw every day, shocked Gwyneth into silence.

He laughed. "Don't worry. I'll see she's kept decent."

Esther frowned. "Indeed I should hope so, Samuel Jacobs."

But Esther never refused her husband anything, and before Gwyneth quite knew what was happening, she was taken upstairs to Esther's bedroom and was trying on a piece of underwear such as Gwyneth had only seen in pictures, a scrap of slippery pink satin that only just covered her breasts and her bottom. Speechless with anxiety, the satin smooth and luxurious and threatening next to her skin, sure she couldn't possibly shed her dress for such a skimpy, seductive garment, she was dispatched with Samuel in the black car with rationed petrol to his factory. When she set eyes on the gloomy, unprepossessing brick building near the docks, she was even more apprehensive. He marched her inside through a gray metal door and she was astonished to find herself in a bright open space alive with the humming of sewing machines. Men and women were bent over the machines, treadles were thundering, wheels flying and bolts of cloth were spilling across large tables, and there were rows of metal hangers crammed with more clothes than Gwyneth had ever seen in one place. Some of the workers looked up and nodded at Samuel's entrance but the hypnotically flashing needles didn't slow.

A small rotund woman came bustling out from behind a wooden partition, almost curtseyed to Samuel, and she spoke in a reverential whisper. "Good morning, Mr. Jacobs. How are you today?" Her accent was just like Mrs. Rubinstein's. Somehow that was reassuring.

Samuel waved a hand casually. "Erica, this is Gwyneth. She's our model for today. Find her a blanket, will you?"

Crooking a finger, Erica said, "Come with me, darling," and she led Gwyneth behind the partition, pulled a thick gray blanket off a shelf, and waited. Gwyneth understood this was the moment she was expected to remove her dress. Very reluctantly and slowly she did so. Erica laughed. "Oh, such pretty frou-frou," she said, and draped the scratchy blanket around the pink satin. Then she took Gwyneth back into the big room, arranged her on a plinth in full view of the workers at the sewing machines, and Samuel began draping dresses in various stages of completion around and about Gwyneth's body. He pinned material, ripped seams out, slashed the fabric here and there as she clutched the scratchy blanket closer for a degree of modesty. But after a while, being exposed in beautiful underwear in a roomful of disinterested people became quite unthreatening, as though she'd been taking her clothes off in public forever, and she stood for hours in the chill of the sewing room as Samuel cut and shaped and lunged at the fabric again and again. Sometime in the early afternoon, he drove her back to the house in time to fetch the children from school. A few days later, he asked if she could come for more fittings.

So it began, Gwyneth's modeling career.

There was a sizable Jewish community in the East End of London. Samuel Jacobs knew every person in it, it seemed. Bit by bit, his business picked up. He was perfectly correct in believing women would want pretty things again, that they were hungry for luxury after years of rationing; several local shops carried his dresses, then a West End department store asked to see them and he took Gwyneth along as his model. He taught her how to walk and stand to show his clothes to their best advantage, and as Gwyneth, too, wanted Sammy to succeed, she was soon strutting and twirling without self-consciousness in front of hard-eyed buyers. She understood they weren't looking at her, only at Sammy's dresses.

But Mrs. Rubinstein hadn't forgotten about the painting. "We have to work on it, because you have talent, Gwyneth." No one had ever before told Gwyneth she had talent, and though she wasn't sure it was true, she enrolled at the Slade School for a couple of classes a week. To please Mrs. Rubinstein as much as to please herself. She understood by then that Carlton Bruce was never coming back to look for her.

Now her life took on a new and different rhythm, some housework, some modeling, some painting, and she discovered that the painting was what gave her life some meaning. Housework gave her a place to live, modeling enough money to pay for the classes at the Slade, but painting was reality. At night she dreamed, not anymore about babies with soft skin, but about the National Gallery and the Tate, about Constable and Turner and Gainsborough and Rembrandt. She grew ambitious with the paints, soon realized her limitations, and despaired of ever being good enough to please her new teachers. But she kept trying, often failing, sometimes succeeding, made new and tentative friendships with other students at the Slade and stayed out late at night, her world expanding, her mind and heart healing. Then, quite suddenly it seemed, as suddenly as the war had come to an end, the fashion industry took off, the New Look came in, live models were in demand, and Gwyneth was thrust willy-nilly into a frenzied world of photograph sessions and dress collections.

She had to make a choice between art classes and modeling. There simply wasn't time for both. Her efforts at painting paled compared this with other new and heady life; art students were shabby and dirty compared with the rich and gleaming world of fashion, with the people who bought fashion. Modeling was glamorous and desirable and men wanted to be seen with models and most models liked to be seen with men. Gwyneth was no exception. One day she would return to the art classes. One day.

After six more months, she moved out of the safe cocoon in the Jacobs house and into a flat in Chelsea with another girl. The Jacobs family was not happy about it. They warned Gwyneth she was only nineteen years old and no match for the kind of men who had money and power and who liked to be seen in the company of beautiful young models. Men with a great deal of charm. And ruthlessness. And wives, usually, somewhere or other. Gwyneth didn't listen.

By the time she was twenty-two, her photo was on the front of magazines and she'd traveled to Paris and Milan and New York. By the age of twenty-four, she'd been in love with two married men, not in love as she was with Carlton Bruce, whom she'd done her best to forget, but in love with the memory of that soaring dizziness, that divine craziness. Gwyneth sought to recapture that feeling and couldn't. At the age of twenty-five she had an abortion, and at twenty-six she was hospitalized for a month with "nervous exhaustion." Somehow it all made her more photogenic, the amber eyes wider and shadowier in the curving hollowed cheeks, hip bones prominent, legs long and slender, arms like delicate reeds. When she was twenty-seven she went to Paris to live with a man called Phillipe de Mentroux, because she wanted to get out of England and because she thought she might be in love with him. After a few months, she decided it was the sound of his name she liked more than him, London that she liked more than Paris, and it was then she got the call from Clarrach that her mother was ill. Dying, the doctor said regretfully. "Come home if you want to see her before it's too late."

In all those years, Gwyneth had been back to Clarrach only

once, when her Uncle Emlyn died. It wasn't a successful visit, if funeral visits can ever be called successful. She'd sat in the parlor of Aunt Ethel's house and tried to converse with the elderly ladies who were drinking tea and eating sponge cake and who looked at her, like her mother, with disapproval. "There's thin you've become, Gwyneth. We'd hardly have known you, that's a fact. Have another piece of cake. We must fatten you up."

"So what is it you do up in London then, Gwyneth? Don't you miss Wales?"

"Your mother is always hoping you'll come back here to live, you know, Gwyneth. You're the only one she's got, after all."

She slept in the same narrow bed in the same tiny room in the flat above the shop and fled the next day, and salved her conscience by sending her mother enough money to buy a bungalow that overlooked the ocean.

But by the time her mother fell ill, Gwyneth was exhausted by the life she was living, and was glad of the excuse to leave Paris and take the train home again to Wales. It was Wales she'd been missing, she decided, the green hills and the shining ocean, the mountain with the crags at the top, the tall hedgerows and the scent of hawthorn.

It was a shock to see how her mother had wasted away. The guilt began then, if it hadn't really begun years ago, and she sat beside her mother's bed for two weeks, holding her hand and trying to feed her, washing her and changing her bedclothes. And crying.

Every day for those two weeks, Dr. Rhys Edwards came to see her mother. He prescribed morphine for his patient and sleeping tablets for Gwyneth, but she didn't take the pills because her mother might die in the night while Gwyneth was sleeping. Rhys Edwards looked at her pale haunted face and the dark circles under her eyes, and when her mother finally slipped quietly away one afternoon, Gwyneth wept on his shoulder and he felt the knobs of her spine and the sharp blades of her scapulae under his fingers, and understood the shaking and the excessive weeping were not normal.

Rhys Ewards was the kindest, most decent, most concerned person she'd ever met. It was ironic that he was right here in Clarrach, the place she'd avoided for all those years. Now it felt this was where she'd belonged all along, as though she'd come home again, to the fields and hedgerows and green hills of Wales. She wanted to give up the rackety life she'd been leading and become Rhys Edwards's wife.

Except she couldn't and wouldn't live in Clarrach. It wasn't until she found the ruined house on the mountain that Gwyneth decided she could settle down and wait for another baby with velvet skin.

Twenty-One

"Except, you see, there was no happy ending. There wasn't any baby and I turned out not to be very good as a doctor's wife."

Somewhere up in the pale blue sky, the larks were still singing, but Tim hadn't the heart to look for them. He didn't know what to say about babies, didn't know what to say about his father having sex with a fifteen-year-old girl. He latched on to the last words. "What's a good doctor's wife?"

"She should be like the vicar's wife. Caring and concerned and involved. Above all, of good moral background. I'm none of those things according to the people in Clarrach."

"What? Because you led a—how did you call it?—a rackety life? Or was it because of the baby? You think your mother told people?"

"Oh no. She'd have died first." A small sound caught in Gwyneth's throat. "Well, she did, didn't she? Die, I mean. No, I'm sure she didn't tell anyone. Mother wasn't the confiding sort. But I bet people suspected. They always did when girls disappeared like that." She sighed. "You can't imagine how the world has changed, Tim. Now there's the pill and there's certainly not the shame. In the old days it was a terrible sin to have a baby outside marriage." Gwyneth smiled, but there was no amusement in her eyes. "No, the baby wasn't what blackened my name. Not as far as Clarrach was concerned."

Propping himself up on one elbow, Tim looked into her eyes, dark and shadowy again, the melancholy back in them. He wanted to put his arms around her, hold her close. Comfort her.

"Don't look at me," she said, and turned her head away. "If you don't look at me, I might be able to tell you the rest. Though I don't think you really want to hear it."

"Yes, I do."

"You might be sorry. It's not a nice story."

"Does it have something to do with my father?"

"In a way."

Tim stared up at the sky. He could feel the damp of the grass seeping through his shirt. "Then I need to know."

Gwyneth didn't say anything for a long time and when he looked at her, her lips were pinched together and her chin was trembling, as if she found the words difficult to say, as if she were about to cry again. He put his hand over hers. "You have to tell me now. It isn't fair not to tell me now."

She took a breath. "All right, Tim. This is what happened. One evening, just before the Americans left, I went to the station to meet your father. Of course, I didn't know then that the Americans were about to leave. They didn't know either."

⁂

That evening, as on many other evenings, she'd walked up through the town to meet Carlton. The train station was a convenient meeting place, people always coming and going around it, nothing conspicuous about a girl waiting alone. Not that she ever had to wait for Carlton; he was always there before her, his face crinkling into a heartwarming smile when he caught sight of her. The station also had the advantage of being away from the square, out of sight of the flat above the shop and her mother's watchful eyes. Gwyneth lied about where she went in the evenings, lied easily and often. "Just for a swim, Mam" or "Got some homework with Ellie Jones" or "Going for a walk with Annie Thomas." It was easier than she'd ever thought to tell lies, much too easy. She almost wanted her mother to be less trusting, not to believe whatever she was told, and she lived in fear of being found out. The lies made Gwyneth uncomfortable, because she'd been brought up to tell the truth, but at the same time they lent an aura of greater excitement to the adventure of love. In any case, the truth would have kept her away from Carlton.

"Just watch out for those American soldiers," her mother warned. "You hear all sorts of stories about them. And don't let me ever hear you've been in a pub. You're not of an age to go drinking, which is a sin and damnation anyway."

"Oh, Mam. Whatever would I want to go to a pub for?"

Gwyneth and Carlton never dreamed of going into the pubs which were crammed with sweaty, uniformed soldiers who drank far too much, flung their money around in a kind of desperation, smoked cheap cigarettes, and picked fights. Or cried into their beer. No, Gwyneth and Carlton preferred their own company. They wandered along the paths at the cliff edge, across fields where the gorse burned in brilliant yellow fire and where there were only sheep to watch them, where they could be alone with each other, lie together in the sweet-smelling new mown hay, where he could tell her how much he loved her, how they'd be together forever when this war was over. He told her about the town where he grew up and where he'd gone to law school and how he planned to join a good law firm once he was out of the army. Philadelphia and Chicago and Boston sounded foreign and exotic to a girl from Clarrach who'd never been anywhere. Gwyneth had very little to say herself because what was there to say? Life in Clarrach had been boring and trivial until Carlton Bruce came along.

He never spoke of the coming invasion of Europe, never raised the possibility of death or injury, of not going home again. The gathering storm of invasion was dim and distant to Gwyneth, unrelated to this new and wonderful existence in Carlton Bruce's arms; to her, war was a permanent state of affairs and the invasion had been talked about for so long it was difficult to believe it would really happen. She'd watched the camps spring up on the surrounding hills, the town throng with soldiers, the supply ships fill the harbor, but she viewed it all through a hazy filter of love. Carlton Bruce was what the war meant to Gwyneth, not death or fighting, not bombs or fear or destruction. Love was what the war meant to Gwyneth.

She didn't really believe Carlton would ever have to leave.

But that evening when Gwyneth arrived at the train station, he wasn't waiting for her. She could pick him out of a crowd instantaneously, tall and fair-haired, distinctive in his smart officer's olive drab, but as she stood on tiptoes to peer among the crowds milling around and about, there was no sign of him. She was a few minutes early, the clock on the station said six-forty, and she didn't mind waiting. She'd wait for him for eternity.

The station at Clarrach was an imposing structure, Victorian and Gothic, a big clock on the tower, a wide courtyard in front, and over the entrance an elaborate glass overhang supported by lacy iron pillars. There was also a café on the platform, open for cups of strong tea and stale sticky buns, but Gwyneth didn't bother with the café, just leaned against one of the pillars beside the entrance and watched the activity. In those days of the war, trains were sporadic and never on schedule, but as they were practically the only means of transportation, no petrol for cars and precious little for buses, a crowd was always milling around the station, either waiting for a train to arrive or waiting for one to depart. The wait was uncertain, often protracted.

Outside the entrance, under the overhang, a few civilians sat on suitcases, faces gray and resigned, as though they'd already been waiting far too long; a company of British sailors in pressed bell bottoms, duffle bags on shoulders, marched briskly past and disappeared inside. On the opposite corner of the courtyard, half a dozen bored-looking, gum-chewing GIs slouched against a wall, hands in pockets, caps tipped over their foreheads, and when they caught sight of Gwyneth, a couple of them whistled and yelled out, "Hey there, good-looking!" She ignored them. American GIs were often to be seen slouching against walls with their hands in their pockets, which was not allowed for uniformed British men, and Americans always whistled at girls, as if it were expected of them.

Thankfully, she saw no one she recognized, because otherwise, she knew, the word might get back to her mother. "Saw your Gwyneth hanging round the station the other evening," and then her mother would want to know what she'd been doing there. When Gwyneth and Carlton met, they'd smile and walk away from each other until there was no one to see them, and then she would take his hand.

More minutes went by. Still no Carlton.

Across the courtyard, two of the GIs detached themselves from the wall and sauntered over to her, catlike and somehow insolent. They came too close, looking her up and down, their jaws moving rythmically. "All alone, beautiful?"

"I'm waiting for someone."

"Hey now, honey, that's too bad. You look kinda lonely." They grinned at her. "Sweetheart, if he doesn't turn up, we'd like you to know we're available. We got nothing else to do. We're just waiting for a war to begin."

Gwyneth moved away, sought shelter behind another pillar.

One of them called after her, "You're much too good-looking to have to wait for anyone," and she turned her back deliberately. From the corner of her eye, she saw the two shrug elaborately, swagger back to the group, say something that made them all laugh, and then they all stared over at her. She felt conspicuous and awkward and stepped inside the entrance, away from their bold eyes.

The station hall was noisy and crowded, canvas kit bags in heaps on the floor, soldiers and sailors stretched out on the bags, some smoking, some sleeping, some just staring into space. The café on the platform beyond was totally full, the wooden benches in the middle of the hall crammed with travelers surrounded by brown paper packages, cardboard suitcases, and small children, most of whom seemed to be crying. Their wails echoed off the high stone ceiling and walls and their mothers wore expressions of exhausted exasperation. "Is everyone waiting for a train?" Gwyneth asked a woman. "Is it late?"

"What the hell else do you suppose we're doing here, ducky? Waiting for Father Christmas?"

Gwyneth retreated to the outside again, where Carlton would be by now, but there was still no sign of him, just the GIs lounging against the wall. Once again they whistled and waved at her and she walked purposefully around the corner, out of their sight.

Around the same corner, a few yards farther away, a lone American soldier was leaning against the high wall; like the others, his hands were in his pockets, but his head was bent and he didn't even glance towards her, just kicked at the ground in a desultory manner with one shiny black shoe. He ignored her and she ignored him and it was several moments before she looked at him again and realized he was one of the colored soldiers. It was unusual to see any colored soldiers in the town, especially one all by himself. If they ever came into the town, there would always be two or three of them together.

This was as close as Gwyneth had ever been to a black man. She didn't intend to stare but he seemed completely absorbed in his own feet, so she felt she could watch him surreptitiously. The hunch of his shoulders and the droop of his head in the angled forage cap lent him a solitary, hopeless appearance, as though he was lonely and very far from home. Which he was, of course. She couldn't help wondering what it must be like to be a different color from everyone else. From everyone in Clarrach, that is. Perhaps where he came from in America, colored people weren't unusual. For the first time, it occurred to Gwyneth that a place like Clarrach might seem strange to a black American. Or to any other kind of American, for that matter. She'd never considered Clarrach in that light before. She'd grown up there, lived most of her life there, took the little town with its meandering streets and tall old stone houses completely for granted, but even Carlton sometimes called it "quaint," and remarked on those things he found peculiar, the driving on the left, the narrowness of the streets, the funny way people spoke. Even the way she spoke. But she knew Carlton liked Clarrach because he said so, often. "It's stunning here, Gwyneth. One of the most beautiful places I've ever seen."

She didn't consider Clarrach stunning or beautiful. She thought the countryside around was lovely, the fields and the hedgerows, the long golden beaches, the hills rising above the town. The farm where she used to live was lovely, but the town of Clarrach itself wasn't anything to write home about.

As she watched the soldier, even the phrase "write home about" took on new meaning for Gwyneth. What, for example, would that Negro soldier there write home about? What would he tell his mother or his sister or whomever about a place like Clarrach? "A cold little town where no one talks to people like us"?

Then she realized the soldier was looking back at her and she was conscious of how she'd been staring. He glanced at her anxiously, warily. "Hey, sister," he said. "What's up?"

She stammered in embarrassment. "Nothing. Nothing. I'm sorry. I . . . I didn't mean to stare."

He tilted his cap lower over his eyes and went back to contemplating his shoes, then after a moment he asked, "You waiting for someone?"

"Yes. Yes, I am," and she turned to look at the station clock, but she couldn't see it from where she was standing. "Do you happen to know what the time is?"

Thrusting back the sleeve of his jacket, he stretched out his left hand to peer at his watch. "Fifteen after seven," he said, and she noticed how frail the bones of his wrist seemed against the heavy metal watchband, how smooth and brown the color of his hand, how startlingly pale and pink his fingernails. She looked at him more carefully and saw he was much younger than she'd thought at first, his face round and unlined and somehow unformed, his eyes very big and black. He didn't seem much older than she was herself. She felt sorry for him.

She said, "My friend is late." And after a moment, "Are you waiting for someone, too?"

He laughed then. His teeth flashed startlingly white in the black of his face. "You could say that, sister. Waiting for the train to carry me off. To Jericho." He had a deep, soft voice, his accent quite different from Carlton's. "I'd wait in the pub if I could but you know they won't let us go in them in this here town. No siree. Good enough to fight in their war but not good enough to spend our money in their pubs." He was silent for a while, kicking his shoe against the ground. Then he said, "Like a cigarette?" and pulled a crumpled packet from inside his jacket, offering it to her, moving a yard or so closer.

"Oh no. No thanks. I don't smoke."

"Good thing." He thrust the packet back into the pocket. "Smokes ain't any good for folks. Coffin nails, they call them." He moved another step closer. "You from round here?"

"Yes." She hesitated for a moment, wondering whether she should move away now, but he seemed so unthreatening, so mild and polite, not like those others around the corner. She wanted to talk to him, if only because no one else talked to people like him. Anyway, she was curious about him. "Where do you come from?"

"Tennessee. You ever been to Tennessee, ma'am?"

"Heavens, no." She was amused to be called ma'am and smiled and saw him blink at her. "To tell you the truth," she said, "I'm not even sure where Tennessee is."

His shoulders relaxed against the wall and he smiled in turn, his teeth dazzling. "Well, I knows how that is, for sure. I hardly knows where this here little town is and I'm right here, ain't I? But I'll tell you something, sister. It is certainly a pleasure to have someone to talk to."

"It must be hard," she sympathized, "to be so far from home." She'd never thought of making such a remark to Carlton.

"Yeah, well, that's war, ain't it?" He stared across the street, looked up and down the road. "Can I say something else, ma'am? You certainly have a pretty smile. My name's Chester. What's yours?"

Gwyneth decided this might be the moment to break off the conversation. She said politely, "It's Gwyneth. Though, honestly, I really should go and look for my friend now. He must be waiting at the station for me," but as she stepped away, he reached out and touched her arm with one finger, as if he just needed to touch someone. She stared down at his hand on her arm, his hand so dark, her arm so white, and he pulled his hand away quickly. "Gwyneth," he said. "That's a pretty name. I like the sound of it. But please don't go, ma'am. I just wants someone to talk to. You don't know how lonely it gets, waiting and waiting for the real war to begin, knowing your days is surely numbered."

"Numbered?"

"Yeah, that's right. Numbered." He shrugged his shoulders

under the army jacket hopelessly, and his face crumpled, almost as if he were going to cry. "Bye bye baby, bye bye. Come all this way over here and for what? To get some Nazi bullet right in the gut, just as soon as we step off them ships. We black boys are no-account soldiers. We're dead meat, that's for sure."

For a moment, Gwyneth found it impossible to say anything, then she blurted out, "Don't say that," and quite suddenly she felt nauseated, faint almost, because this was the first time she'd come face-to-face with someone who thought he might actually get killed in this invasion everyone talked about so lightly.

"Hey, you all right, ma'am? I didn't mean to upset you. You look kinda sick," and he caught hold of her arm, grasping it tightly.

"I'm sorry," she gasped. "I think I do feel a bit funny," and she closed her eyes and sagged back against the wall. It was only the black soldier's hand that seemed to be holding her up, and she was glad he was there, but at that moment, without warning, she was jostled aside, and she opened her eyes to find herself surrounded by the same gang of GIs who'd been in the courtyard. A couple of them shoved the Negro boy away roughly.

"He bothering you?"

She shook her head in surprise. "No. We were just talking."

"You sure?"

"I'm sure."

But they didn't seem to want to listen to her. Three or four of them pushed the black soldier hard against the wall, flattening him against it, grabbing and pulling at his uniform jacket; one of them had his hands around the boy's slender neck, and two had hold of his arms, and they were all glaring at him, jaws set, faces angry and flushed. She saw his eyes roll in alarm. "I weren't doing nothing," he stammered.

"Damn nigger," one of them growled, and his voice was low

and threatening. "We saw you touching her. Keep your filthy hands off the lady."

"But he wasn't doing anything," Gwyneth protested. "I told you, we were just talking."

"Yeah? But you wouldn't talk to us, would you? What are you, some kind of nigger lover?" She had no idea what they could mean, and quite suddenly, without any warning, the men around the black boy started hitting him, hard thudding punches that knocked the air out of him in great wheezing sighs. Gwyneth heard the crunch of bone on bone and was terrified.

"Don't," she screamed. "Stop it, stop it," but it seemed she was only making it worse, because they didn't stop, just kept on hitting and hitting him in a kind of mad frenzy that lasted until he slid down the wall and lay on the ground, his hands over his head. One of the soldiers slung a boot at the side of his head and Gwyneth saw blood spurt from his mouth. She screamed again.

Then there were other people, running from around the corner, and thank God, one of them was Carlton. He yelled, "Hey, what the hell's going on here?" and as he ran towards the melee, she threw herself at him. "Make them stop, Carlton. Make them stop," and it seemed that once the GIs caught sight of his officer's uniform, they did stop, drawing away from the inert heap on the ground.

"He was bothering her," one of them said. "He had his hands on her."

"He wasn't bothering me," she cried. "He wasn't. We were only talking."

As she attempted to kneel down beside the boy, Carlton put his arms around her waist and pulled her away. "Don't get involved," he hissed in her ear. "I'll get you out of here."

"But we have to do something! Look at him, poor thing. Look at the blood. It's all over his head. My God! Carlton! We've got to do something for him." She could hear herself screaming and crying, frightened and hysterical, out of control.

"Don't worry," Carlton said calmly. "The MPs will take care of it."

A crowd gathered in a circle, some servicemen, some townspeople, and for a moment everyone just stood there, staring at the boy on the ground, the blood gushing from his mouth and his head, staining the pavement. They looked from him to Gwyneth and she sobbed, "They just started hitting him, for no reason. No reason. He wasn't doing anything. We were just talking." She was trying to make them understand, had to keep repeating the same thing over and over, and she looked around to point her finger at the attackers. But they were gone, disappeared, melted away in the crowd. "You saw them, Carlton, didn't you?"

She couldn't believe such a thing could have happened, so fast, so brutal, so unnecessary, couldn't believe Carlton was trying to drag her away, was doing nothing to help the injured boy. When she tried to look back, she saw men kneeling beside him. He lay very still at the foot of the wall.

"Hush now, Gwyneth," Carlton was saying, his arms tight around her. "It's better not to think about it. They'll get him to the field hospital. He'll be all right. Don't worry about it. It's not your fault. You don't understand about these things. Some of the men feel very strongly about a white girl and a black boy. It's not something you people here can understand."

He was pulling her further and further away, and her knees were buckling under her, hardly holding her up. Her stomach churned and she felt faint and nauseated again and suddenly she knew she was going to be sick. She managed to loosen Carlton's grip and right there, right on the street in front of him and in front of all those other people, she threw up, retching miserably, humilatingly, disgustingly. And then she did faint, slipping soundlessly to the ground, and Carlton had to pick her up and carry her home, through the streets of Clarrach, back to her mother in the flat about the shop, and everyone knew about it, about the black soldier who was beaten to death in the streets of Clarrach, and how it was Gwyneth Griffith's fault because she'd led him on.

Twenty-Two

If the phone rang in the night for Rhys, some odd instinct usually woke Gwyneth immediately beforehand, as if her nerve endings were, after all, alert to the demands of his profession. But that night, as her eyes opened in the darkness, she could hear the steady and regular rhythm of Rhys's breathing beside her and she wasn't expecting the phone to ring. She knew it was her conscience that was scratching her awake, the memory of the hurt in Tim Bruce's eyes when she'd spilled out that whole wretched saga. Why in heaven's name had she needed to burden him with it, the old, old story of the abandoned baby and the dead soldier? She'd kept quiet about it all for so long, why on earth had she needed to speak now? To Carlton Bruce's son, of all people?

Then the telephone did start ringing, clamoring loudly on the other side of the bed, as if it was after all the presentiment of its summons that had disturbed her. Not the shame of confession, not the fear of having done harm to Tim Bruce. To herself.

Rhys's easy breathing ceased abruptly and he lay very still for a moment, then he fumbled for the phone and muttered, "Dr. Edwards," and was silent for a long while. Gwyneth wondered, as she often did, if he'd fallen back to sleep.

"All right. I'll be there in less than ten minutes. Hang on. Keep her as quiet as possible."

Dropping the receiver back on the hook, Rhys fell out of bed and Gwyneth reached to snap the light on. He was already dragging his shirt over his head, the tie still in a knot under the collar, the way he always left it when he undressed. He blinked at the light. "Sorry. Did the phone wake you?"

"I wasn't asleep. What's happened?"

"Eileen Williams. The midwife's says she's in full blown labor but the baby's not due for at least another six weeks. We may be able to slow it down."

Gwyneth looked at the clock on the bedside table. "It's one A.M., Rhys."

"Yes, well, unfortunately, babies aren't much good at telling time. Go back to sleep, *cariad*. There's no sense in both of us being awake." He leaned over the bed, brushed his lips against hers, and switched off the lamp.

She heard his footsteps running down the stairs, the sound of the car accelerating on the gravel, pausing at the gate, fading away down the hill. Silence descended on the house once again. Poor Rhys. Though he didn't seem to mind, seemed to relish it, in fact, jumping out of bed almost eagerly, running so lightly down the stairs. Was he glad to escape, even in the middle of the night, go and find someone he could really help, someone to whom he could make a difference? Was she such a weight around his neck, the proverbial ball and chain, a wife who asked for more than he was able to give? She'd tried not to demand too much of him, had wanted to be content, not let him know she was disappointed, but something was slipping away from both of them, from her and from Rhys. It was the promise of different things to come that was slipping away. There was nothing different to come. This was what it was. He had his patients and she had her paintings. That was it. They would grow old together, she and Rhys. Alone together. Once she'd believed that would be enough. She'd learn to live with it.

Tossing in the bed, eyes opening and closing again, Gwyneth pulled the covers over her head. Why, why, why had she told that story? Had she been hoping for some sort of forgiveness, some sort of redemption? Tim Bruce was the last person she should have told. Though, of course, she understood it was exactly *because* he was who he was, Carlton's son, that the words had spewed out of her in a dense cloud like an eruption of volcanic ash. She'd done exactly what she'd sworn not to do, visit the sins of the father on the son. God knew how he would cope with it.

Wide awake now, Gwyneth fixed her eyes on the bedroom window, at the faint glimmer of moonlight in the gap between the curtains, imagined Rhys arriving at Eileen Williams's house, delivering her baby, everyone congratulating everyone else, mother and father, doctor and midwife. They'd sit around drinking tea, telling each other how wonderful they were, how wonderful the baby was, until Rhys decided it was time to get in his car and drive back home again to crash asleep in the bed beside her so that he could get up again tomorrow and go to the surgery and see all those other people who thought he was wonderful. Everyone thought Rhys was wonderful. Mavis thought so. Even she, Gwyneth, thought so.

She'd never get back to sleep. Throwing aside the bedcovers and pulling on her dressing gown, she crept along the landing to the bathroom, very conscious of the closed door at the other end, of Tim Bruce asleep in the spare room, the stranger in the house who wasn't a stranger. She wanted to tell him, right now, how sorry she was, how mortified, for relating that old history, but the damage was done and she had done it and that was that. Tomorrow she might be able to apologize, if he'd let her. Tomorrow she might work on his portrait. If he'd let her do that.

In the bathroom, she opened the door of the medicine cupboard and searched among the containers for the sleeping pills she tried not to take these days.

In the mirror, Gwyneth saw her hair wild about her head, like a madwoman's, put her hands up to smooth it back. She stared at her own face, at her eyes, the shadows beneath them, the lines flaring away from the corners, and pulled the skin under her chin taut. One day soon this flesh would be flaccid and sagging. One day soon. She'd never considered herself beautiful, had never been completely convinced she was, but now she didn't think she could bear to melt into wrinkles and sagging skin. Except how could it not happen? It's what happened to everyone. It was said to be worse, if once you'd been considered beautiful, to look into the mirror every day and see the steady deterioration.

She shook a couple of the blue and green capsules into the palm of her hand. If she took a dozen, would she sleep forever? Two dozen? How many would it take? Gwyneth emptied all the capsules into her hand and counted them. Fifteen.

She would never finish his portrait. It was over, the painting of the faces. Finished. Done. Not completed. Just over and done with.

Then she heard a clumping noise along the landing and knew that Tim Bruce was also awake, and was heading for the bathroom. Quickly, she dropped the pills back into the container, washed two down with water, cracked open the door. He stared at her through the opening, thick blond hair tousled, eyes bleary, swaying on the crutches, wearing only his undershorts.

Gwyneth opened the door wider. "Did the phone wake you? I'm sorry. Rhys had to go out on a call."

"I wasn't asleep. What time is it?"

"After one o'clock. Why weren't you asleep?" She was whispering, though there was no need to whisper. "I'm going downstairs to make some warm milk. Do you want some?"

"No thanks. I hate warm milk."

As Gwyneth stepped out onto the landing, the light from the bathroom went streaming into his eyes and he flinched away from it. She reached behind the door to switch it off and then everywhere was too dark, so she switched it on again. He didn't move and she tried to squeeze past him, sidling against the wall, clutching the neck of her robe tightly. "Tim, I want to say how sorry I am for spilling out all that old history. There was no need to have told you, no need for you to have heard it. I apologize. Will you forgive me?"

He squinted at her. "Forgive *you?* Surely you're not the one who needs to be forgiven."

"It was all so long ago. Life has gone on. You won't say anything to your father, will you?"

Pulling himself up on the crutches, very tall and straight, Tim stared down at her. "Damn it, Gwyneth, you think I should just forget it? Forget you had a child? Forget you were fifteen, for God's sake. That's statutory rape, isn't it? You think I should forget my own father ran away from the scene of a crime? From murder?" He banged a crutch on the floor, and all along the landing the pictures shook on the walls. "He's supposed to uphold the law. He teaches that stuff at the university, for God's sake. He's taken an oath."

Gwyneth regretted every word she'd spoken and would have taken every one of them back if she could, but somehow it seemed absurd to be standing at the bathroom door in the middle of the night, whispering about it. "I'm going to get some milk. I'll make you a cup. Maybe we can both sleep then."

"How can I sleep?"

Brushing past her into the bathroom, he shut the door in her face. She hesitated outside for another moment, then went down to the kitchen and heated milk in a saucepan, as though she was doing something useful, as one made tea in an emergency. Not to cure anything, just to be doing something. She placed two mugs on a tray, and some sugar, because warm milk and sugar did help you to sleep, that's what her mother always said, and she carried the tray back up the stairs. The door to his room was ajar, and when she knocked lightly and walked in, he was sitting on the edge of the bed, just sitting there, the battered old crutches beside him, his elbows on his knees, his face in his hands.

She said. "Perhaps it would be better if we talked about it. Tim, it wasn't your father who did harm to that Negro soldier."

His face was haggard and drawn, years older, no longer cheerful and eager. "He didn't do anything to help him either, did he?"

She put the tray on the bedside table and because there was nowhere else to sit, sat down beside Tim on the bed. "He helped me. Perhaps that was his first concern. And we don't know what happened afterwards, do we? The next day, everyone was confined to the camp and then everyone was gone. Off to France. Where so many of them died. You have to remember how many of those young men died, Tim. Perhaps he told the authorities what happened and who did what. Perhaps it was all taken care of before they left and perhaps there wasn't time before they went off to die. It was a military matter, people said, not a civilian matter, and anyway there was no one left to answer for it. As far as Clarrach was concerned, the incident went away with the Americans, as though it never happened." She paused, thought about it. "Except for those who chose not to forget, of course."

Tim moaned, in some sort of pain. "Now I understand why he never came back. If he'd come back to Clarrach, the whole wretched story would surely have been resurrected." He thumped a fist on his knee and threw the crutches to one side, crashing them to the floor. "You don't understand how it is with my father and me. I've spent half my life apologizing to him for those few minor transgressions that he makes so much of, that little bit of pot smoking, the protest marches, the night in jail. It feels as though we've spent years arguing about this damn war, the rights and the wrongs of it. Wrong as far as I'm concerned. And all the time he was hiding something far worse. He, Carlton Bruce, holier than holy. So damned upright, so damned hypocritical. Now he'll have to explain himself to me." Tim kneaded the flesh of his forehead and rubbed his hand over his eyes. "It's as though I've become the father and he the son. To tell you the truth, I don't think I can handle it."

Gwyneth rested a hand on his arm lightly, and then she put both arms around him and held his head in her hands. The thick springing hair rested against her neck and she could feel his bare body warm and strong and firm under her hands. "You don't *have* to say anything. After all, it isn't always wisest to tell the truth, the whole truth, nothing but the truth. Sometimes it's wiser just to keep quiet." She wished to heaven she'd heeded her own advice.

"Shit, oh shit." His voice was muffled against her shoulder. "How can I pretend I never heard it? I can't do that. Somehow I've got to face it."

She patted his back mindlessly, thoughtlessly, like a mother patting a child, and Tim pulled away from her, his mouth set into a grim line.

"I've made up my mind. I'll go off to my own war. I'll stop thinking of ways to get out of it. If I go off to this stupid war, I'll be able to speak to him man to man. In his day, he didn't have the luxury of deciding whether he was fighting for the right cause. Easy now to pretend I've been making a moral choice, as if I'm more righteous than he is. Perhaps after all I'm merely a coward. I don't want to be thought of as a coward. Especially by my father. Especially now I know he acted like one."

Gwyneth looked into his face, such a familiar face, the green-gray eyes, the strong planes of his cheekbones, the fading bruise above the blond eyebrows. Everything about him was so familiar now. So dear. "Oh no," she whispered. "Please don't go to the war, Tim. Please. For my sake."

He was staring into her eyes. "For your sake? I'd do anything for your sake, Gwyneth. Anything. Because . . . because I'm crazy about you. Right from the first moment I saw you." He grabbed hold of her shoulders with both hands and drew her closer so his breath was against her mouth, clutching her so tightly that the breath was squeezed out of her. "So beautiful," he muttered. "The most beautiful woman I ever laid eyes on."

For a second, one brief second, she made a halfhearted effort to resist, and just as quickly all wish for resistance fled away. She knew suddenly that this was the answer to some unlikely, forgotten hope, to be holding this warm young body in her arms once again, as if all those years had never passed, as if all those consequences had never happened. As if she were young again, in love the way she'd once been. As if she were being given a second chance. Until this moment, she hadn't completely understood that she'd been waiting for this forever, the chance to love someone all over again and get it right this time. As the strong arms enfolded her, it was as though she was drowning in some ocean, battered by a great wave crashing over her head, and she gasped for air and heard someone moaning, the sound coming from a great distance, as if it didn't belong to her, heard her own voice crying aloud, "Yes, yes, oh yes. Please. Please."

His arms were crushing her and he was drawing her down on the bed impatiently, dragging away her robe and running his hands over her body, kissing her, licking her, devouring her, and then he lifted himself on top of her, pulling her up, up into him, and in a moment he had entered her, as though this was meant to be, as though they had both been waiting forever for this moment. Which she knew was true, from the first second they'd set eyes on each other. She had looked at him in the hallway of the house in that very first moment, seen the sunshine on his hair, the smile on his face, and the deep sound of his voice, and had known, known she would end up making love to him. Sinfully, wonderfully, treacherously. It came so rarely in a lifetime, this urgency, this deep and unreasonable pleasure, this frenzy, this abandonment.

Drifting away, Gwyneth fell over an edge into some deep dark dream, a dream that was somehow too familiar, too sinful and erotic, the kind of dream she never allowed herself to have anymore. She had to force herself to struggle out of it, deliberately wake herself, but it was difficult, her mind too fuzzy, her body too satiated. Slowly, slowly, she rose to the surface out of the haze and found she was stretched out on the narrow bed alongside a naked male body and for a moment couldn't imagine where she was, what had happened. She gazed at the peaceful face on the pillow, the naked body beside her, the white cast below his knee, and was awake, suddenly, shockingly. Dear God!

Rhys! She hadn't given Rhys a single thought. Hadn't given anyone or anything a thought, had just wallowed in this glorious, wilfull lovemaking, this wonderful, awful, sinful desire. Now her heart plummeted within her, like the proverbial stone, thudding in her chest, banging against her ribs. "Oh my God! What have I done? Tim! Rhys! Oh God, forgive me."

Tim Bruce lifted his head, blinked and smiled at her, and gradually the beatific smile faded and the expression on his face changed to dismay. He sat bolt upright. "Rhys! Whatever are we going to say to Rhys?"

They stared at each other, at the bed that reeked of sweat and lust. The enormity of her own conduct shattered Gwyneth, and she fell off the bed, scrabbled around for her robe, hurried her arms into it, tightened the belt around her waist. But she felt dizzy and slightly sick and the room seemed to be swaying around her and she remembered the sleeping pills. If only she could blame it all on the sleeping pills. How long had she been there? How long had she slept? Oh God. Her mouth wouldn't work right, the words difficult to form. "We aren't going to say a word to Rhys. Of course not. You think he'd want to know?"

Tim reached out with his arms and she shook him away.

"What was I thinking? This never happened, you understand? It never should have happened. You know it and I know it. You'll be on your way soon and I'll be left here with Rhys and life will go on in the same old way, so it really wouldn't be a good idea to say anything at all, would it?"

Tim swung his legs over the side of the bed, clutching the sheet around his body. "Goddamn it, Gwyneth. How can you say forget it? You keep saying it. I can't forget just like that. Especially this. Don't tell me you can forget this, too."

"I'm going to pretend it didn't happen."

"Well, I'm no good at pretending."

Stepping away giddily, she had to put out a hand to support herself against the wall. "How very American of you, Tim. How very youthful. As you get older, you'll acquire the trick."

His face flushed and he raised his voice, almost yelling at her. "Is that what you always do? Pretend?"

"Doesn't everyone?"

"No, Gwyneth. No. Not everyone. I wasn't pretending. Is that what you've been doing all your life? Pretending? Is that all this was to you? The way you made love to me? Just some sort of pretense, some game?"

She said desperately, "Tim. I love Rhys. And he loves me. We're married. Married." She wanted to cry. "For better or for worse. Maybe one day you'll understand such things."

He groaned. "What is there to understand? What would Rhys do if he found out? Aren't you worried about that?" Sinking back against the pillows, collapsing against them, Tim covered his head with his hands. "I'll leave tomorrow. I should have gone before. I should never have come."

The room was swaying dangerously now, but she managed to smile sadly, and she leaned forward and brushed her fingers against his head. "Ah well, *cariad,* that might very well be true."

He didn't look up. "*Cariad.* That's means lover, doesn't it? At least you said it once. At least."

Twenty-Three

The delivery turned out to be a breech, fraught with peril, a procedure Rhys normally wouldn't have attempted in the home, but by the time he got to the house, the mother was already in the second stage and it was too late to send her to the hospital. Placing two hands on her belly, he felt the frequent drum-tight contractions and the baby's position and tried not to sweat. He'd taken care of this young woman, Eileen Williams, for all of this pregnancy and her previous one, and hadn't foreseen any problems. Now the baby was at least six weeks premature and had flipped in the uterus.

The midwife pulled Rhys aside. "I called as soon as I got here. She'd only had a few contractions. She seems to have gone into precipitate labor. There wasn't a chance to turn the baby."

"Give her plenty of trilene. We'll have to try and deliver it this way." He washed his hands hurriedly, snapped on a pair of gloves, reached in and felt the thin rim of a fully dilated cervix, the baby's bottom against his fingers, the pressure from the contractions. "We'll have to try the forceps."

The midwife carried equipment for emergencies, drums of sterile instruments and gowns, suction for the post-delivery, bags of IV fluid; he had drugs in his bag, but they always hoped never to have to use any of it. Now there was no choice. While Eileen breathed the inadequate anesthetic, Rhys quickly injected novocaine into her perineum, made a large episiotomy, slid the curved forceps up until he judged the baby's head was between the forceps, closed them, held them there, pulled gently and firmly and prayed. Normally he didn't pray, and never out loud, but now he repeated over and over inside his head, Please, please let it be all right. Please don't let the head be stuck. Don't let it come too quickly. Please God.

The baby came slithering out, a poor struggling infant, not ready for the world, limp and hardly breathing. The midwife snatched him up, sucked out his airway, and breathed into the tiny mouth, and at last he gasped for air, turned pink instead of blue, and uttered thin, piercing cries.

"A boy," Rhys announced to Eileen. "A boy." As he massaged her belly to help the placenta on its way, the nurse placed the child in her arms and Eileen wept and panted with relief. But afterwards, when they examined the baby more closely, they discovered the tiny defect. An imperforate anus. No opening from the rectum.

Rhys pointed to the dimpled skin in the baby's bottom where there should have been a hole. "It's not a big defect, you understand, but maybe that's why he arrived early. It needs to be taken care of. Soon. Surgery, I mean. Unfortunately, that little hole in one's bottom is another of those things we take for granted but which are essential to life."

Eileen and her husband stared blankly at each other, at the baby. "But will he be all right?"

An eternal question from parents. Unanswerable, really. How to say how all right a baby would ever be? Rhys tried not to make heavy weather of it. "With any luck, they'll only have to make a little nick in the skin and then everything will be just fine."

"Well, thank the Lord it's nothing more serious," Eileen said, and Rhys didn't tell her it could be a whole lot more serious. Plenty of time for those kind of explanations later. If the rectum stopped too far short of the anus, there'd be multiple reconstructive surgeries. He wasn't happy with the outcome of the night's work. A premature baby and a breech presentation and an imperforate anus. Breech delivery meant the head hadn't time to mold correctly for the birth passage so there could be damage to delicate cerebral membranes. Prematurity meant unformed lungs. Imperforate anus meant surgery. That everything had seemed perfectly normal beforehand didn't make Rhys feel any better.

Eileen and her husband kept apologizing for dragging him out in the middle of the night, which only made him feel worse. "We'd no idea it would happen so quickly," they said. "Should we have known? The first one took a lot longer."

"Who knows why babies want to arrive in the middle of the night? In a way, it's more convenient for me. At least I wasn't busy doing anything else."

Except sleeping, of course.

Rewrapping the baby in its warm blankets, Rhys peered into its premature face and handed him back to Eileen. "Mothers," he said reassuringly, "are the best medicine for babies."

If only it were that simple. If only being held in a mother's arms could solve all the problems. There were so many things that could go wrong. He never delivered a baby without marveling at the miracle of nature that usually got the bits and pieces of complicated anatomy joined up and arranged in symbiotic harmony; the cells that divided and redivided and ended up as a perfect human being, the genes and chromosomes that somehow organized themselves into a correct and specific order. And it all started with a tiny sperm and a tiny egg. Usually all that was needed was a good sperm and a good egg.

Pity he didn't have any decent sperm himself.

As a rule, Rhys didn't allow himself to dwell on that particular aspect of nature. Some things were the way they were and there was nothing to be done about it. The trivial and somewhat ridiculous infection of mumps, *epidemic parotitis,* had ruined his own sperm production. He hadn't even known about it until after he and Gwyneth were married, until they wondered why no baby came along. When he did think about it, he comforted himself with the thought that no child of his could come into the world with those defects that made hell of their lives. Cleft lip and palate, Down's syndrome, spina bifida. He'd seen them all, grieved over them all. At the very least, a child should start out intact; God knew there were enough hurdles in life without the curse of congenital defects. He couldn't bear the thought that any child of his and Gwyneth's would be less than perfect. So perhaps it was just as well they couldn't have children. He'd accepted the fact. He wasn't entirely sure if Gwyneth had. She never spoke of it anymore.

They sat around in the bedroom in the middle of the night, mother and father, doctor and nurse, drinking the inevitable tea, waiting for the ambulance. Rhys earnestly desired a stiff scotch. Eileen cuddled the baby and attempted to suckle him, though he was too feeble to hang onto her breast, and she gazed down at him with the familiar new mother mixture of pride and satisfaction and concern.

His own wife would never wear that expression on her face.

He explained to Eileen, "You'll have to go with him to the hospital and stay with him for a couple of days. They'll put him in an incubator to keep him warm and to make sure he's getting enough oxygen and you can talk to the surgeon and see what they plan to do."

"That's all right, then," Eileen said and clutched the baby closer.

Patients seemed to accept without question whatever he told them, as if he had all the answers, which he didn't, of course. And though Rhys never lied or made up answers, he didn't always tell the complete truth straight away because, in his opinion, the bald and complete truth could be a burdensome commodity.

At three-thirty A.M., the ambulance arrived, mother and baby were packed off with the midwife for the long ride, father went back to bed, and Rhys got in his car to drive home. He never allowed himself the luxury of exhaustion on the way home, not until the car was parked in front of the house and he was opening the front door, then the waves of weariness would overcome him and he'd just manage to stumble up the stairs and fall into bed. As quietly as possible. No reason to disturb Gwyneth when he came home, no reason for both of them to be awake in the middle of the night, but usually she'd stir when he got into bed, turn sleepily, ask how things had gone.

Tonight she made absolutely no movement, sleeping as though comatose, sprawled out, arms flung wide, mouth slightly open. He prodded her gently to make room for him, and she curled up on her side and muttered something incomprehensible. Rhys warmed himself against the warmth of her body, better than an electric blanket, and thought he should have showered because the smell of amniotic fluid and afterbirth still lingered around him. He fell asleep immediately.

When he opened his eyes it was broad daylight, and Gwyneth was shaking his shoulder, standing by the bed with a cup of tea in her hand. "You must have been very late. What time did you get home?"

He groaned. "Oh Lord, I don't know. Past four, I suppose. What time is it now?"

"Eight-thirty. I let you sleep as long as possible."

Grabbing the cup from her, Rhys crashed out of bed, slurping the tea down as he headed for the bathroom. "Dammit, Gwyneth, don't I always tell you not to let me sleep late? Late, late. I hate being late for morning surgery. I never get caught up."

Following him to the bathroom, she leaned against the doorjamb. "You work too hard, Rhys. You don't do anything except work. Isn't it time you took a break?"

He slathered his face with shaving cream, scraped the razor across it, muttering impatiently, "Damn nuisance, shaving. I'd save at least ten minutes in the mornings if I didn't have to shave," and then he nicked himself with the razor and drew blood and swore. "Damnation!"

"A break," Gwyneth repeated. "A holiday. We could go away somewhere together. Somewhere nice and warm, where you could relax, not be disturbed by the phone all the time. I mean it, Rhys. You need a holiday. And so do I."

"You?" Turning away from the mirror, Rhys stared at her. "You never want a holiday. You always say you don't want to go anywhere."

"Well, I've changed my mind."

He flung down the shaving brush. "Well, if that's what you want, I'll have to look into it, won't I? Why don't you arrange something? Italy, why not? Or maybe the south of France. Paris? Wherever. I'll talk to Mavis. She knows who's booked for when. She'll have to find someone to cover the practice."

"I'm not asking for myself, Rhys. And while we're on the subject, what about a partner? Have you ever thought about a partner? Then there'd always be someone to cover for you."

Splashing his face with cold water, Rhys rubbed it vigorously with the towel and dashed past her into the bedroom. "Since when have you become so interested in my practice?"

Gwyneth picked the towel off the floor. "You can't keep up this pace, Rhys. Nights without sleep. Always on call. A treadmill, a never-ending rat race. What sort of life do we have?"

Snatching up the clothes he'd worn in the night, he struggled into them, cursing. "Ah, that's the rub, isn't it, being married to the local GP? Not quite the glamorous life you were used to, is it? Don't say I didn't warn you beforehand."

Gwyneth's voice went flat and cool. "Yes, you did. Of course you did," and she turned away and headed downstairs. Rhys realized his fraying temper had spilled over on to her. Too little sleep. She was right. He probably could do with a holiday. He probably could do with a partner. And perhaps Gwyneth could do with a holiday, too. She did look rather pale this morning, dark circles below her eyes, cheeks more hollow. Sometimes he forgot she, too, was wakened by the phone in the night. Sometimes he worried about her.

As he snatched a piece of toast from the breakfast table he said, "I'll look into the holiday thing. I will," and he pulled on his jacket. "Where's the boy? Not up yet?"

Gwyneth stared around the kitchen vaguely, as though she wasn't quite sure who he was talking about. "It's only late for you, Rhys. Not for the likes of him."

"Ah yes, the joys of youth. Once I could sleep like that. Until midday sometimes. Oh God, to be young like that again. I might take him with me on my rounds again this afternoon. He seems interested. And he's good company. Doesn't talk too much but seems to take it all in."

"He says he's going to leave today."

Rhys paused in his flight to the door. "He did? When did he say that? I'm not at all sure that ankle is fit to travel on. I want to check that cast before he sets off for God knows where. Bring him down to the surgery, will you? Don't let him leave without getting it checked." He opened the door. "Anyway, I wouldn't want him to leave without saying good-bye to him."

He was surprised to be disappointed that the boy was leaving. He'd liked having him around. After all, it had been good to have a stranger in the house.

Twenty-Four

Because Rhys was late getting to the surgery, the waiting room was inevitably stacked with patients and he was immediately even more irritable and aggrieved. Gwyneth knew very well what time he should be there; he didn't ask much of her, for God's sake, just a meal occasionally and to be woken at the correct hour of the morning. She could at least manage that.

After the surgery and before leaving on rounds, he called the hospital about Eileen's baby, a long, drawn-out process requiring persistence and patience. As he waited, he scribbled at the forms that constantly cluttered his desk and when the house surgeon came on the phone, he, too, sounded distracted and harrassed.

"The Williams baby? Came in last night? Let's see, we've scheduled him for a simple colostomy later this afternoon. But if there's too much rectum missing, he'll have to go to the pediatric surgeons down in Cardiff. We'll let you know how it goes."

Rhys had been hoping for a definite diagnosis, some reassurance that all was going to be well. His early morning mood grew more sour. He didn't linger over the house visits or stay for the usual chats with the relatives, and didn't remember until the last visit that Gwyneth was supposed to bring Tim Bruce to see him. Impatient with himself, Rhys drove back to the surgery, peered round the door into the waiting room, ready with some sort of excuse. The waiting room was deserted.

Mavis came bustling into his room with a tray of coffee and his favorite chocolate biscuits.

"Did my wife show up with that American boy?"

"The American boy? No, I haven't seen sight nor sign of him. Or Mrs. Edwards, either." Mavis's careful nurse's face betrayed a flicker of curiosity. "Is he still with you, then? I imagined he'd be well on his way by now."

"Did she call?"

"Haven't heard a word."

Rhys ate half a chocolate biscuit, picked up the phone, and dialed the house. No answer. He caught sight of a new pile of forms on his desk and pushed them aside with one hand impatiently. "If there's one thing I detest about the NHS, it's all this paper nonsense. I'm going to take the afternoon off. Late nights wreak havoc on me these days," and he yawned ostentatiously to prove his point. "Gwyneth thinks we should have a holiday. I don't particularly care for holidays myself, but I suppose if she thinks we should, then we should. It'll mean finding a locum, though. Call that place in Cardiff, will you? See if anyone's available. And when."

Mavis clasped her hands over the starched apron front and regarded him with maternal solicitude. "A holiday sounds like a very good idea, Dr. Edwards. When did you last go away?" She rustled around the desk to tidy up the heap of forms. "Don't worry about these. I can't imagine what they possibly do with all these little bits of paper anyway."

"They pay me with them, that's what they do."

"Yes, well, maybe it was better in the old days, when the doctor was paid directly. At least we knew where we were in the old days."

"Oh, come on, Mavis. You know very well it was always a struggle for the poor damn patients to pay anything at all. Take Eileen Williams and her baby. You think she and Billy could ever afford what that baby's going to need? The operations, the long-term follow-up? It's going to be a hell of a burden for them anyway, without being in debt for the rest of their lives. In the good old days their baby would probably have been allowed to quietly expire. Is that what you'd prefer?"

Mavis set her lips in a tight line. "Of course not. I remember how it was better than you do, doctor. I've been here longer than you. People would bring eggs or butter or chickens when they didn't have money. We'd get home-cured bacon and often rabbit, before the myxomatosis." Her frown changed to a fond smile, as if to forgive him. "Your father couldn't abide rabbit. He said that if he saw one more dead rabbit in the waiting room, he'd personally throw it off Carew Head."

"There you are, then. But I wouldn't say no to a nice fresh rabbit now and then." Rhys knew the patients still brought little gifts, small offerings of gratitude, but unlike his father and his grandfather, he didn't have to live off such offerings. No, these days were much better than the old ones.

Mavis kept fiddling around on his desk, straightening the blotter, tidying the in-and-out tray, and she peered sideways at him. "I know it isn't my place to say so, Dr. Edwards, but isn't it time you found someone to share the work? It's not just a holiday you need, it's another doctor. The practice keeps getting bigger and bigger. Too much for one man." Little spots of color flared in her papery cheeks. "If you don't mind my saying so."

He did mind, actually, but he was intrigued at hearing the same suggestion twice in one day. "Well, Mavis, you might be interested to know that's exactly what my wife suggested this very morning. Are you two hatching something up between you?"

The color ran higher in her face. "Mrs. Edwards and I don't hatch things up between us. No, doctor, that's just my own personal opinion."

"Partners can be a lot of damn trouble, Mavis. You don't really want a stranger coming in and changing the way we run things, do you?"

"You could find a nice young doctor straight out of training. Someone who wouldn't mind being up all night."

Rhys laughed bitterly. "Oh, good luck in finding someone who doesn't mind being up all night! The young ones need more sleep than I do. Look at that boy who's staying with us. He's always sleeping late." He swallowed the rest of the coffee in a gulp, picked up his bag and his jacket. "I don't care for change, Mavis, that's the truth. I like things to go on in the same old way." He paused with his hand on the door. "But, you know, having that boy around the house has made me wonder if change might not be all bad. Is it because he's from the land of constant reinvention? Or is it merely because he's young? Maybe I don't see enough young people." Rhys shrugged and yawned again. "Anyway, I'm going home now to rest my ancient bones for the afternoon."

As he made his way out through the waiting room, half hoping Gwyneth might have materialized with the boy, he was struck for the first time in a long while by the shabbiness of the room, the ill-assorted chairs, the dingy paint. "This place could do with a bit of a change, for instance. It's pretty dreary, isn't it? Why don't we get it painted and smartened up?"

Mavis looked around in faint surprise, as though also noticing the waiting room for the first time. "Nobody ever complains."

"But that's the trouble, isn't it? People don't complain enough. I don't complain enough and neither do you, never mind the patients."

"As a matter of fact, Mrs. Edwards said something about it the other day. Talked about new furniture."

"Did she now? She's taking a lot of interest in my practice these days. And did she suggest how to pay for it?"

Mavis said doubtfully, "I suppose I could ask Richards the painters. They might do it in a weekend, so as not to disturb us too much."

"Good. That's settled then." Rhys was suddenly cheered with all the decisions he was making. New paint. A locum. Maybe he'd even talk to Gwyneth about new furniture. She'd be good at that. "Call me if anything urgent turns up. Otherwise, I'll be back at five."

"I'll try not to disturb you, doctor. You need your rest."

Mavis was a good stick. Forebearing, competent. Everyone should have a Mavis in his life. If she thought he needed help, then he probably did. But the practice had been his father's and his grandfather's before that, passing down through the family in the traditional way of country doctors, and Rhys had to answer to no one. A distant and impersonal Ministry of Health left day-to-day details to the local doctor. He didn't want some young upstart coming in and telling him how to run things. Because that's what would happen. New brooms always swept clean. Though eventually, he supposed, sooner or later, he'd have to do it. Sooner rather than later, if Gwyneth and Mavis had their way. Maybe they *were* conspiring against him. No, that was ridiculous. Gwyneth wouldn't ever do anything behind his back.

Rhys drove out of town, puffy white clouds scudding across a pale blue sky, the Irish Sea shining and empty, the cliffs and bays sharply delineated in the bright light. He wished he had energy for something more exciting on this unexpectedly free afternoon other than just to go home and put his feet up. Not so long ago, he'd have taken the dinghy around the headland and along the coast for a mile or so. Get in a bit of fishing. The mackerel were running at this time of the year. Nothing like fresh mackerel. But the dinghy had been hauled at the quay since last winter and he hadn't taken it out once this year. Gwyneth was right. All he did was run on a treadmill of his own choosing. He wasn't unhappy with the treadmill, didn't mind the hours, couldn't imagine doing anything else. How on earth would he occupy his time without the constant demands on it? But he supposed it wasn't much fun for Gwyneth. It was a wonder she didn't complain more often. She'd always seemed content enough, drifting along, messing around with her garden and with her painting.

Rhys tried to envisage himself lying on a beach in the south of France. Traipsing around the ruins of Pompeii. The Vatican. The Louvre. He'd be wondering all the time about Eileen Williams's baby or some other baby and mother or someone like old Johnnie Watkins, worrying that his replacement wasn't taking good care of them, doing the right thing for them. Old habits were hard to break.

When he reached the house, the front door was locked. Which was unusual. Rhys couldn't remember when he'd last used the key to open his own front door. If Gwyneth went out, she rarely locked up because no one locked doors in this part of the world. And if she was out, she couldn't have gone far because her car was still in the driveway.

Inside the house all was quiet, the ticking of the grandfather clock loud in the stillness, the fragrance of flowers heavy in the undisturbed air. "Anyone home?" Rhys called out, but he knew no one was there. The house was palpably empty. He wandered through the hallway and into the kitchen, out into the garden at the back. The garden, as always, was green and inviting, warm sun trapped inside the walls, perfumed by lavender and the stocks and roses. Rhys smiled for the first time that day. Beside the back door, under the trellis and a yellow climbing rose, the old striped lounge chair sat as if waiting for him, and he lowered himself into it, stretched his arms and legs, turned his face to the sun. This is the life, he thought. This is what I should do more often. Come home early, put my feet up, sit in the sun, smell the roses.

But this being the month of June in the country of Wales, a cloud soon slipped over the sun and the air cooled, and after a few more minutes Rhys climbed out of the chair and went back inside the house. "Hey, Gwyneth, you here?" It was perfectly obvious she wasn't. Gazing vaguely around the kitchen, he peered in the oven to see what was cooking for lunch, found nothing, sat down at the table and started to read the newspaper. It was full of the death of Robert Kennedy. Rhys chucked the paper aside, depressed by the story, felt oddly abandoned. He'd expected Gwyneth to be home waiting for him. He wasn't only disconcerted to find her missing. He realized he resented her for being missing.

Rhys got up to stand by the window expectantly, as though Gwyneth and the boy might appear at any moment. Where the hell could they be? They couldn't have gone far, not without the car, not with that cast on the boy's leg. Then the shadow of a cloud raced across the roof of the old barn and it occurred to him they just might be out there in the studio. Not likely, of course. Gwyneth never took anyone into her studio, but Rhys strode purposefully out of the house anyway, through the gate in the wall and along the path around the side.

The two halves of the door into the studio were firmly closed. Rhys contemplated the door. It was painted a pale washed blue, the color of doors in Provence. Perhaps Gwyneth fancied herself as Cezanne or Monet? He found it difficult to take this painting business seriously, one reason he never pressed to see her paintings, because what would he say about them? The truth was that Gwyneth didn't have enough to do. If she had children . . . it would be different. If they had children, everything would be different.

He rarely came here, had never been inside since the barn was converted to a studio, found the very word "studio" pretentious. Nevertheless, Gwyneth considered it her place of work. If you could call what Gwyneth did work. She didn't come inspecting his place of work, so he didn't inspect hers. Though he had to admit he was curious. She seemed to be taking more interest in his line of work those days, so maybe it was time for him to take an interest in hers. Standing before the closed door, Rhys was suddenly impatient to see inside, as if inside there might be a revelation.

He rapped on the door with his knuckles, and without waiting lifted the latch.

A sudden burst of sunlight shot through the clear skylights, blinding him for a second, and it wasn't until another cloud raced across to dim the sun once more that he realized Gwyneth was at the far end of the space, in a long blue smock that reached to her ankles, standing before a tall easel, staring intently at it. "Gwyneth, you *are* here!" he said, and pushed the door wider. She turned her head at the sound of his voice and peered at him vaguely, as if he were a stranger, as if she inhabited some other world and didn't quite recognize who he was.

She stood in silence, a dripping brush in her hand, her eyes distant and abstracted. The door swung shut behind Rhys, cutting off more light, and as he moved across the concrete floor, he was surprised to see all the stuff accumulated in there. He wondered where it had all come from and when, the sofa and small tables, the upholstered chairs with loose covers, the easel, a tall wooden stool, a long wooden bench cluttered with pots and paint and brushes. He thought he remembered that bench used to be in the garden shed. Somehow he'd assumed it would be bare and uninviting in here, not cozy like this, warm and comfortably furnished. Better than his own waiting room.

"Hey, this isn't bad," he said, stopping to look around. "I decided to come home early. There weren't many calls. I tried to phone but there was no answer. I thought you were bringing the boy to the surgery."

Gwyneth shook her head slowly. "He's gone."

"Gone? What do you mean gone?"

"I took him to the train."

"Good God, Gwyneth, he can't manage with that damn cast. I wanted to check it. What were you thinking of, to let him go?"

"How would you suggest I stop him?"

"You could have called me. Why didn't you call me? Where's he gone?"

She shrugged. "London? Paris? It was time for him to leave, Rhys. That's what he wanted. But I was painting his face. He'd promised not to leave until it was finished."

"His face?"

Striding across to the easel, Rhys was brought up short in astonishment. For a moment he couldn't say anything, just stood and stared at the painting. "Gwyneth! I had no idea . . ." Indeed, he'd had absolutely no idea she could paint like this. It wasn't just the likeness that captured the boy's personality and features subtly and yet distinctively; it was the liveliness in the face and hands, the long, strong brush strokes and bold striking colors, the vigorous, thick layering on of paint. There was a strength and individuality to the portrait that took Rhys completely aback, as though it had been painted by someone he didn't know at all.

"Good God, woman. This is quite brilliant! Why on earth would you hide this away from everyone, never showing your work to anyone? Not even to me. What did you think? That I'd not approve or something?"

Gwyneth wiped the brush with a rag and laid it carefully on the ledge of the easel. "You know, Rhys, it didn't occur to me to ask whether you'd approve or not. You don't ask me my opinion of your patients."

"Oh, come on! That's not the same thing. Not at all. Paintings aren't people. And anyway, paintings are nothing if they're not seen. Like an unread book."

She shrugged slightly. She was in a strange mood.

At last Rhys managed to drag his eyes away from the painting and he looked around the room again, the space, the studio, whatever it was she wanted to call it. Then he spotted the canvases stacked against the wall and headed towards them. "What else do you have here?"

"Rhys." There was a warning note in Gwyneth's voice "I'd rather you didn't."

Stopping, he swiveled on his heel. "Why ever not?"

"Do I have to give a reason?"

"Well, no, I suppose you don't have to give a reason. If you really don't want me to look at them . . ."

She'd told him often enough she didn't want anyone to see her paintings. He'd always supposed it was a lack of confidence, but the boy's picture evinced a great deal of confidence. He didn't pretend to know anything about painting, but he recognized that much. He'd always imagined, if he'd ever thought about it at all, that Gwyneth would be trying nice little watercolors or sweet little flower arrangements or little local landscapes.

Rhys came back to look at the painting on the easel once more. It was impressive. Humbling almost. He owed her an apology. As he gazed at the painting, he wondered how she could possibly have finished it in such a short space of time; the brush strokes didn't seem painstaking and careful and slow, but even so, it surely took days and days to get to this stage? He reached out a cautious finger to touch the paint. It was quite dry.

"Don't," Gwyneth snapped. "Don't touch it."

The sharpness of her tone surprised him again. She turned away, avoiding his eyes, and Rhys was suddenly aware of a crackling tension in her, in the air all around her, an odd, almost physical sensation as though electricity was surging amongst the rafters, prickling the hairs on the back of his neck.

"What exactly is going on here?" he asked, puzzled.

Gwyneth snatched the painting off the easel and carried it across the concrete floor to where the others leaned against the wall. "I'm not going to paint faces anymore, Rhys. This is absolutely the last one," and she stacked the canvas with the others, against the wall, stretchers outwards, brushed off her hands decisively. She stood back and surveyed the stack. "That's it," she announced. "The end."

Rhys frowned. "The end of what exactly? You're telling me you're not going to paint again? When you're so good at it?"

She looked over her shoulder at him, as if he were stupid, and suddenly she leapt forward and began turning the canvases towards him roughly, almost angrily, one after another, more and more of them. Rhys was struck into silence as they were revealed to him, dozens of them, the colors in the paintings jumping out at him, the bright, splashed strokes, an eerie repetition of features repeating again and again, the eyes fixed on him, gazing steadily across the room at him. The boy's face. Tim Bruce's face. Someone who'd come here only two days ago.

"What the hell . . . ?" Rhys sucked in his breath, moved closer, and stared some more. "Who is it?" But even as he asked the question, he thought he'd already guessed the answer. "The child? This is the child, isn't it?"

There was another silence. After a while Gwyneth said, "Yes. The child. The father and the son. And apparently the brother." She sighed heavily, wearily.

Rhys looked from her to the paintings. "This is what you imagined he'd look like? Just like Tim Bruce?" It dawned on him rather slowly. He *was* stupid. "Was the father of your child Tim Bruce's father?"

"Yes."

"So is Tim Bruce . . . ?" He couldn't quite form the question for a moment. "Is he the child?"

"Oh no." Gwyneth's eyes opened wide in alarm. "Oh no, of course not. That would make me his mother. Of course I'm not his mother." She laughed, the sound catching in her throat, more a sob than a laugh. "Oh God, no. Not his mother."

And though Rhys understood it couldn't be true because he knew when it was that Gwyneth's child had been born, he was sorry in a way it wasn't so. Because if it had been true, they could almost have claimed Tim Bruce as their own.

Twenty-Five

Tim hadn't wanted her to take him to the station. "I'll hitchhike. That's the way I came, that's the way I'll leave."

"From here? You know there aren't many cars up here on the mountain."

He was attempting to behave with some sort of dignity. It would have been better if he'd gone in the middle of the night, except he'd crashed asleep the instant she left the room, spinning back on the bed into total unconsciousness. He couldn't believe he had such a capacity for sleeping, couldn't believe he hadn't stayed awake for even a few seconds to relive the excitement of her body, the touch of her hands, the incredible, unbelievable sensation of making love to her. Of taking possession at last. What he'd been dreaming about from the first moment he'd set eyes on her. Instead he'd gone straight off to sleep like a child. At the very least, he could have stayed awake to feel guilty about Rhys.

How did he imagine he could have left in the night, struggling down the lane in the dark with the stupid crutches and the backpack on his shoulders? It was a ludicrous, stupid, idiotic picture. Everything was stupid and ludicrous when it should have been triumphant and glorious.

He hadn't wakened until Rhys's car was pulling away in the morning, when he caught the sound of tires screeching on the gravel. His first cowardly thought was that now he wouldn't have to face Rhys. Now there was only Gwyneth to face and he wasn't sure how he was going to manage that.

Tim had crept out of the bed, stuffed his belongings in the backpack, and inched his way down the stairs. He found her waiting in the kitchen, poised, perfectly cool and calm and collected, as if the situation was quite normal, as if it was something that happened every morning. He hadn't counted on this coolness, this distance. He hardly dared look in her eyes because he was fearful of her scorn, fearful his resolve would melt away and that he'd beg to be allowed to stay.

"Don't you want some breakfast?" she wanted to know. Playing the polite hostess. Not the wild creature of the night.

"No, of course not." He knew he had to leave immediately, but he couldn't bear the thought of never seeing her again. He'd be haunted by her face forever. Just like his father.

"There's no train for hours," she said.

"It doesn't matter. I'll wait for the first one." But he realized it was a foolish idea to try and hitchhike from the house. "Can't we call a cab?"

"I'll take you to the station, at least. Please let me do that, Tim."

So he climbed in the Mini with her one more time, the humiliating crutches and the huge backpack stuffed in the seat behind, and allowed her to drive him down the winding lane between the high hedgerows, the ocean a shining arc on the horizon. He couldn't speak and she, too, said nothing. There really was nothing to say.

In silence, they turned onto the main road, the green hills rising to the crags on one side, the small whitewashed cottages dotting the fields, the sheep grazing, the cliffs and shining ocean on the other side. They snaked down the steep road into Clarrach, over the humped-back bridge, up into the square, past the door of the surgery and the carved stone soldiers in the center, along a narrow street to the train station.

Tim hadn't seen the train station before, only heard about it from Gwyneth's story. It was larger than he'd imagined, built of dark stone, a pointed Gothic tower in the middle, a clock on four sides of the tower. The clock didn't seem to be working, but the wide, deserted cobblestoned courtyard was there in front and the lacy metal pillars supporting the ornate glass overhang, and when Gwyneth pulled into the courtyard and jerked on the hand brake, Tim sat quite still for a moment. He stared through the windshield at the station building. "So it was here it happened?"

"Over there," she said. Her mouth was set into a firm line and she pointed to a wall that curved away from the station on the opposite side of the courtyard. Tim tried not to look at the shape of her hand. "Further down there," she said.

"I want to see it," he said, and climbed out of the car.

The wall was high, of the same dark stone as the station building, and after a few yards, it arced away from the courtyard and round the side of the station. Swinging rapidly on the crutches, Tim went past the station, around the curve, and found he was on a long quiet street that seemed to lead nowhere. On the opposite side, an elderly woman with a cane limped painfully and slowly along the sidewalk, but otherwise there was no one about, no shops, nothing happening, just an empty stretch of street that didn't seem to lead anywhere in particular. He glanced back over his shoulder and realized he could no longer see the station or the clock, just as Gwyneth had said. A white van drove by, fast, and Tim wondered briefly if it could be Billy Price's van.

Gwyneth stood at the corner watching.

"Here?" he called out.

She walked slowly towards him, skirts flicking against her legs, feet pacing deliberately as though measuring the distance, and stopped beside him. "Right here."

There was nothing to see, of course. Gazing at the wall, higher than a man's head, Tim tried to visualize a young black soldier leaning against it, a young Gwyneth watching him surreptitiously. It wasn't difficult to imagine Gwyneth when she was young; she wouldn't have looked much different from now. Shutting his eyes, Tim imagined the GIs coming around the corner, the thump of fists, the cries, her screams, the black man in his American uniform slumping to the ground, bleeding. To death.

He opened his eyes. Such a thing didn't seem possible, not here on a quiet street in a quiet town.

They both stared at the wall for a while, then Gwyneth reached out her hand to touch it, as she had touched the stone of the burial chamber. She bent her neck and rested her forehead against the wall for a moment, her eyes closed as if in prayer, and when she straightened up she said, "It was a long time ago. But perhaps I'm glad, after all, that I told you. Such things shouldn't be forgotten."

"What did you say his name was?"

"Chester. I never knew his last name."

"I could try and find it. It must be possible, even after so many years. There must be records. I'll find it and let you know."

Gwyneth wiped at her eyes with the back of her hand. "No, Tim. I don't think I want to know his name. I don't think either of us need to know anything more. We know more than enough now."

That was probably true. He probably knew more than enough.

They walked back to the car and Tim reached into the backseat and hauled out his backpack. As he hoisted it onto his shoulders, the weight of it made him stagger and he had to grab hold of the door to catch his balance.

Gwyneth said, "You'll never manage."

"Sure I will. I'll manage just fine from now on." He pulled the crutches out of the backseat. "I should pay for these, shouldn't I?"

"Don't worry. The National Health Service is free, remember?"

"I'll remember everything. I'll remember you and I'll remember Rhys. And old Mr. Watkins and his cows and the burial chamber. Those damn rocks I fell off. Maybe I'll even remember the height of the doorways."

The entrance to the station was high above his head and he wouldn't have to duck, and as Gwyneth walked to the entrance alongside him, he had the absurd hope she might get on the train with him. But she stopped beneath the overhang, the glass refracting the sunshine across her face, shimmering across her wide forehead and the flyaway light hair. "I have to say good-bye now," she said.

Tim shifted the weight of the backpack on his shoulders. "I'll always remember you, Gwyneth. I'll never be able to forget you. But I wonder if you'll remember me?"

She put her hand to her mouth and stared at him for a moment, took her hand away and reached up to kiss him on the lips, a feathery brief touch, soft and delicate, gone as quickly as it came. Then she turned on her heel and walked away without a backward glance, got into the ridiculous little car, and drove away.

Twenty-Six

The envelope, long and white and with an American stamp in the corner, lay on the desk amongst all the government forms. Though Rhys didn't recognize the large scrawling handwriting on the front of the envelope, it wasn't exactly a surprise to find Tim Bruce's name on the back. He'd always been sure he'd hear from him sometime, from someplace, but when he turned the envelope over and saw the return address, Boston, Massachusetts, he sat down with sudden unexpected relief. The boy had not gone off to war, after all.

Rhys picked up the silver letter opener to slit the envelope, paused, and put it aside. He would save it for later. Any minute now, the fellow from Bristol would be arriving to look over the job, to be looked over himself. This process of selecting a new partner had become protracted and dispiriting. So far he hadn't cared for any of the candidates, either too young or too old, too clever or not clever enough, too this or that. Rhys was relying on his gut rather than his head in this interview process, well aware he'd taken against some of the candidates unreasonably, judging them by the clothes they wore or the way they spoke, never mind if they were qualified or not. He had to live with them, after all. The patients had to live with them. Mavis had to live with them.

This chap, Gwillam Hopkins, whose résumé lay on the desk together with the forms and the letter from America, seemed more promising. Welsh born, if nothing else, from North Wales, which wasn't quite as good as West Wales or even the valleys, but Welsh nevertheless. Bristol qualified, a trainee-assistant in a general practice in Somerset, with stellar references. Though that didn't necessarily mean too much. Doctors in practice were apt to write glowing references for trainees they wanted to get rid of.

What if he liked this one? He might actually have to take him on. He'd have to brace himself for more changes.

Picking up Tim Bruce's letter again, turning it over in his hands, Rhys wanted to read it and was almost afraid to. It might have been better not to know where the boy had got to because now he'd be tempted to get in touch with him. But it was a relief to know he hadn't gone off to that damned war. That he was safe. Or was he? Maybe he was still waiting to be called up. Had his ankle healed properly? How had he managed, going off like that to God knew where with that clumsy great cast and those ridiculous old crutches?

Rhys opened the envelope.

Dear Dr. Edwards, (So formal! Surely he could have called him Rhys?)

Of course I should have written sooner. Of course. If for nothing else to thank you for making such a good job of my ankle, for offering me hospitality at your house, for introducing me to the National Health Service. I know I left rather precipitously, without saying good-bye to you, and for that I'm sorry, but I thought you might like to know that I did go to medical school, after all.

*The decision was a direct result of my stay in Wales, an experi-
ence I will never forget.*

Mavis rapped with her knuckles on the open door. "That Dr.
Hopkins is here to see you." .

Reluctantly, Rhys put down the letter. Medical school, after
all. Good, good. The boy had the makings of a decent doctor.

Walking briskly to the door, he offered his hand to the fellow
hovering behind Mavis, received a firm handshake in return, neither too bone-crushing nor too feeble.

"Gwillam Hopkins. From Bristol. Thank you for seeing me,
Dr. Edwards."

Rhys recognized immediately the guttural North Wales accent,
the decent gray suit, respectful, not flashy, the starched white
shirt, and striped Bristol University tie. So far, so good.

"Come in, come in," he said heartily, and ushered him to the
chair where the patients sat. Rhys wanted to be welcoming, yet
not overeager, and he sat solemnly behind the desk, put his finger-
tips together, and regarded the young man carefully, the suit, the
tie, the polished black shoes. Suddenly, without quite meaning to,
he asked, *"Y dych chi 'n siarad Cymraeg?"*

Hopkins smiled. *"Ydw. Wrth gwrs."*

Clearing his throat, Rhys forced his face into a deliberately pas-
sive expression. He had to go through the motions, of course,
knew it would be unutterably stupid to take anyone on simply because he spoke Welsh, for God's sake, but somehow he was ready
to find nothing amiss with this one. He mouthed the questions already answered on the résumé, training, experience, schooling,
marital status, so on and so forth, and forced himself to listen to
the answers. This young man looked and sounded like someone he
already knew, himself as a young doctor, similar thin smile, similar confident but deprecating manner, as though he didn't take
himself too seriously, as though he was comfortable in his skin.

Could it really be that he, Rhys, had at last stumbled across a kindred spirit?

When he'd asked as many questions as he could think of and allowed Hopkins to ask some of his own straightforward, sensible questions, Rhys took him on a brief tour of the premises and introduced him to Mavis.

"I couldn't help noticing the waiting room as I came in," Hopkins remarked. "Nice. I do think it's important to give the patients a cheerful place to wait. As long as they don't have to wait too long, of course."

Mavis beamed approval. "We did it up recently," she said. "It does look ever so much better, doesn't it? Everyone says so."

"We're making a few changes around here," Rhys said. "It was certainly time for a few changes." He took hold of Hopkins's gray-suited arm. "Can you stay for lunch? I'd like you to meet my wife."

"I'd be delighted," Hopkins murmured. "Most kind."

"Gwyneth doesn't speak Welsh, mind, but she understands enough, so be careful what you say."

Hopkins flashed a modest smile. "I always try to be careful what I say."

At one o'clock Rhys drove his candidate up the mountain. If he was going to offer the job to Hopkins, which he surely was, and if Hopkins was going to accept, which Rhys hoped he would, he had to meet Gwyneth. Wives needed to approve of newcomers to a general practice.

He'd have liked the weather to be better to show off the glories of the countryside but these were the middle days of December, the sky thick with dark heaping clouds, heavy rain lashing in on the wind from the southwest, bending and flattening the trees and shaking the hedgerows. It wasn't possible to see much further than the length of the car, let alone to catch a glimpse of the coastline or the sweep of the hillside up to the rocks at the top.

"Rotten day," Rhys apologized. "But beautiful it is here in the summer."

"I know. My family used to come down this way for holidays. It's just one more reason I was interested in your practice. I wanted to come back to Wales."

Rhys could hardly believe his good luck.

The rain soaked them as they dashed the few yards from the car to the house, in through the blue-painted front door and into the hallway with the black and white tiles. Taking Hopkins's coat, Rhys shook it out and hung it on the rack by the front door, called out, "Gwyneth, I'm home. I've brought our visitor."

At the end of the hallway, the door from the kitchen swung open and the light shone on Gwyneth's hair as she came through the doorway, wiping her hands on an apron stretched tight across her swelling belly.

"Gwyneth, this is Dr. Gwillam Hopkins, come all the way from Bristol to look at our little job," and when she came up to Hopkins and shook his hand and smiled at him, Rhys saw him blink with the same startled expression all strangers had when they first set eyes on her. She was, if it was possible, even more beautiful now, eyes serene, hair shining, skin thick and creamy.

"Lunch is nearly ready," she said. "Why don't you take Dr. Hopkins in the sitting room and offer him a glass of sherry?"

In the sitting room, a fire was burning in the grate and the lamps were lit against the darkness of the day. "What a pleasant house," Gwillam Hopkins said, and accepted a glass of sherry. "When's the baby due?"

"Two months. It's another of the changes around here."

"Congratulations," Hopkins said.

"Thank you. It's come rather late in our lives. We're hoping it's a boy. Or a girl." Rhys laughed. "Just as long as it's healthy. That's what all parents hope, isn't it?"

As he and Hopkins sipped their sherry, they discussed the local setup for deliveries and home care, the district midwives and the prenatal care, the hazards of a distant hospital, some of the details of the practice that Hopkins would need to know if he was going to take the job.

"So you'd probably like me to start before the baby comes?"

Rhys breathed a silent sigh of relief. "That would be most convenient."

⁂

Gwyneth told him eight weeks after the boy left. He wasn't going to pretend he'd suspected such an extraordinary thing before she sat down opposite him at the kitchen table that Sunday morning, poured him a cup of coffee, and said quietly and calmly, "Rhys, I have something to tell you."

But as soon as she told him, he realized he should have recognized the signs. His first reaction, oddly enough, was relief. For one terrible moment he'd thought she was about to tell him she was ill. He'd noticed her pallor in the mornings, her unusual fatigue and lack of interest in food, a new habit of lingering in the bathroom with the door firmly closed, and yet he had done nothing about it. He'd asked her once or twice, "Gwyneth, do you feel all right?" and she'd brushed it off. If he'd been sharp enough he might have recognized that part of it, added it up and come to a rational if unlikely conclusion, one any doctor of any worth should have been able to make. But the other part of it, the fact that his wife was informing him she'd had sexual intercourse with Tim Bruce and thus was pregnant, and the fact that such an idea would never have crossed his mind, left Rhys dumbfounded. To have been so blind, so unwitting an accomplice, to have been idiotic enough to throw a virile young man together with his beautiful wife and never to have contemplated for a single moment that anything like that would occur, made him feel a complete and utter fool. And if she hadn't become pregnant, he'd have remained as ignorant and unthinking as before.

"I never meant it to happen. He didn't either, Rhys. It wasn't his fault. You mustn't blame him."

"No? So who should I blame? You? You think that will make it easier?"

"It happened only once. The night you went off to deliver Eileen Williams's baby. I wouldn't have thought it was possible to get pregnant just like that."

"Once is all it ever takes," Rhys said grimly. "One sperm, one shot."

He supposed he was glad to know it was only once. Somehow that made it less unforgiveable. But he didn't want to hear the details, even though he couldn't help remembering the poor little Williams baby, scrawny and defective, still undergoing surgeries, who'd come into life that very night.

Rhys had stared at the untouched coffee in his cup, at the table set with breakfast things, then stared around the kitchen, through the window into the garden where the leaves were turning color. Finally his eyes had come back to Gwyneth, to her pale face and to her shining eyes. It was himself he should blame, perhaps. Not Gwyneth. Not Tim Bruce. Rhys realized that Tim Bruce recognized Gwyneth for what she was, a beautiful and lonely woman, while he, Rhys, had taken her for granted, assumed she was content alone here in the house on the mountain. He'd been too absorbed in his patients and his fascinating line of work and had put the barrenness of her life and body out of his mind.

"What are you going to do about it?" he wanted to know.

A fleeting expression flickered across her smooth face. "Me? I'm not going to do anything about it, Rhys. It's what you're going to do, isn't it? Whatever it is you want to do, I'll understand. Except don't expect me to get rid of it because I won't. But I'm very sorry for the hurt this has caused you. Of course I am."

"Are you, Gwyneth? Are you quite sure you're sorry?"

Slowly she shook her head. "I can't be sorry about the baby. It's a miracle."

A miracle? Yes, he supposed that's what it was. She was going to have what he couldn't give her. A child. He knew he should be outraged and angry and betrayed, and yet the extraordinary, miraculous reality of it caught in his chest and drowned the sense of outrage and betrayal. As Rhys struggled with the astonishment at his own stupidity and cupidity, in the same moment he was strangely grateful to be offered a second chance at a more fulfilled life with his beautiful wife. She'd been drifting away from him and now she would be anchored. Now she would need him more than she had ever needed him. Rhys realized it was what he wanted most of all, to be needed. And a baby would need both of them.

"One sperm," he said. "So ironic I couldn't give you even that. But don't forget, Gwyneth. A sperm carries all that genetic coding. The child will probably grow up to look just like our American visitor. That should give Clarrach something to talk about."

She shrugged. "They've always talked about me, Rhys. I'm used to it now. Will you mind?"

He thought about it. A child who looked like the boy? Like those paintings in the studio? "It will be a beautiful child," he said.

After lunch, after he offered Gwillam Hopkins the job and Hopkins accepted it, and they shook hands on it, Rhys drove him back down the mountain and Hopkins got into his own car to drive off to Bristol in the pouring rain. Rhys sat down at his desk to read the rest of Tim Bruce's letter.

"I made up my mind to go to medical school during those few days with you. I'll never forget that baby being born or old Mr. Watkins and his cows. Even the ankle was some sort of amazing luck. The draft board wouldn't pass me because of it. It mended perfectly well, of course, but it gave me the chance to go off to

school instead of to war. You did your job well. The wretched war drags on. There can be no good end to it and I'm just grateful not to be part of it. But this has been a terrible year in our country, such ferment, such continuing strife. I look back on those few days in Wales as a peaceful interlude in all the turmoil. I hope to come back one day.

I'm planning to take up obstetrics when I qualify. You gave me a hint of what it could be like. Perhaps I'll even campaign for a National Health Service!

Please give my best regards to Gwyneth and tell her I never looked for the name of that soldier and never spoke to my father about him. Perhaps someday, when the time is right, though for some things the time may never be right. She will understand.

I want to have a life that makes a difference to people. Like yours.

My very best wishes,

Tim Bruce

He showed the letter to Gwyneth. "Are we going to tell him about the difference he made to our lives?"

She held her hands to her belly. "I think that would be very foolish, Rhys. As he says, for some things the time may never be right."

But Rhys knew he'd have to be told one day. He didn't know when, or how, but one day the time would surely be right. Even Gwyneth couldn't keep secrets forever.

It was May again. Another end of term gathering. Another stint as waiter.

Carlton said, "Do you remember my son Tim? Didn't you meet him at this same party last year?"

The stranger smiled. "Why, yes, of course. Another lovely

evening like this. Weren't you just off to Europe? Did you ever get to Wales?"

Tim held the tray of drinks close to his chest. "Wales? Yes, I did, as a matter of fact. Smashed my ankle there. It saved me from the draft."

"Believe it or not, he's in medical school now," Carlton said. "Surprising what one's kids can aspire to eventually, isn't it? Well, I suppose the world needs doctors more than it needs soldiers, but I'm sorry he's missed the experiences I had in the services."

"Are you, Dad?" Tim put down the drink tray. There would never be a good time. "Funny, that wasn't what I heard in Wales. In Clarrach. You remember Clarrach, don't you, Dad? You remember Gwyneth? I never told you that I met her, did I?"

Carlton stared at his son. "Gwyneth? What Gwyneth?"

The crowd of guests jostled around and about and the smoke from the barbecue stung Tim's eyes. "I seem to recall the sound of her name at this very party this time last year. You might be interested to know that she hasn't forgotten you. She told me quite a lot about you."

Carlton looked away. He sighed. "Ah, my boy, it's probably wiser not to believe everything you hear. The Welsh, I've been told, have very lively imaginations."

"Don't you want to hear what I heard?"

Carlton peered into his glass. "Would there be any point in hearing it?"

Tim saw the torchlight flickering on his father's face, on the rhododendrons and azaleas. The stranger stood close by, smiling. The students drank wine. Tim could hear his sister laughing somewhere not far away and he saw his mother approaching with a tray of food.

"No," he said. "I suppose, after all, there wouldn't be any point."